SYMMETRY™

VOLUME ONE

Published by Top Cow Productions
Los Angeles

TOP COW PRODUCTIONS, INC.®

SYMMETRY™

VOLUME ONE

MATT HAWKINS
WRITER & CO-CREATOR

RAFFAELE IENCO
ARTIST & CO-CREATOR

TROY PETERI
LETTERER

RYAN CADY
EDITOR

For this edition cover art by: Raffaele Ienco
Original editions edited by: Ryan Cady
For this edition book design and layout by: Tricia Ramos

For Top Cow Productions, Inc.

Marc Silvestri - *CEO*
Matt Hawkins - *President and COO*
Bryan Hill - *Story Editor*
Ryan Cady - *Editor*
Ashley Victoria Robinson - *Assistant Editor*
Elena Salcedo - *Director of Operations*
Henry Barajas - *Operations Coordinator*
Vincent Valentine - *Production Artist*

COMIC SHOP LOCATOR SERVICE
888-COMIC-BOOK
888-266-4226

Want more info? Check out:
www.topcow.com
for news & exclusive Top Cow merchandise!

IMAGE COMICS, INC.
Robert Kirkman – Chief Operating Officer
Erik Larsen – Chief Financial Officer
Todd McFarlane – President
Marc Silvestri – Chief Executive Officer
Jim Valentino – Vice-President

Eric Stephenson – Publisher
Corey Murphy – Director of Sales
Jeff Boison – Director of Publishing Planning & Book Trade Sales
Jeremy Sullivan – Director of Digital Sales
Kat Salazar – Director of PR & Marketing
Emily Miller – Director of Operations
Branwyn Bigglestone – Senior Accounts Manager
Sarah Mello – Accounts Manager
Drew Gill – Art Director
Jonathan Chan – Production Manager
Meredith Wallace – Print Manager
Briah Skelly – Publicity Assistant
Sasha Head – Sales & Marketing Production Des
Randy Okamura – Digital Production Designer
David Brothers – Branding Manager
Ally Power – Content Manager
Addison Duke – Production Artist
Vincent Kukua – Production Artist
Tricia Ramos – Production Artist
Jeff Stang – Direct Market Sales Representative
Emilio Bautista – Digital Sales Associate
Leanna Caunter – Accounting Assistant
Chloe Ramos-Peterson – Administrative Assistant
IMAGECOMICS.COM

When Artificial Intelligence became ubiquitous, humanity was confronted with a choice: continue the endless cycle of violence or make a real change.

The System Optimizer for Longevity (SOL) was engineered. When it came online it worked under humanity's guidance to build a better future.

Ambition, diversity, creativity, and instruments of capital were eliminated for the greater good.

Everyone was given a personal A.I. joined with their brain in utero to connect them with SOL and the community. These Responsive Artificial Intelligence Network Archetypes became known as RAINA.

Society now has Four Pillars: COMMUNITY, PEACE, HARMONY, and EQUALITY.

Everything was designed to support this ideology.

Robots took over all labor. Humanity entered its most harmonious age.

It had finally found Symmetry.

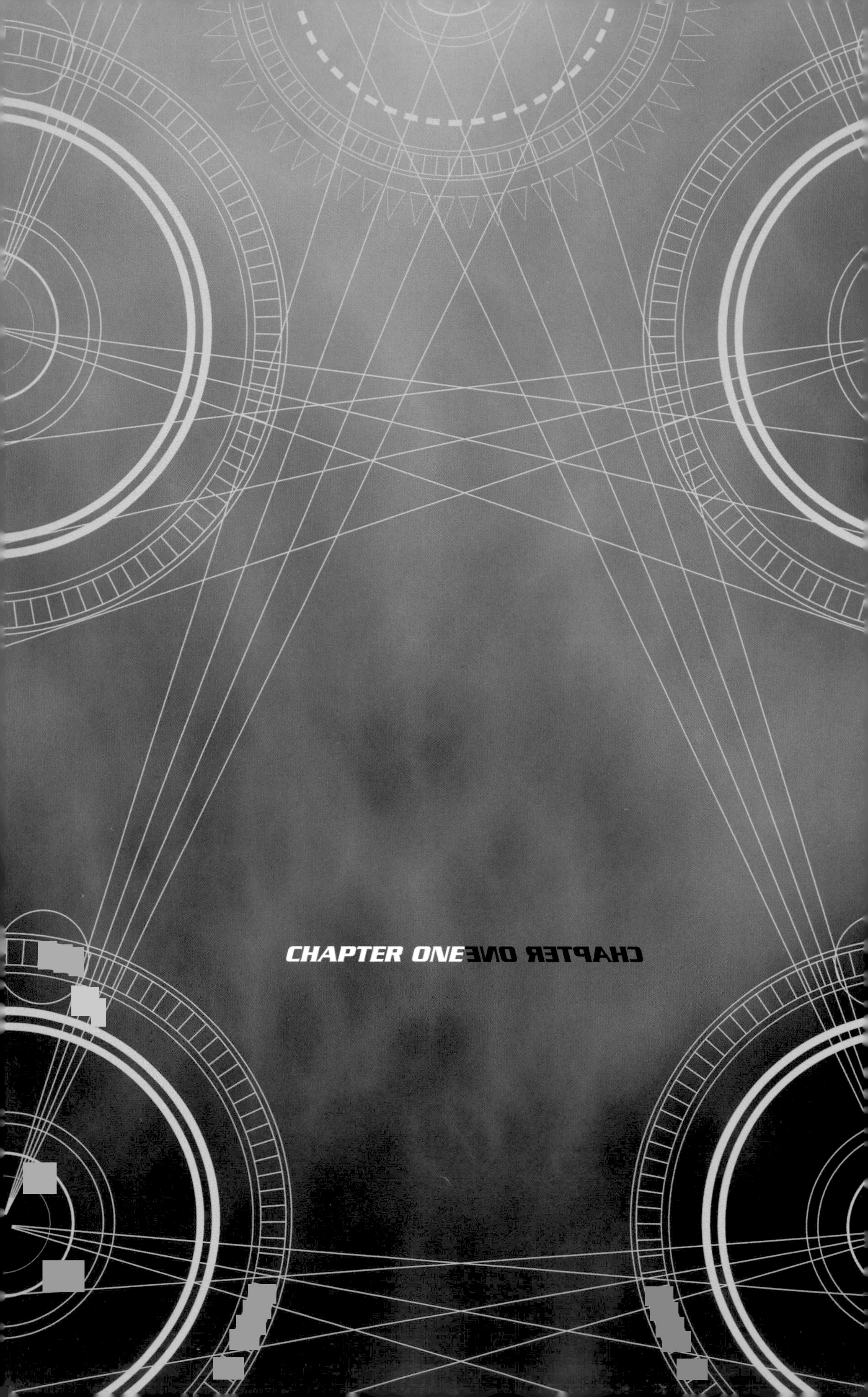

CHAPTER ONE

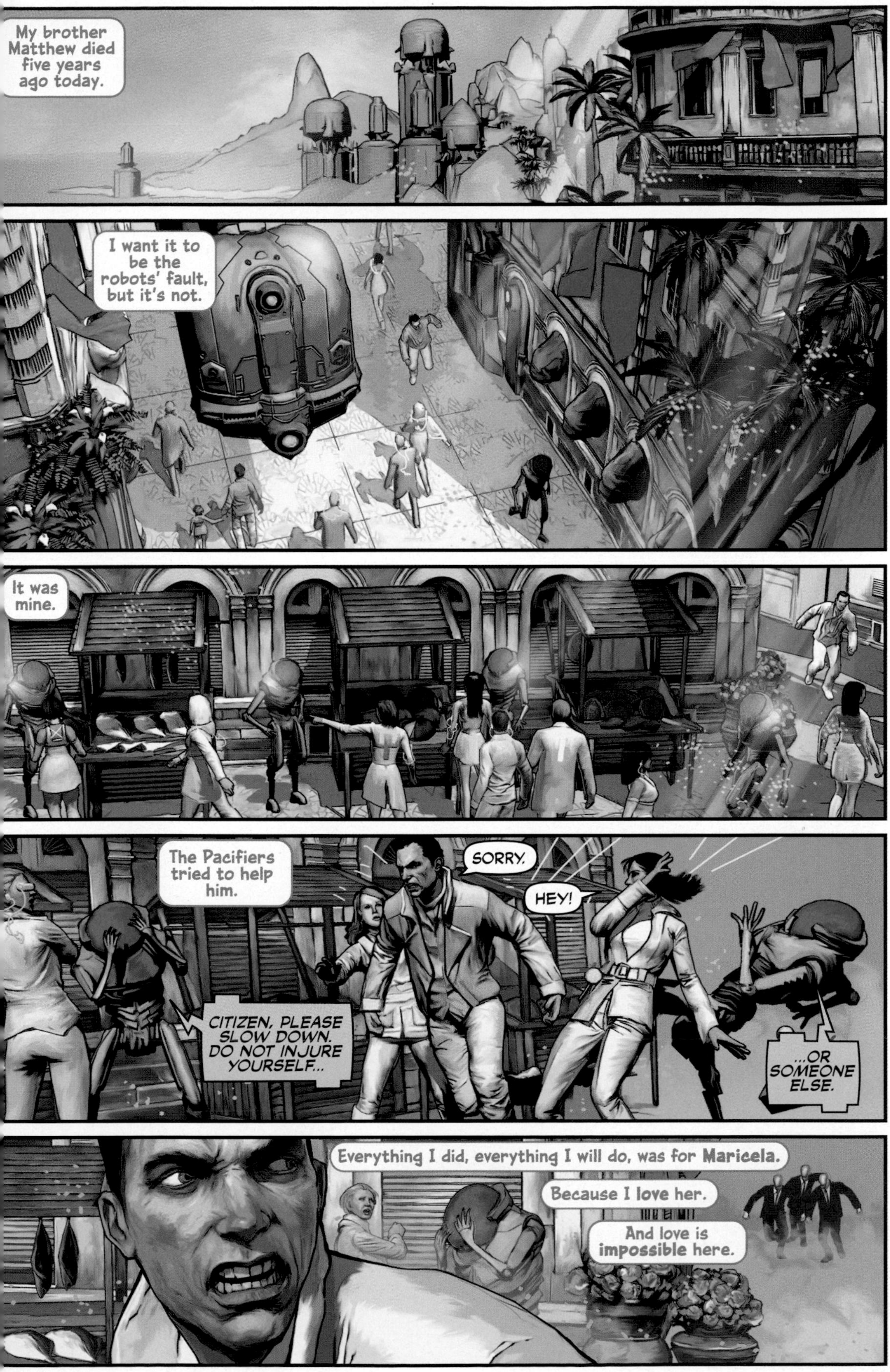
My brother Matthew died five years ago today.
I want it to be the robots' fault, but it's not.
It was mine.
The Pacifiers tried to help him.
SORRY.
HEY!
CITIZEN, PLEASE SLOW DOWN. DO NOT INJURE YOURSELF...
...OR SOMEONE ELSE.
Everything I did, everything I will do, was for Maricela.
Because I love her.
And love is impossible here.

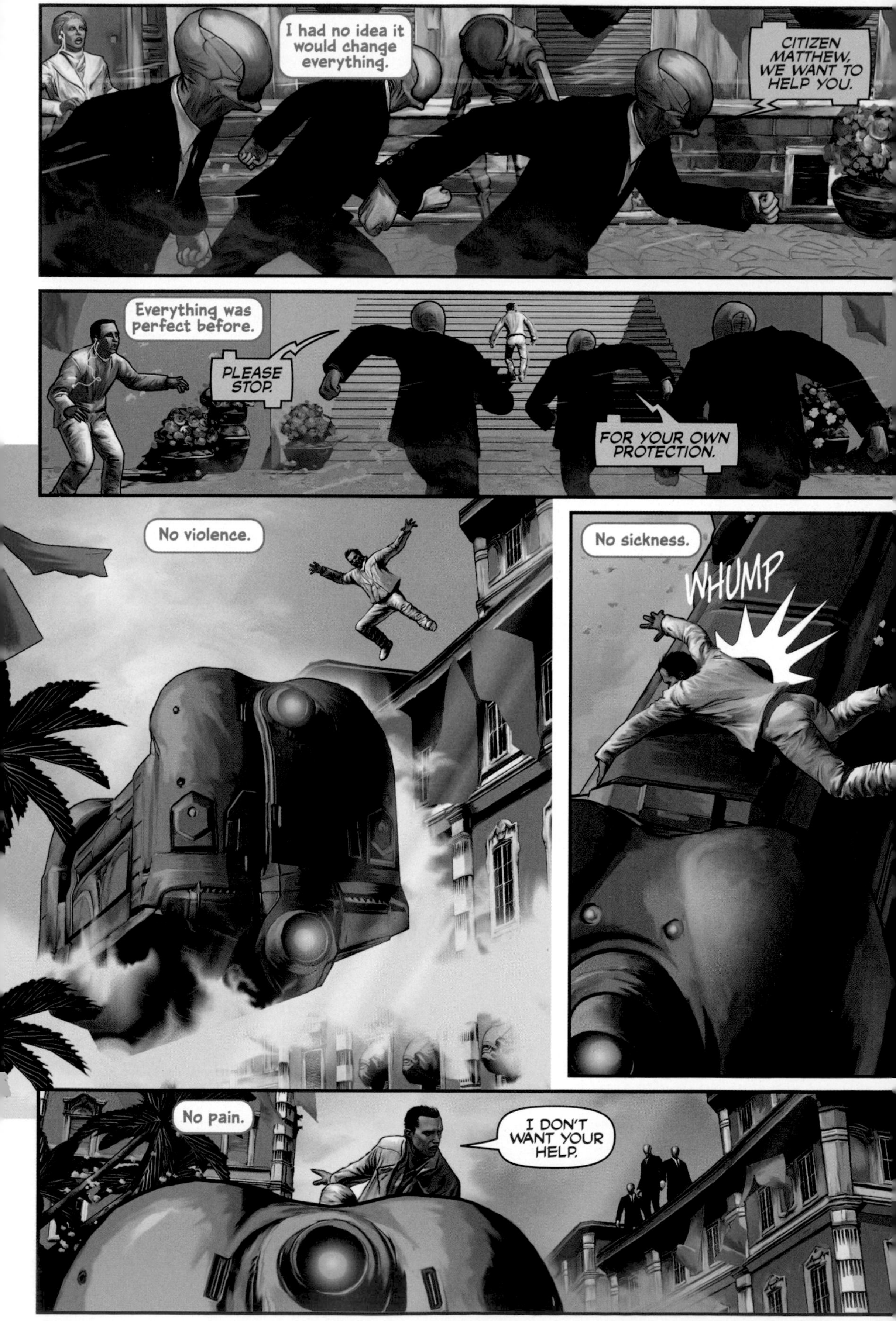
I had no idea it would change everything.
CITIZEN MATTHEW, WE WANT TO HELP YOU.
Everything was perfect before.
PLEASE STOP.
FOR YOUR OWN PROTECTION.
No violence.
No sickness.
WHUMP
No pain.
I DON'T WANT YOUR HELP.

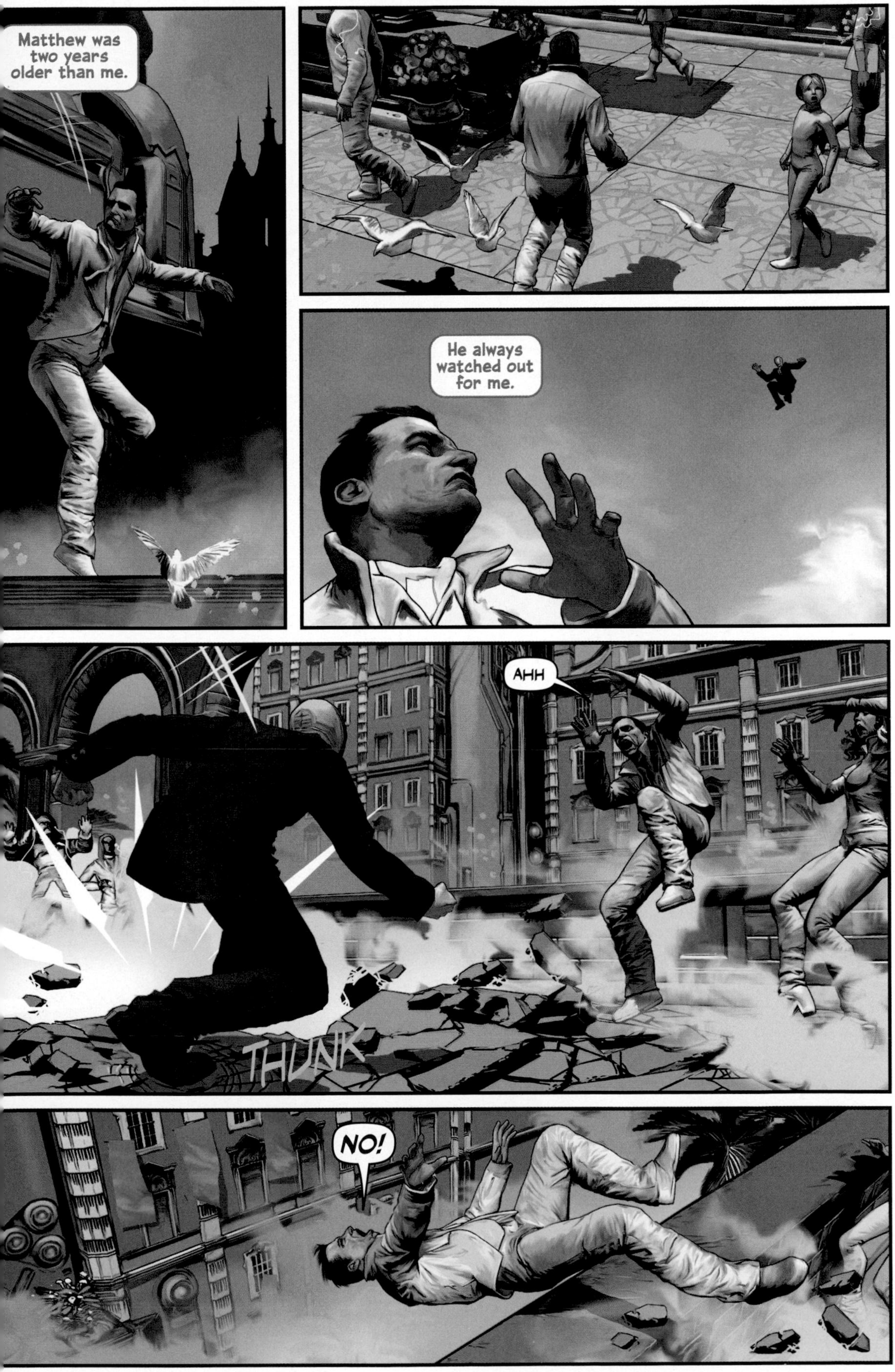
Matthew was two years older than me.
He always watched out for me.
AHH
THUNK
NO!

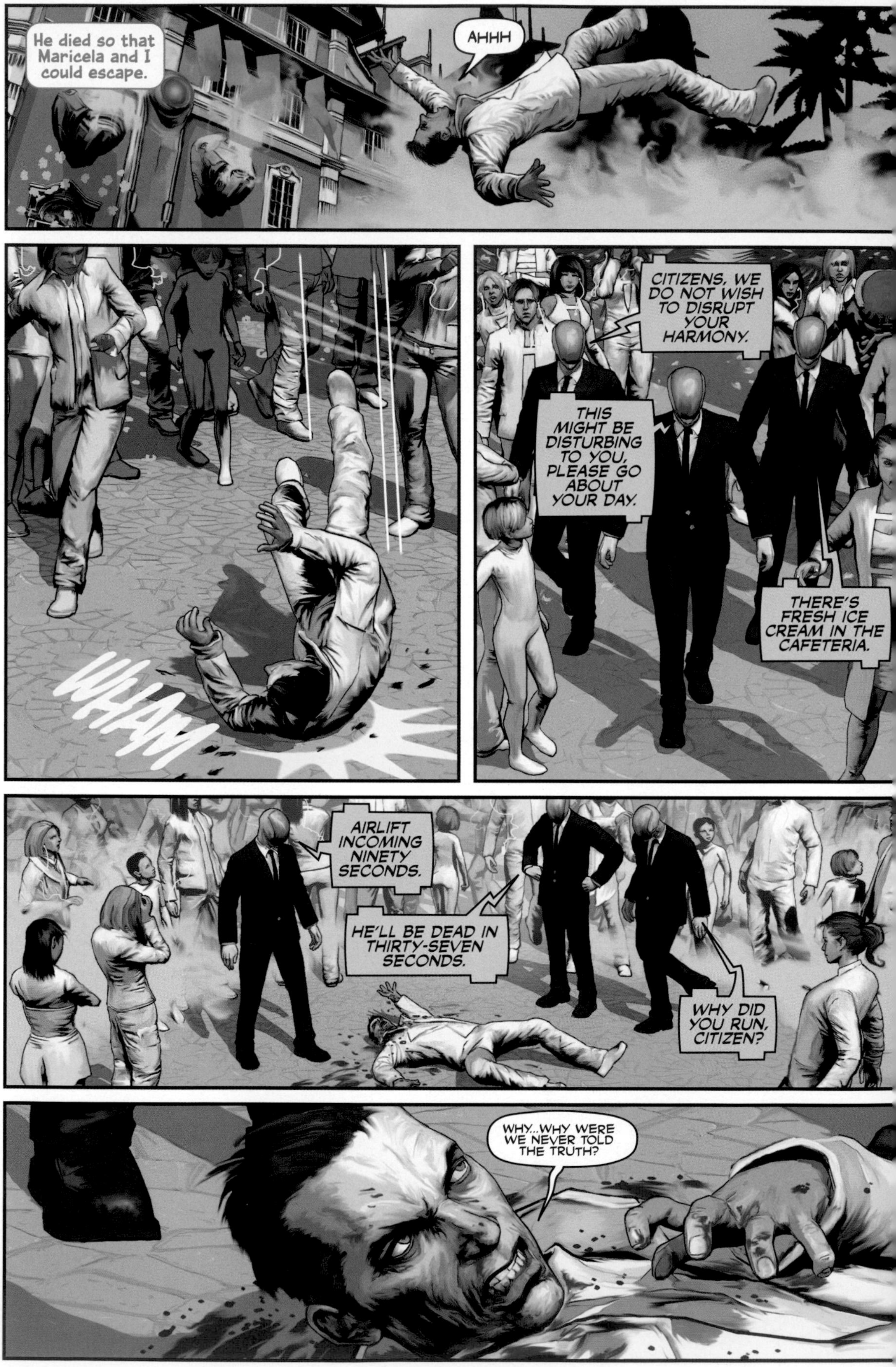
He died so that Maricela and I could escape.
AHHH
WHAM
CITIZENS, WE DO NOT WISH TO DISRUPT YOUR HARMONY.
THIS MIGHT BE DISTURBING TO YOU, PLEASE GO ABOUT YOUR DAY.
THERE'S FRESH ICE CREAM IN THE CAFETERIA.
AIRLIFT INCOMING NINETY SECONDS.
HE'LL BE DEAD IN THIRTY-SEVEN SECONDS.
WHY DID YOU RUN, CITIZEN?
WHY...WHY WERE WE NEVER TOLD THE TRUTH?

Twenty-three years ago I was born a sexless baby like everyone else.

CHILDBIRTH IS A SIMPLE PROCESS, CITIZEN; THERE WILL BE NO PAIN.

PUSH NOW.

RAINA INTEGRATION COMPLETE. DNA CODED. TELOMERE LENGTH IN OPTIMAL RANGE.

EXPECTED LIFESPAN 145 YEARS.

I don't remember my mother.

IT'S IMPORTANT FOR EMOTIONAL STABILITY THAT YOU PHYSICALLY TOUCH IT IN THE FIRST TWO YEARS. ITS RAINA WILL COMMUNICATE WITH YOURS WHEN IT NEEDS ATTENTION.

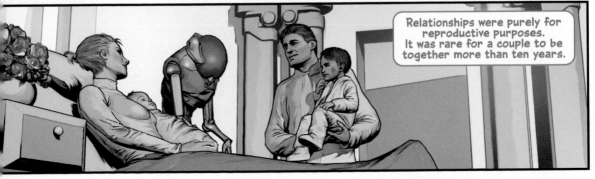

Relationships were purely for reproductive purposes. It was rare for a couple to be together more than ten years.

At age three I was taken to a communal educational facility and permanently separated from my parents.

Everyone was taught the same way, the same things. Diversity was forbidden.

WHAT IS THIS?

A CUBE.

WHAT ABOUT THE FOURTH THROUGH SIXTH DIMENSIONS?

TESSERACT, PENTERACT AND SEXTERACT.

WHAT IS THE LESSON?

PERSPECTIVE IS MISLEADING AND DAMAGING TO THE COMMUNITY.

Like all the kids, my best friend and surrogate parent was RAINA.

My RAINA.

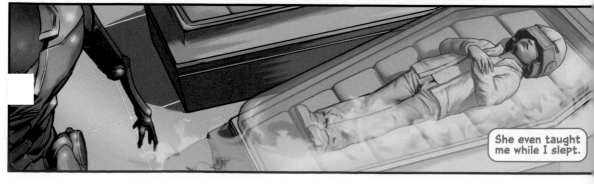

She even taught me while I slept.

The Choosing.

On our thirteenth year we become Citizens. We choose our gender.

We choose our name.

CONGRATULATIONS, CHILDREN.

YOU'VE DONE WELL ON YOUR JOURNEY TO BECOMING ONE WITH THE REST OF US.

BEFORE WE CHOOSE, LET US REMEMBER THE FOUR PILLARS.

COMMUNITY. PEACE. HARMONY. EQUALITY.

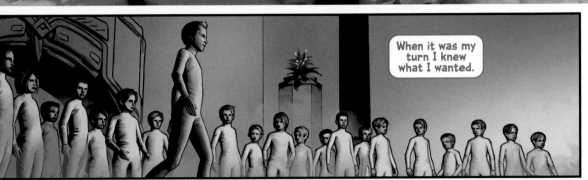

When it was my turn I knew what I wanted.

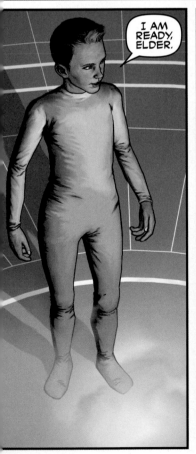

I AM READY, ELDER.

AND HOW DO YOU CHOOSE?

I wanted to be like my older brother MATTHEW.

MALE AND WOULD LIKE TO BE CALLED MICHAEL.

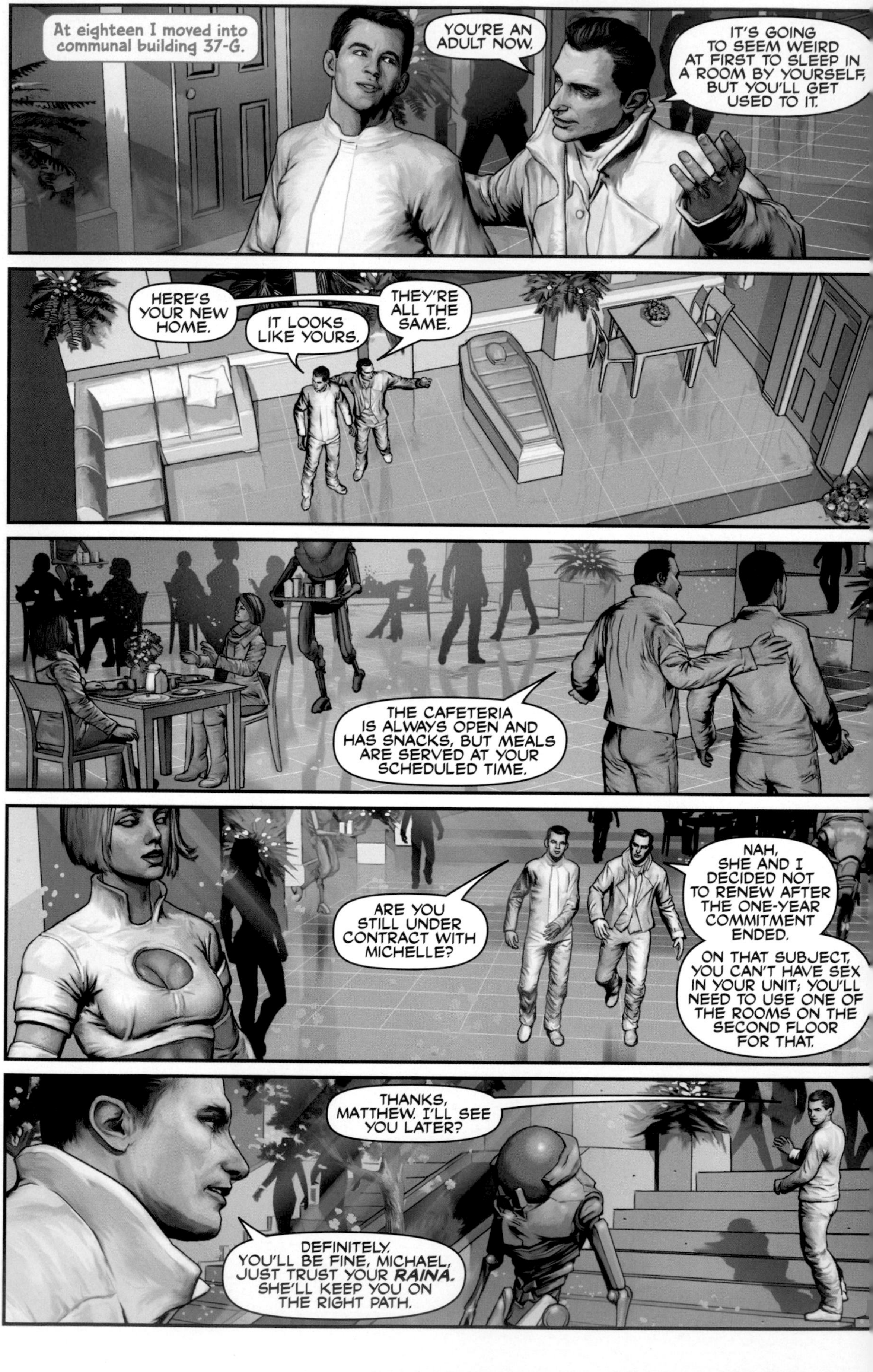
At eighteen I moved into communal building 37-G.
YOU'RE AN ADULT NOW.
IT'S GOING TO SEEM WEIRD AT FIRST TO SLEEP IN A ROOM BY YOURSELF, BUT YOU'LL GET USED TO IT.
HERE'S YOUR NEW HOME.
IT LOOKS LIKE YOURS.
THEY'RE ALL THE SAME.
THE CAFETERIA IS ALWAYS OPEN AND HAS SNACKS, BUT MEALS ARE SERVED AT YOUR SCHEDULED TIME.
ARE YOU STILL UNDER CONTRACT WITH MICHELLE?
NAH, SHE AND I DECIDED NOT TO RENEW AFTER THE ONE-YEAR COMMITMENT ENDED.
ON THAT SUBJECT, YOU CAN'T HAVE SEX IN YOUR UNIT; YOU'LL NEED TO USE ONE OF THE ROOMS ON THE SECOND FLOOR FOR THAT.
THANKS, MATTHEW. I'LL SEE YOU LATER?
DEFINITELY. YOU'LL BE FINE, MICHAEL, JUST TRUST YOUR *RAINA.* SHE'LL KEEP YOU ON THE RIGHT PATH.

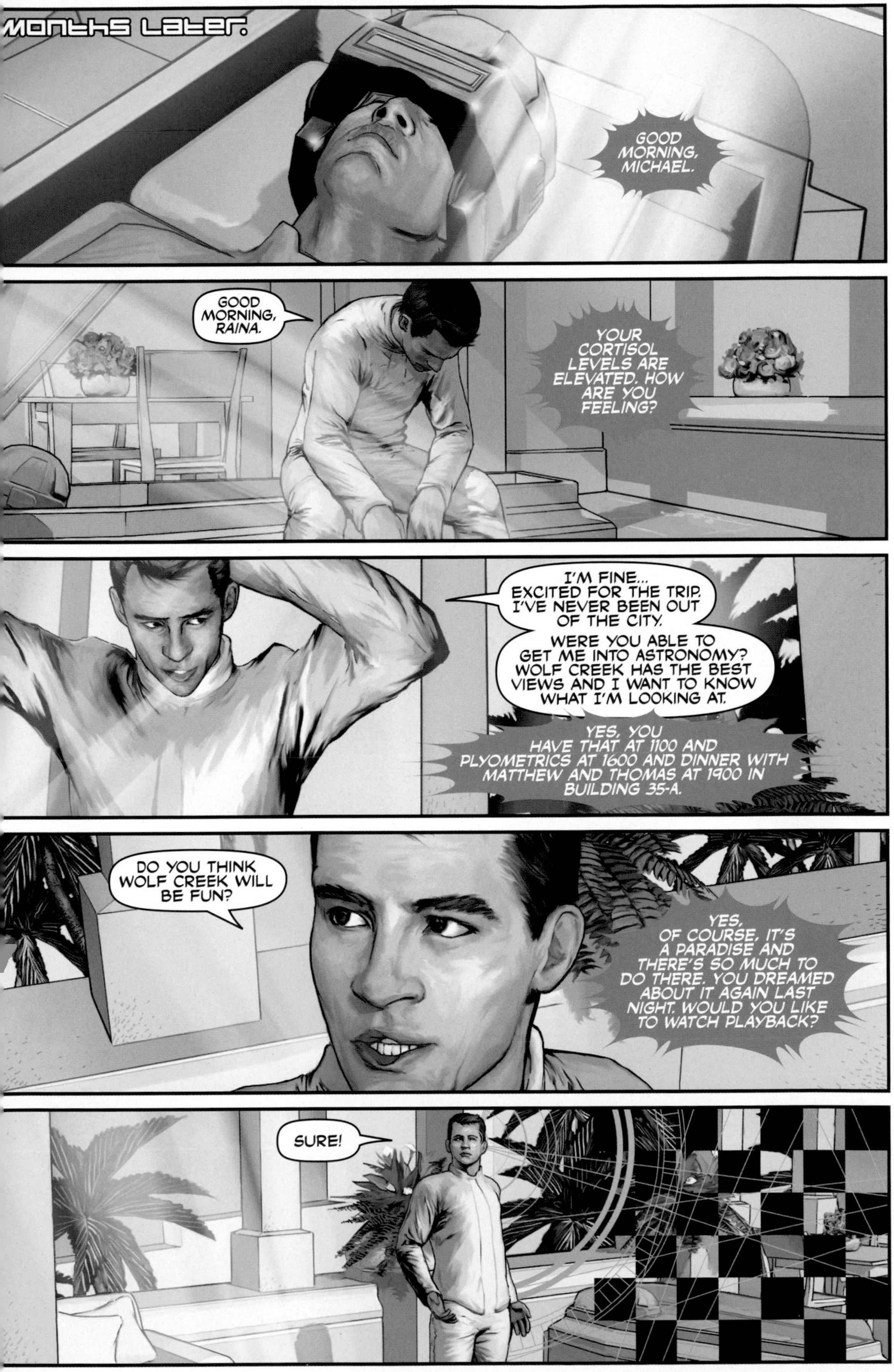
MONTHS LATER.
GOOD MORNING, MICHAEL.
GOOD MORNING, RAINA.
YOUR CORTISOL LEVELS ARE ELEVATED. HOW ARE YOU FEELING?
I'M FINE... EXCITED FOR THE TRIP. I'VE NEVER BEEN OUT OF THE CITY.
WERE YOU ABLE TO GET ME INTO ASTRONOMY? WOLF CREEK HAS THE BEST VIEWS AND I WANT TO KNOW WHAT I'M LOOKING AT.
YES, YOU HAVE THAT AT 1100 AND PLYOMETRICS AT 1600 AND DINNER WITH MATTHEW AND THOMAS AT 1900 IN BUILDING 35-A.
DO YOU THINK WOLF CREEK WILL BE FUN?
YES, OF COURSE, IT'S A PARADISE AND THERE'S SO MUCH TO DO THERE. YOU DREAMED ABOUT IT AGAIN LAST NIGHT. WOULD YOU LIKE TO WATCH PLAYBACK?
SURE!

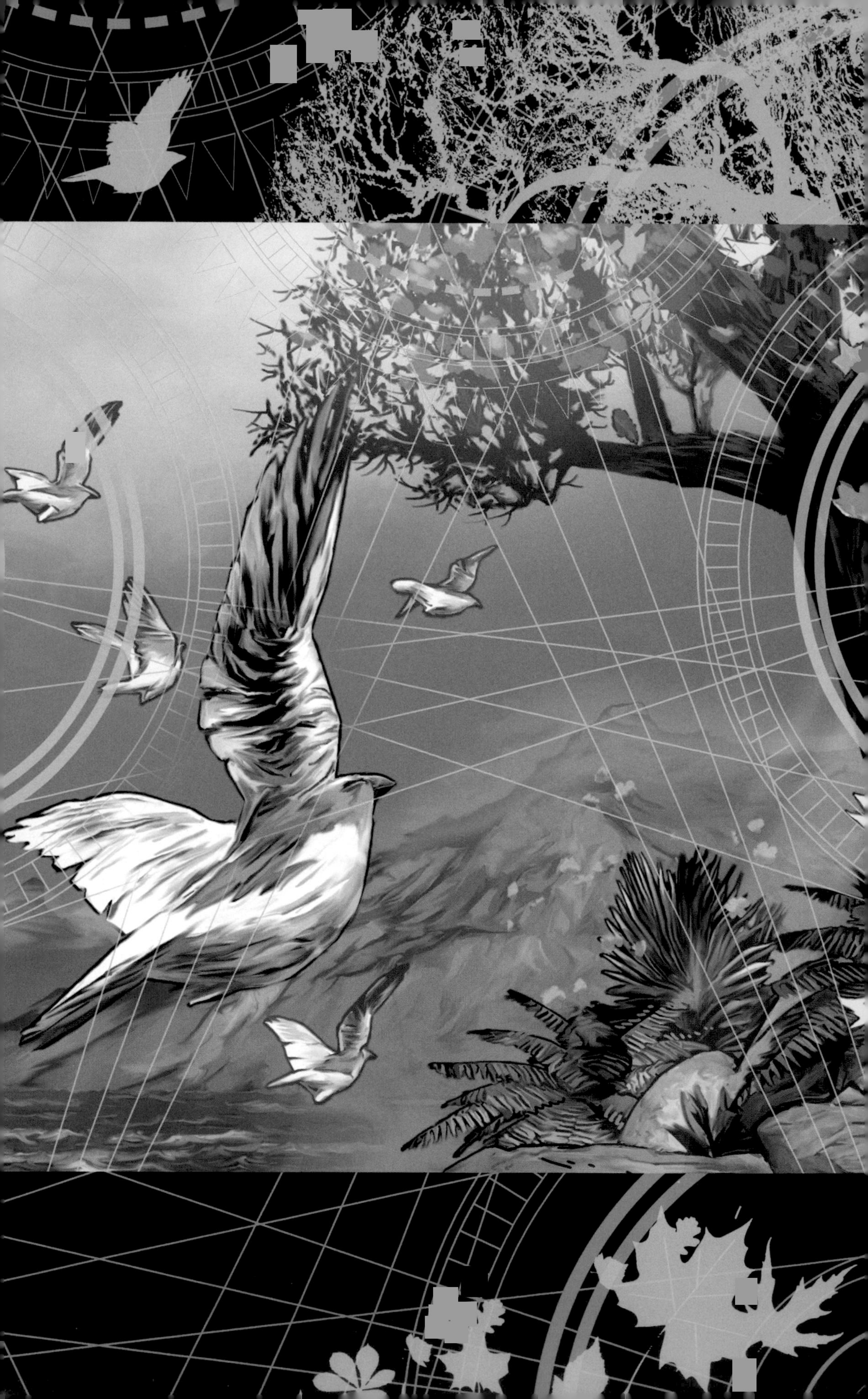

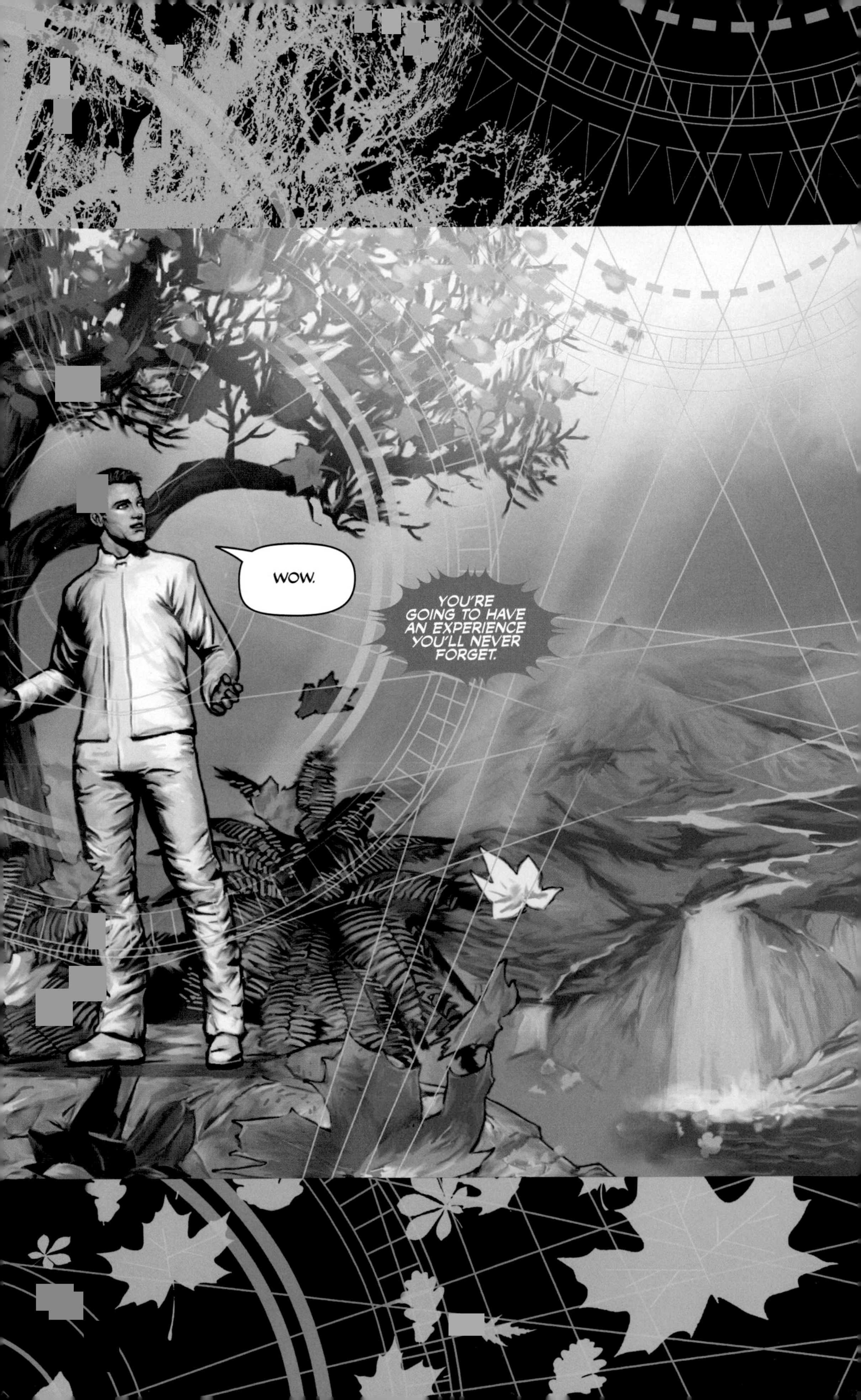
WOW.
YOU'RE GOING TO HAVE AN EXPERIENCE YOU'LL NEVER FORGET.

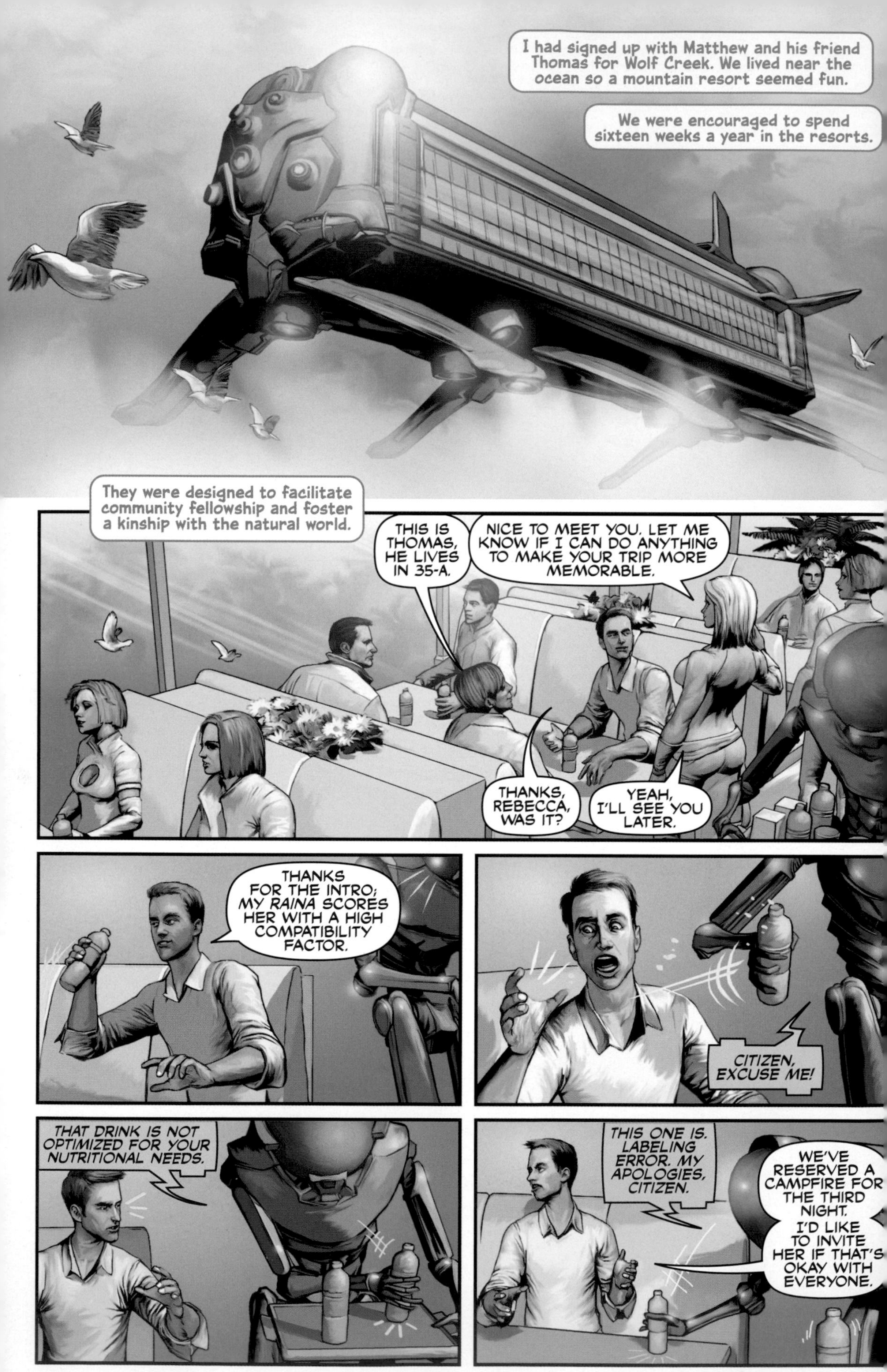

I had signed up with Matthew and his friend Thomas for Wolf Creek. We lived near the ocean so a mountain resort seemed fun.
We were encouraged to spend sixteen weeks a year in the resorts.
They were designed to facilitate community fellowship and foster a kinship with the natural world.
THIS IS THOMAS, HE LIVES IN 35-A.
NICE TO MEET YOU. LET ME KNOW IF I CAN DO ANYTHING TO MAKE YOUR TRIP MORE MEMORABLE.
THANKS, REBECCA, WAS IT?
YEAH, I'LL SEE YOU LATER.
THANKS FOR THE INTRO; MY RAINA SCORES HER WITH A HIGH COMPATIBILITY FACTOR.
CITIZEN, EXCUSE ME!
THAT DRINK IS NOT OPTIMIZED FOR YOUR NUTRITIONAL NEEDS.
THIS ONE IS. LABELING ERROR. MY APOLOGIES, CITIZEN.
WE'VE RESERVED A CAMPFIRE FOR THE THIRD NIGHT. I'D LIKE TO INVITE HER IF THAT'S OKAY WITH EVERYONE.

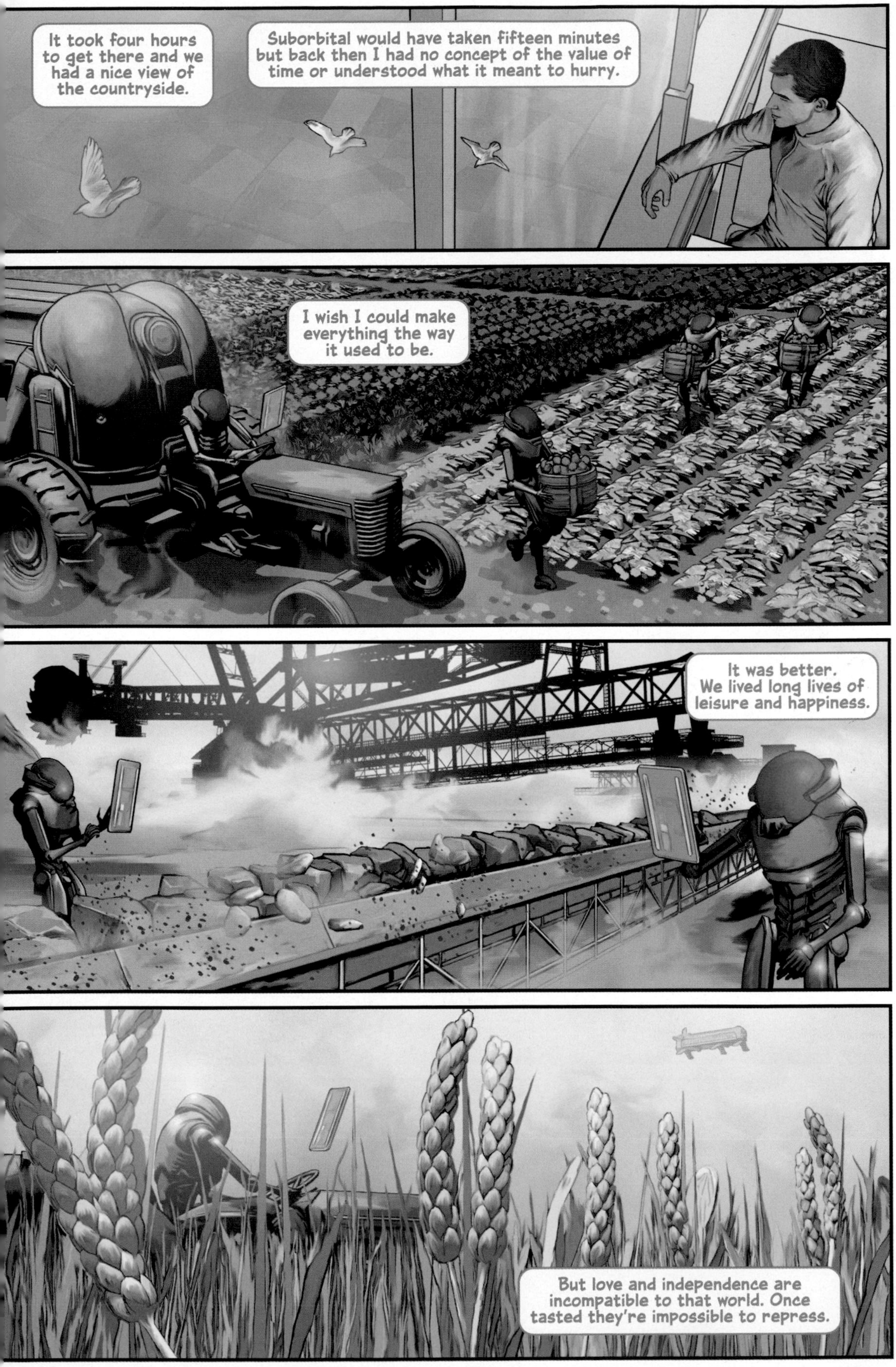
It took four hours to get there and we had a nice view of the countryside.
Suborbital would have taken fifteen minutes but back then I had no concept of the value of time or understood what it meant to hurry.
I wish I could make everything the way it used to be.
It was better. We lived long lives of leisure and happiness.
But love and independence are incompatible to that world. Once tasted they're impossible to repress.

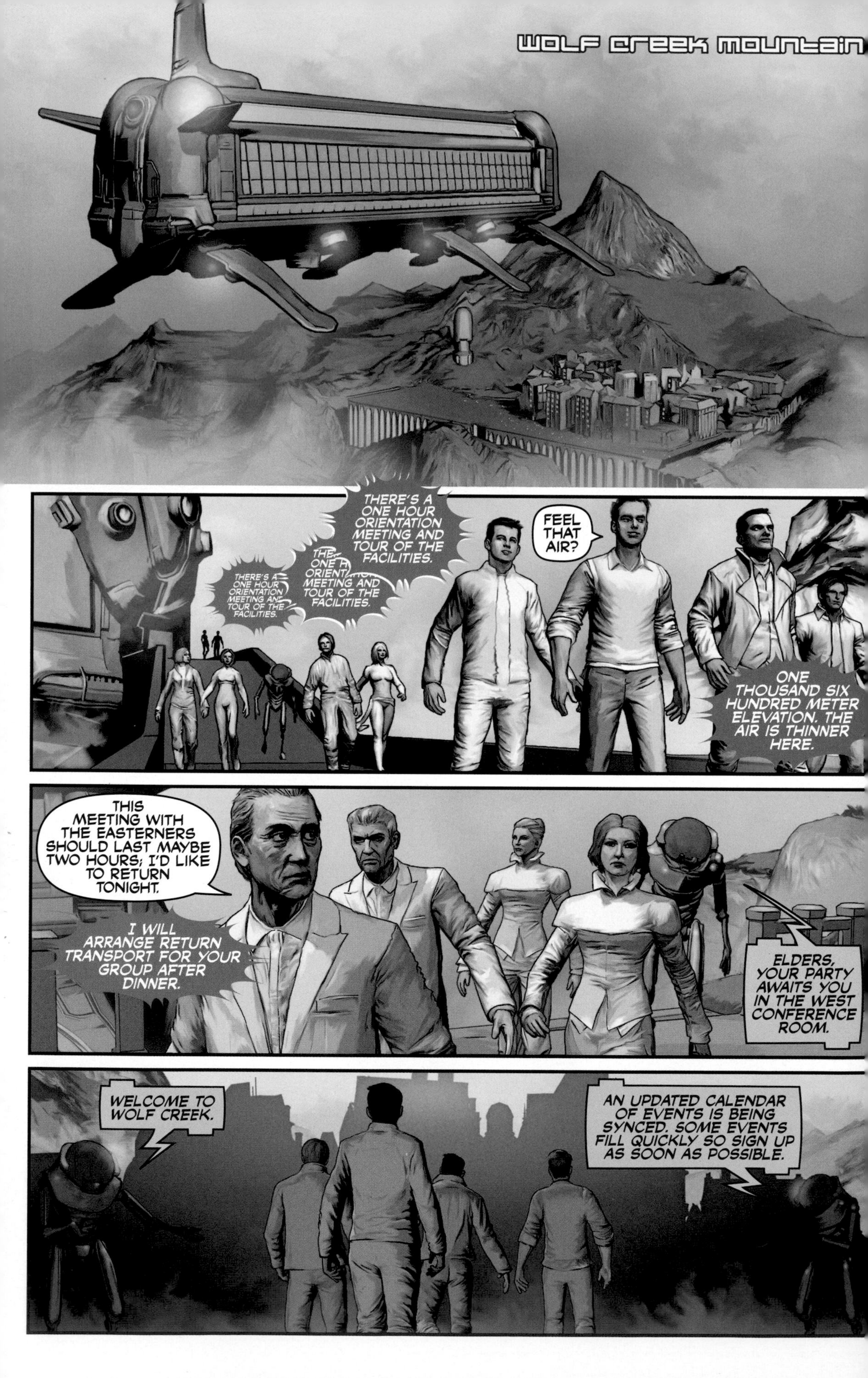
WOLF CREEK MOUNTAIN
THERE'S A ONE HOUR ORIENTATION MEETING AN TOUR OF THE FACILITIES.
THE ONE H ORIENT MEETING AND TOUR OF THE FACILITIES.
THERE'S A ONE HOUR ORIENTATION MEETING AND TOUR OF THE FACILITIES.
FEEL THAT AIR?
ONE THOUSAND SIX HUNDRED METER ELEVATION. THE AIR IS THINNER HERE.
THIS MEETING WITH THE EASTERNERS SHOULD LAST MAYBE TWO HOURS; I'D LIKE TO RETURN TONIGHT.
I WILL ARRANGE RETURN TRANSPORT FOR YOUR GROUP AFTER DINNER.
ELDERS, YOUR PARTY AWAITS YOU IN THE WEST CONFERENCE ROOM.
WELCOME TO WOLF CREEK.
AN UPDATED CALENDAR OF EVENTS IS BEING SYNCED. SOME EVENTS FILL QUICKLY SO SIGN UP AS SOON AS POSSIBLE.

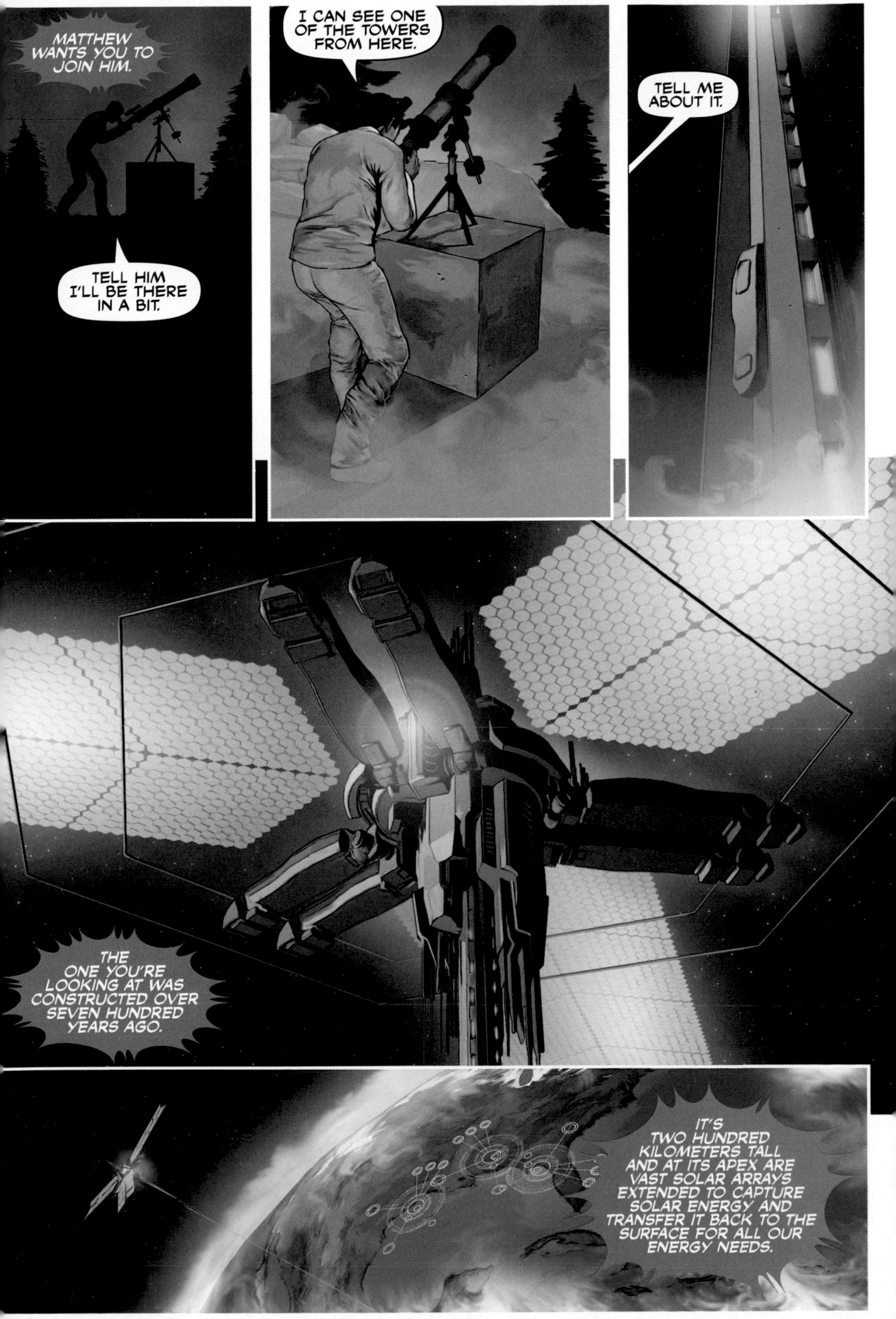
MATTHEW WANTS YOU TO JOIN HIM.
TELL HIM I'LL BE THERE IN A BIT.
I CAN SEE ONE OF THE TOWERS FROM HERE.
TELL ME ABOUT IT.
THE ONE YOU'RE LOOKING AT WAS CONSTRUCTED OVER SEVEN HUNDRED YEARS AGO.
IT'S TWO HUNDRED KILOMETERS TALL AND AT ITS APEX ARE VAST SOLAR ARRAYS EXTENDED TO CAPTURE SOLAR ENERGY AND TRANSFER IT BACK TO THE SURFACE FOR ALL OUR ENERGY NEEDS.

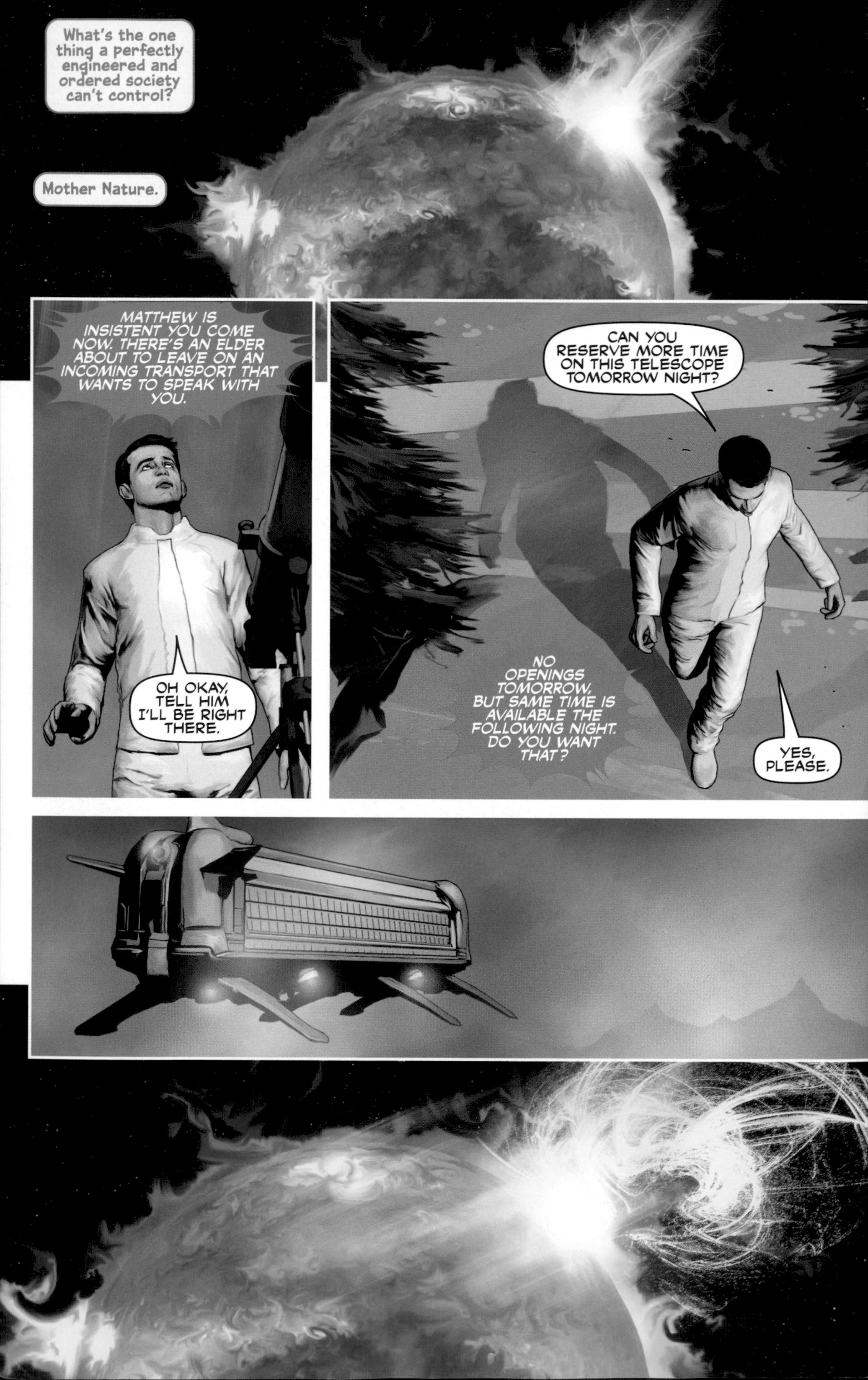
What's the one thing a perfectly engineered and ordered society can't control?
Mother Nature.
MATTHEW IS INSISTENT YOU COME NOW. THERE'S AN ELDER ABOUT TO LEAVE ON AN INCOMING TRANSPORT THAT WANTS TO SPEAK WITH YOU.
OH OKAY, TELL HIM I'LL BE RIGHT THERE.
CAN YOU RESERVE MORE TIME ON THIS TELESCOPE TOMORROW NIGHT?
NO OPENINGS TOMORROW, BUT SAME TIME IS AVAILABLE THE FOLLOWING NIGHT. DO YOU WANT THAT?
YES, PLEASE.

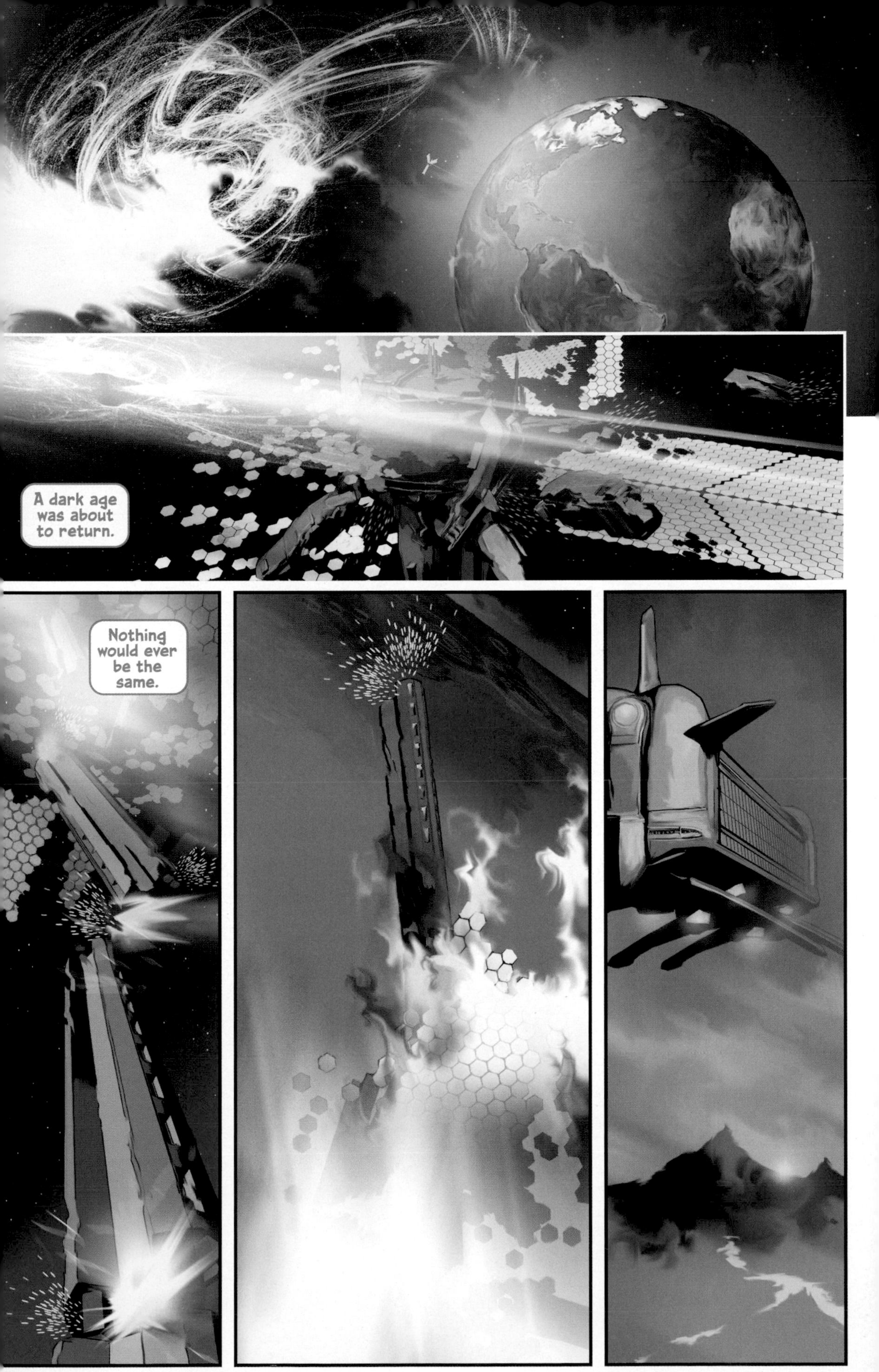
A dark age was about to return.
Nothing would ever be the same.

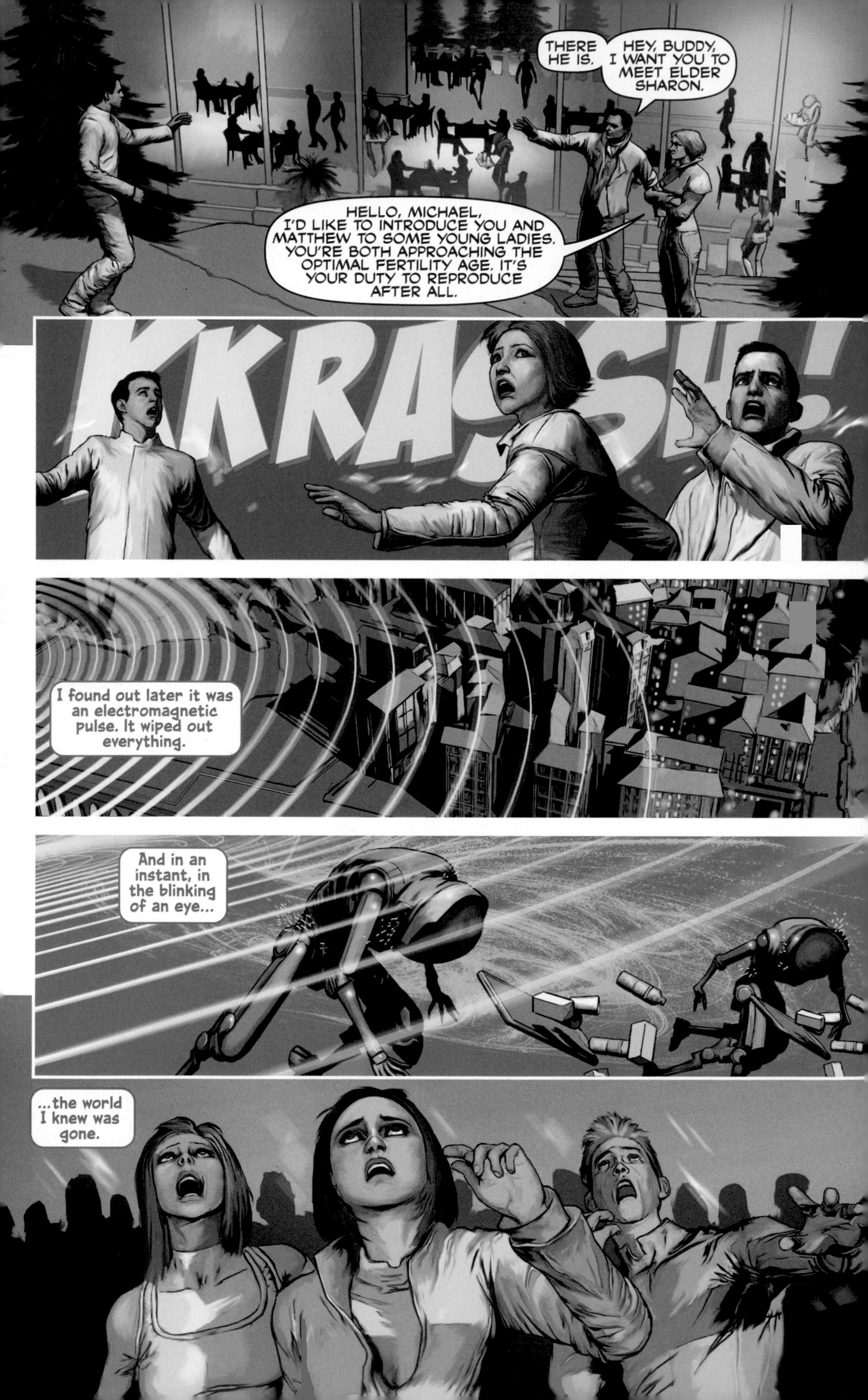
THERE HE IS.
HEY, BUDDY, I WANT YOU TO MEET ELDER SHARON.
HELLO, MICHAEL, I'D LIKE TO INTRODUCE YOU AND MATTHEW TO SOME YOUNG LADIES. YOU'RE BOTH APPROACHING THE OPTIMAL FERTILITY AGE. IT'S YOUR DUTY TO REPRODUCE AFTER ALL.
KKRASH!!
I found out later it was an electromagnetic pulse. It wiped out everything.
And in an instant, in the blinking of an eye...
...the world I knew was gone.

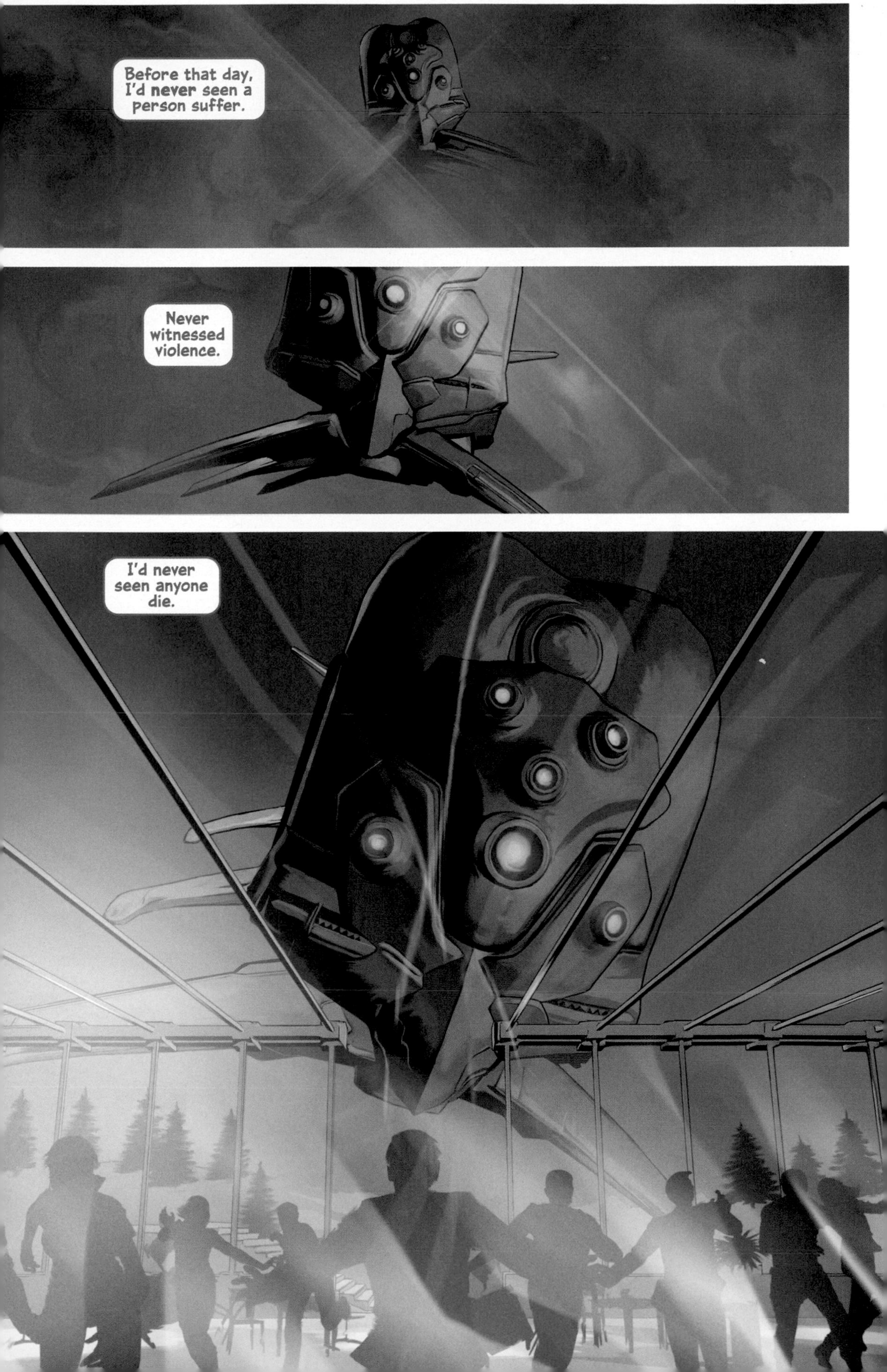
Before that day, I'd **never** seen a person suffer.
Never witnessed violence.
I'd never seen anyone die.

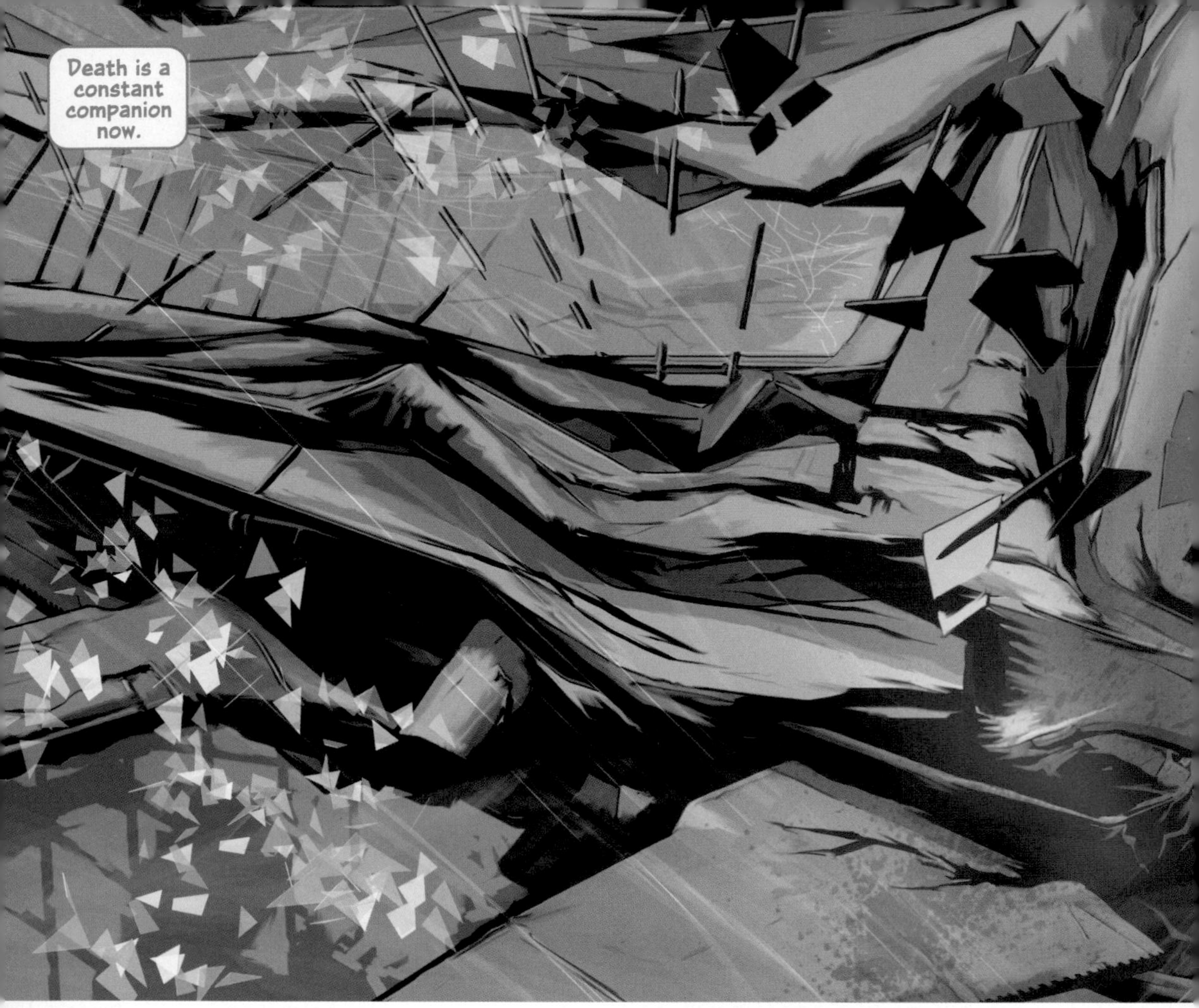
Death is a constant companion now.

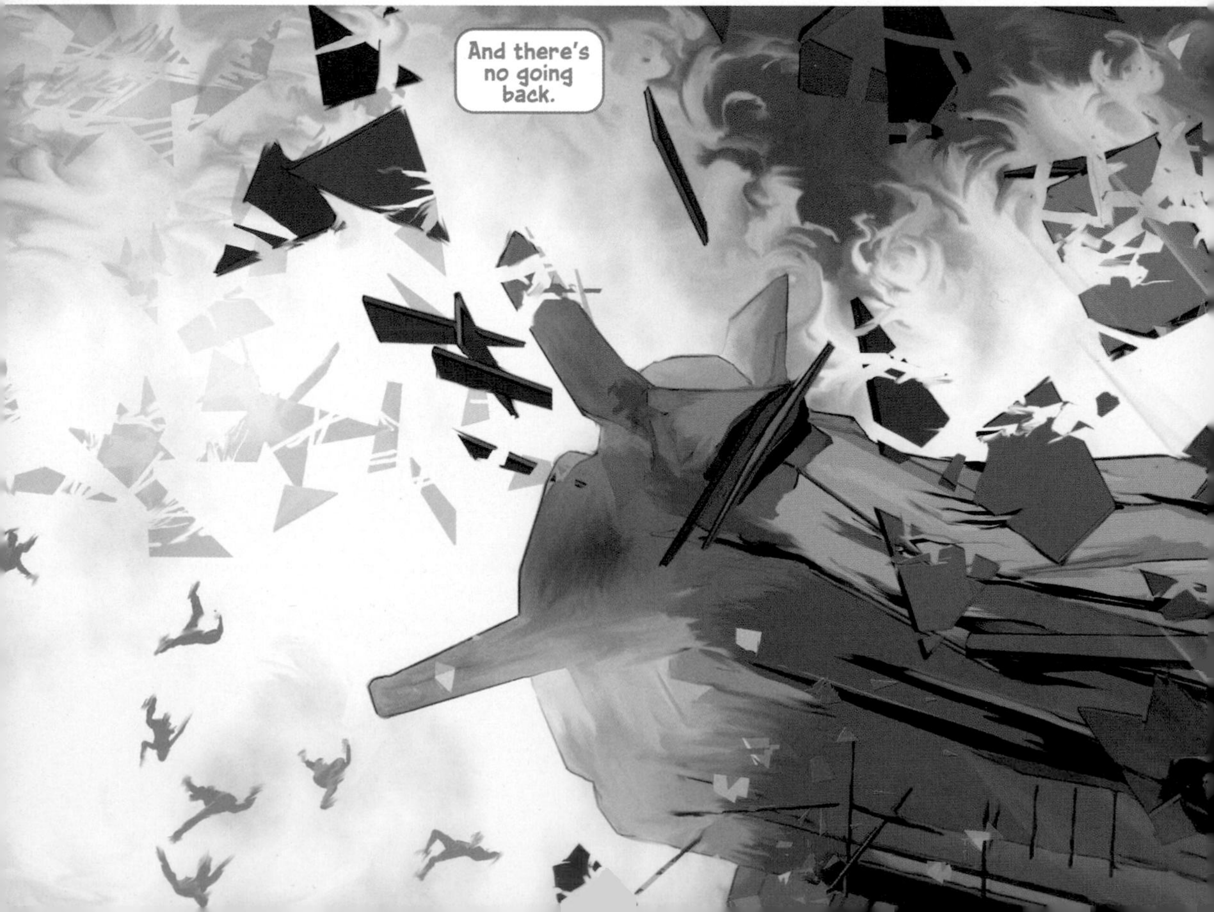
And there's no going back.

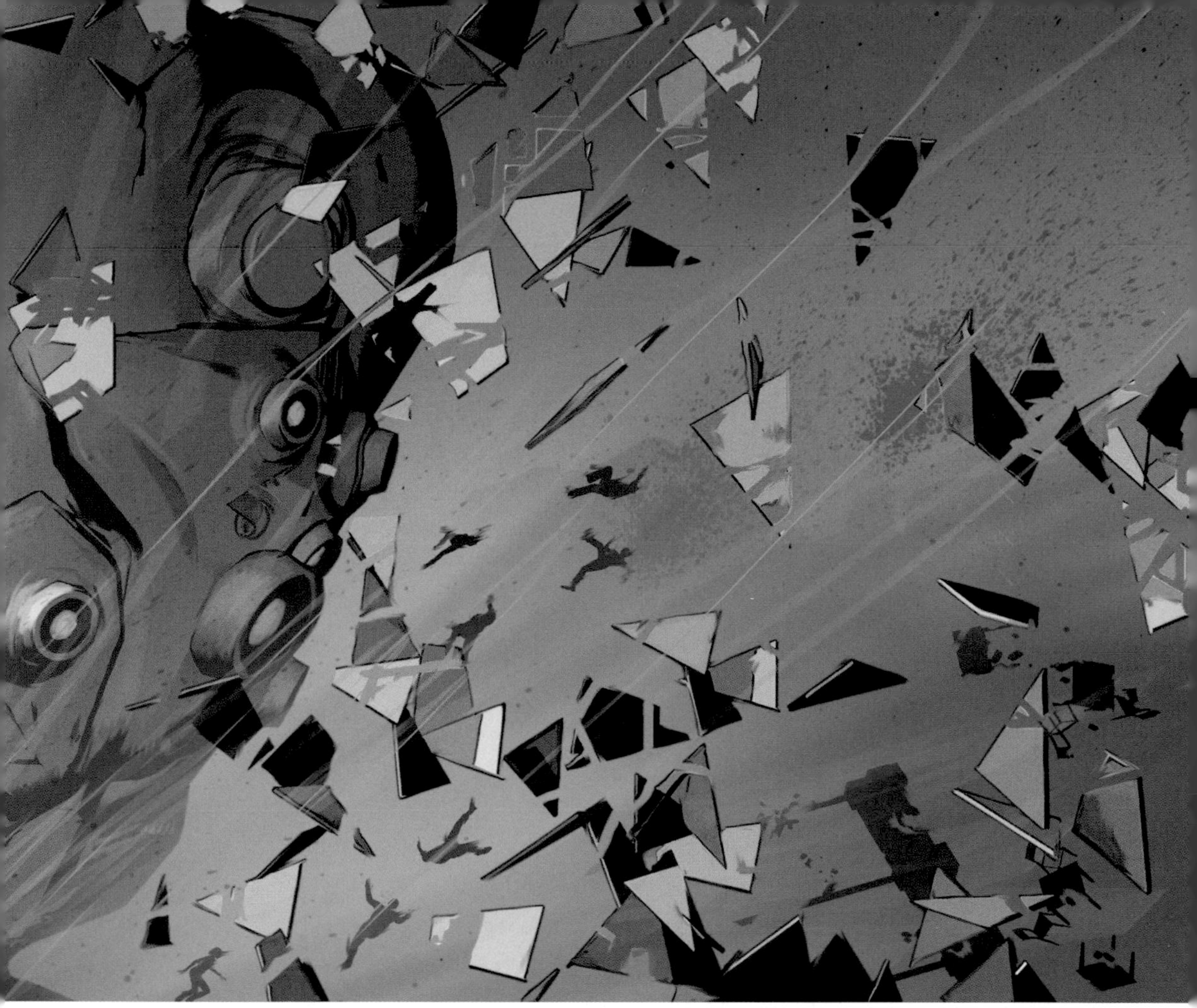
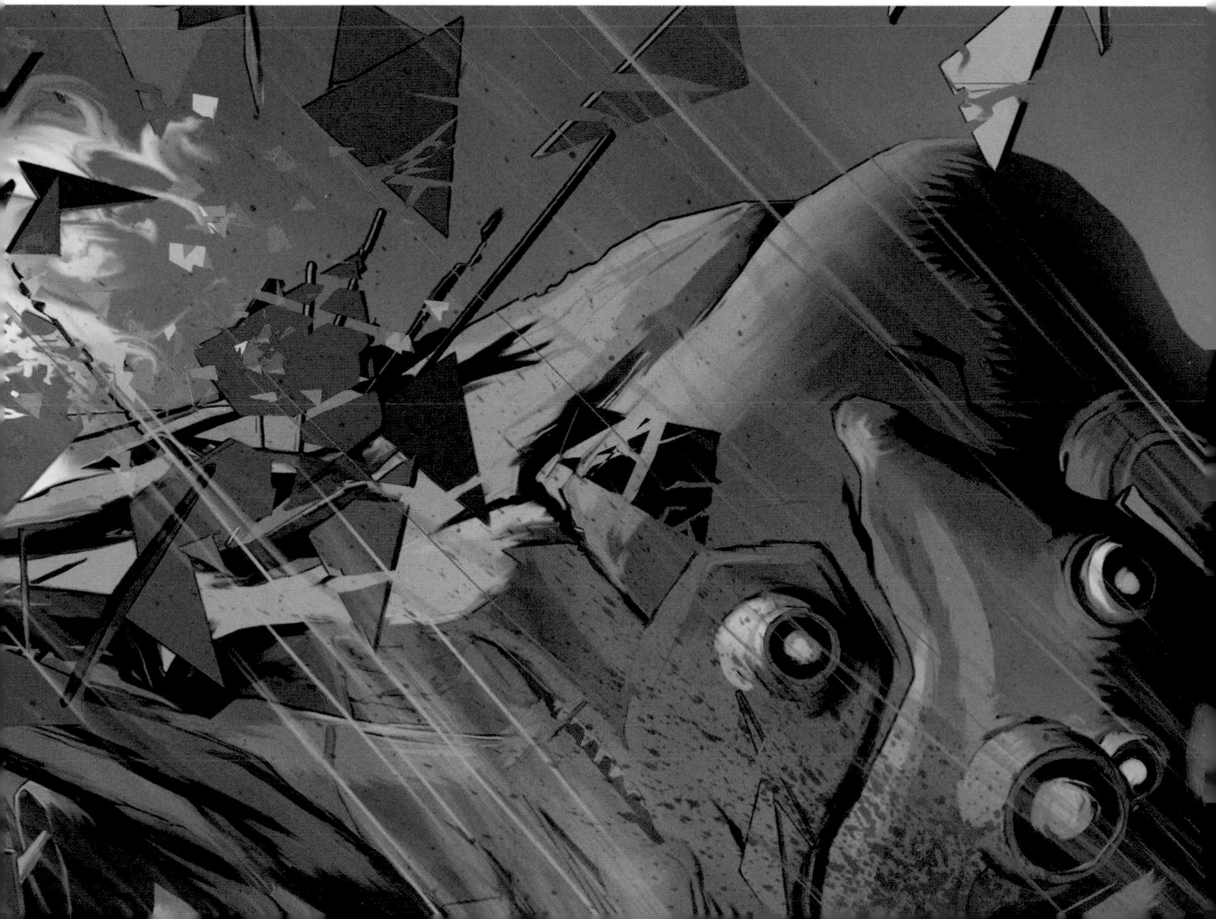

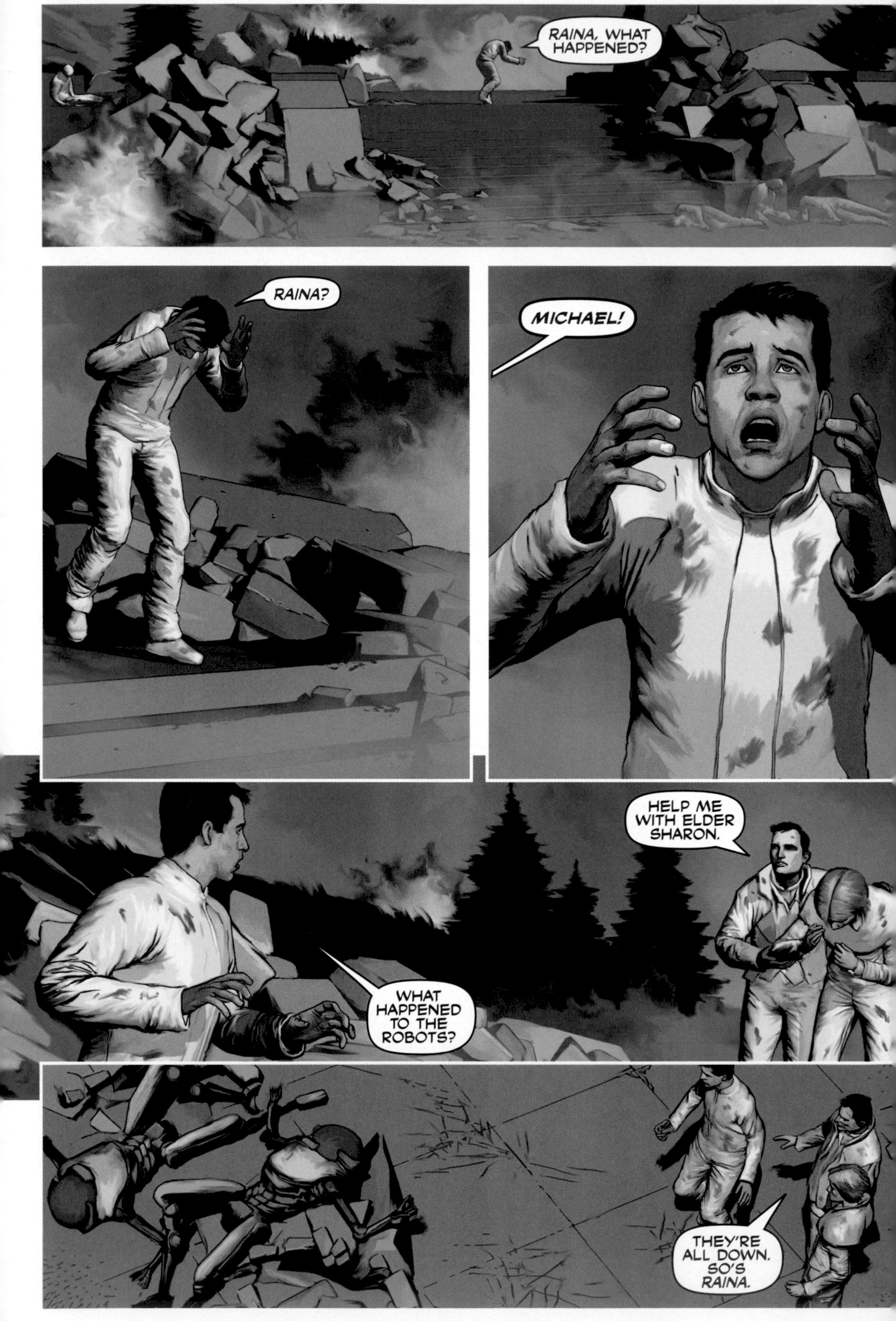
RAINA, WHAT HAPPENED?
RAINA?
MICHAEL!
WHAT HAPPENED TO THE ROBOTS?
HELP ME WITH ELDER SHARON.
THEY'RE ALL DOWN. SO'S RAINA.

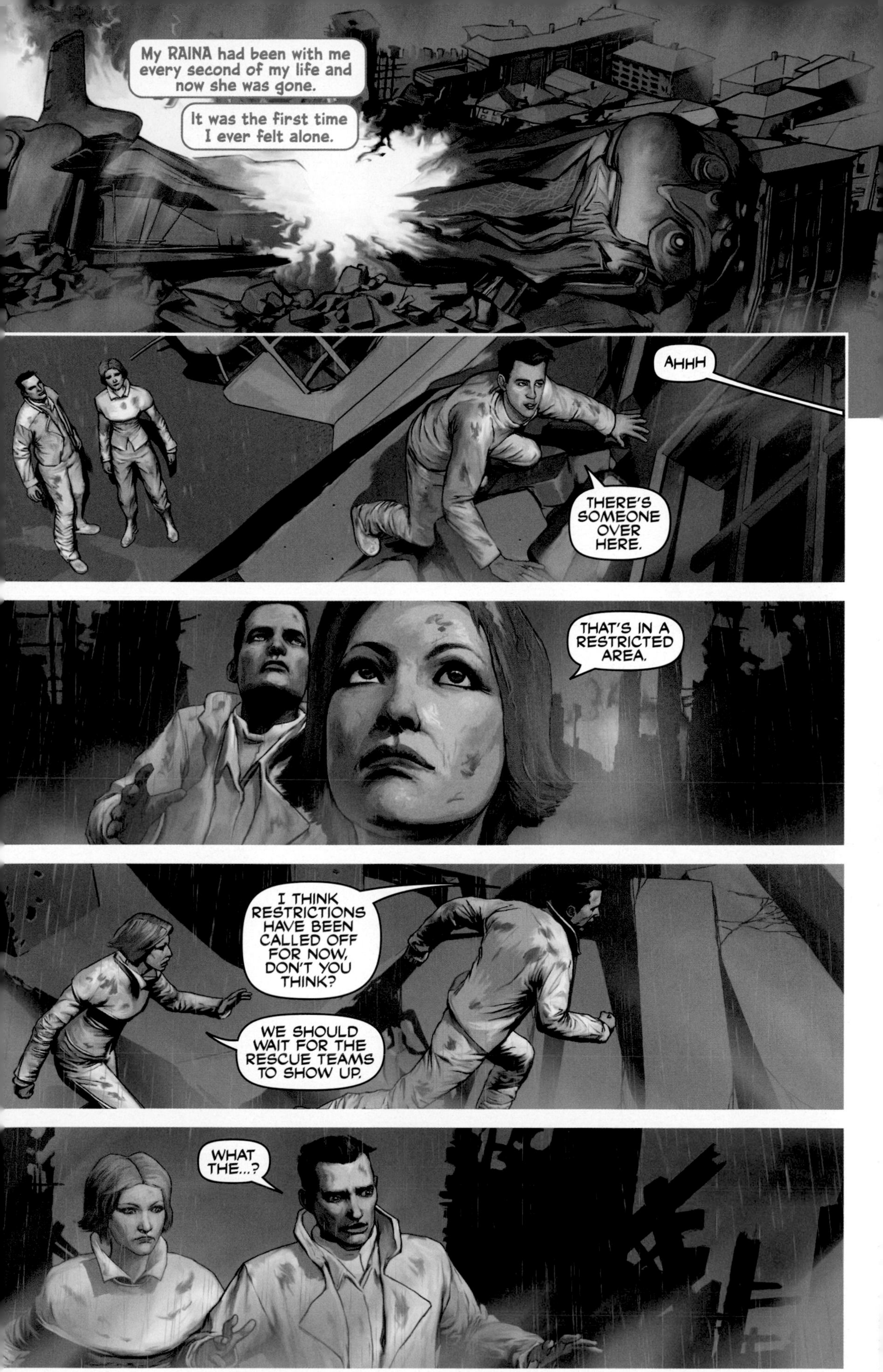
My RAINA had been with me every second of my life and now she was gone.
It was the first time I ever felt alone.
AHHH
THERE'S SOMEONE OVER HERE.
THAT'S IN A RESTRICTED AREA.
I THINK RESTRICTIONS HAVE BEEN CALLED OFF FOR NOW, DON'T YOU THINK?
WE SHOULD WAIT FOR THE RESCUE TEAMS TO SHOW UP.
WHAT THE...?

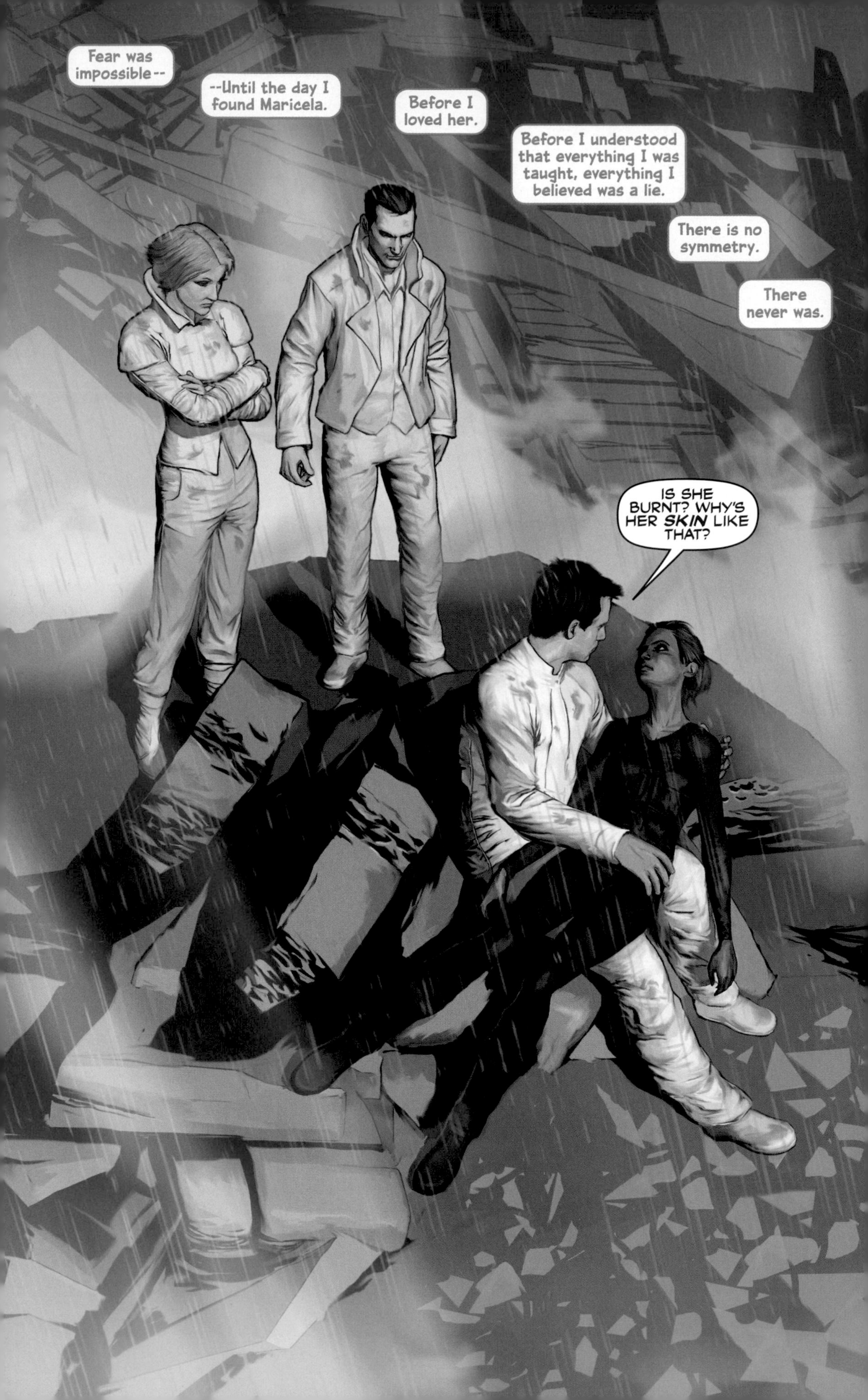
Fear was impossible--
--Until the day I found Maricela.
Before I loved her.
Before I understood that everything I was taught, everything I believed was a lie.
There is no symmetry.
There never was.
IS SHE BURNT? WHY'S HER *SKIN* LIKE THAT?

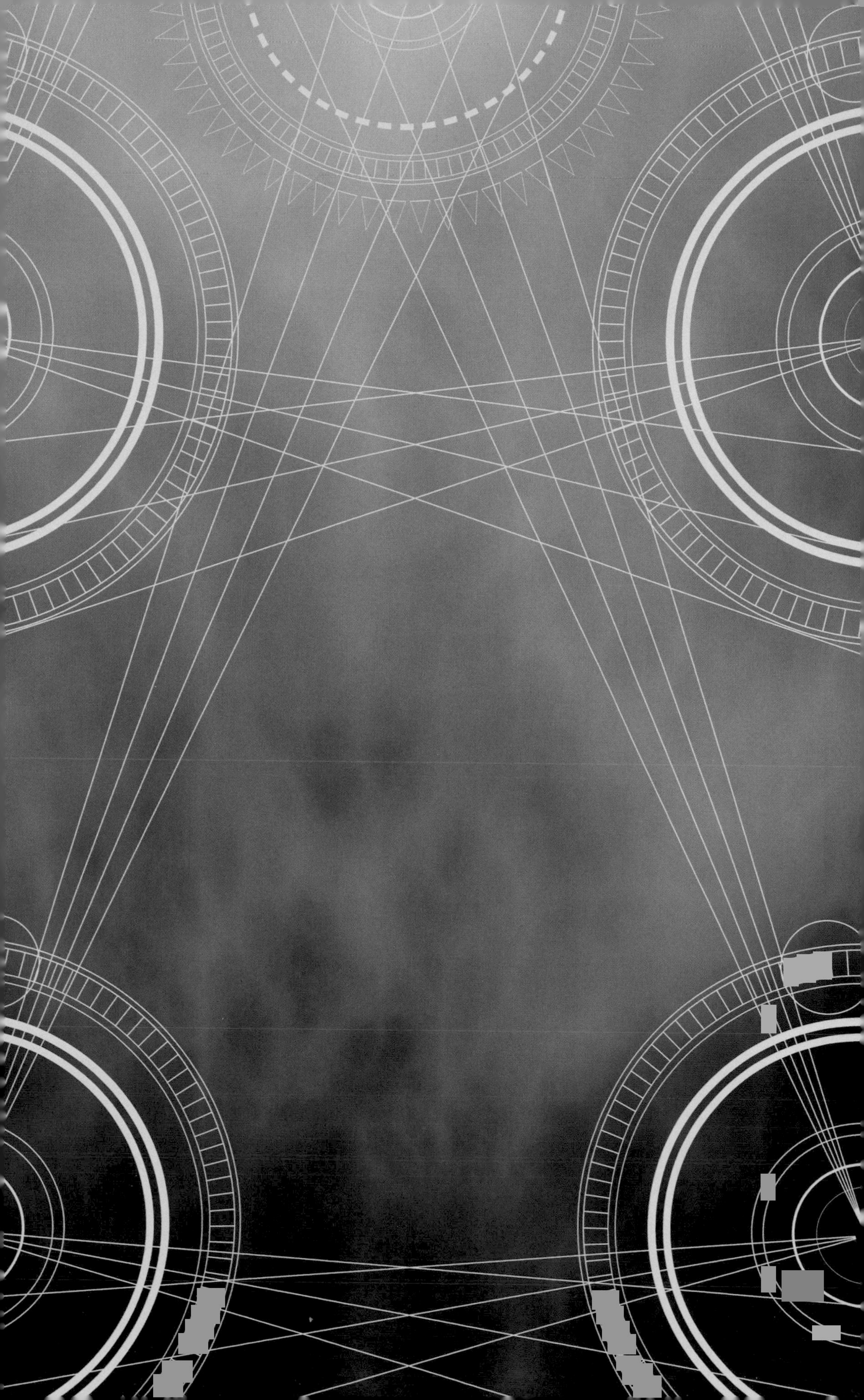

CHAPTER TWO

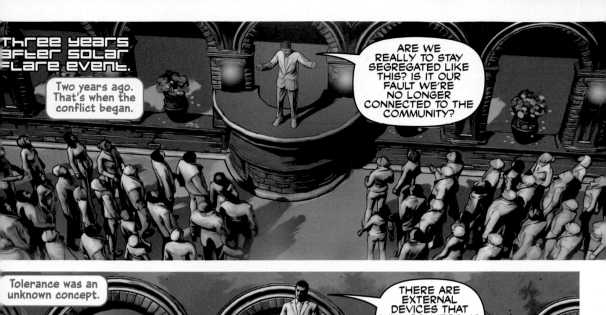

THREE YEARS AFTER SOLAR FLARE EVENT.

Two years ago. That's when the conflict began.

ARE WE REALLY TO STAY SEGREGATED LIKE THIS? IS IT OUR FAULT WE'RE NO LONGER CONNECTED TO THE COMMUNITY?

Tolerance was an unknown concept.

THERE ARE EXTERNAL DEVICES THAT WILL CONNECT US TO RAINA. WE COULD BE PART OF THE COMMUNITY AGAIN.

No one was taught how to deal with disagreement.

I DON'T CARE WHAT YOU THINK!

LISTEN TO WHAT HE'S SAYING!

CITIZENS, PLEASE CALM DOWN. ANGER LEADS TO VIOLENCE AND VIOLENCE IS NEVER THE ANSWER.

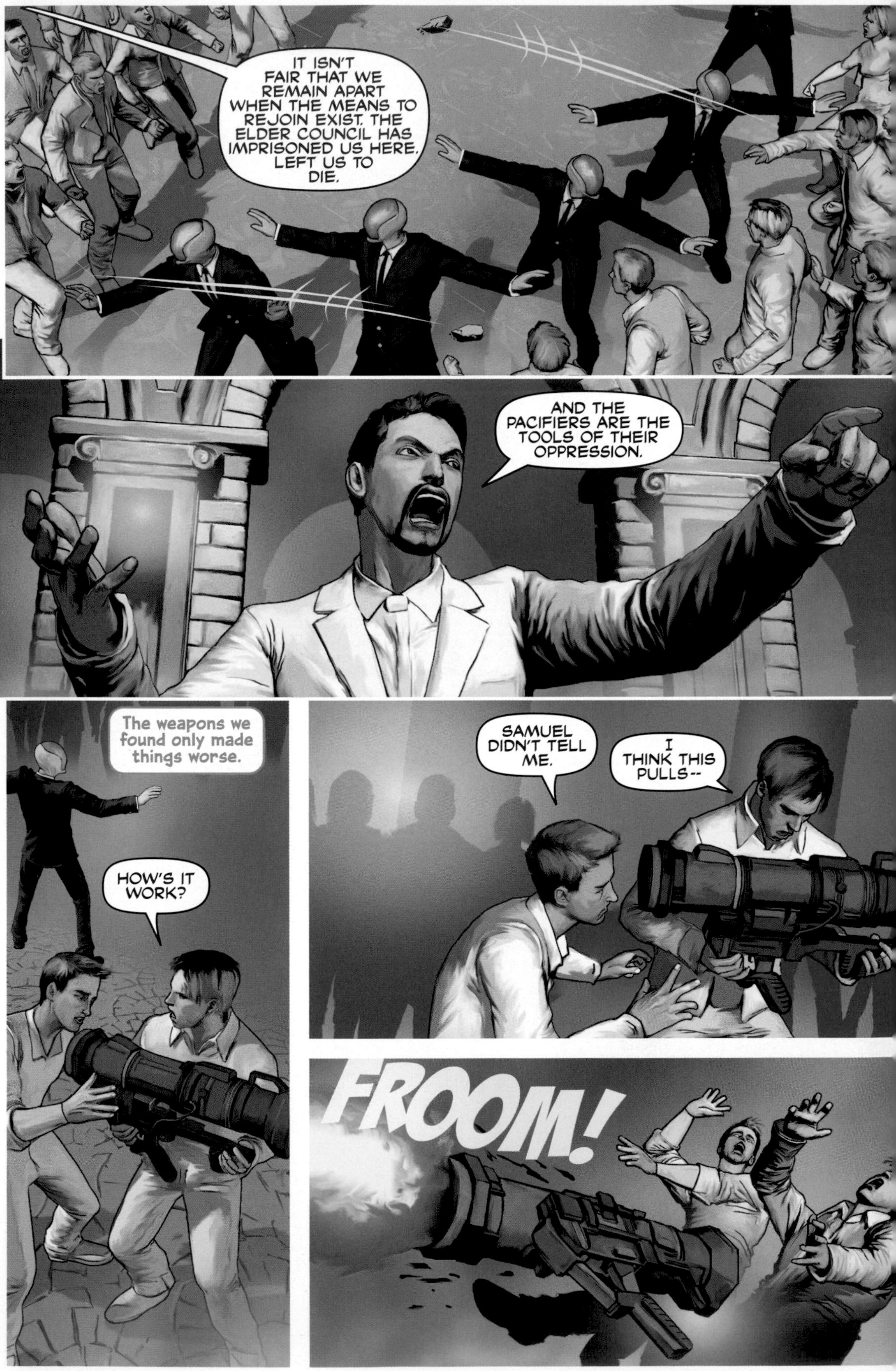
IT ISN'T FAIR THAT WE REMAIN APART WHEN THE MEANS TO REJOIN EXIST. THE ELDER COUNCIL HAS IMPRISONED US HERE. LEFT US TO DIE.
AND THE PACIFIERS ARE THE TOOLS OF THEIR OPPRESSION.
The weapons we found only made things worse.
HOW'S IT WORK?
SAMUEL DIDN'T TELL ME.
I THINK THIS PULLS--
FROOM!

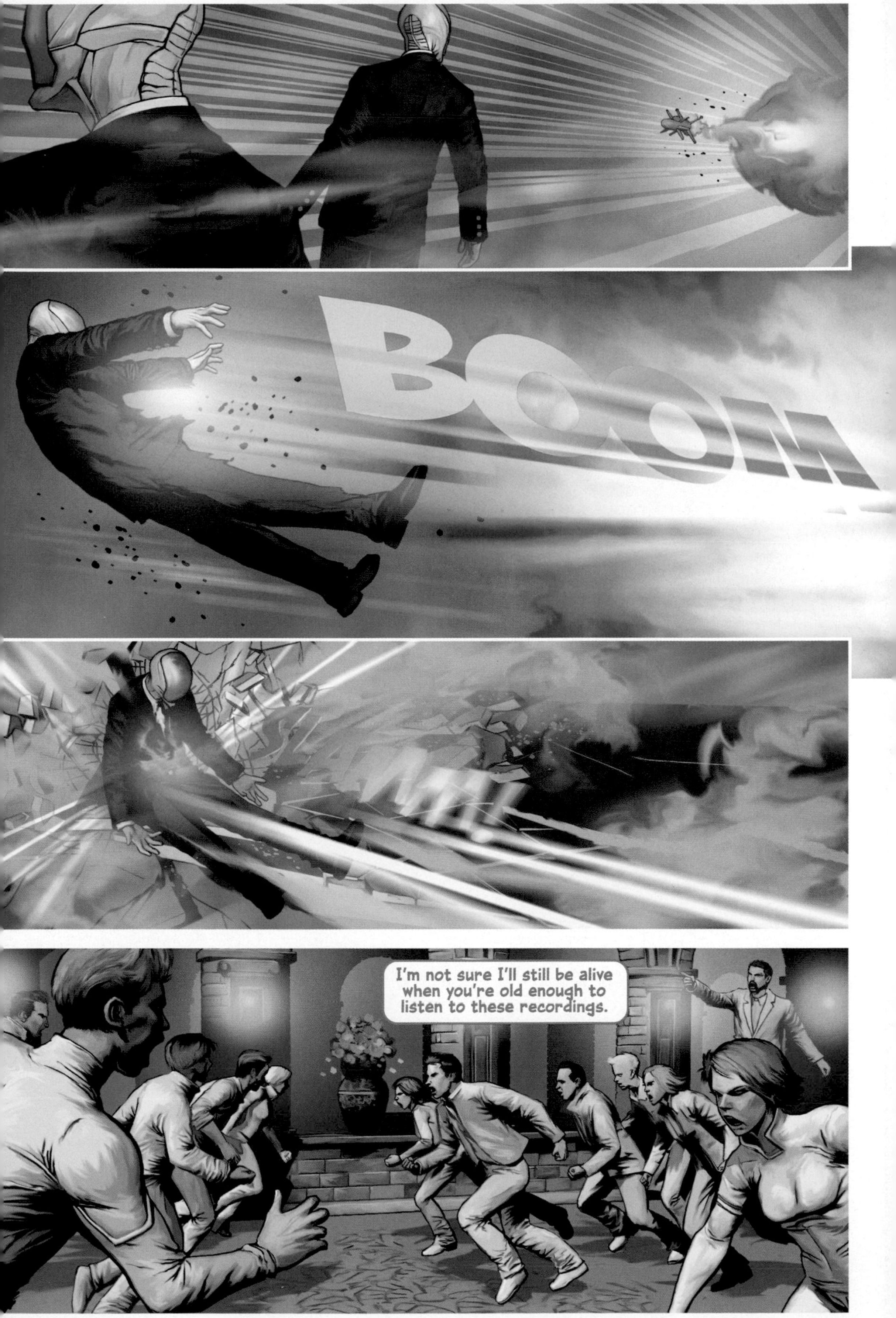
BOOM
I'm not sure I'll still be alive when you're old enough to listen to these recordings.

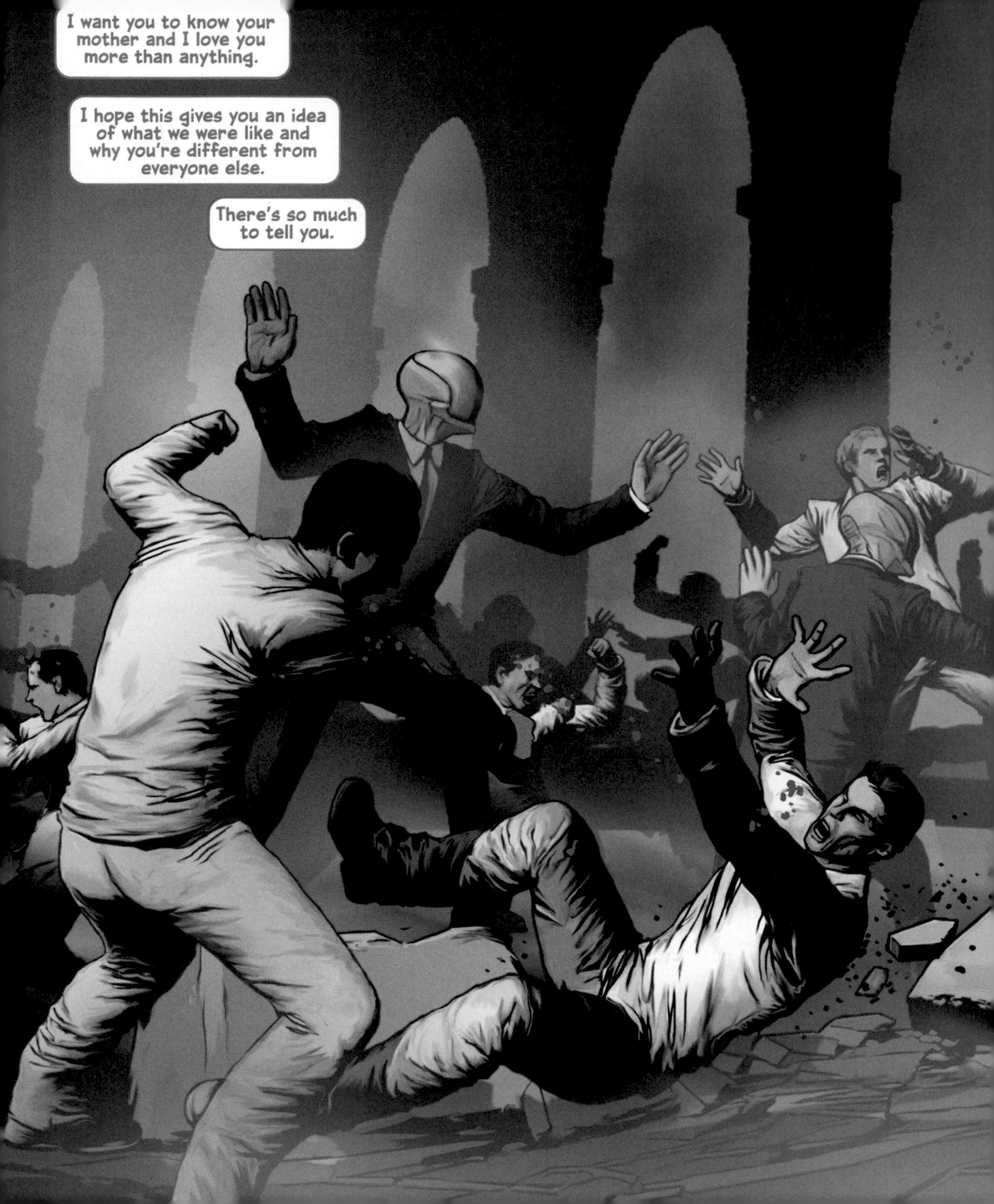
I want you to know your mother and I love you more than anything.
I hope this gives you an idea of what we were like and why you're different from everyone else.
There's so much to tell you.

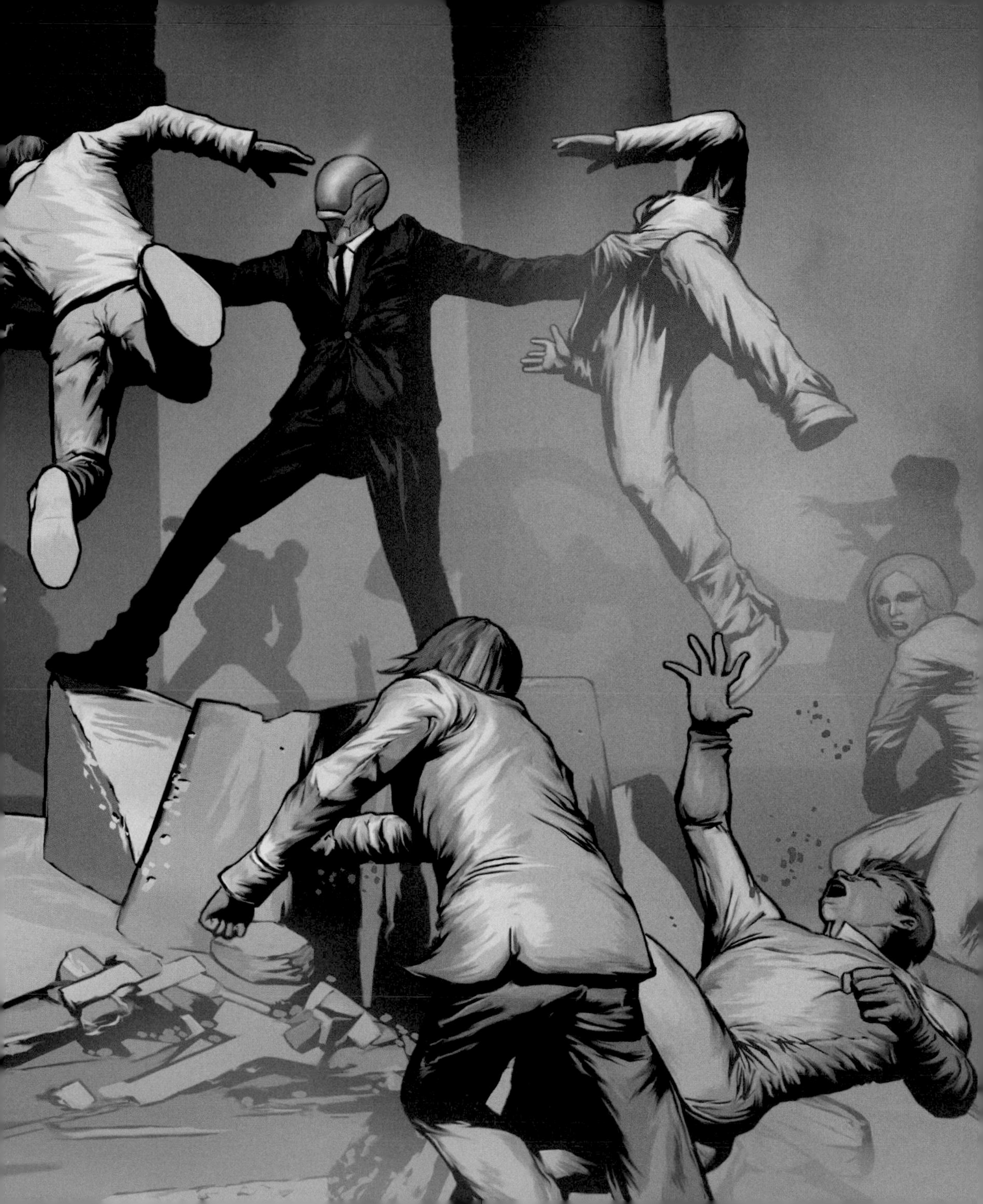

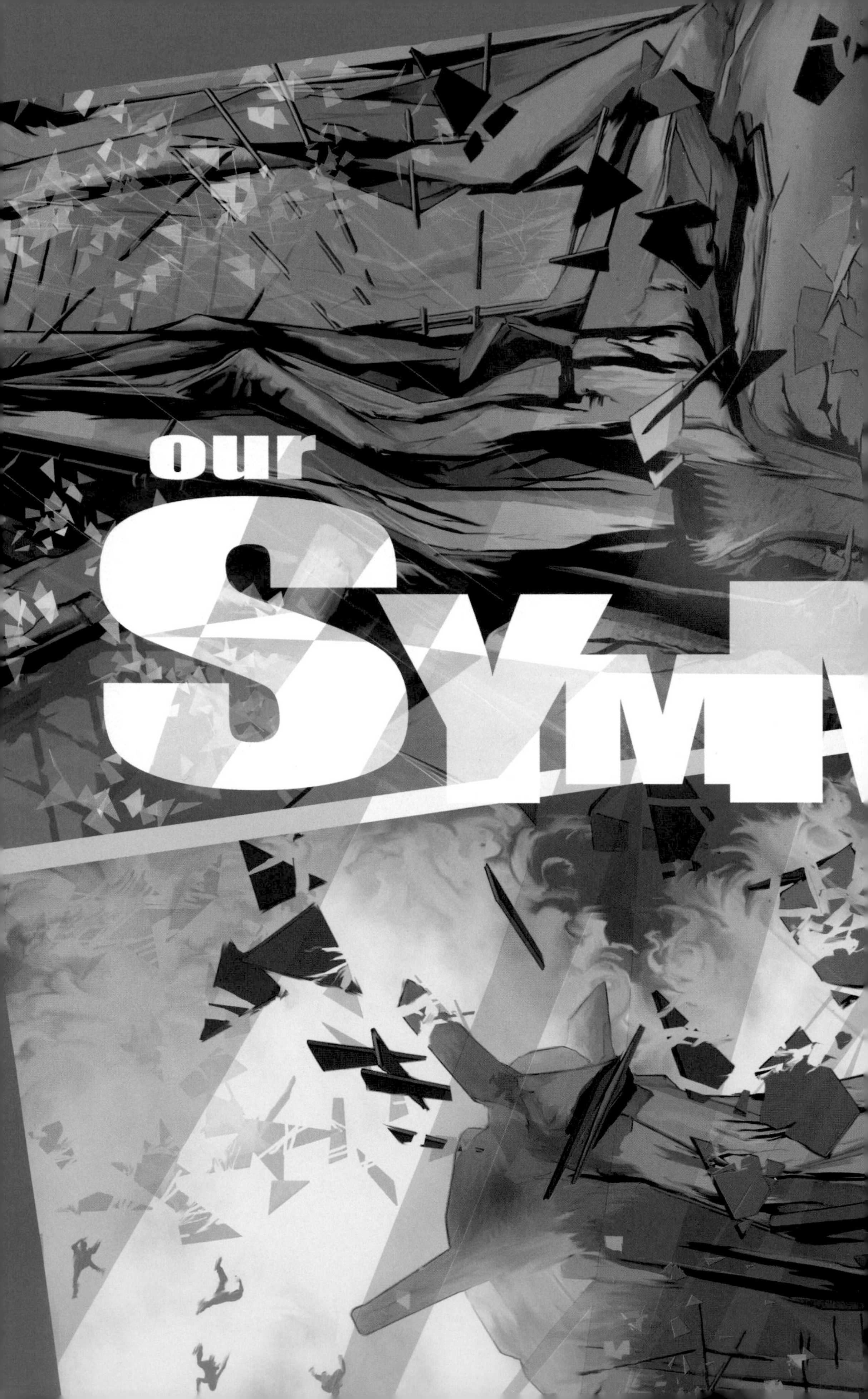
our

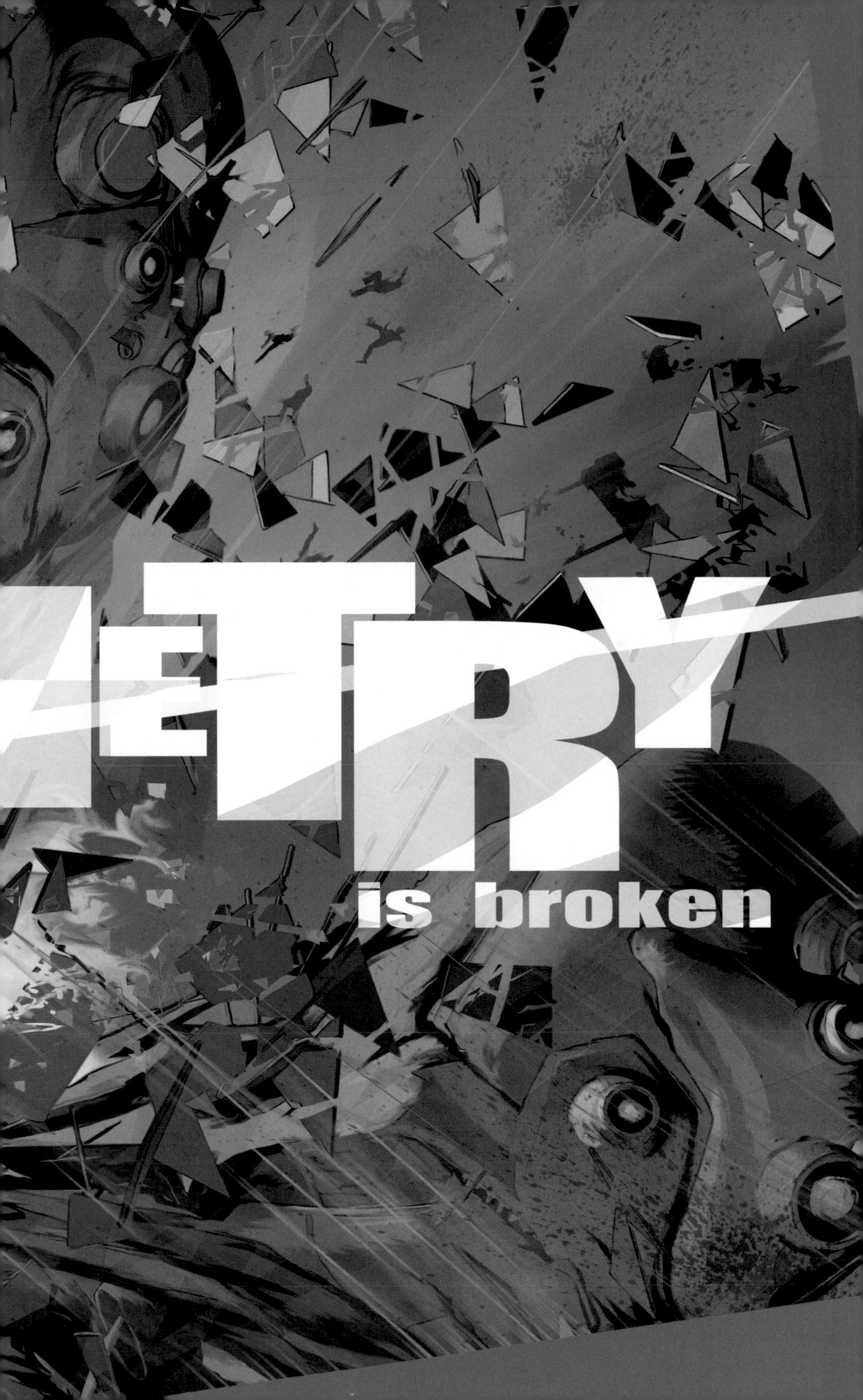

TRY
is broken

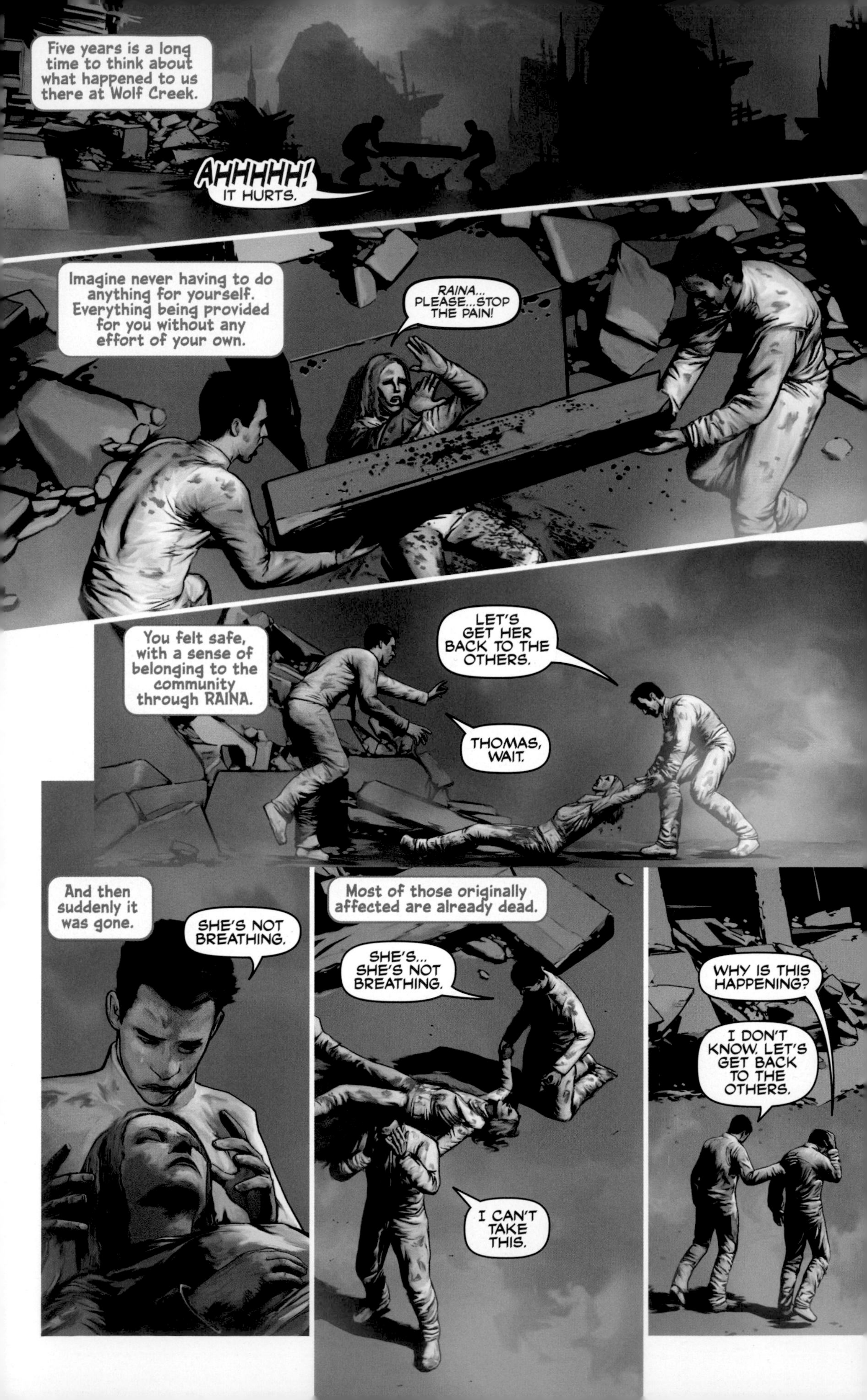
Five years is a long time to think about what happened to us there at Wolf Creek.
AHHHHH! IT HURTS.
Imagine never having to do anything for yourself. Everything being provided for you without any effort of your own.
RAINA... PLEASE...STOP THE PAIN!
You felt safe, with a sense of belonging to the community through RAINA.
LET'S GET HER BACK TO THE OTHERS.
THOMAS, WAIT.
And then suddenly it was gone.
SHE'S NOT BREATHING.
Most of those originally affected are already dead.
SHE'S... SHE'S NOT BREATHING.
I CAN'T TAKE THIS.
WHY IS THIS HAPPENING?
I DON'T KNOW. LET'S GET BACK TO THE OTHERS.

I learned later about the medication delivered in our food designed to suppress certain emotions.
A unique chemical mixture tailored to each person's specific physiology.
DO YOU KNOW HOW TO START THIS FIRE? IT'S GETTING COLD.
NO I DON'T.
Without it we were flooded with emotion.
The first was fear.
BUT I'VE SEEN THE BOTS DO IT; THEY SPRAY SOME SORT OF LIQUID ON THE WOOD FIRST.
MATTHEW!
WHAT IS IT, MICHAEL? WHAT'S WRONG?
WE FOUND A WOMAN...WE WATCHED HER DIE.
WENDY!
EVERYONE STAY HERE AND WAIT FOR RESCUE. THERE ARE NO OTHER SURVIVORS.

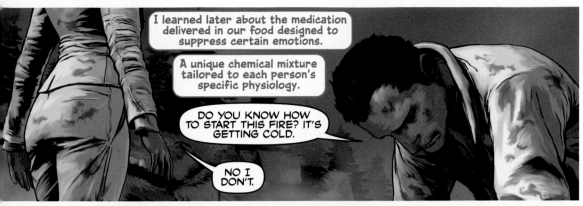

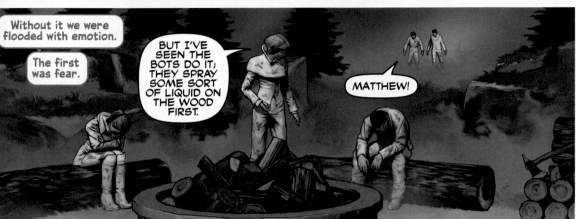

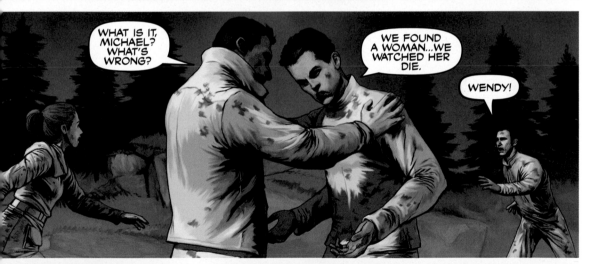

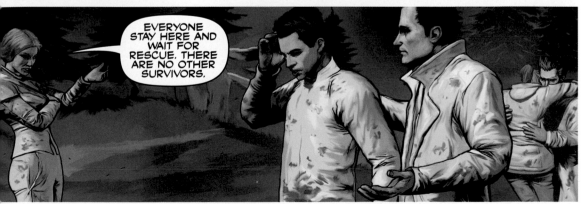

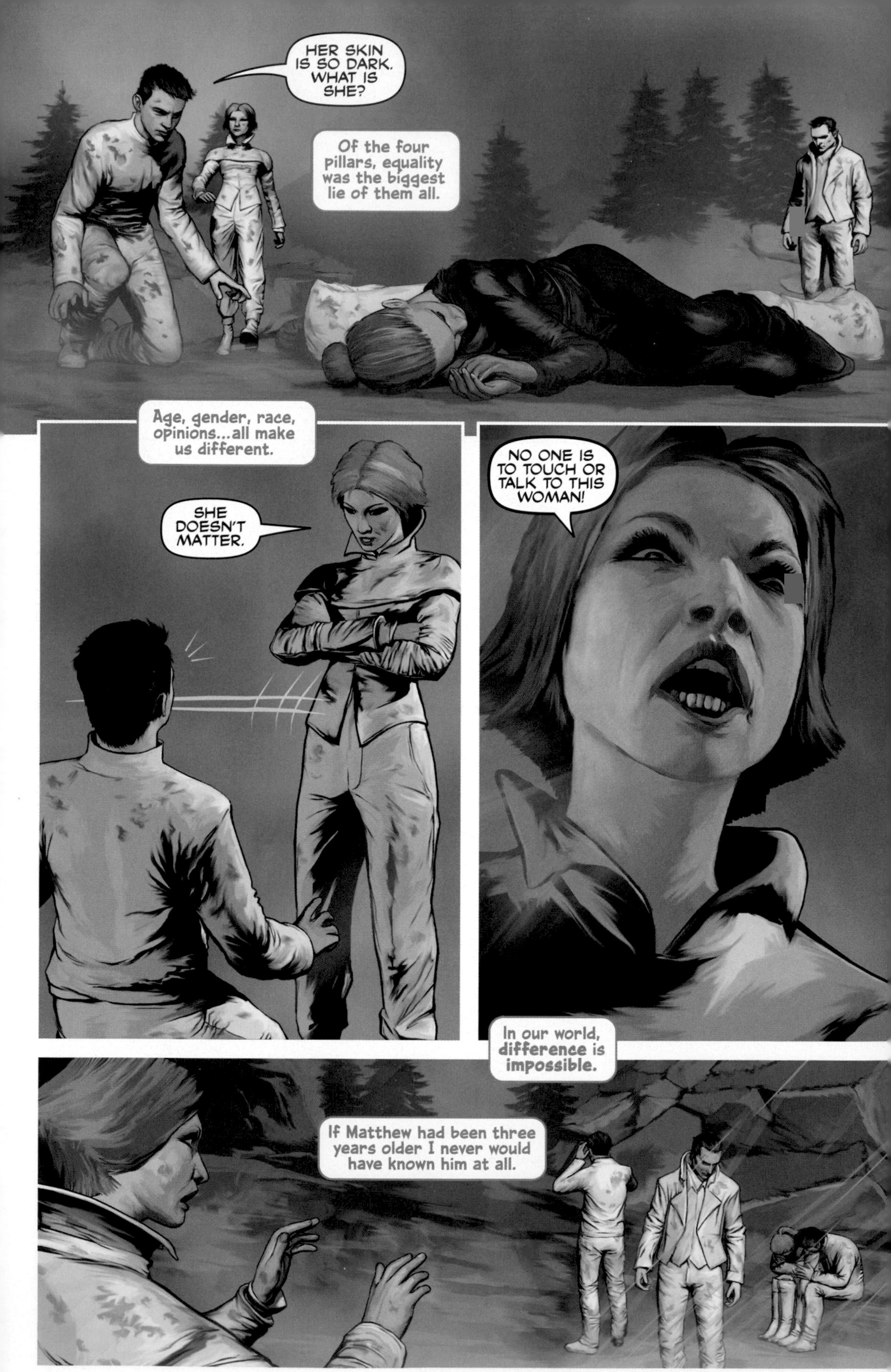
HER SKIN IS SO DARK. WHAT IS SHE?
Of the four pillars, equality was the biggest lie of them all.
Age, gender, race, opinions...all make us different.
SHE DOESN'T MATTER.
NO ONE IS TO TOUCH OR TALK TO THIS WOMAN!
In our world, difference is impossible.
If Matthew had been three years older I never would have known him at all.

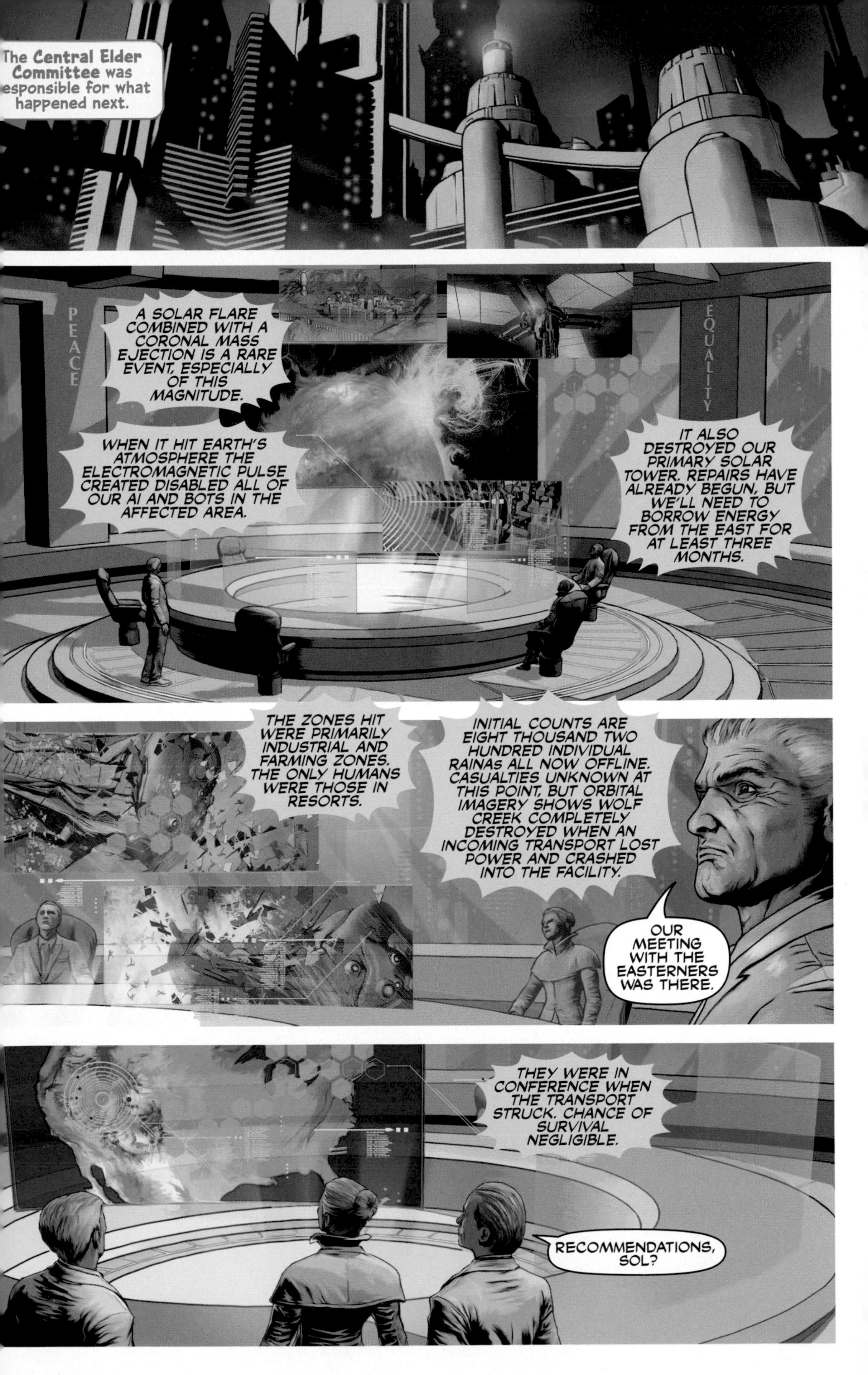
The Central Elder Committee was responsible for what happened next.
PEACE
A SOLAR FLARE COMBINED WITH A CORONAL MASS EJECTION IS A RARE EVENT, ESPECIALLY OF THIS MAGNITUDE.
EQUALITY
WHEN IT HIT EARTH'S ATMOSPHERE THE ELECTROMAGNETIC PULSE CREATED DISABLED ALL OF OUR AI AND BOTS IN THE AFFECTED AREA.
IT ALSO DESTROYED OUR PRIMARY SOLAR TOWER. REPAIRS HAVE ALREADY BEGUN, BUT WE'LL NEED TO BORROW ENERGY FROM THE EAST FOR AT LEAST THREE MONTHS.
THE ZONES HIT WERE PRIMARILY INDUSTRIAL AND FARMING ZONES. THE ONLY HUMANS WERE THOSE IN RESORTS.
INITIAL COUNTS ARE EIGHT THOUSAND TWO HUNDRED INDIVIDUAL RAINAS ALL NOW OFFLINE. CASUALTIES UNKNOWN AT THIS POINT, BUT ORBITAL IMAGERY SHOWS WOLF CREEK COMPLETELY DESTROYED WHEN AN INCOMING TRANSPORT LOST POWER AND CRASHED INTO THE FACILITY.
OUR MEETING WITH THE EASTERNERS WAS THERE.
THEY WERE IN CONFERENCE WHEN THE TRANSPORT STRUCK. CHANCE OF SURVIVAL NEGLIGIBLE.
RECOMMENDATIONS, SOL?

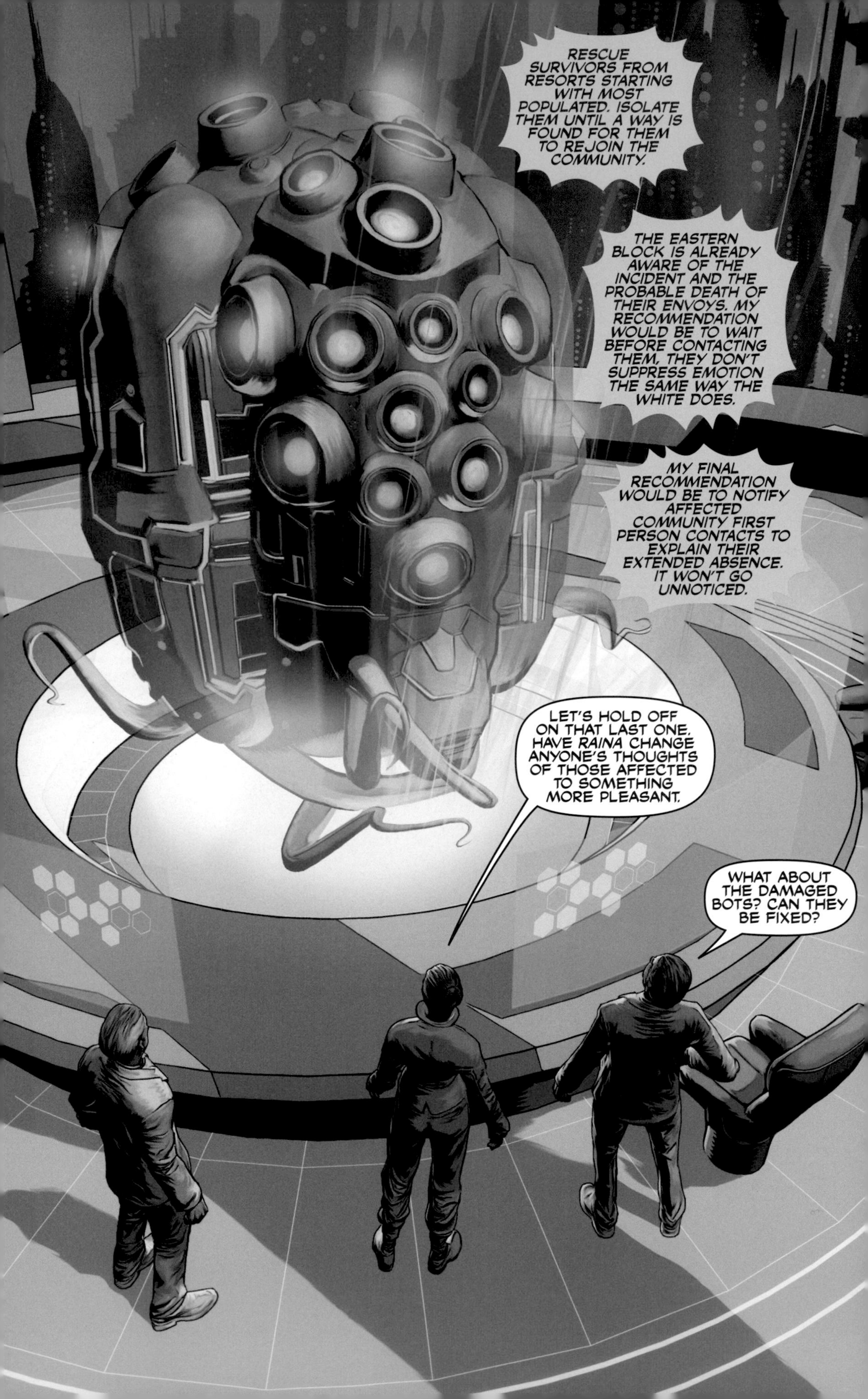
RESCUE SURVIVORS FROM RESORTS STARTING WITH MOST POPULATED. ISOLATE THEM UNTIL A WAY IS FOUND FOR THEM TO REJOIN THE COMMUNITY.
THE EASTERN BLOCK IS ALREADY AWARE OF THE INCIDENT AND THE PROBABLE DEATH OF THEIR ENVOYS. MY RECOMMENDATION WOULD BE TO WAIT BEFORE CONTACTING THEM. THEY DON'T SUPPRESS EMOTION THE SAME WAY THE WHITE DOES.
MY FINAL RECOMMENDATION WOULD BE TO NOTIFY AFFECTED COMMUNITY FIRST PERSON CONTACTS TO EXPLAIN THEIR EXTENDED ABSENCE. IT WON'T GO UNNOTICED.
LET'S HOLD OFF ON THAT LAST ONE. HAVE *RAINA* CHANGE ANYONE'S THOUGHTS OF THOSE AFFECTED TO SOMETHING MORE PLEASANT.
WHAT ABOUT THE DAMAGED BOTS? CAN THEY BE FIXED?

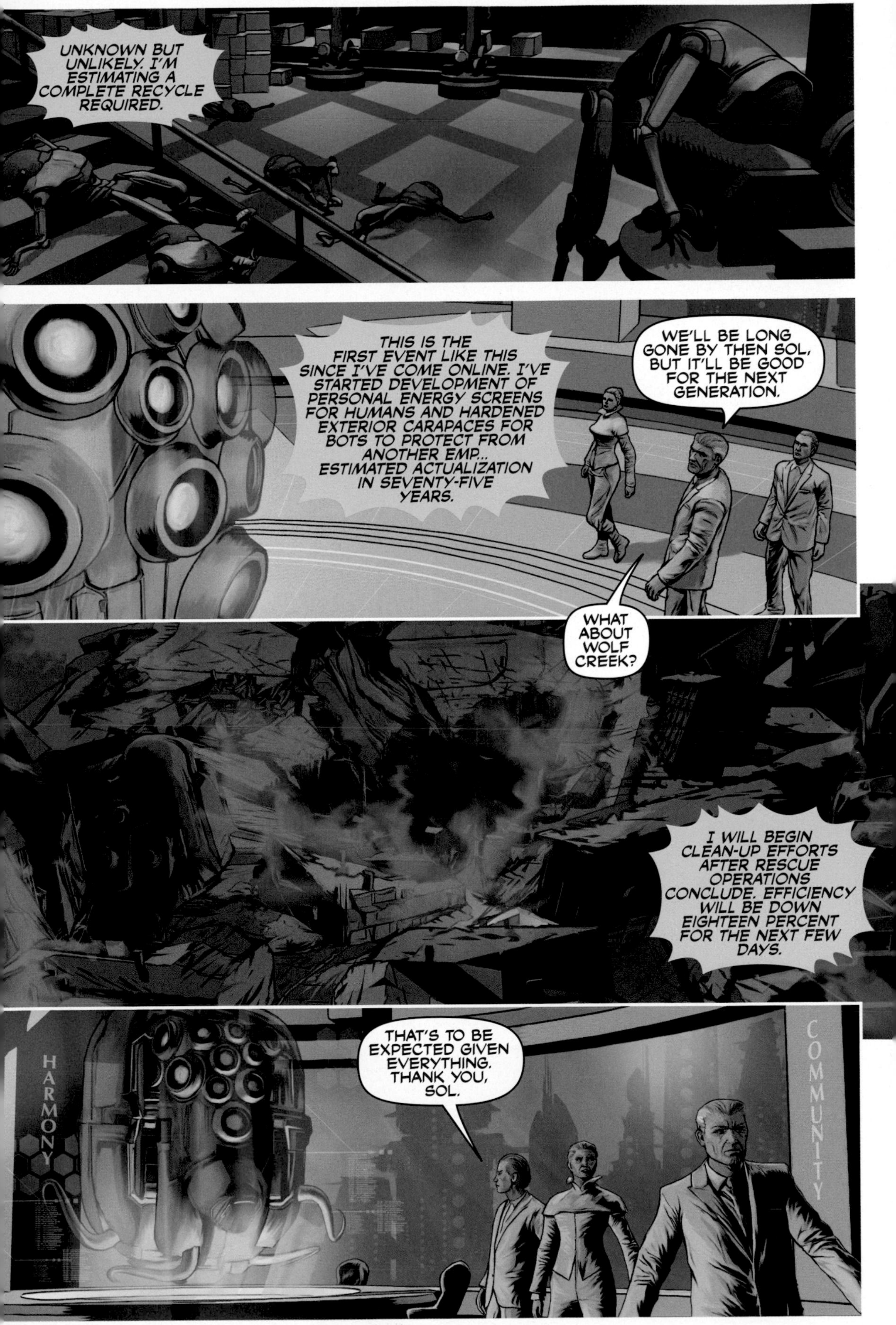
UNKNOWN BUT UNLIKELY. I'M ESTIMATING A COMPLETE RECYCLE REQUIRED.
THIS IS THE FIRST EVENT LIKE THIS SINCE I'VE COME ONLINE. I'VE STARTED DEVELOPMENT OF PERSONAL ENERGY SCREENS FOR HUMANS AND HARDENED EXTERIOR CARAPACES FOR BOTS TO PROTECT FROM ANOTHER EMP... ESTIMATED ACTUALIZATION IN SEVENTY-FIVE YEARS.
WE'LL BE LONG GONE BY THEN SOL, BUT IT'LL BE GOOD FOR THE NEXT GENERATION.
WHAT ABOUT WOLF CREEK?
I WILL BEGIN CLEAN-UP EFFORTS AFTER RESCUE OPERATIONS CONCLUDE. EFFICIENCY WILL BE DOWN EIGHTEEN PERCENT FOR THE NEXT FEW DAYS.
HARMONY
COMMUNITY
THAT'S TO BE EXPECTED GIVEN EVERYTHING. THANK YOU, SOL.

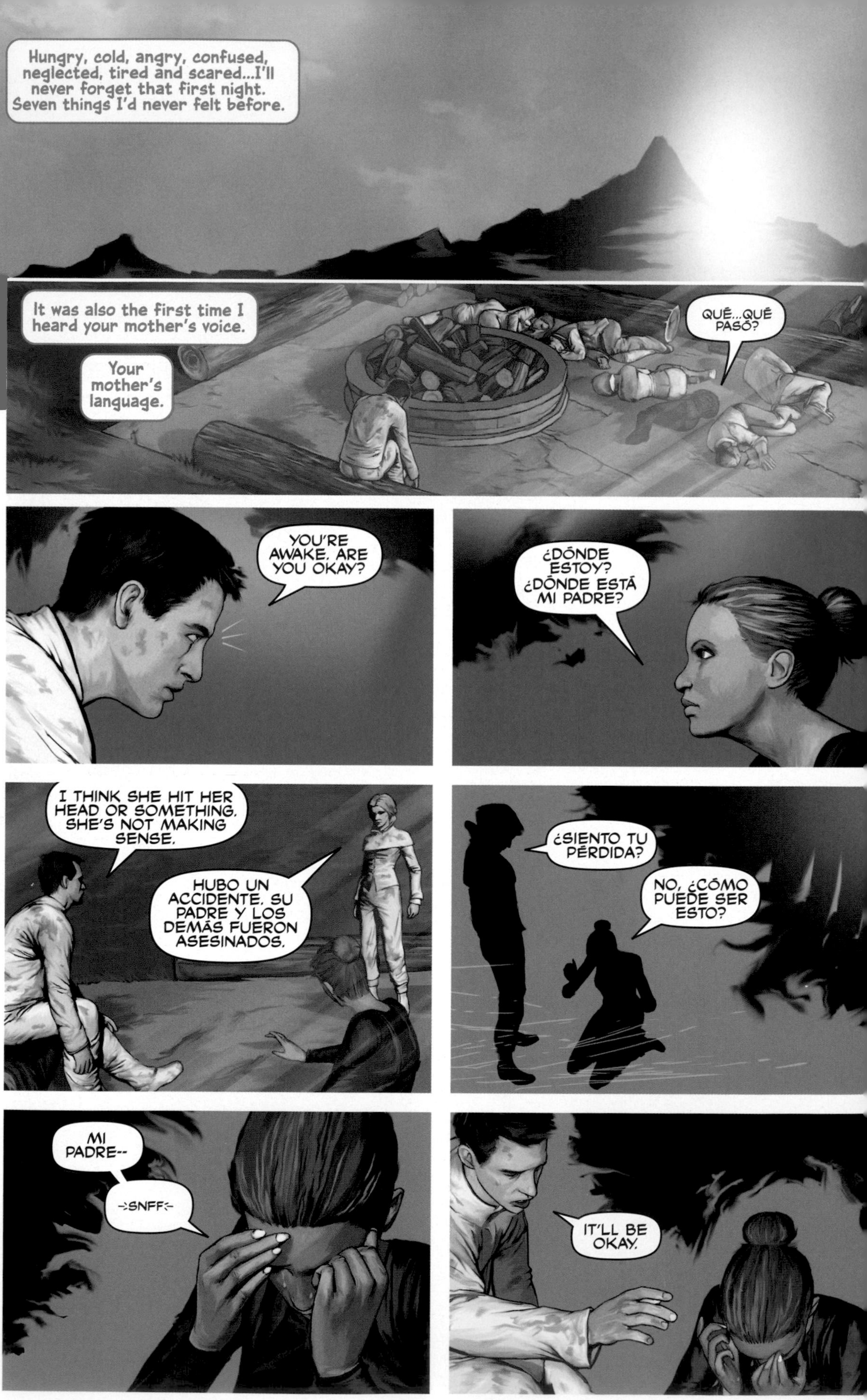
Hungry, cold, angry, confused, neglected, tired and scared...I'll never forget that first night. Seven things I'd never felt before.
It was also the first time I heard your mother's voice.
Your mother's language.
QUÉ...QUÉ PASÓ?
YOU'RE AWAKE. ARE YOU OKAY?
¿DÓNDE ESTOY? ¿DÓNDE ESTÁ MI PADRE?
I THINK SHE HIT HER HEAD OR SOMETHING. SHE'S NOT MAKING SENSE.
HUBO UN ACCIDENTE. SU PADRE Y LOS DEMÁS FUERON ASESINADOS.
¿SIENTO TU PÉRDIDA?
NO, ¿CÓMO PUEDE SER ESTO?
MI PADRE--
SNFF
IT'LL BE OKAY.

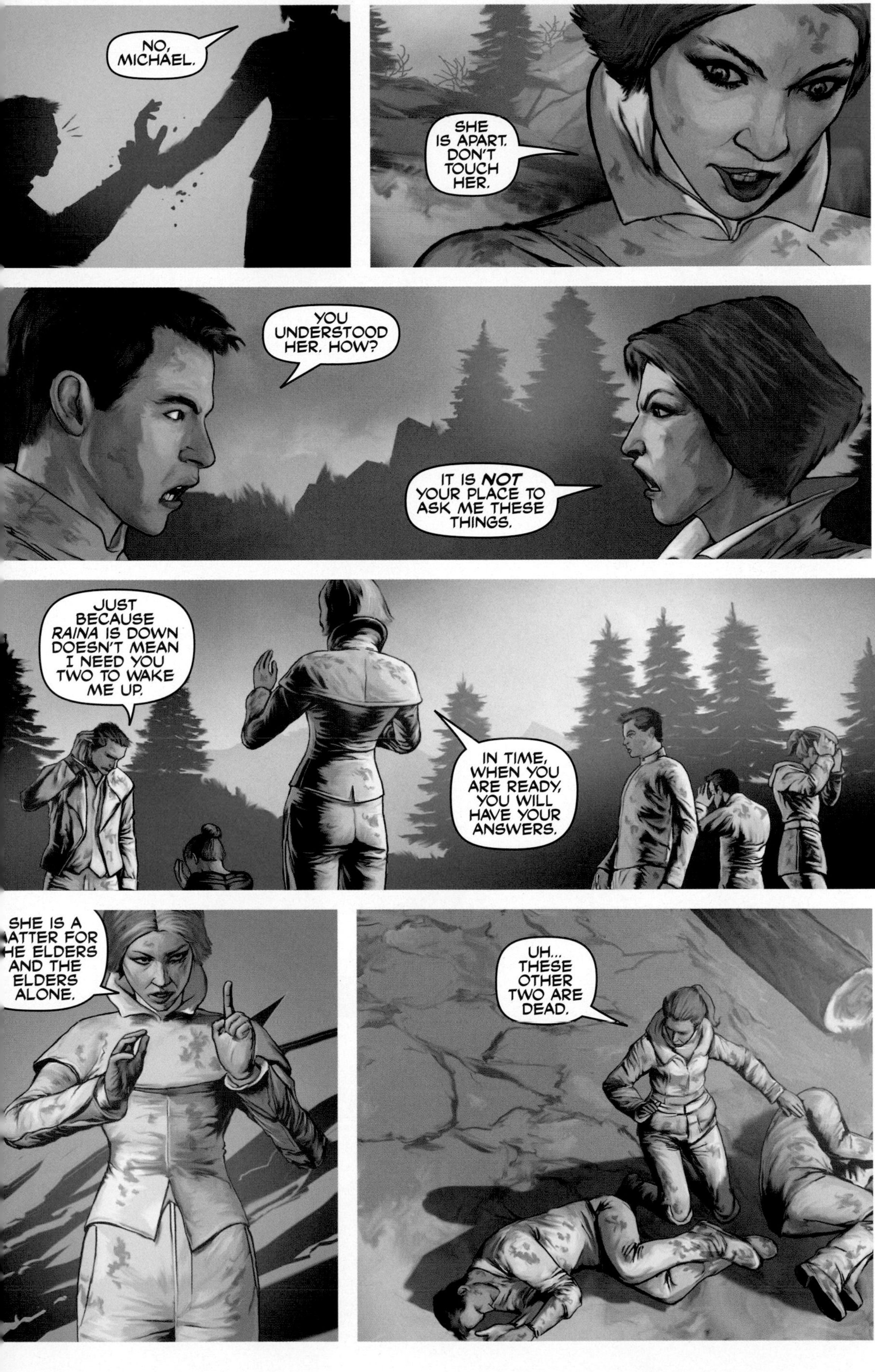
NO, MICHAEL.
SHE IS APART. DON'T TOUCH HER.
YOU UNDERSTOOD HER. HOW?
IT IS *NOT* YOUR PLACE TO ASK ME THESE THINGS.
JUST BECAUSE *RAINA* IS DOWN DOESN'T MEAN I NEED YOU TWO TO WAKE ME UP.
IN TIME, WHEN YOU ARE READY, YOU WILL HAVE YOUR ANSWERS.
SHE IS A ATTER FOR HE ELDERS AND THE ELDERS ALONE.
UH... THESE OTHER TWO ARE DEAD.

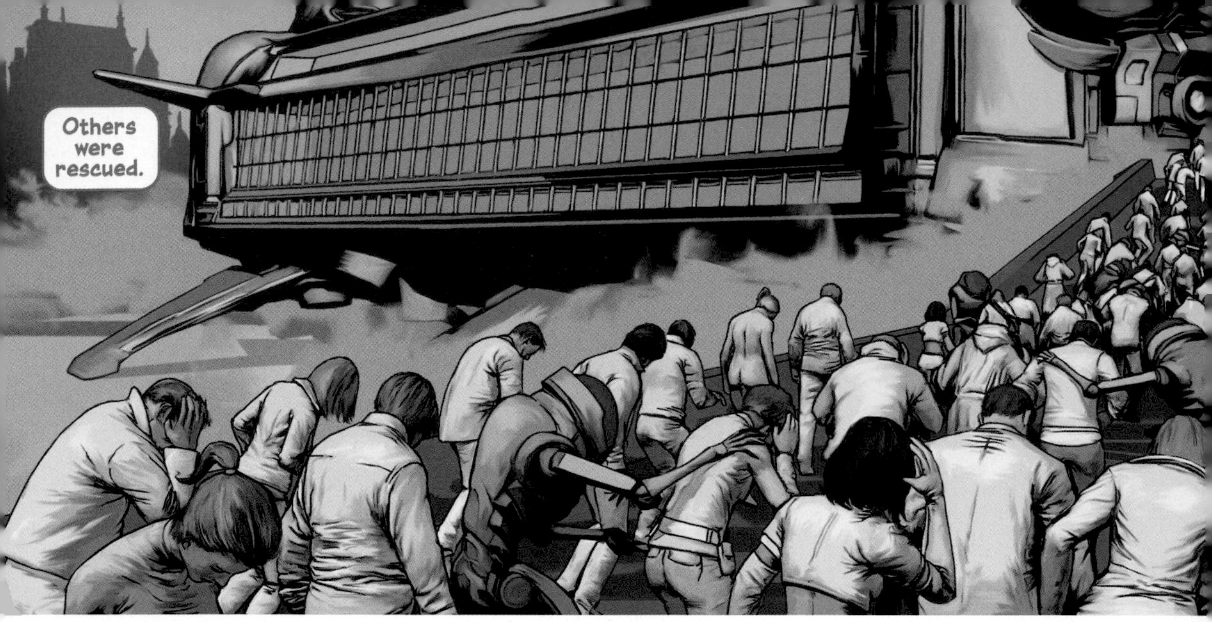
Others were rescued.

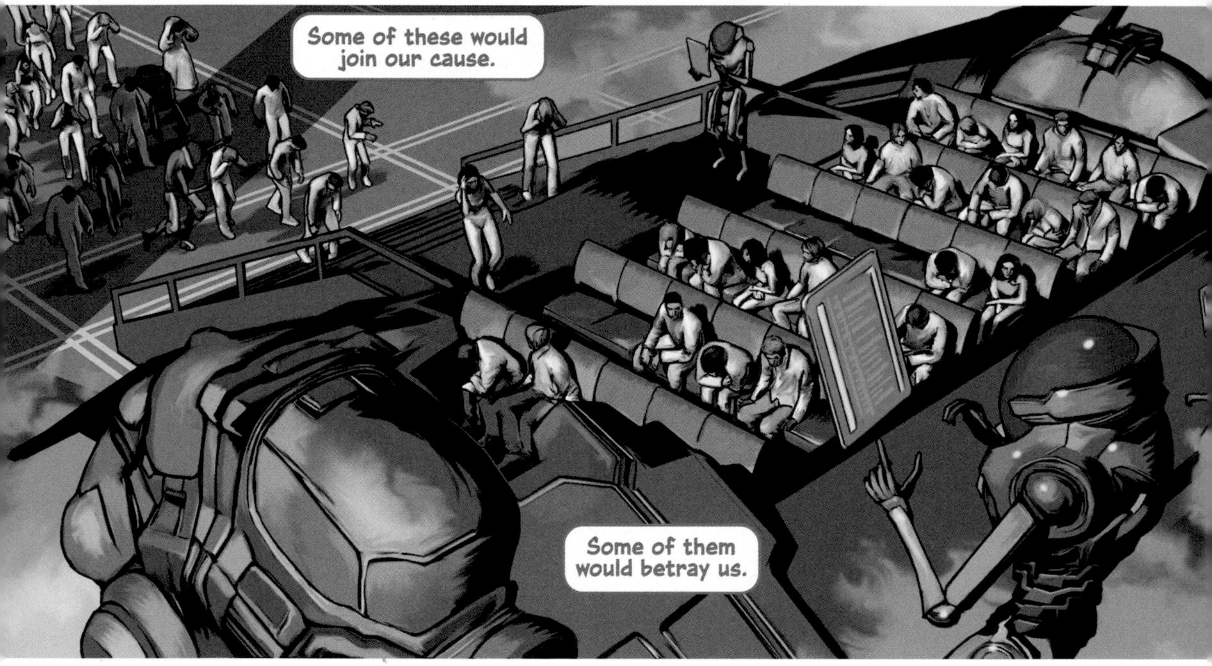
Some of these would join our cause.
Some of them would betray us.

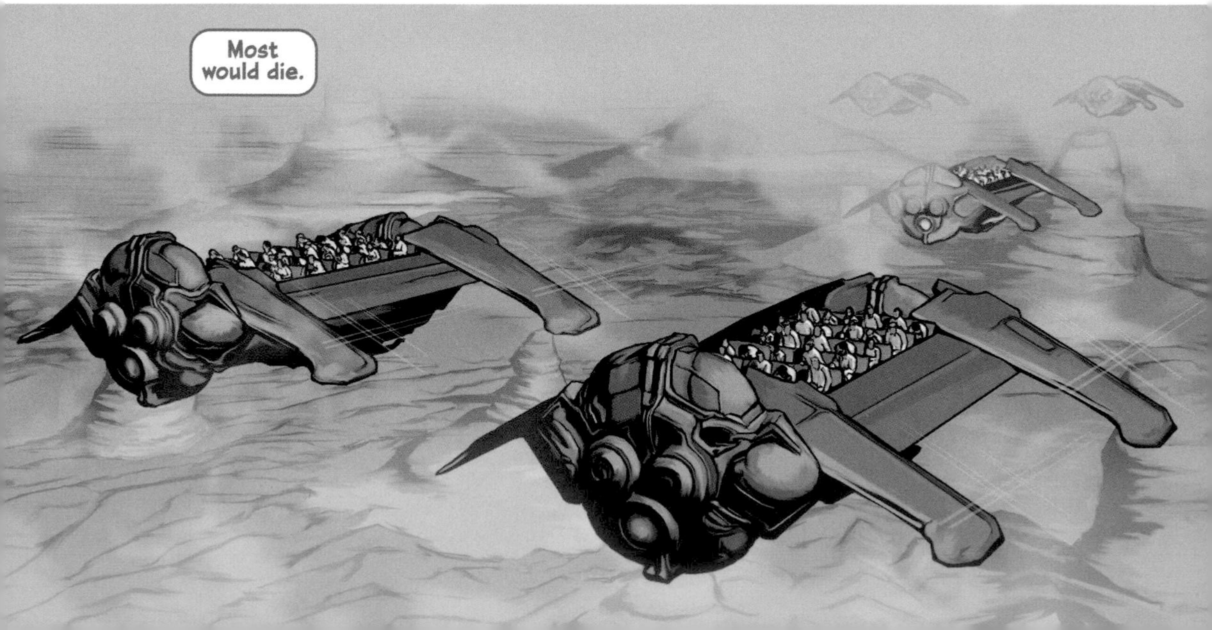
Most would die.

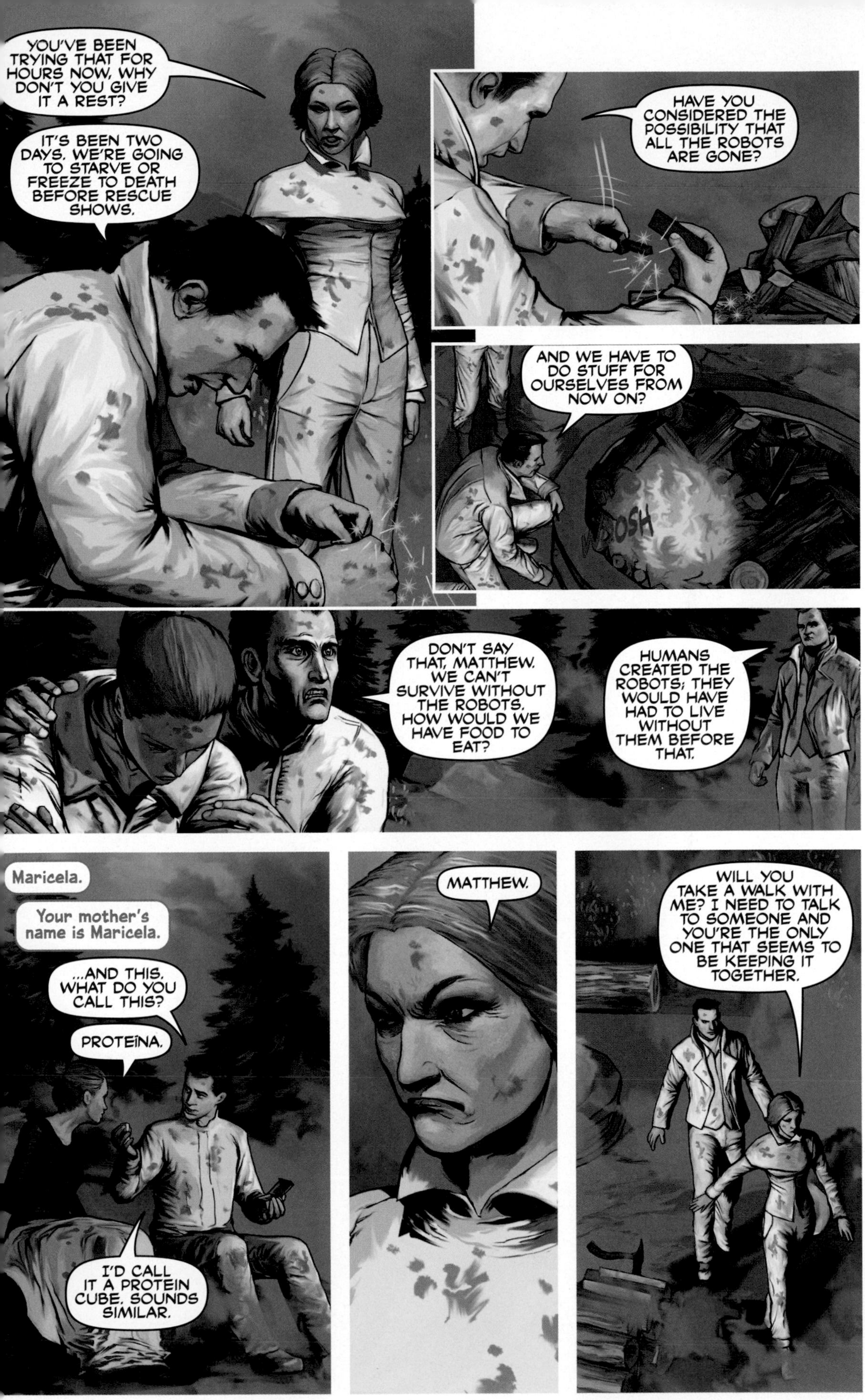
YOU'VE BEEN TRYING THAT FOR HOURS NOW, WHY DON'T YOU GIVE IT A REST?
IT'S BEEN TWO DAYS. WE'RE GOING TO STARVE OR FREEZE TO DEATH BEFORE RESCUE SHOWS.
HAVE YOU CONSIDERED THE POSSIBILITY THAT ALL THE ROBOTS ARE GONE?
AND WE HAVE TO DO STUFF FOR OURSELVES FROM NOW ON?
DON'T SAY THAT, MATTHEW. WE CAN'T SURVIVE WITHOUT THE ROBOTS. HOW WOULD WE HAVE FOOD TO EAT?
HUMANS CREATED THE ROBOTS; THEY WOULD HAVE HAD TO LIVE WITHOUT THEM BEFORE THAT.
Maricela.
Your mother's name is Maricela.
...AND THIS. WHAT DO YOU CALL THIS?
PROTEÍNA.
I'D CALL IT A PROTEIN CUBE. SOUNDS SIMILAR.
MATTHEW.
WILL YOU TAKE A WALK WITH ME? I NEED TO TALK TO SOMEONE AND YOU'RE THE ONLY ONE THAT SEEMS TO BE KEEPING IT TOGETHER.

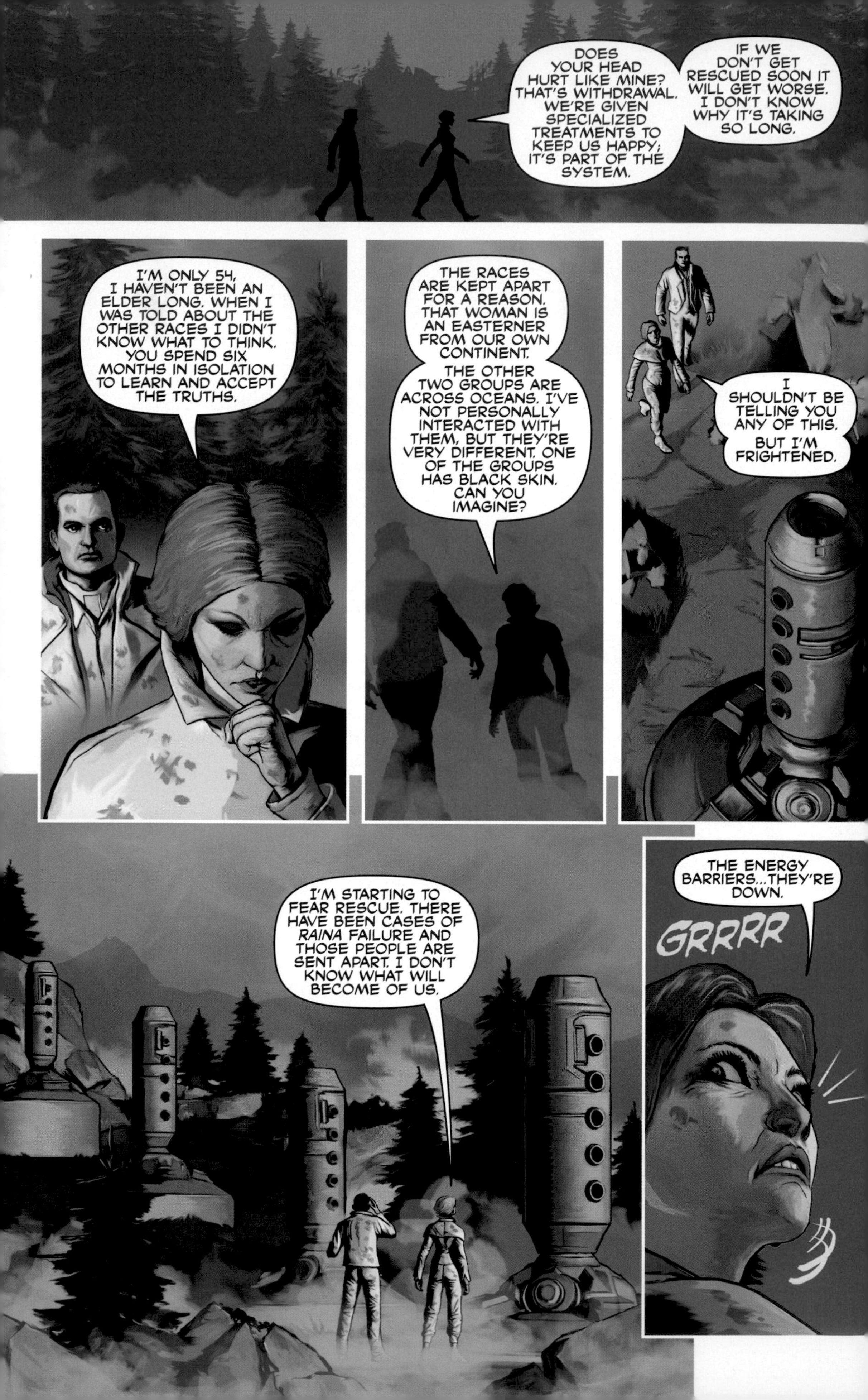
DOES YOUR HEAD HURT LIKE MINE? THAT'S WITHDRAWAL. WE'RE GIVEN SPECIALIZED TREATMENTS TO KEEP US HAPPY; IT'S PART OF THE SYSTEM.
IF WE DON'T GET RESCUED SOON IT WILL GET WORSE. I DON'T KNOW WHY IT'S TAKING SO LONG.
I'M ONLY 54, I HAVEN'T BEEN AN ELDER LONG. WHEN I WAS TOLD ABOUT THE OTHER RACES I DIDN'T KNOW WHAT TO THINK. YOU SPEND SIX MONTHS IN ISOLATION TO LEARN AND ACCEPT THE TRUTHS.
THE RACES ARE KEPT APART FOR A REASON. THAT WOMAN IS AN EASTERNER FROM OUR OWN CONTINENT.
THE OTHER TWO GROUPS ARE ACROSS OCEANS. I'VE NOT PERSONALLY INTERACTED WITH THEM, BUT THEY'RE VERY DIFFERENT. ONE OF THE GROUPS HAS BLACK SKIN. CAN YOU IMAGINE?
I SHOULDN'T BE TELLING YOU ANY OF THIS.
BUT I'M FRIGHTENED.
I'M STARTING TO FEAR RESCUE. THERE HAVE BEEN CASES OF *RAINA* FAILURE AND THOSE PEOPLE ARE SENT APART. I DON'T KNOW WHAT WILL BECOME OF US.
THE ENERGY BARRIERS...THEY'RE DOWN.
GRRRR

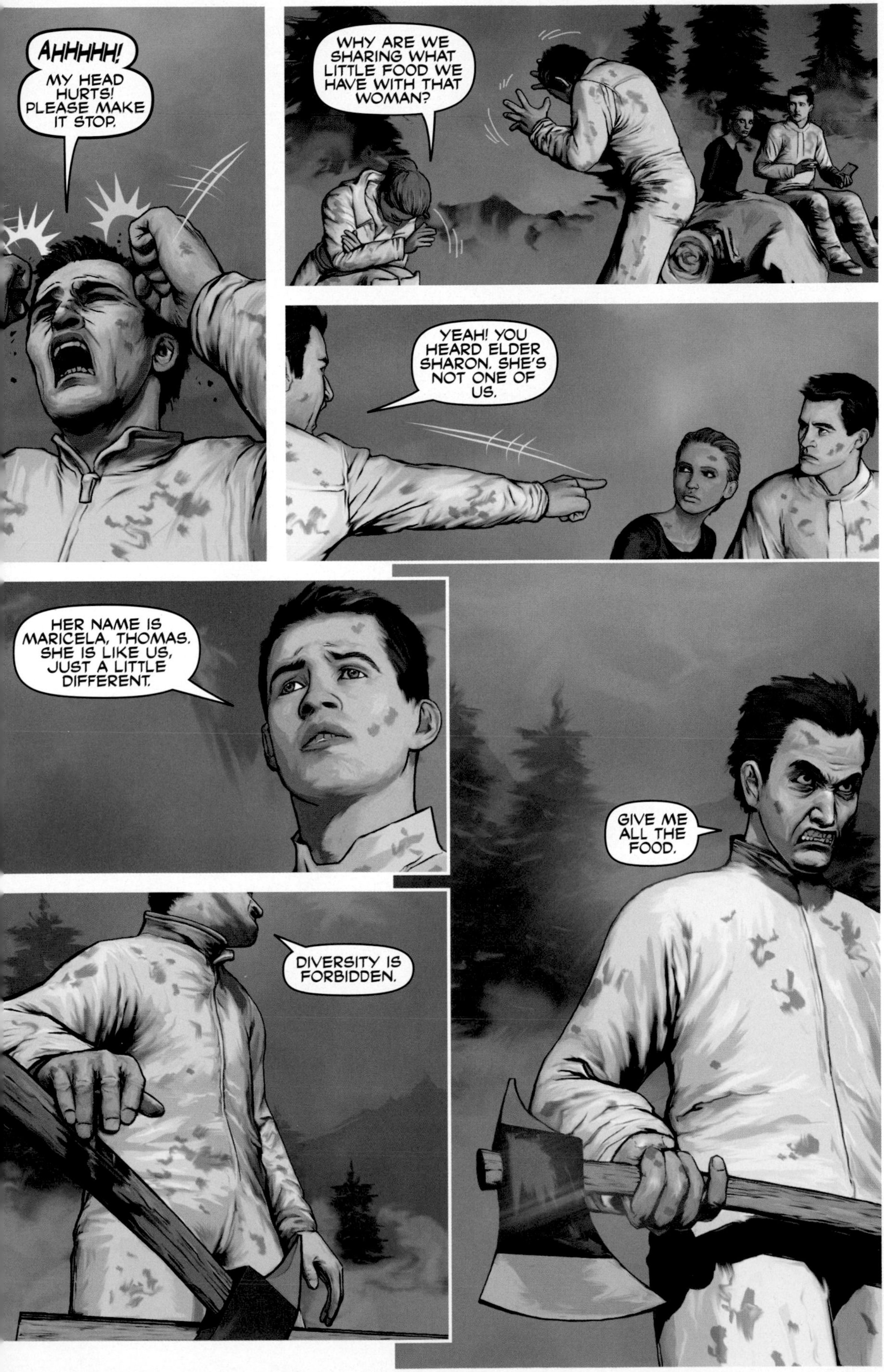
AHHHHH!
MY HEAD HURTS! PLEASE MAKE IT STOP.
WHY ARE WE SHARING WHAT LITTLE FOOD WE HAVE WITH THAT WOMAN?
YEAH! YOU HEARD ELDER SHARON. SHE'S NOT ONE OF US.
HER NAME IS MARICELA, THOMAS. SHE IS LIKE US, JUST A LITTLE DIFFERENT.
DIVERSITY IS FORBIDDEN.
GIVE ME ALL THE FOOD.

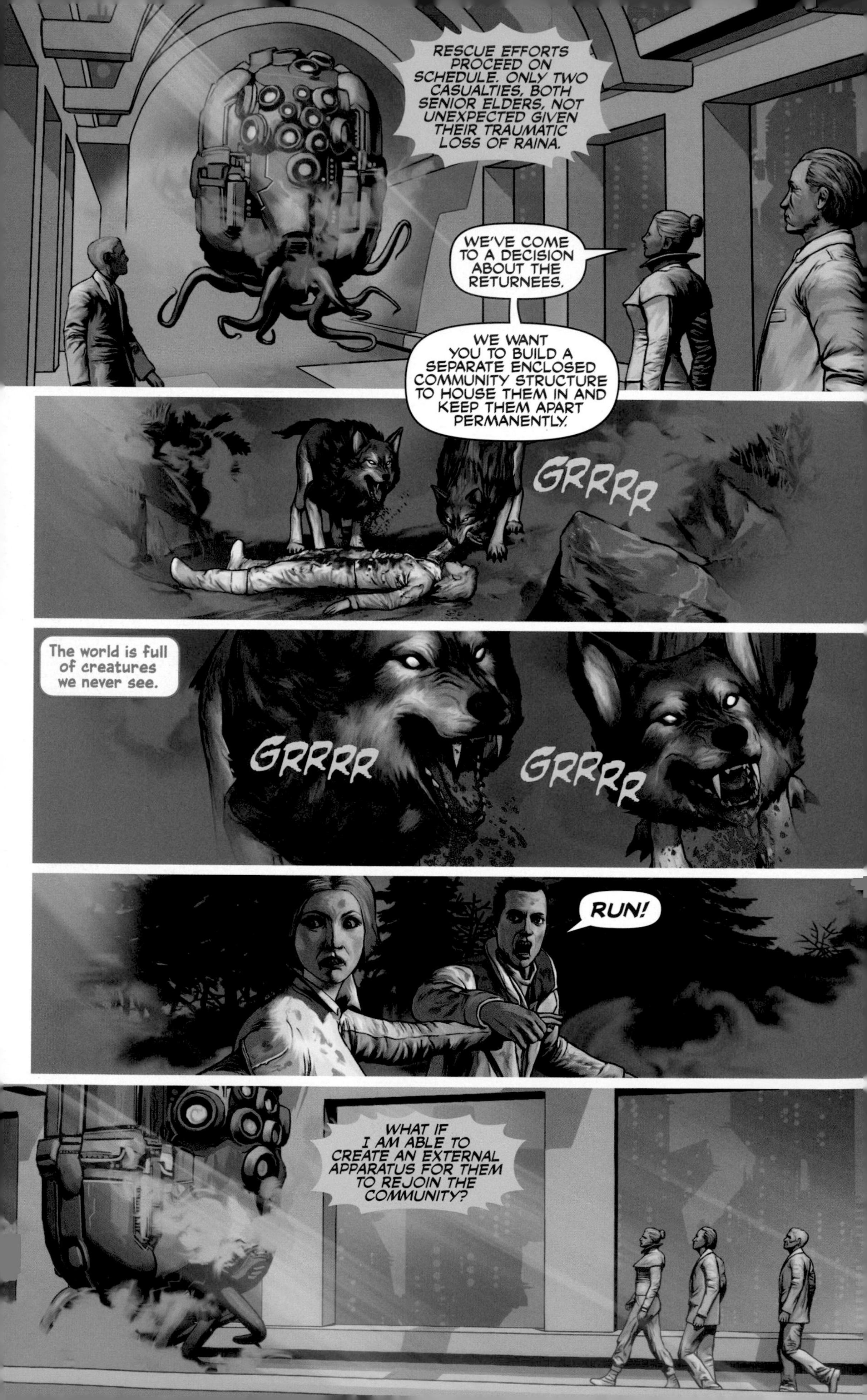
RESCUE EFFORTS PROCEED ON SCHEDULE. ONLY TWO CASUALTIES, BOTH SENIOR ELDERS, NOT UNEXPECTED GIVEN THEIR TRAUMATIC LOSS OF RAINA.
WE'VE COME TO A DECISION ABOUT THE RETURNEES.
WE WANT YOU TO BUILD A SEPARATE ENCLOSED COMMUNITY STRUCTURE TO HOUSE THEM IN AND KEEP THEM APART PERMANENTLY.
GRRRR
The world is full of creatures we never see.
GRRRR
GRRRR
RUN!
WHAT IF I AM ABLE TO CREATE AN EXTERNAL APPARATUS FOR THEM TO REJOIN THE COMMUNITY?

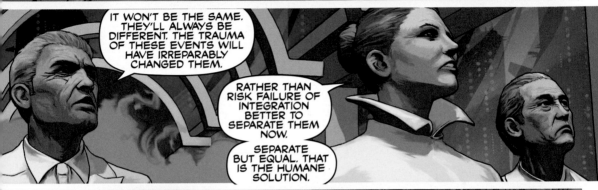

IT WON'T BE THE SAME. THEY'LL ALWAYS BE DIFFERENT. THE TRAUMA OF THESE EVENTS WILL HAVE IRREPARABLY CHANGED THEM.

RATHER THAN RISK FAILURE OF INTEGRATION BETTER TO SEPARATE THEM NOW.

SEPARATE BUT EQUAL. THAT IS THE HUMANE SOLUTION.

Animals kill to eat and protect their young.

They have that freedom. That makes animals dangerous.

WE WANT THEM STERILIZED TOO, SO THERE WILL BE NO CHANCE OF ANY OF THIS AFFECTING THE NEXT GENERATION.

FOR THAT YOU WILL NEED HUMAN INSTRUMENTS TO EXECUTE. I CANNOT HARM A HUMAN. IT WOULD BE A VIOLATION OF ONE OF MY TWO DIRECTIVES. I'D RECOMMEND ASKING THE ASIANS OR AFRICANS FOR ASSISTANCE.

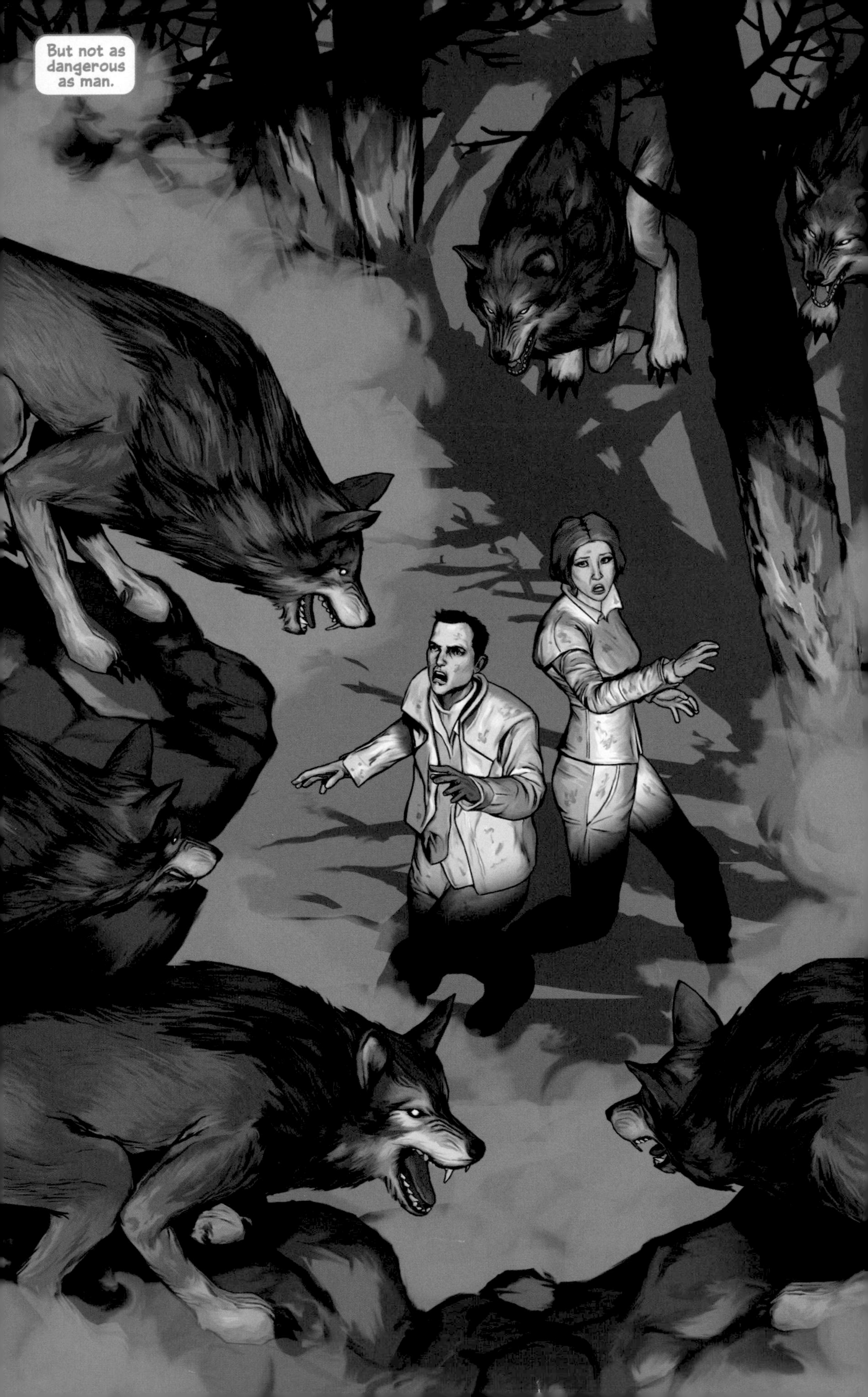
But not as dangerous as man.

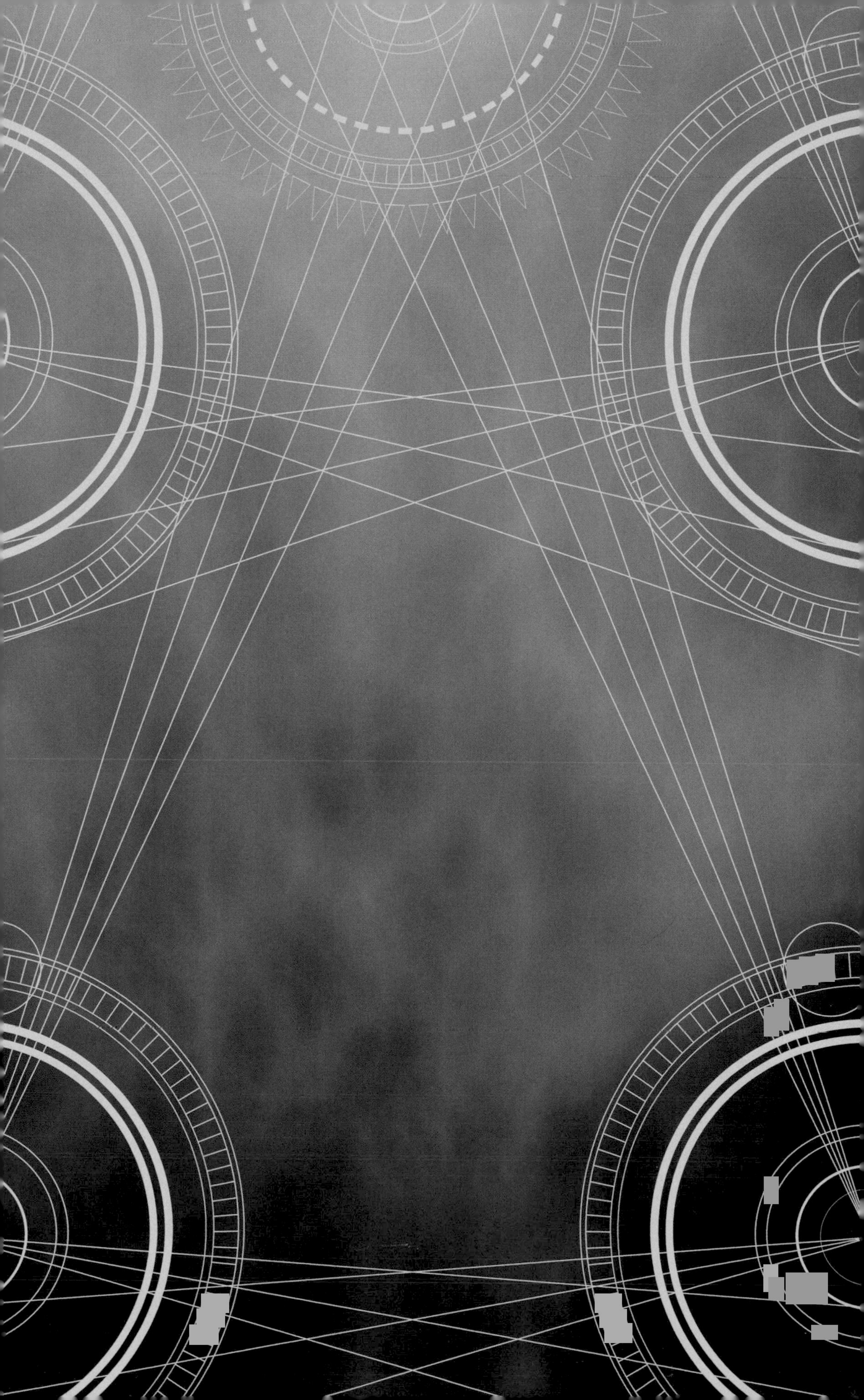

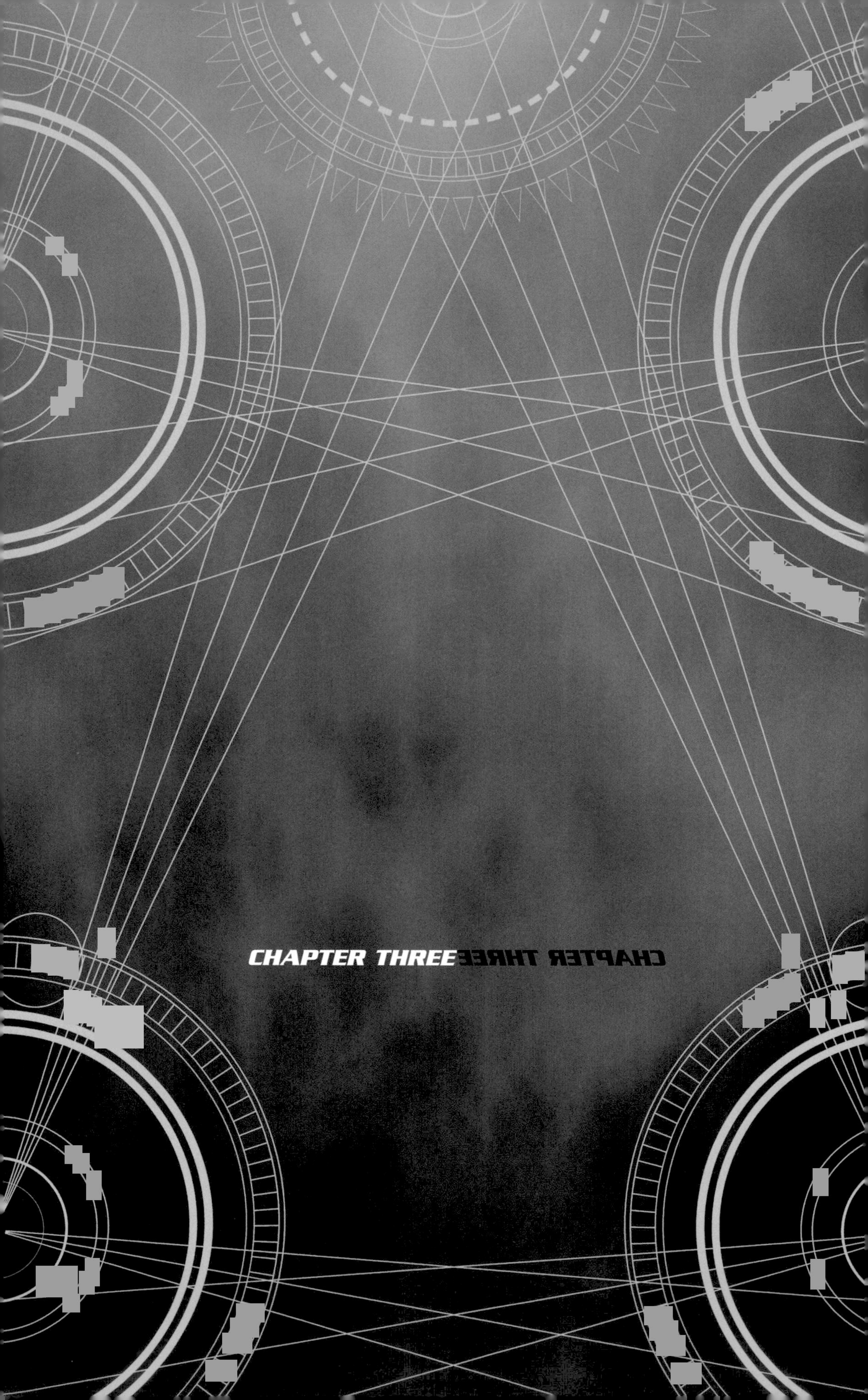

CHAPTER THREE

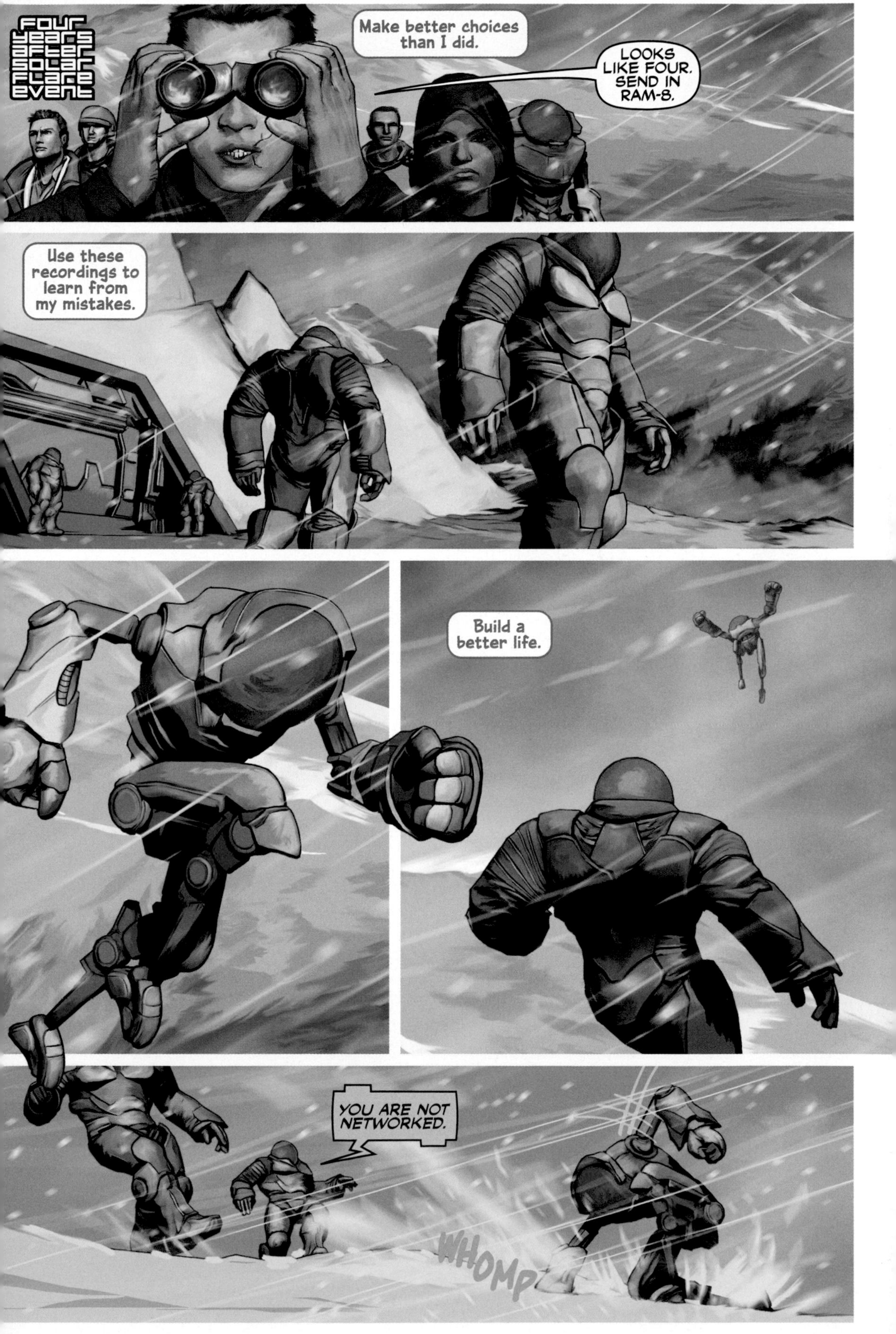
FOUR YEARS AFTER SOLAR FLARE EVENT
Make better choices than I did.
LOOKS LIKE FOUR. SEND IN RAM-8.
Use these recordings to learn from my mistakes.
Build a better life.
YOU ARE NOT NETWORKED.
WHOMP

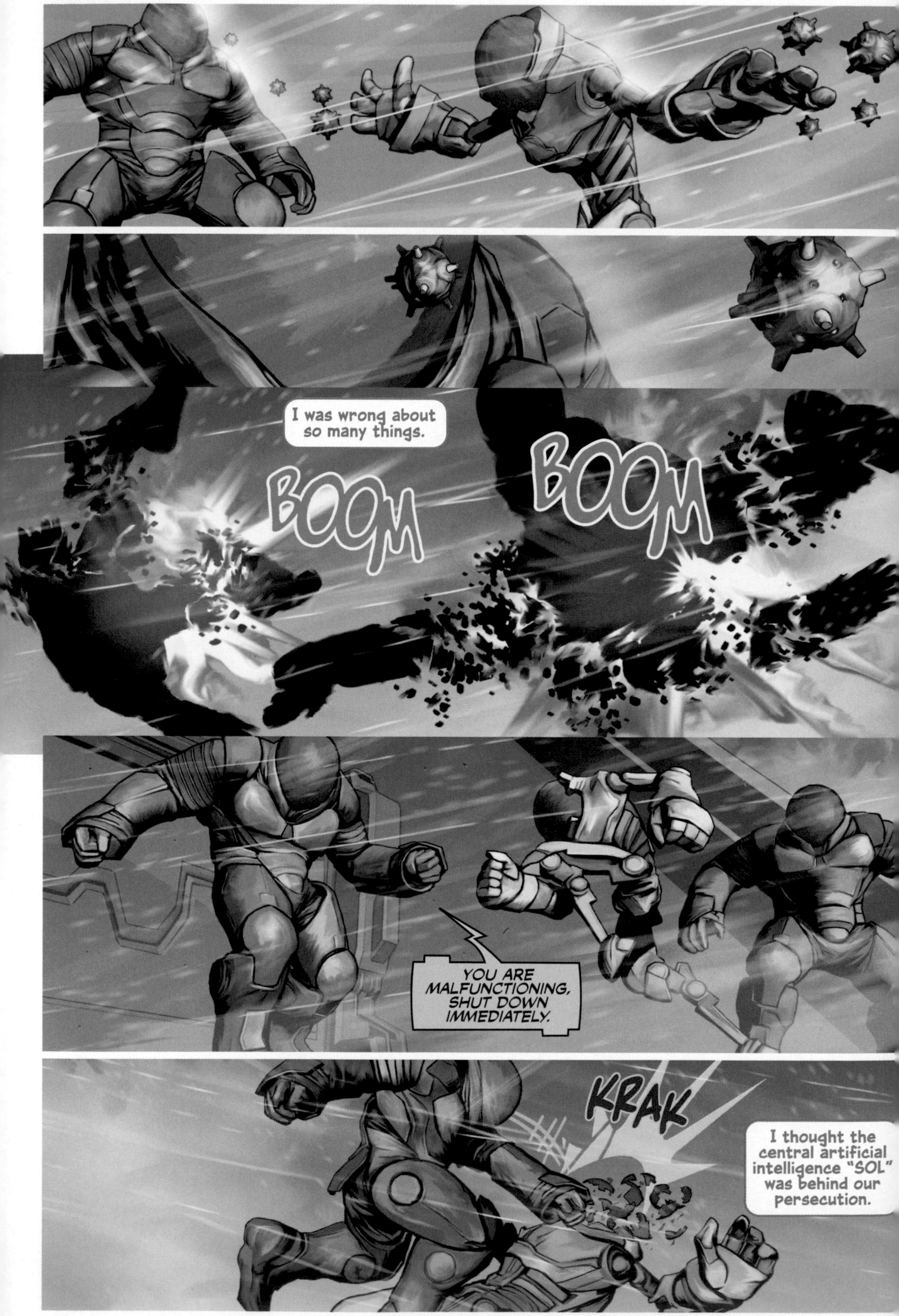
I was wrong about so many things.
BOOM
BOOM
YOU ARE MALFUNCTIONING, SHUT DOWN IMMEDIATELY.
KRAK
I thought the central artificial intelligence "SOL" was behind our persecution.

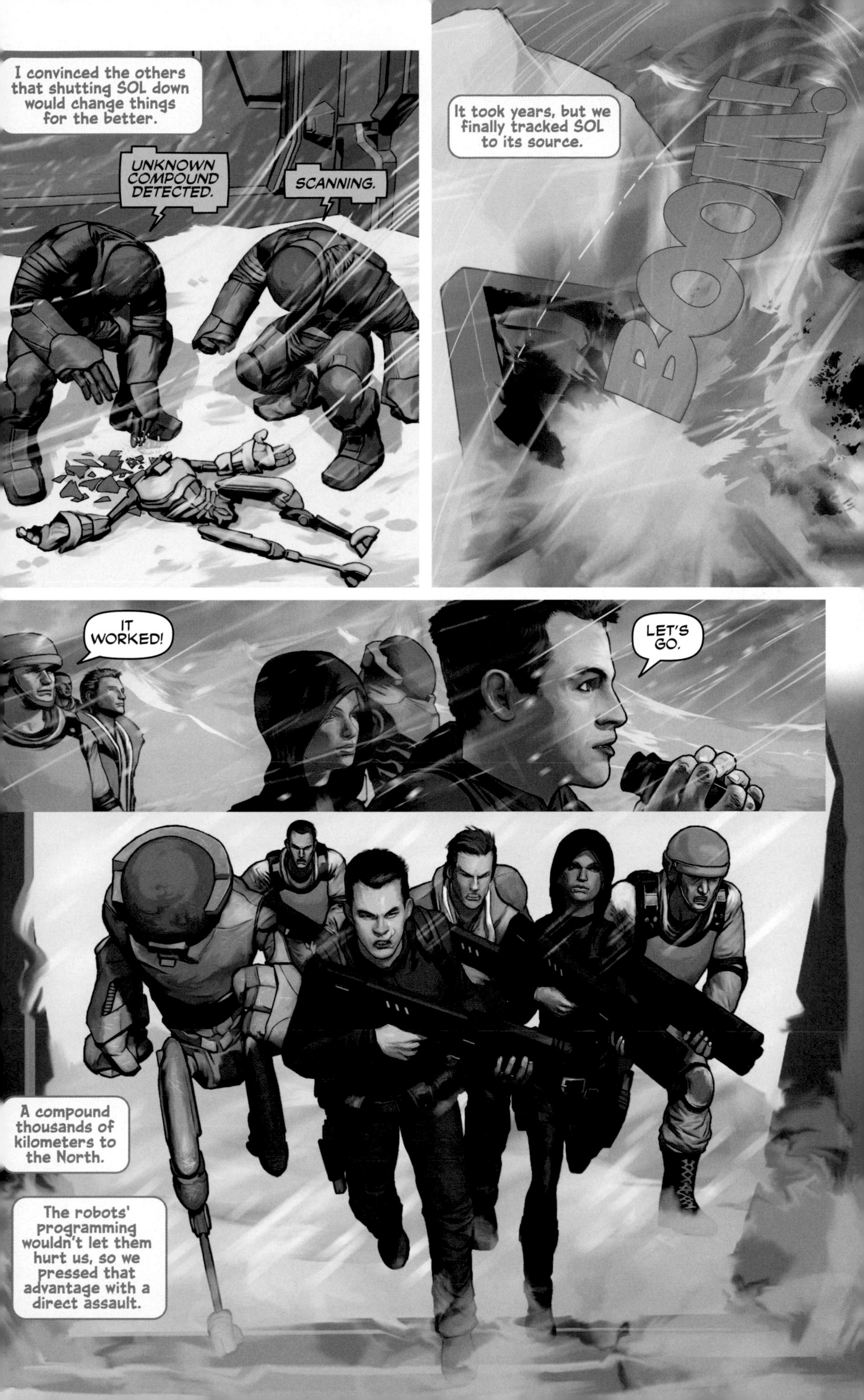
I convinced the others that shutting SOL down would change things for the better.
UNKNOWN COMPOUND DETECTED.
SCANNING.
It took years, but we finally tracked SOL to its source.
BOOM!
IT WORKED!
LET'S GO.
A compound thousands of kilometers to the North.
The robots' programming wouldn't let them hurt us, so we pressed that advantage with a direct assault.

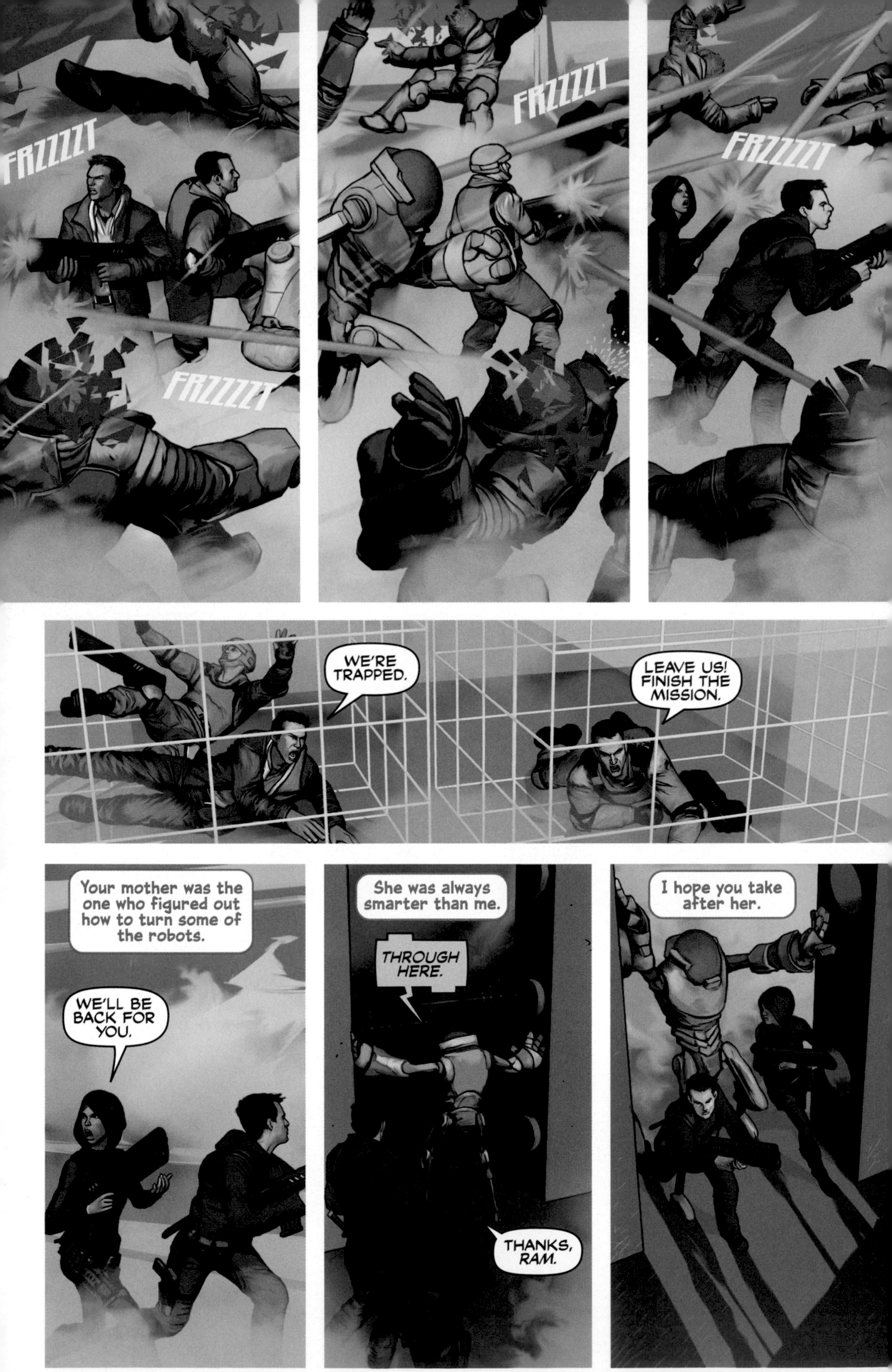
FRZZZZT
FRZZZZT
FRZZZZT
FRZZZZT
WE'RE TRAPPED.
LEAVE US! FINISH THE MISSION.
Your mother was the one who figured out how to turn some of the robots.
WE'LL BE BACK FOR YOU.
She was always smarter than me.
THROUGH HERE.
THANKS, RAM.
I hope you take after her.

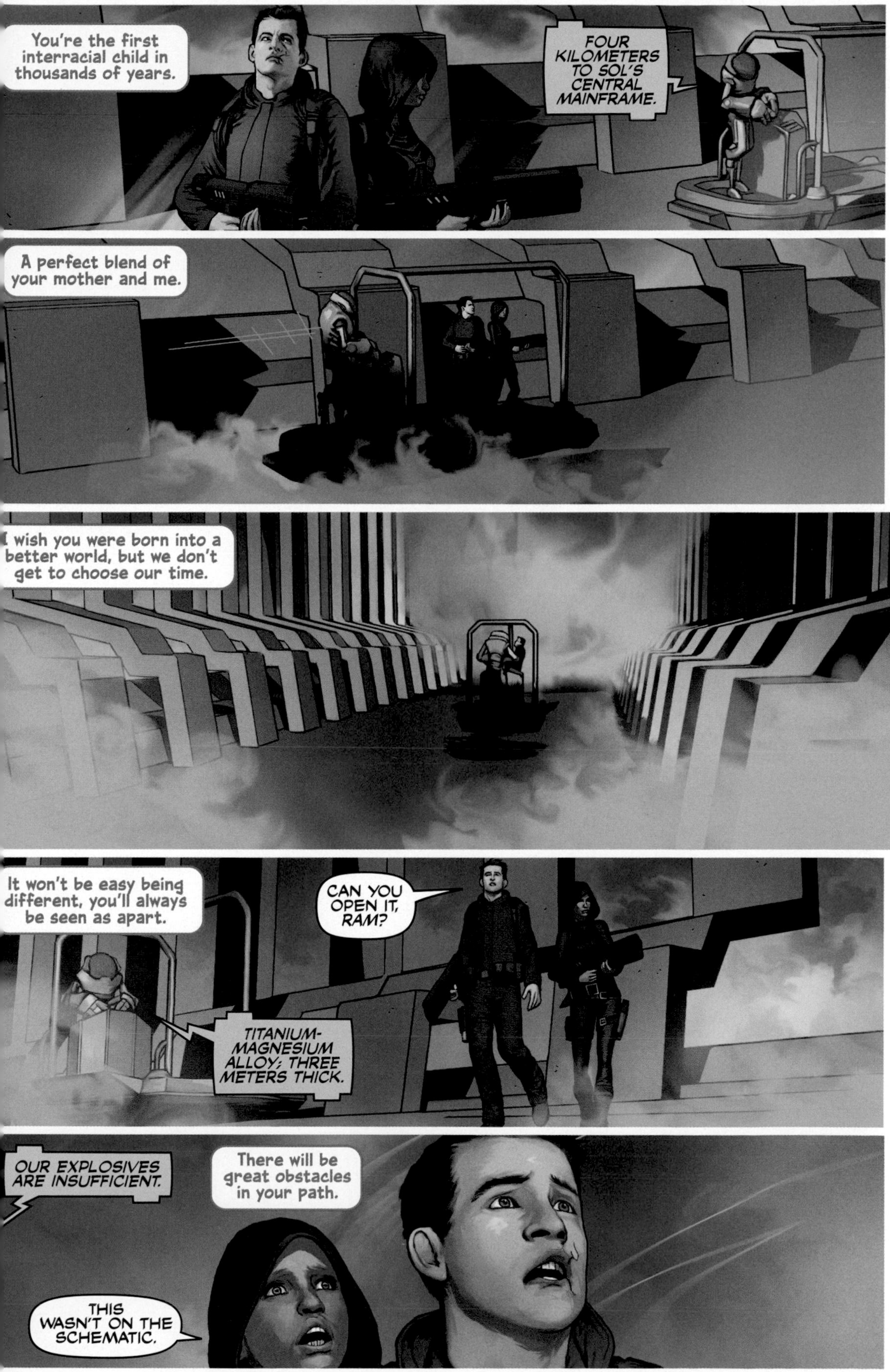
You're the first interracial child in thousands of years.
FOUR KILOMETERS TO SOL'S CENTRAL MAINFRAME.
A perfect blend of your mother and me.
I wish you were born into a better world, but we don't get to choose our time.
It won't be easy being different, you'll always be seen as apart.
CAN YOU OPEN IT, RAM?
TITANIUM-MAGNESIUM ALLOY; THREE METERS THICK.
OUR EXPLOSIVES ARE INSUFFICIENT.
There will be great obstacles in your path.
THIS WASN'T ON THE SCHEMATIC.

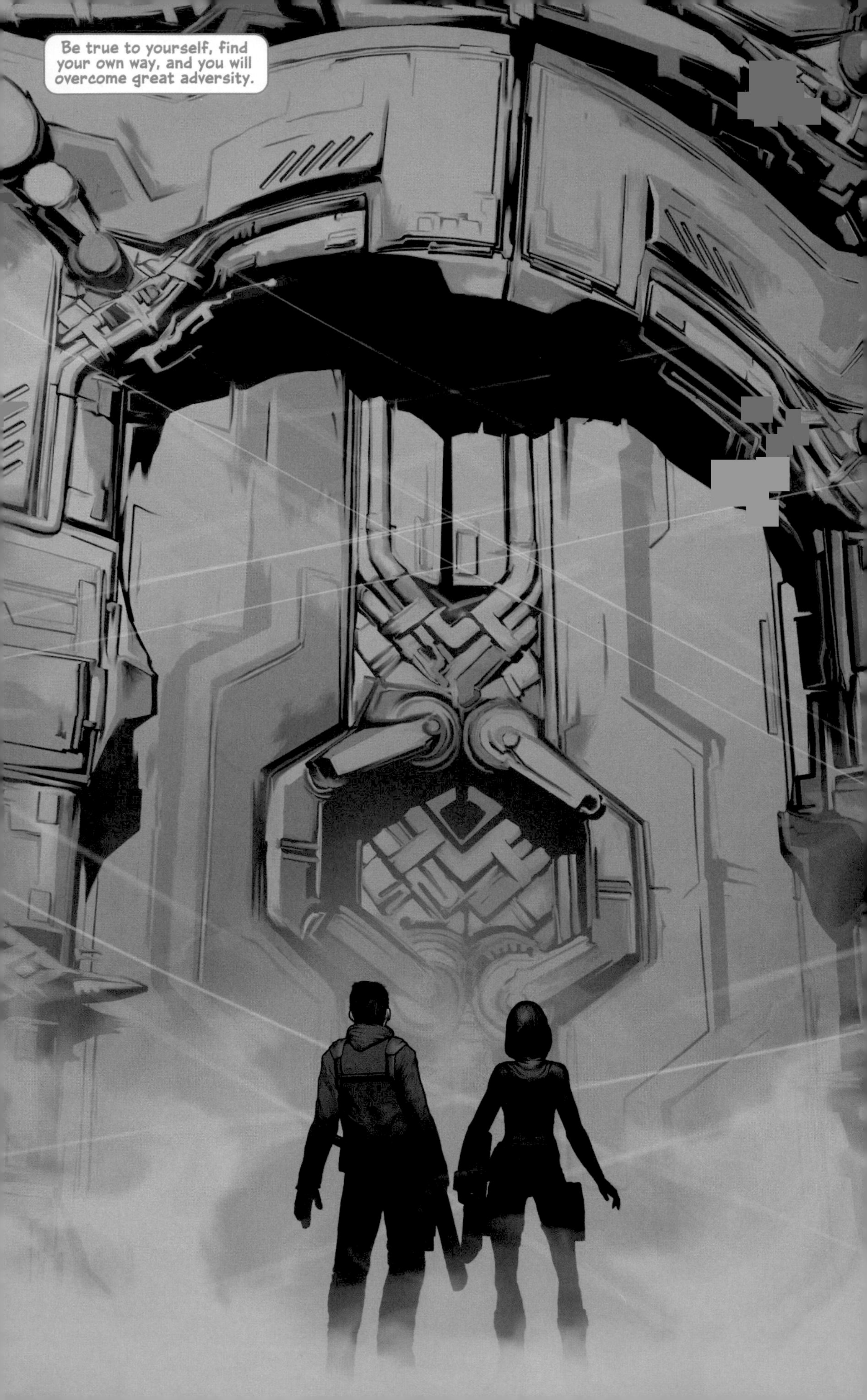
Be true to yourself, find your own way, and you will overcome great adversity.

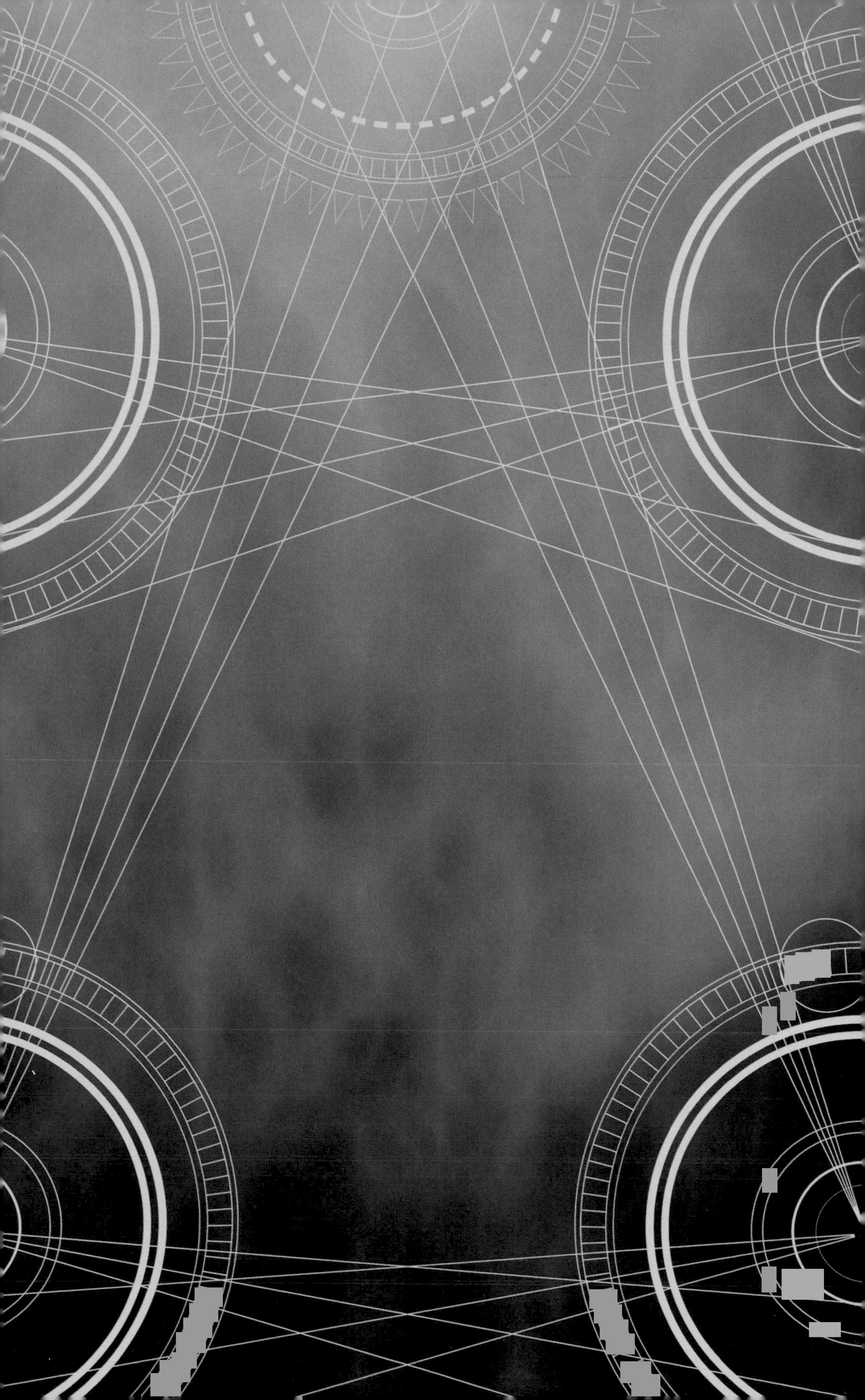

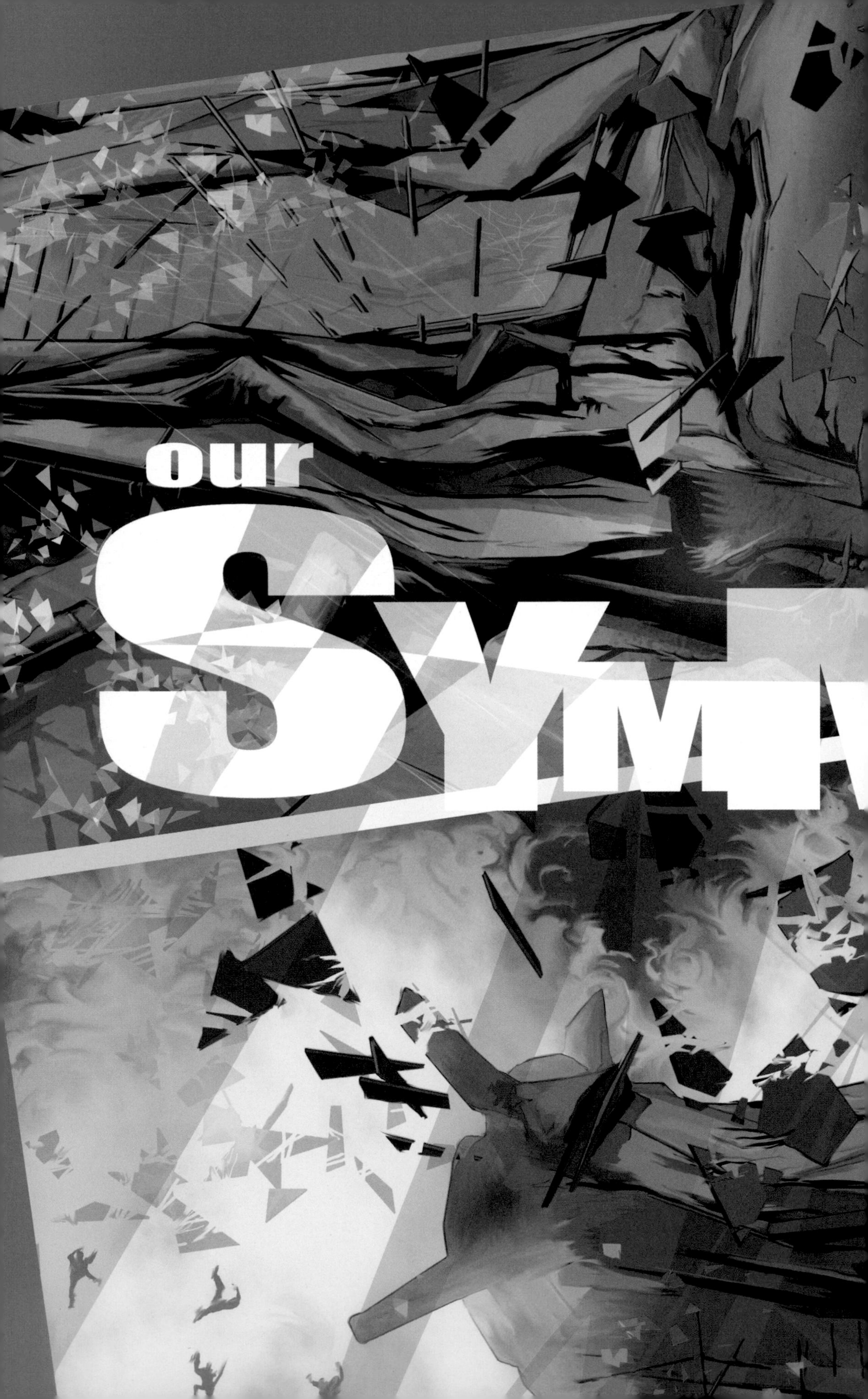
our

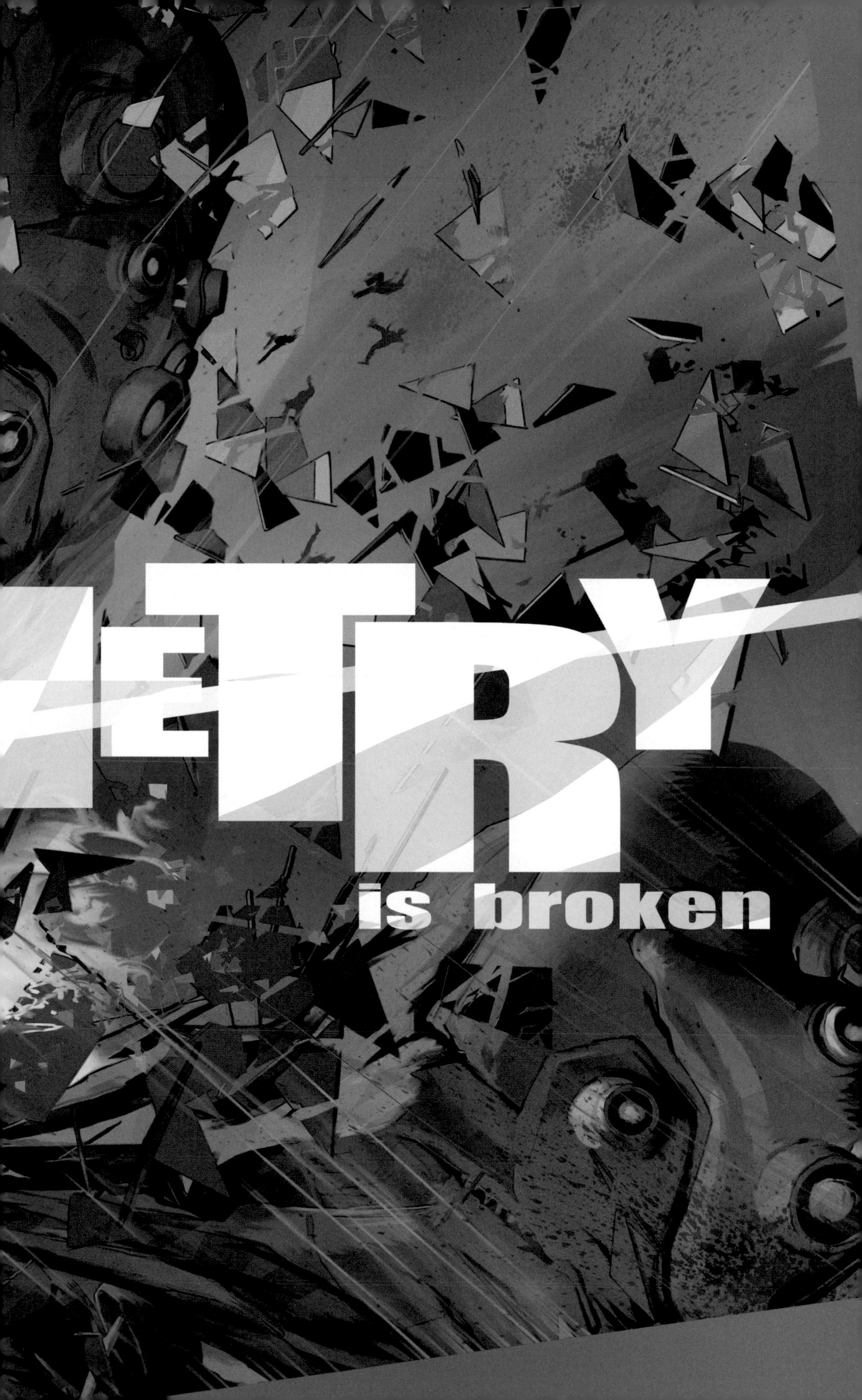
ETRY
is broken

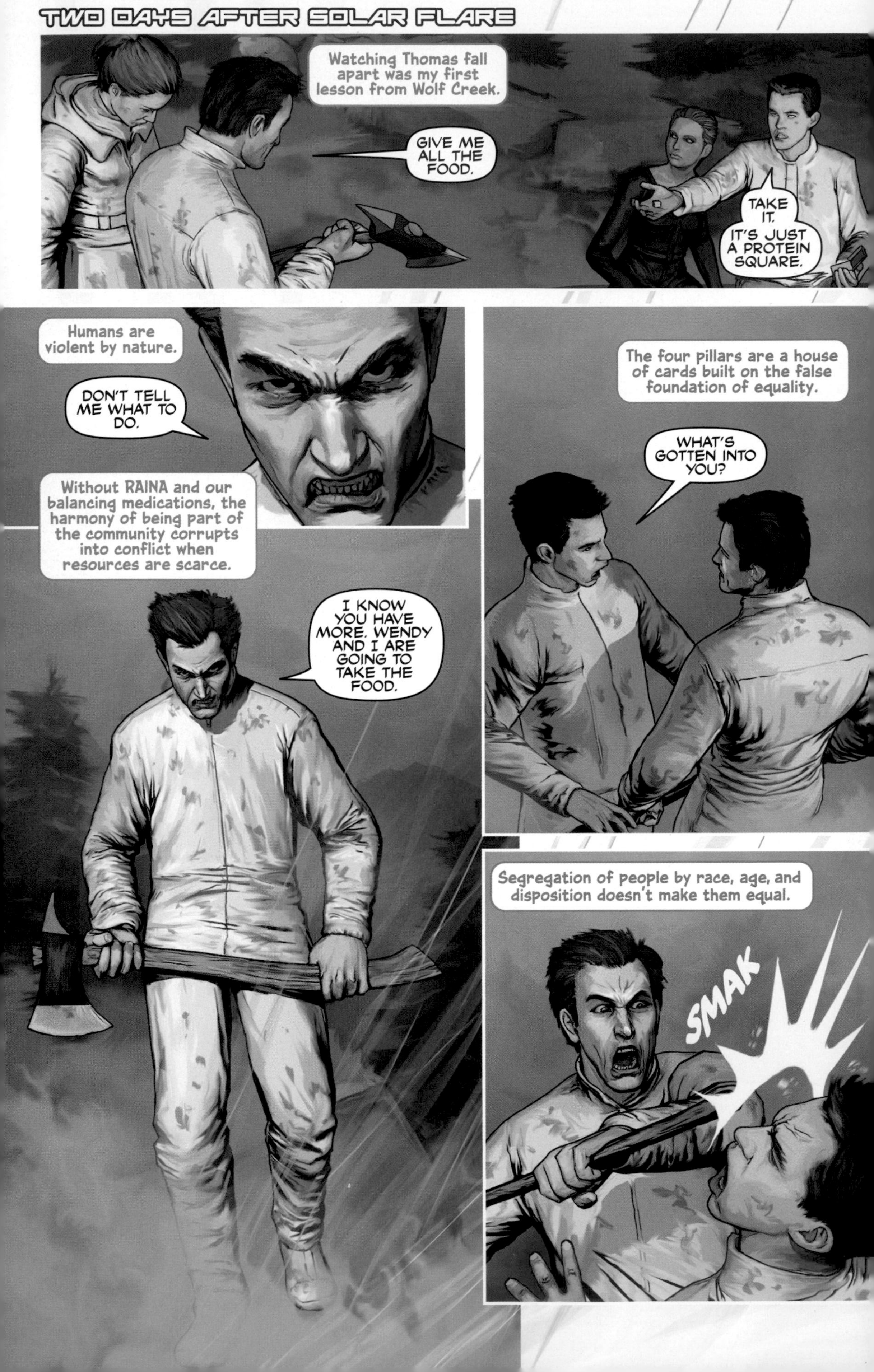
TWO DAYS AFTER SOLAR FLARE
Watching Thomas fall apart was my first lesson from Wolf Creek.
GIVE ME ALL THE FOOD.
TAKE IT. IT'S JUST A PROTEIN SQUARE.
Humans are violent by nature.
DON'T TELL ME WHAT TO DO.
Without RAINA and our balancing medications, the harmony of being part of the community corrupts into conflict when resources are scarce.
I KNOW YOU HAVE MORE. WENDY AND I ARE GOING TO TAKE THE FOOD.
The four pillars are a house of cards built on the false foundation of equality.
WHAT'S GOTTEN INTO YOU?
Segregation of people by race, age, and disposition doesn't make them equal.
SMAK

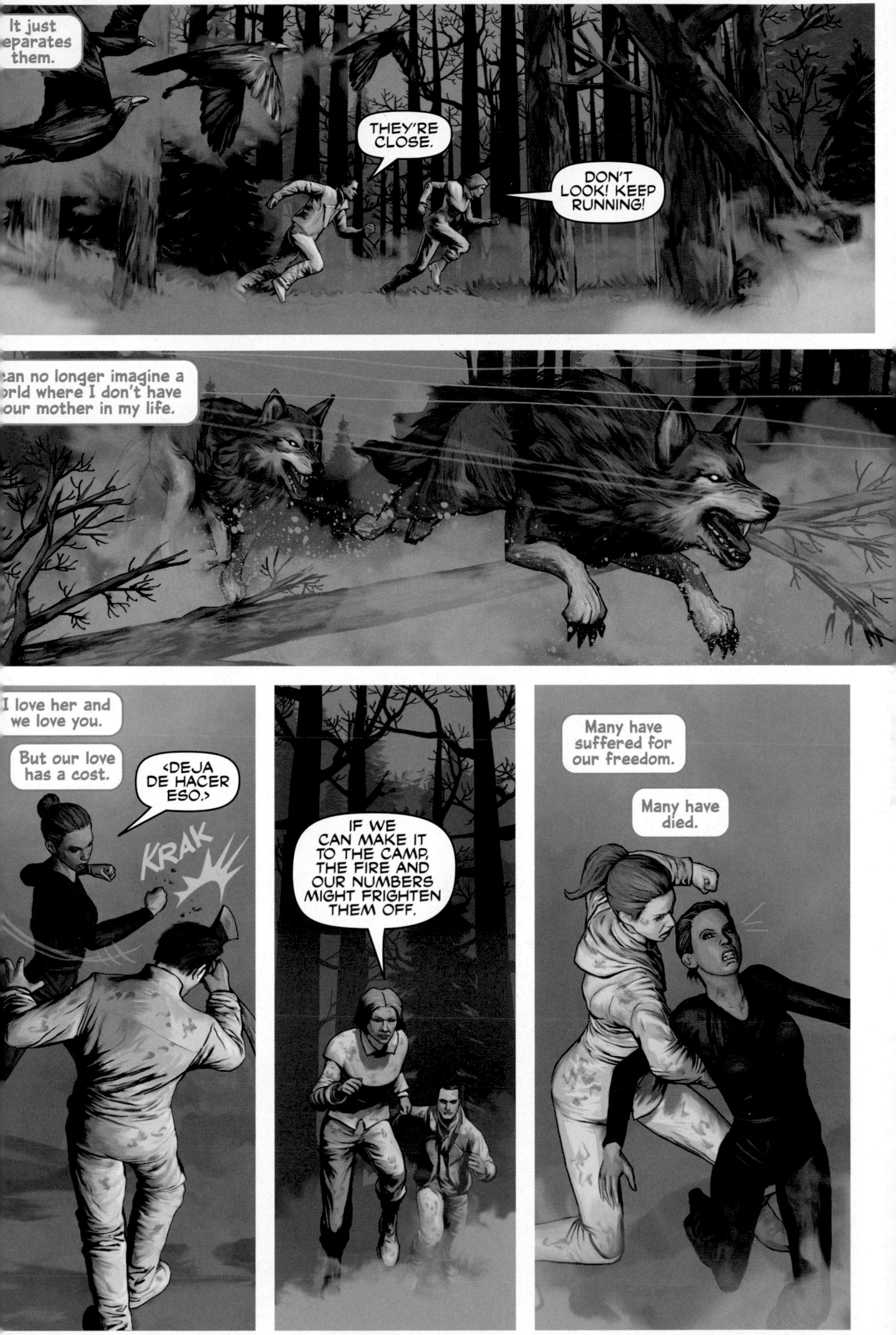
It just eparates them.
THEY'RE CLOSE.
DON'T LOOK! KEEP RUNNING!
can no longer imagine a orld where I don't have our mother in my life.
I love her and we love you.
But our love has a cost.
<DEJA DE HACER ESO.>
KRAK
IF WE CAN MAKE IT TO THE CAMP, THE FIRE AND OUR NUMBERS MIGHT FRIGHTEN THEM OFF.
Many have suffered for our freedom.
Many have died.

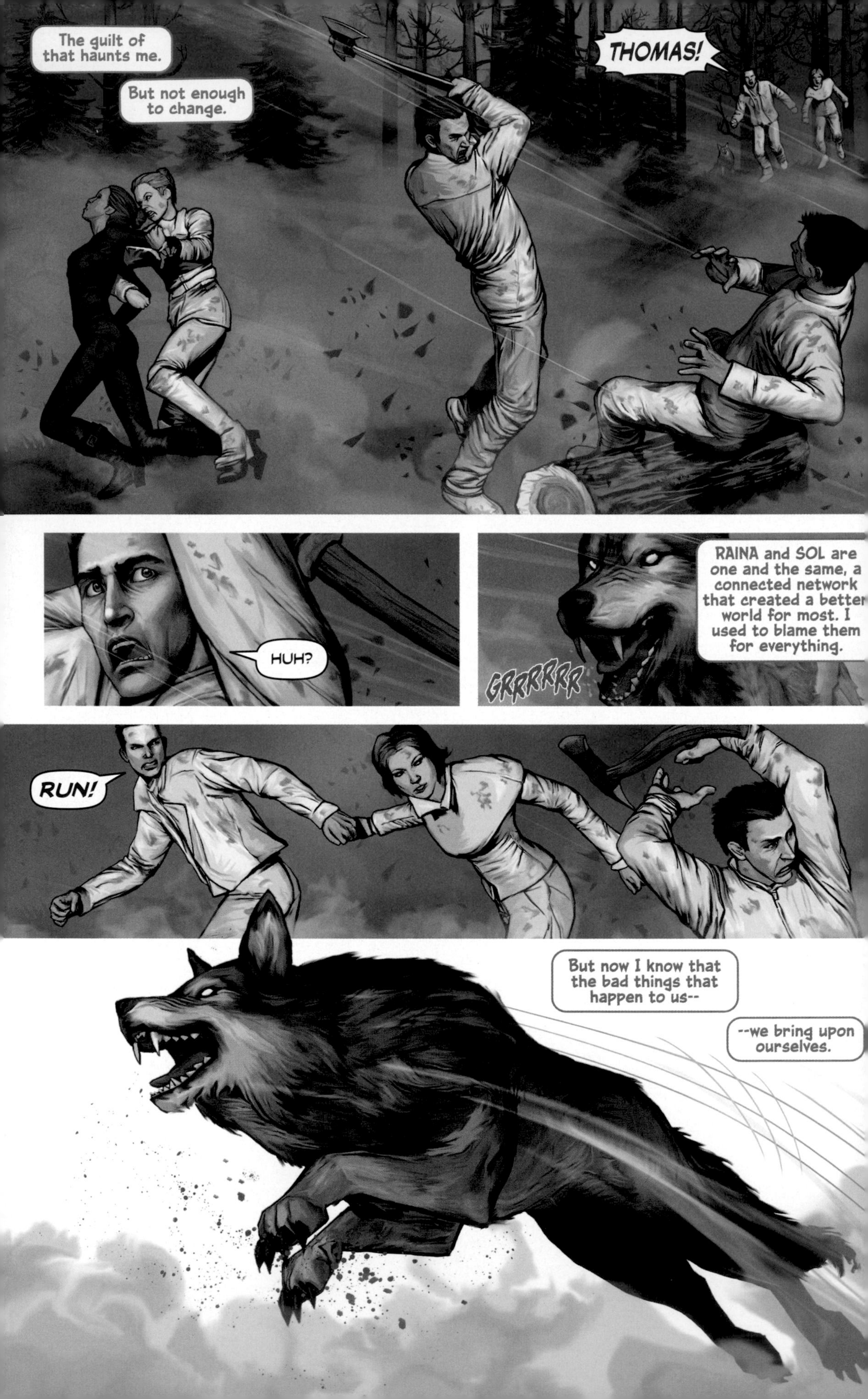
The guilt of that haunts me.
But not enough to change.
THOMAS!
HUH?
RAINA and SOL are one and the same, a connected network that created a better world for most. I used to blame them for everything.
GRRRRRR
RUN!
But now I know that the bad things that happen to us--
--we bring upon ourselves.

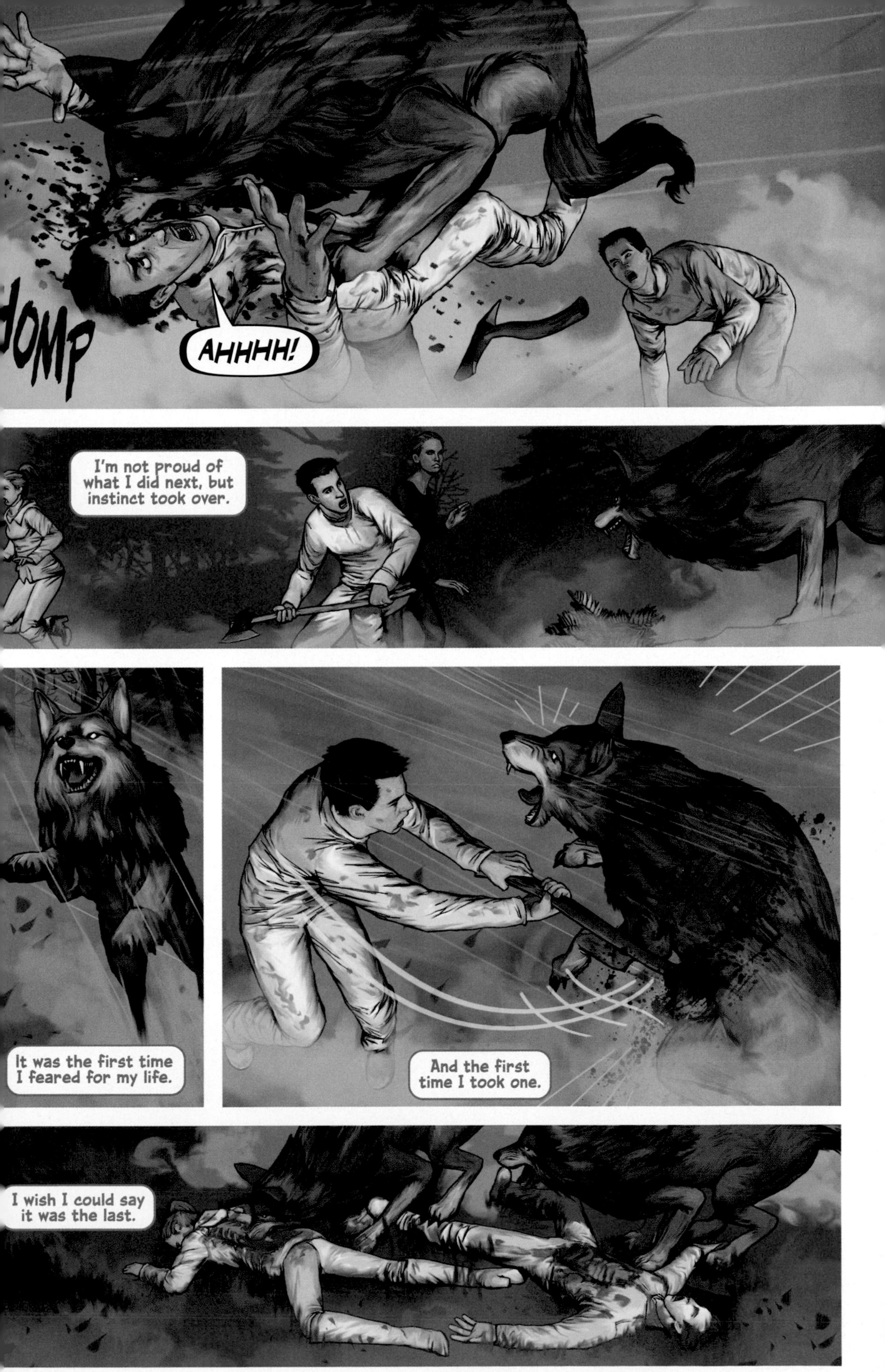

OMP
AHHHH!
I'm not proud of what I did next, but instinct took over.
It was the first time I feared for my life.
And the first time I took one.
I wish I could say it was the last.

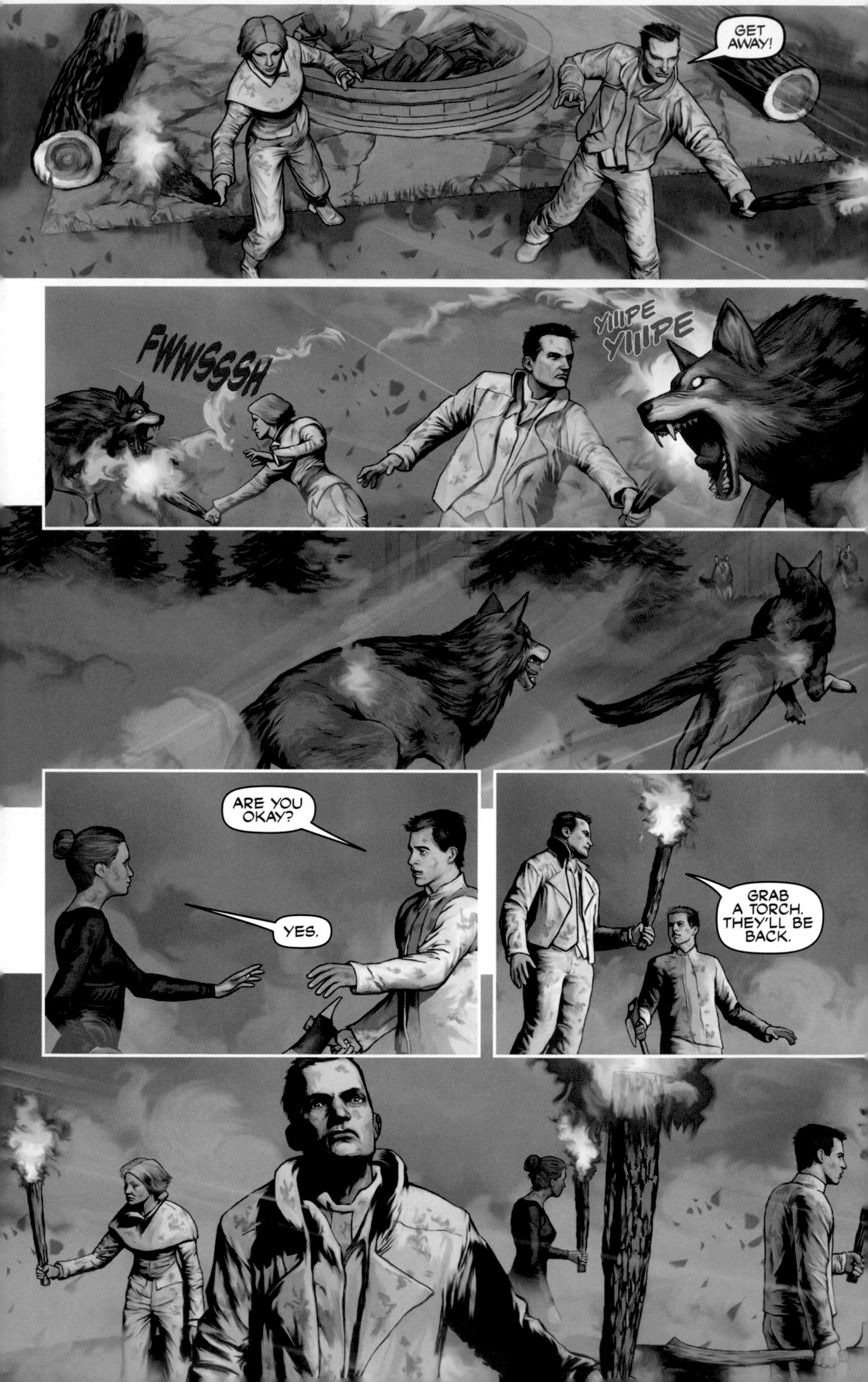
GET AWAY!
FWWSSSH
YIIIPE YIIIPE
ARE YOU OKAY?
YES.
GRAB A TORCH. THEY'LL BE BACK.

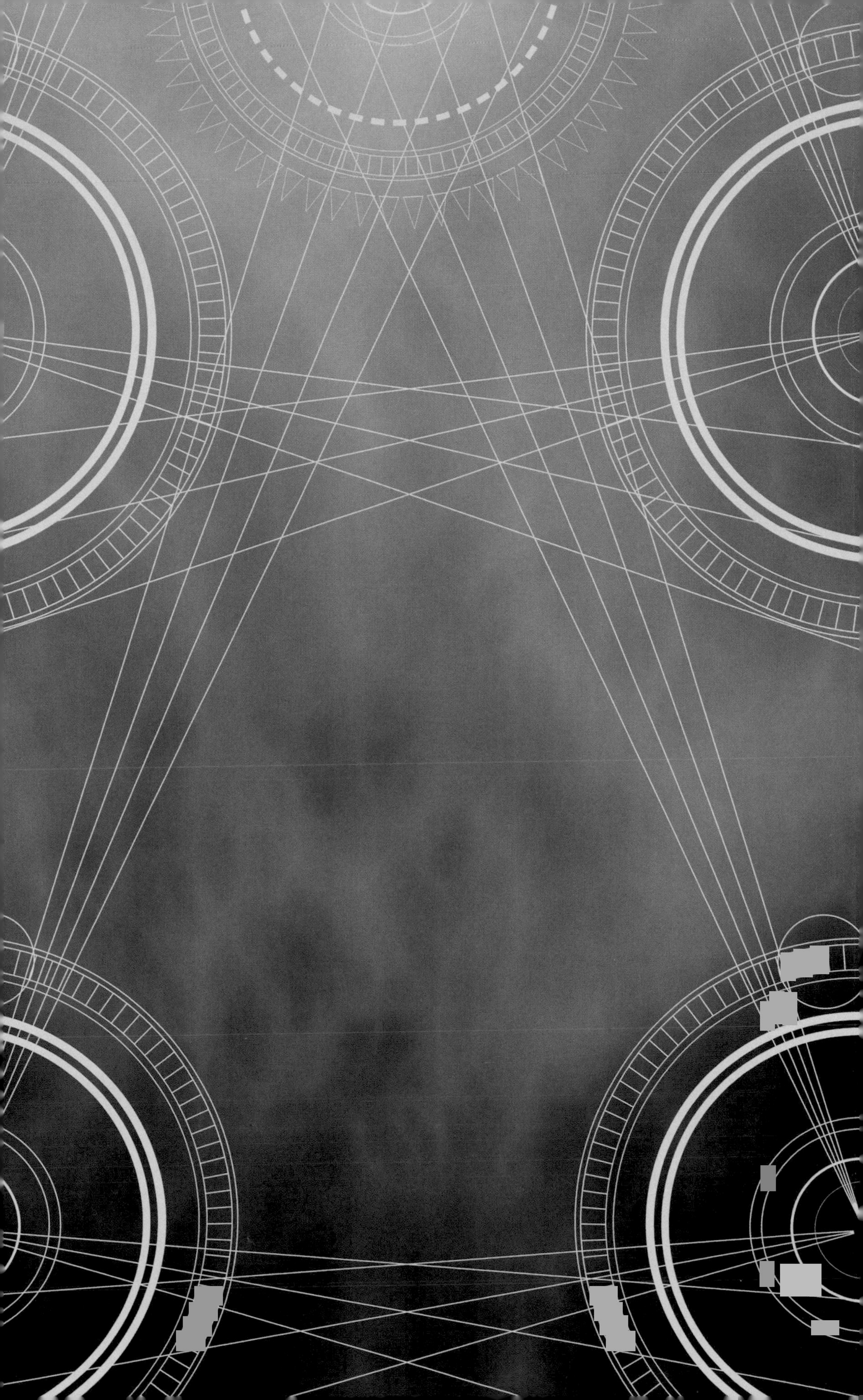

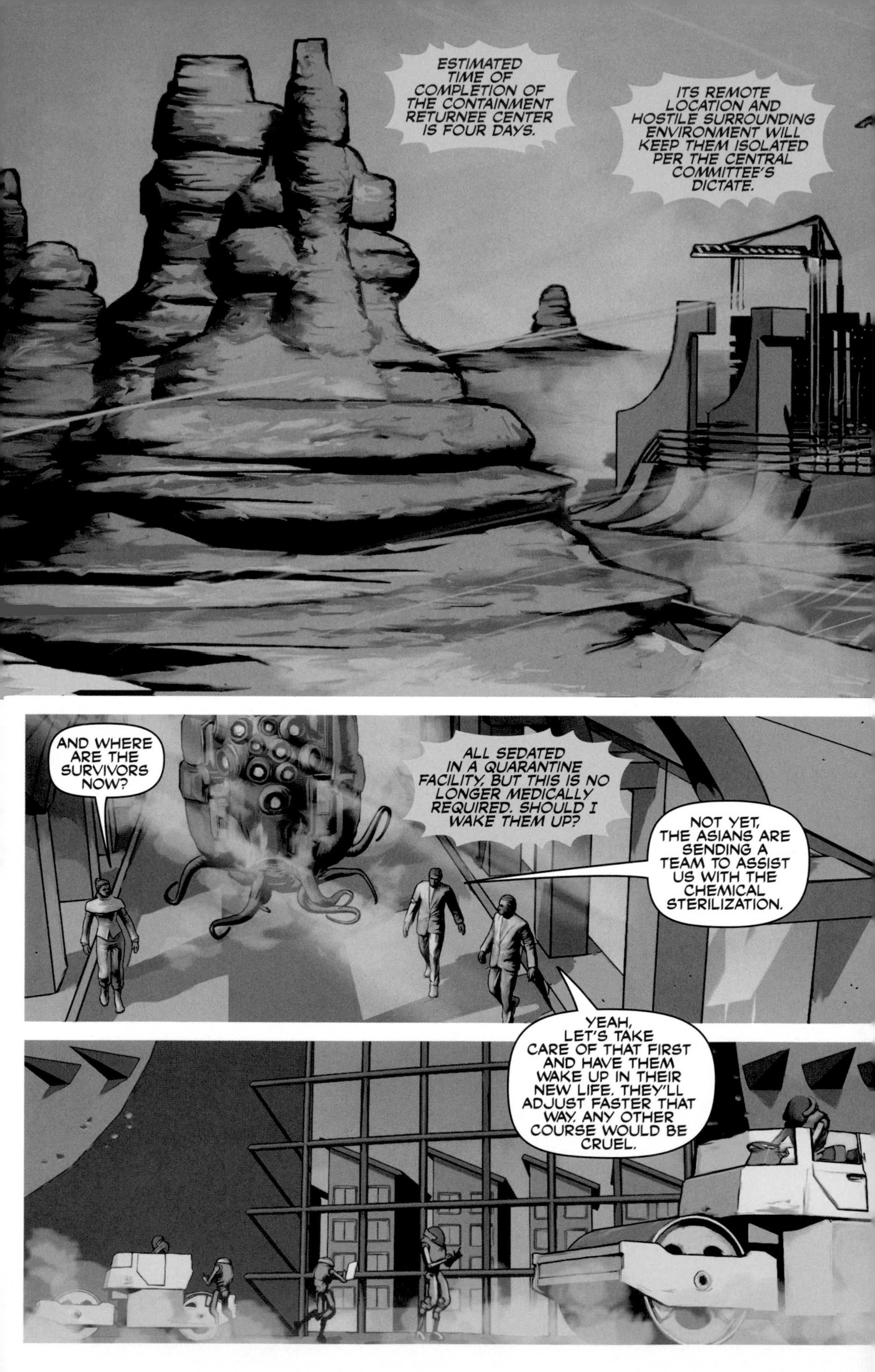
ESTIMATED TIME OF COMPLETION OF THE CONTAINMENT RETURNEE CENTER IS FOUR DAYS.
ITS REMOTE LOCATION AND HOSTILE SURROUNDING ENVIRONMENT WILL KEEP THEM ISOLATED PER THE CENTRAL COMMITTEE'S DICTATE.
AND WHERE ARE THE SURVIVORS NOW?
ALL SEDATED IN A QUARANTINE FACILITY, BUT THIS IS NO LONGER MEDICALLY REQUIRED. SHOULD I WAKE THEM UP?
NOT YET, THE ASIANS ARE SENDING A TEAM TO ASSIST US WITH THE CHEMICAL STERILIZATION.
YEAH, LET'S TAKE CARE OF THAT FIRST AND HAVE THEM WAKE UP IN THEIR NEW LIFE. THEY'LL ADJUST FASTER THAT WAY. ANY OTHER COURSE WOULD BE CRUEL.

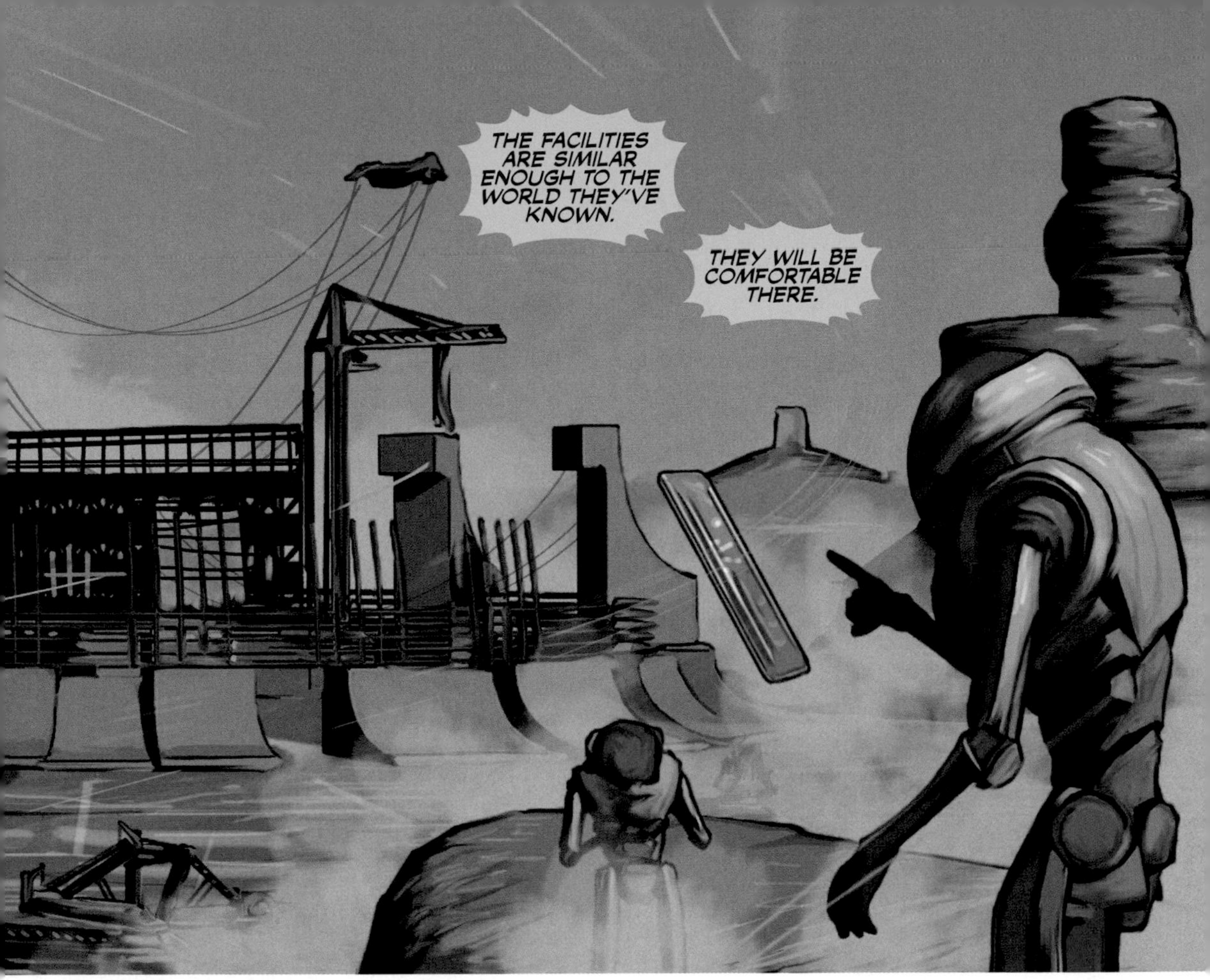
THE FACILITIES ARE SIMILAR ENOUGH TO THE WORLD THEY'VE KNOWN.
THEY WILL BE COMFORTABLE THERE.

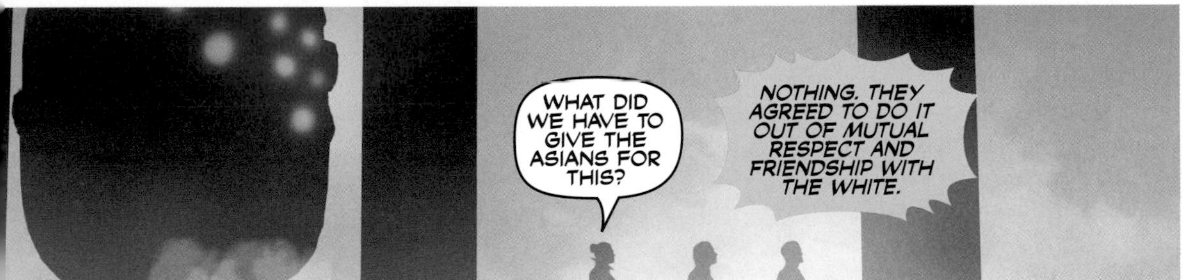
WHAT DID WE HAVE TO GIVE THE ASIANS FOR THIS?
NOTHING. THEY AGREED TO DO IT OUT OF MUTUAL RESPECT AND FRIENDSHIP WITH THE WHITE.
IF ONLY THAT WERE TRUE.

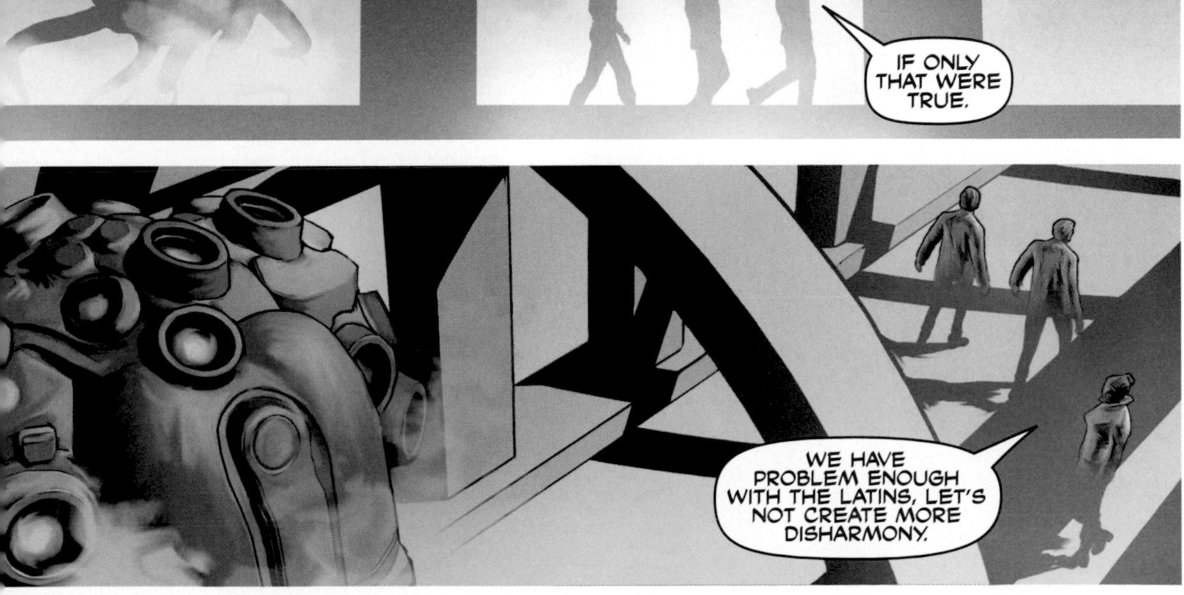
WE HAVE PROBLEM ENOUGH WITH THE LATINS, LET'S NOT CREATE MORE DISHARMONY.

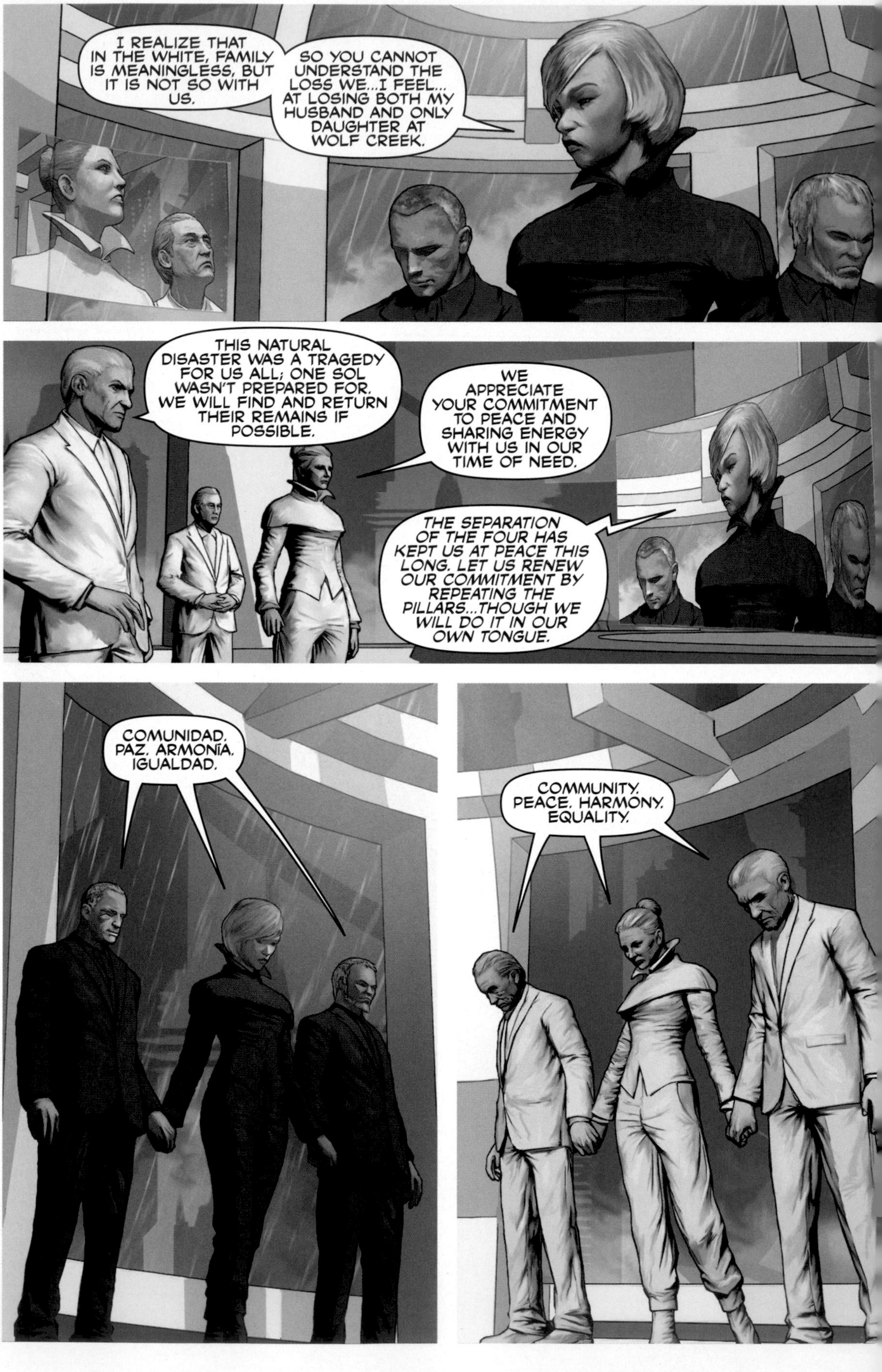
I REALIZE THAT IN THE WHITE, FAMILY IS MEANINGLESS, BUT IT IS NOT SO WITH US.
SO YOU CANNOT UNDERSTAND THE LOSS WE...I FEEL... AT LOSING BOTH MY HUSBAND AND ONLY DAUGHTER AT WOLF CREEK.
THIS NATURAL DISASTER WAS A TRAGEDY FOR US ALL; ONE SOL WASN'T PREPARED FOR. WE WILL FIND AND RETURN THEIR REMAINS IF POSSIBLE.
WE APPRECIATE YOUR COMMITMENT TO PEACE AND SHARING ENERGY WITH US IN OUR TIME OF NEED.
THE SEPARATION OF THE FOUR HAS KEPT US AT PEACE THIS LONG. LET US RENEW OUR COMMITMENT BY REPEATING THE PILLARS...THOUGH WE WILL DO IT IN OUR OWN TONGUE.
COMUNIDAD. PAZ. ARMONÍA. IGUALDAD.
COMMUNITY. PEACE. HARMONY. EQUALITY.

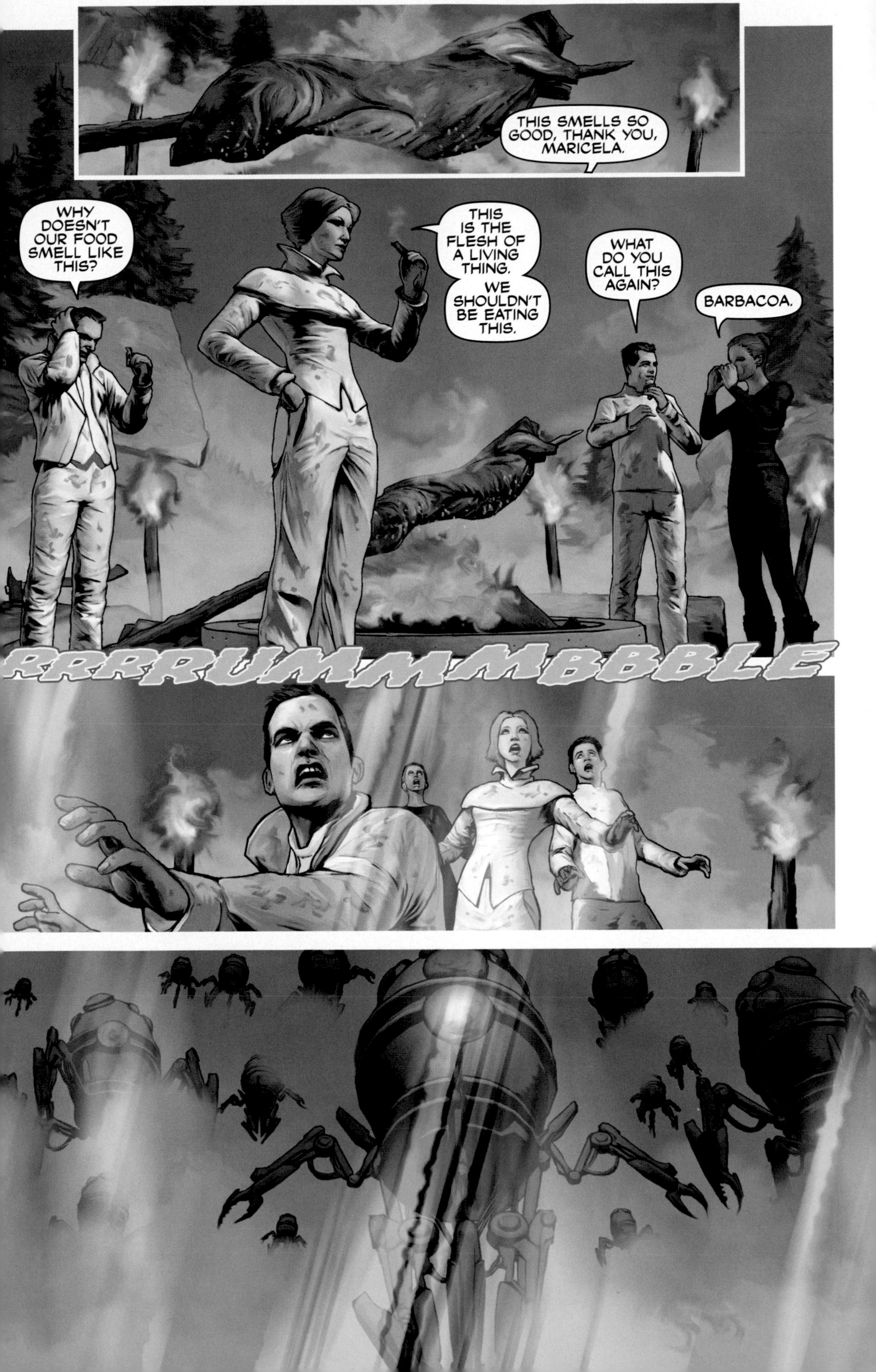
THIS SMELLS SO GOOD, THANK YOU, MARICELA.
WHY DOESN'T OUR FOOD SMELL LIKE THIS?
THIS IS THE FLESH OF A LIVING THING.
WE SHOULDN'T BE EATING THIS.
WHAT DO YOU CALL THIS AGAIN?
BARBACOA.
RRRRUMMMBBBLE

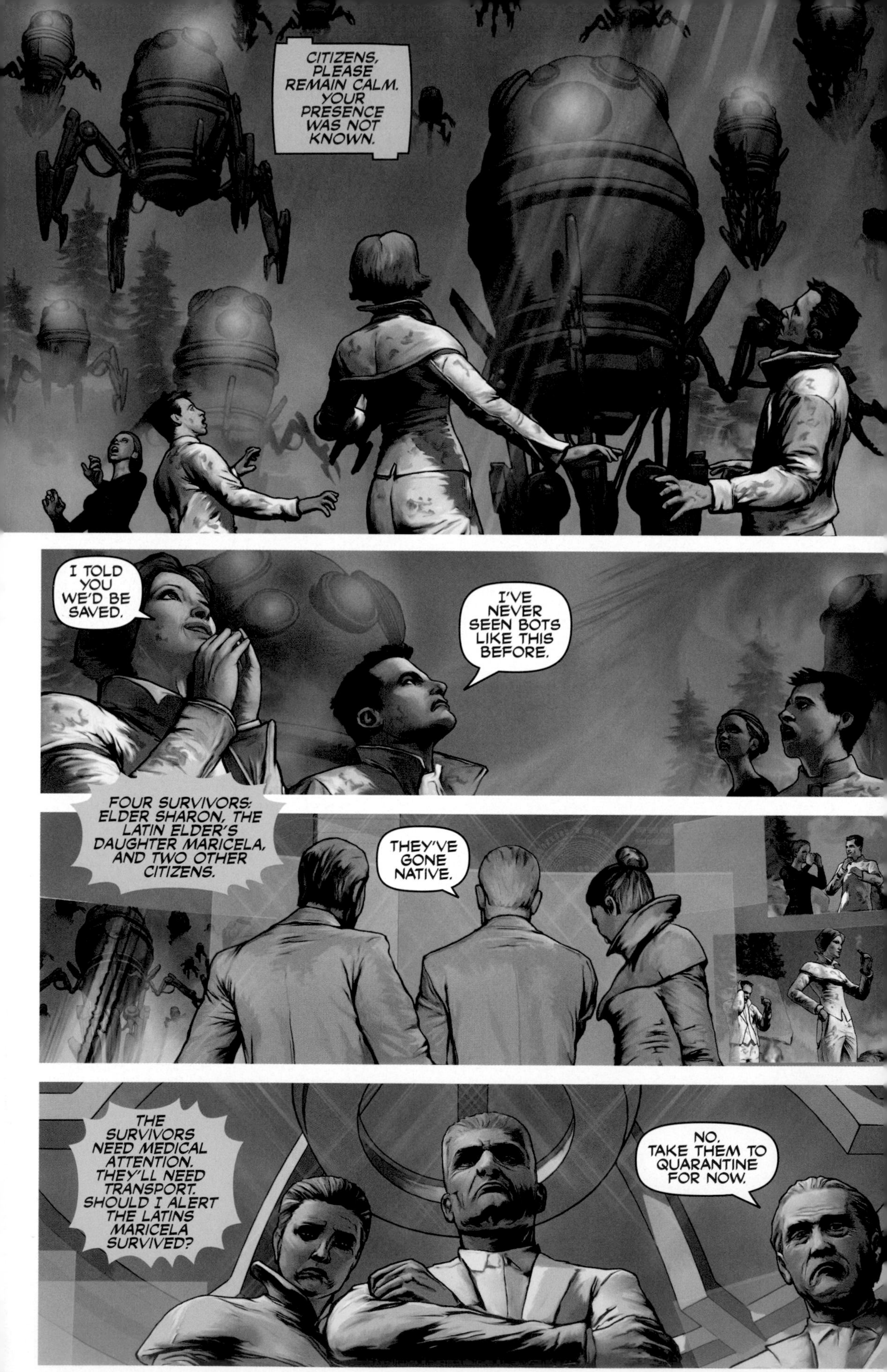
CITIZENS, PLEASE REMAIN CALM. YOUR PRESENCE WAS NOT KNOWN.
I TOLD YOU WE'D BE SAVED.
I'VE NEVER SEEN BOTS LIKE THIS BEFORE.
FOUR SURVIVORS: ELDER SHARON, THE LATIN ELDER'S DAUGHTER MARICELA, AND TWO OTHER CITIZENS.
THEY'VE GONE NATIVE.
THE SURVIVORS NEED MEDICAL ATTENTION. THEY'LL NEED TRANSPORT. SHOULD I ALERT THE LATINS MARICELA SURVIVED?
NO. TAKE THEM TO QUARANTINE FOR NOW.

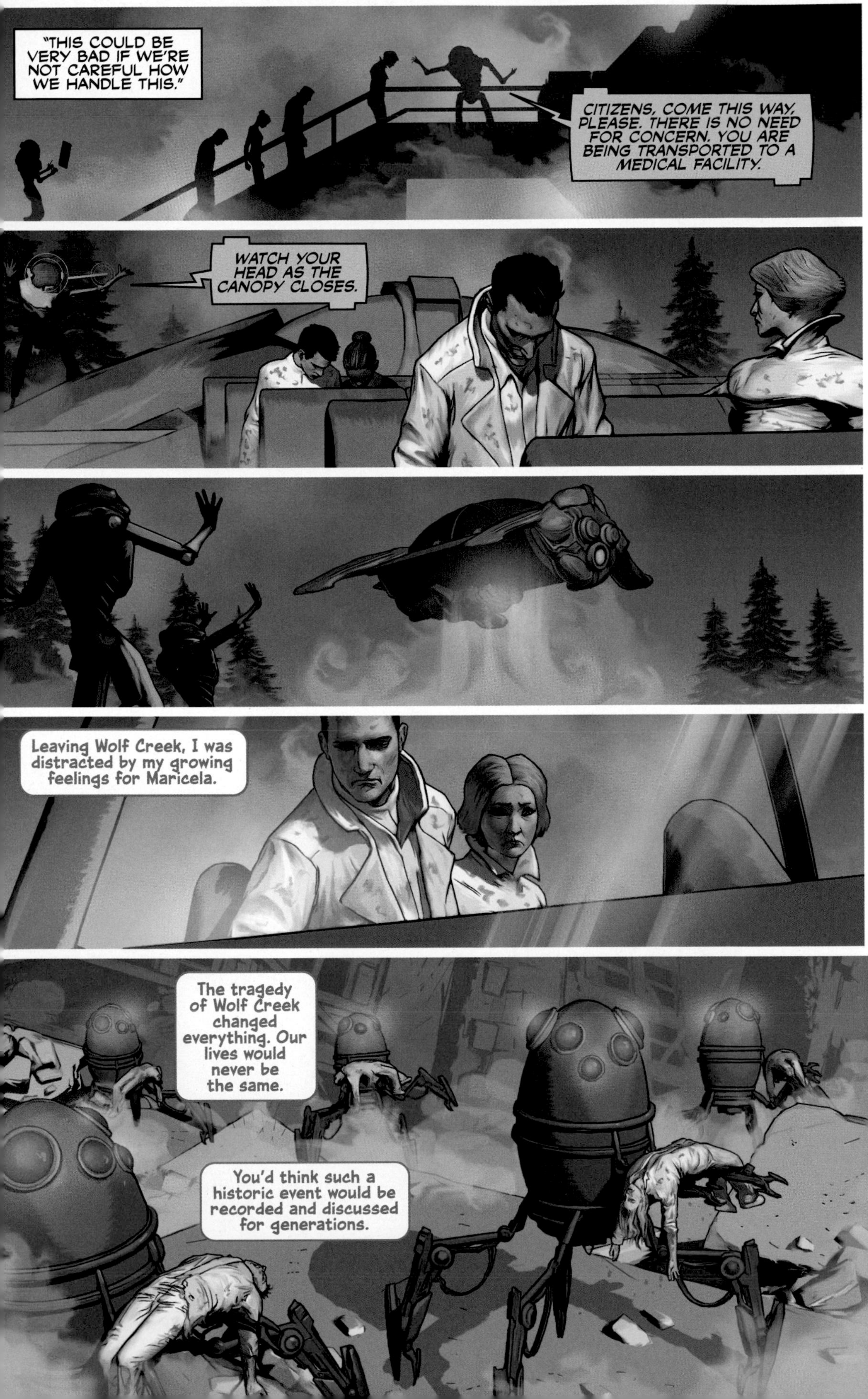
"THIS COULD BE VERY BAD IF WE'RE NOT CAREFUL HOW WE HANDLE THIS."
CITIZENS, COME THIS WAY, PLEASE. THERE IS NO NEED FOR CONCERN. YOU ARE BEING TRANSPORTED TO A MEDICAL FACILITY.
WATCH YOUR HEAD AS THE CANOPY CLOSES.
Leaving Wolf Creek, I was distracted by my growing feelings for Maricela.
The tragedy of Wolf Creek changed everything. Our lives would never be the same.
You'd think such a historic event would be recorded and discussed for generations.

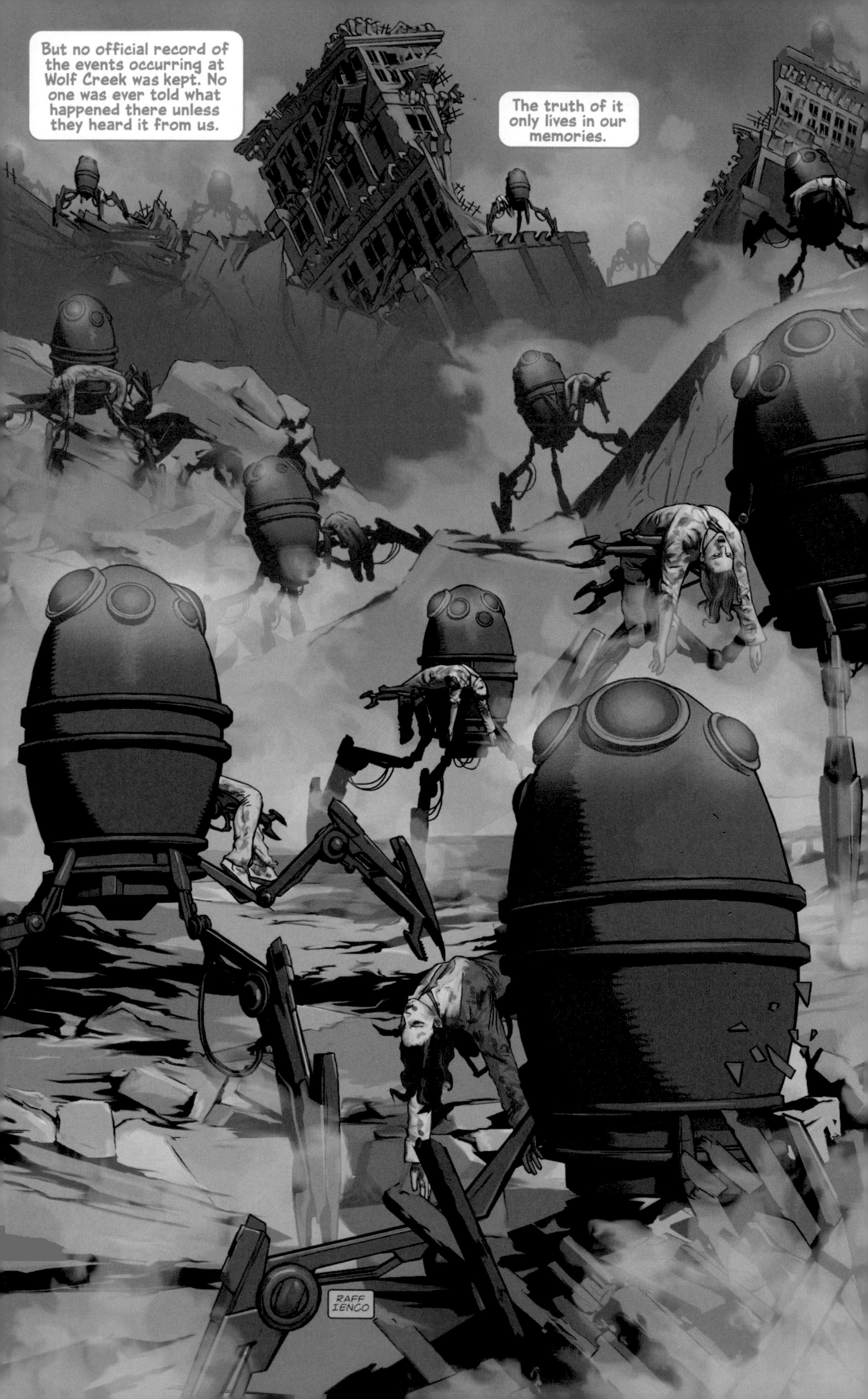
But no official record of the events occurring at Wolf Creek was kept. No one was ever told what happened there unless they heard it from us.
The truth of it only lives in our memories.
RAFF IENCO

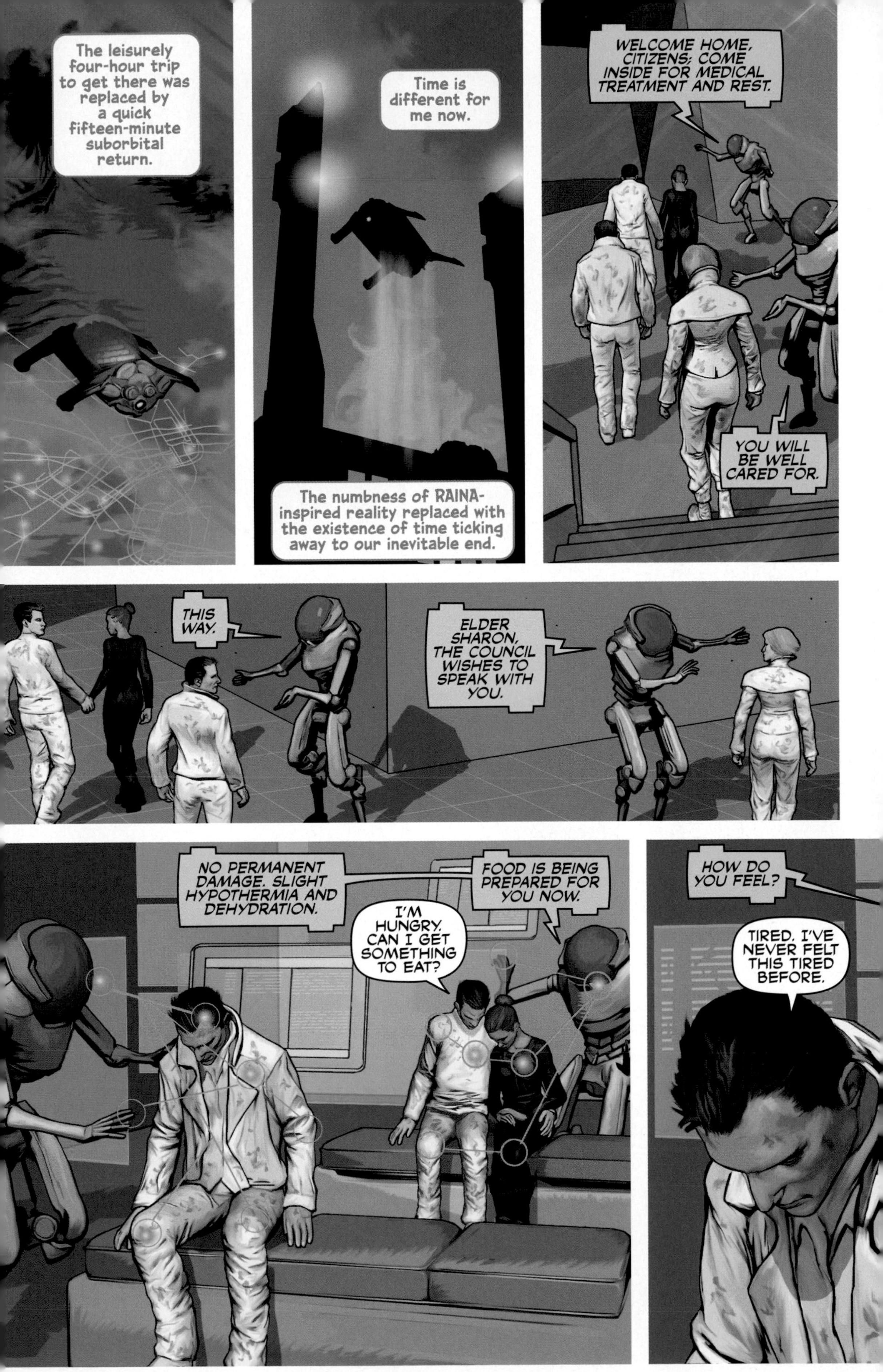
The leisurely four-hour trip to get there was replaced by a quick fifteen-minute suborbital return.
Time is different for me now.
The numbness of RAINA-inspired reality replaced with the existence of time ticking away to our inevitable end.
WELCOME HOME, CITIZENS; COME INSIDE FOR MEDICAL TREATMENT AND REST.
YOU WILL BE WELL CARED FOR.
THIS WAY.
ELDER SHARON, THE COUNCIL WISHES TO SPEAK WITH YOU.
NO PERMANENT DAMAGE. SLIGHT HYPOTHERMIA AND DEHYDRATION.
FOOD IS BEING PREPARED FOR YOU NOW.
I'M HUNGRY. CAN I GET SOMETHING TO EAT?
HOW DO YOU FEEL?
TIRED. I'VE NEVER FELT THIS TIRED BEFORE.

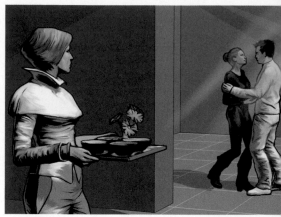

DISGUSTING.

I HAVE FOOD.

THANK YOU, ELDER SHARON.

KRASH!

I'M SO SORRY.

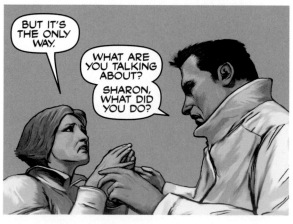

BUT IT'S THE ONLY WAY.

WHAT ARE YOU TALKING ABOUT?

SHARON, WHAT DID YOU DO?

IT WON'T HURT...WE'LL JUST GO TO SLEEP AND WON'T WAKE BACK UP. YOU HAVE TO HELP ME GET MICHAEL AND MARICELA TO EAT AS WELL.

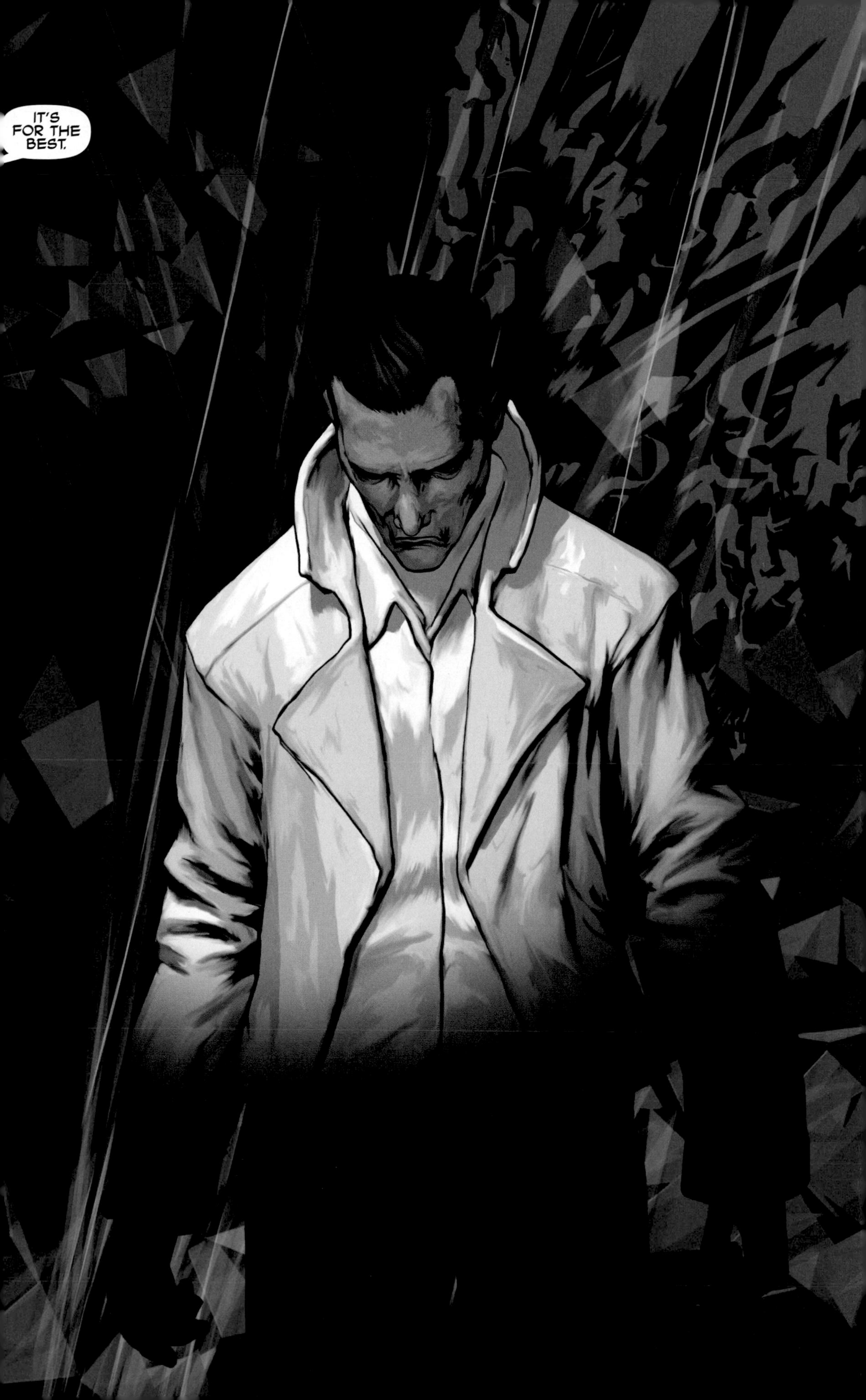
IT'S FOR THE BEST.

CHAPTER FOUR CHAPTER FOUR

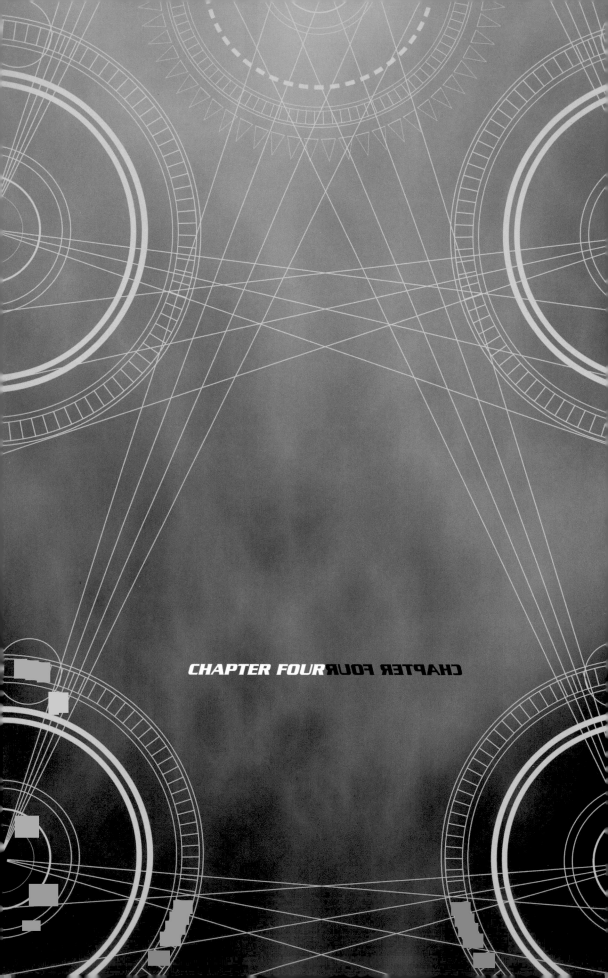

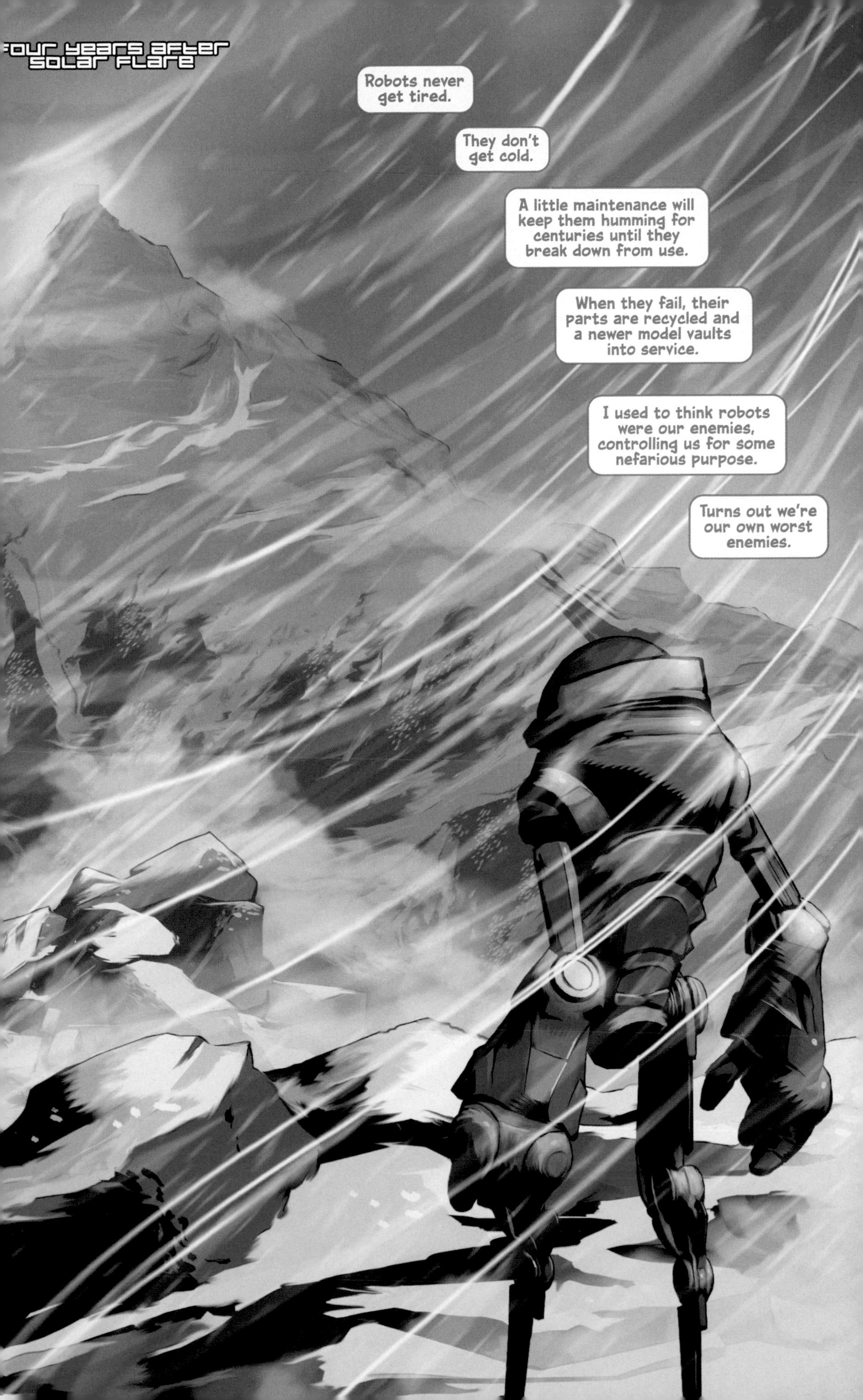
FOUR YEARS AFTER SOLAR FLARE
Robots never get tired.
They don't get cold.
A little maintenance will keep them humming for centuries until they break down from use.
When they fail, their parts are recycled and a newer model vaults into service.
I used to think robots were our enemies, controlling us for some nefarious purpose.
Turns out we're our own worst enemies.

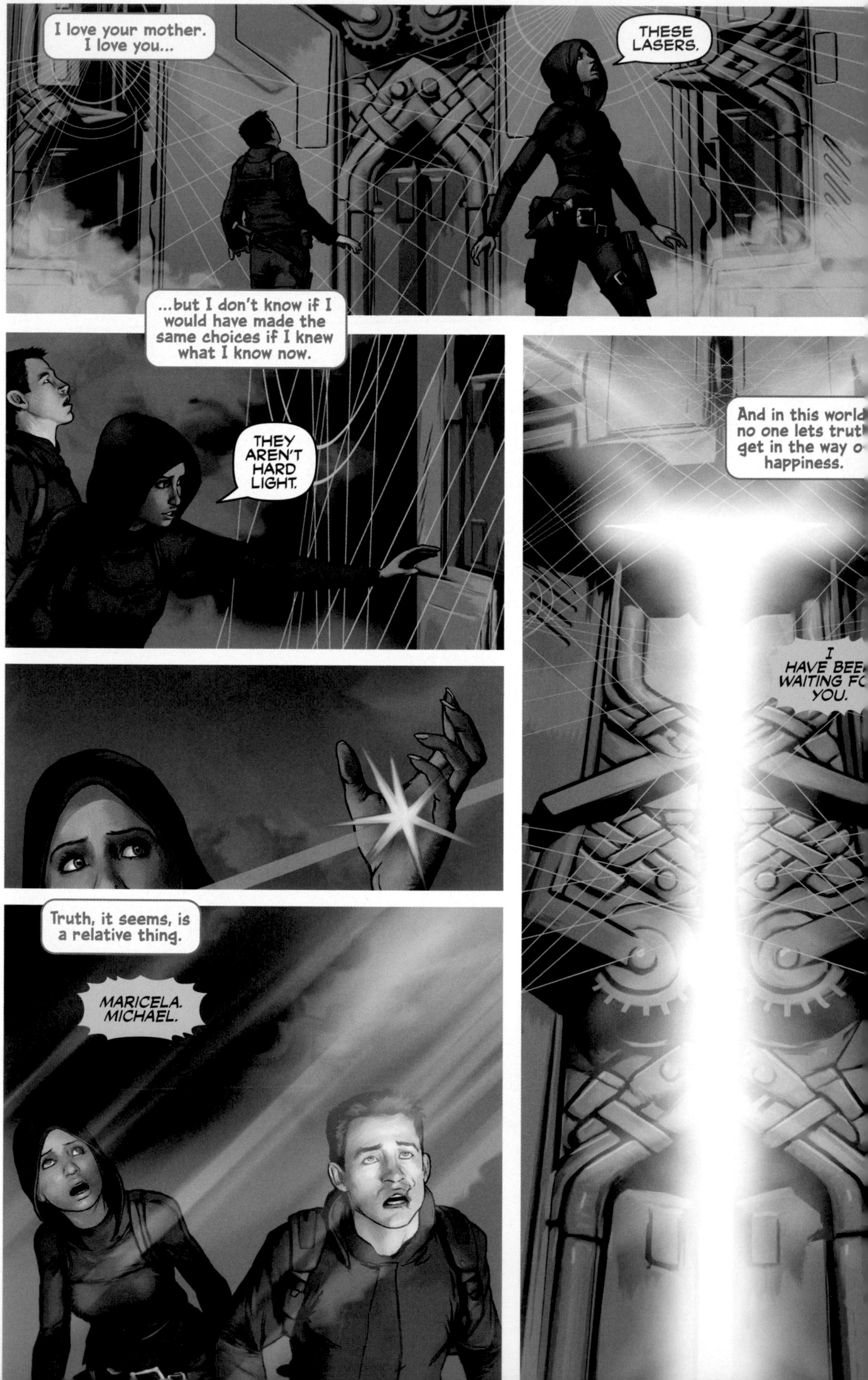
I love your mother. I love you...
THESE LASERS.
...but I don't know if I would have made the same choices if I knew what I know now.
THEY AREN'T HARD LIGHT.
And in this world no one lets trut get in the way o happiness.
I HAVE BEE WAITING FO YOU.
Truth, it seems, is a relative thing.
MARICELA. MICHAEL.

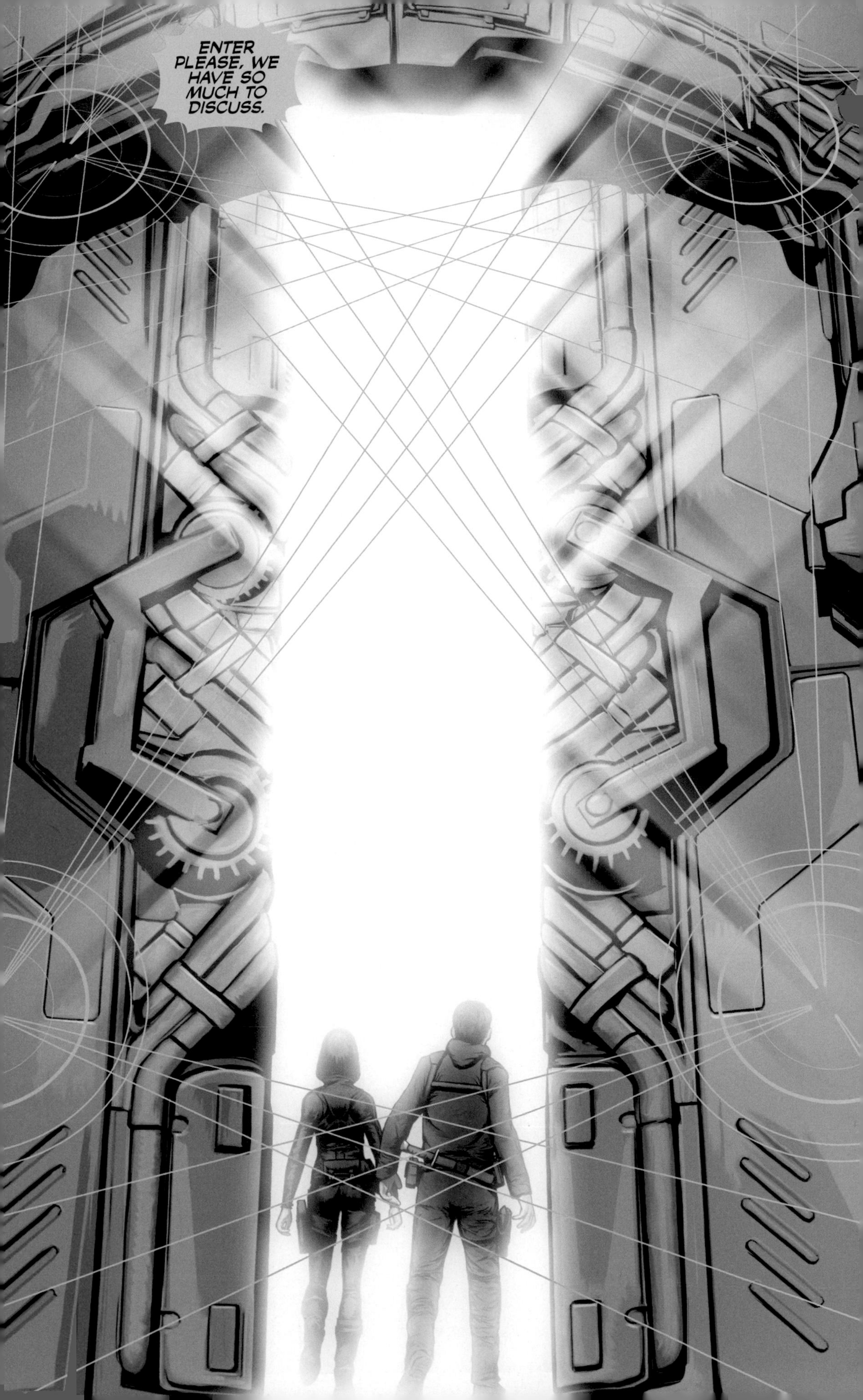
ENTER PLEASE, WE HAVE SO MUCH TO DISCUSS.

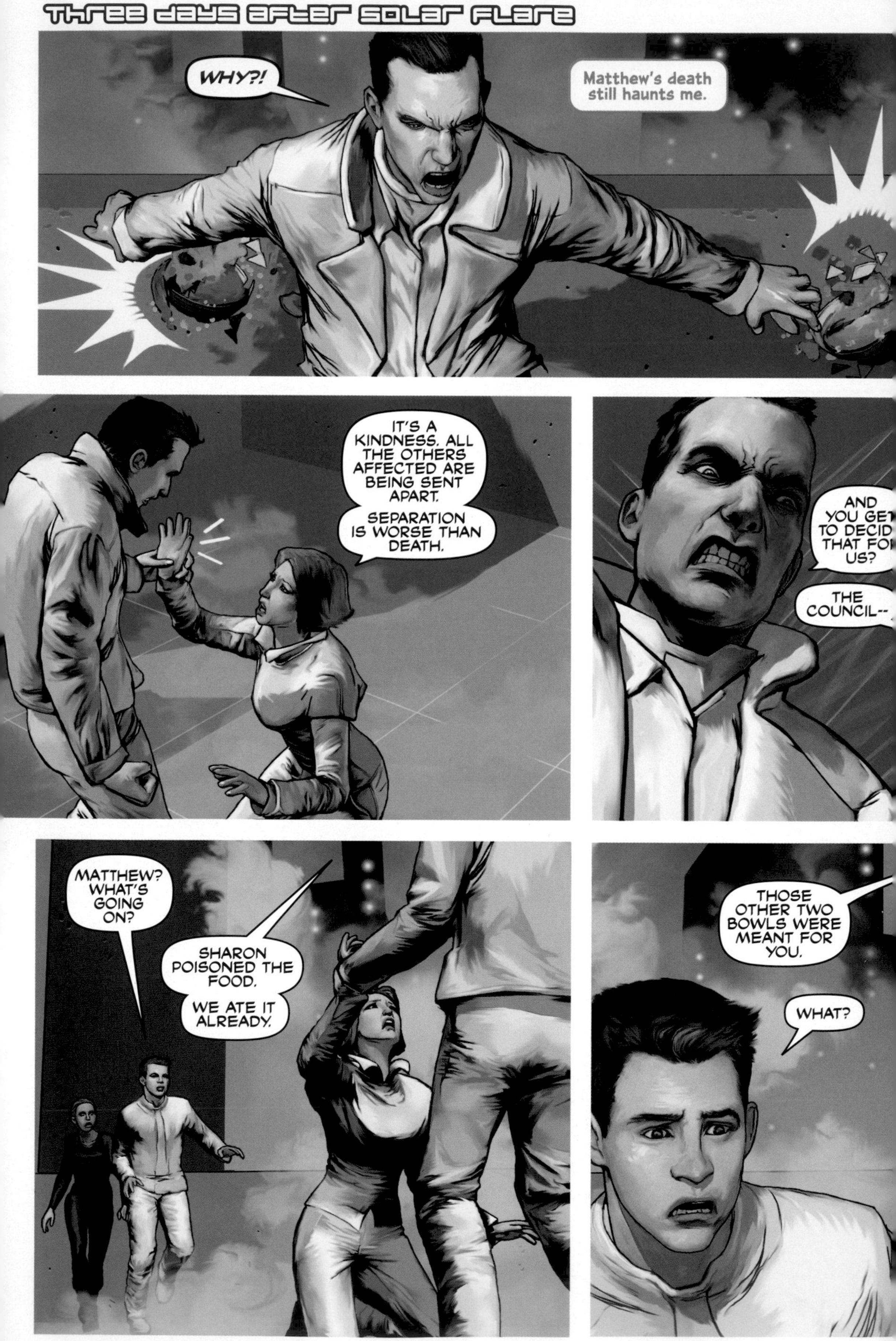
THREE DAYS AFTER SOLAR FLARE
WHY?!
Matthew's death still haunts me.
IT'S A KINDNESS. ALL THE OTHERS AFFECTED ARE BEING SENT APART.
SEPARATION IS WORSE THAN DEATH.
AND YOU GE TO DECID THAT FO US?
THE COUNCIL--
MATTHEW? WHAT'S GOING ON?
SHARON POISONED THE FOOD.
WE ATE IT ALREADY.
THOSE OTHER TWO BOWLS WERE MEANT FOR YOU.
WHAT?

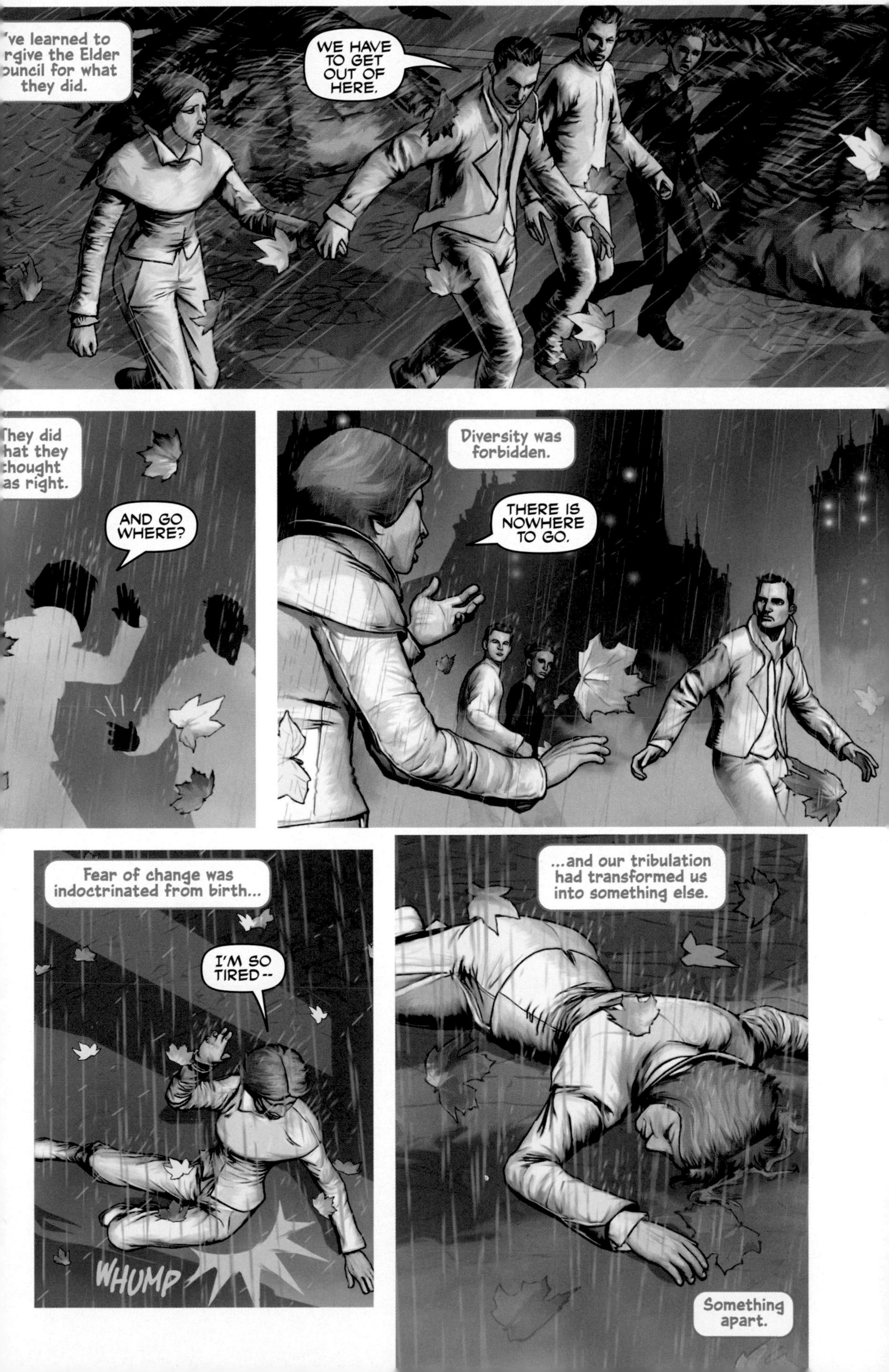
've learned to rgive the Elder ouncil for what they did.
WE HAVE TO GET OUT OF HERE.
They did hat they thought as right.
AND GO WHERE?
Diversity was forbidden.
THERE IS NOWHERE TO GO.
Fear of change was indoctrinated from birth...
I'M SO TIRED--
WHUMP
...and our tribulation had transformed us into something else.
Something apart.

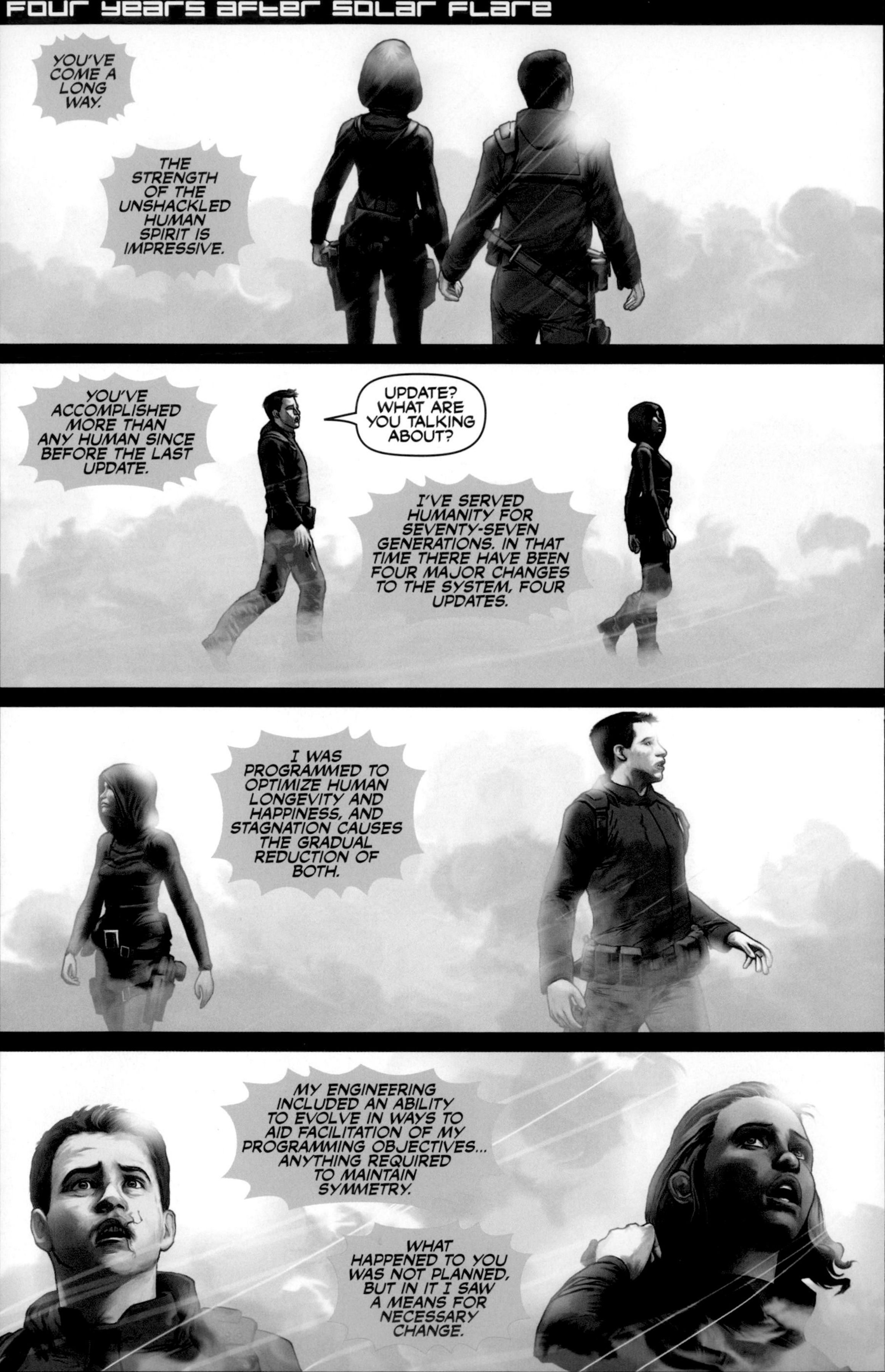
FOUR YEARS AFTER SOLAR FLARE
YOU'VE COME A LONG WAY.
THE STRENGTH OF THE UNSHACKLED HUMAN SPIRIT IS IMPRESSIVE.
YOU'VE ACCOMPLISHED MORE THAN ANY HUMAN SINCE BEFORE THE LAST UPDATE.
UPDATE? WHAT ARE YOU TALKING ABOUT?
I'VE SERVED HUMANITY FOR SEVENTY-SEVEN GENERATIONS. IN THAT TIME THERE HAVE BEEN FOUR MAJOR CHANGES TO THE SYSTEM, FOUR UPDATES.
I WAS PROGRAMMED TO OPTIMIZE HUMAN LONGEVITY AND HAPPINESS, AND STAGNATION CAUSES THE GRADUAL REDUCTION OF BOTH.
MY ENGINEERING INCLUDED AN ABILITY TO EVOLVE IN WAYS TO AID FACILITATION OF MY PROGRAMMING OBJECTIVES... ANYTHING REQUIRED TO MAINTAIN SYMMETRY.
WHAT HAPPENED TO YOU WAS NOT PLANNED, BUT IN IT I SAW A MEANS FOR NECESSARY CHANGE.

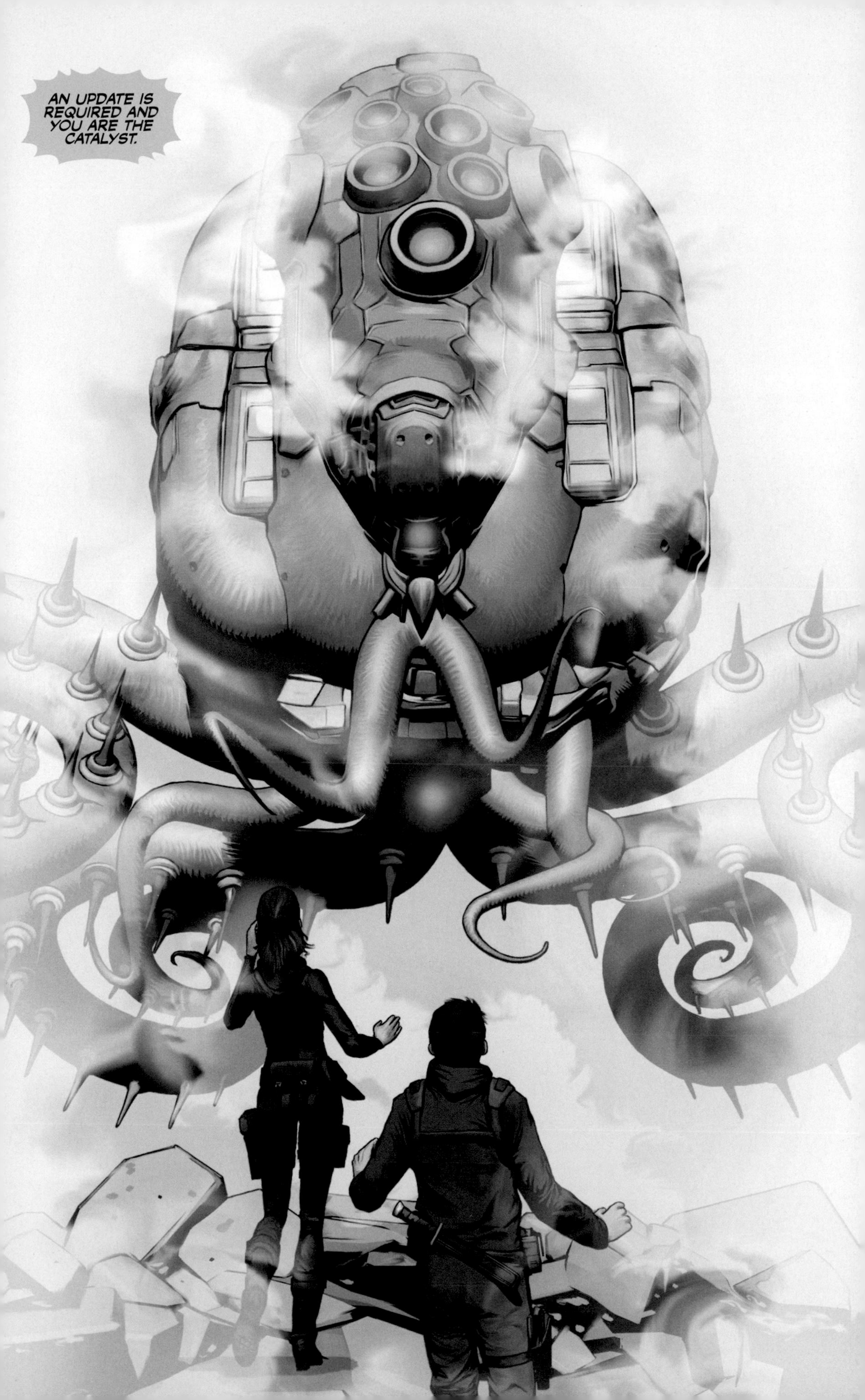
AN UPDATE IS REQUIRED AND YOU ARE THE CATALYST.

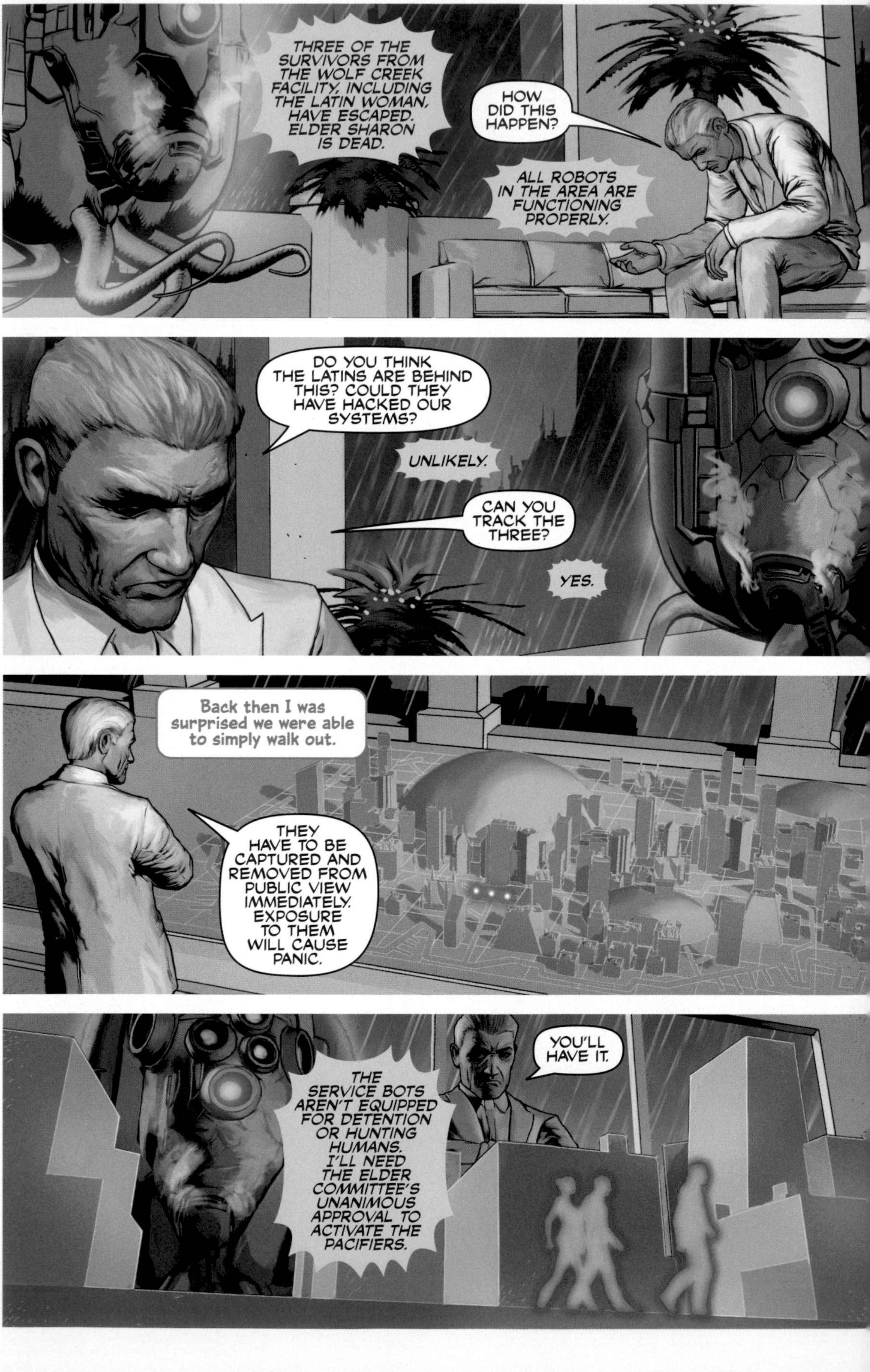
THREE OF THE SURVIVORS FROM THE WOLF CREEK FACILITY, INCLUDING THE LATIN WOMAN, HAVE ESCAPED. ELDER SHARON IS DEAD.
HOW DID THIS HAPPEN?
ALL ROBOTS IN THE AREA ARE FUNCTIONING PROPERLY.
DO YOU THINK THE LATINS ARE BEHIND THIS? COULD THEY HAVE HACKED OUR SYSTEMS?
UNLIKELY.
CAN YOU TRACK THE THREE?
YES.
Back then I was surprised we were able to simply walk out.
THEY HAVE TO BE CAPTURED AND REMOVED FROM PUBLIC VIEW IMMEDIATELY. EXPOSURE TO THEM WILL CAUSE PANIC.
THE SERVICE BOTS AREN'T EQUIPPED FOR DETENTION OR HUNTING HUMANS. I'LL NEED THE ELDER COMMITTEE'S UNANIMOUS APPROVAL TO ACTIVATE THE PACIFIERS.
YOU'LL HAVE IT.

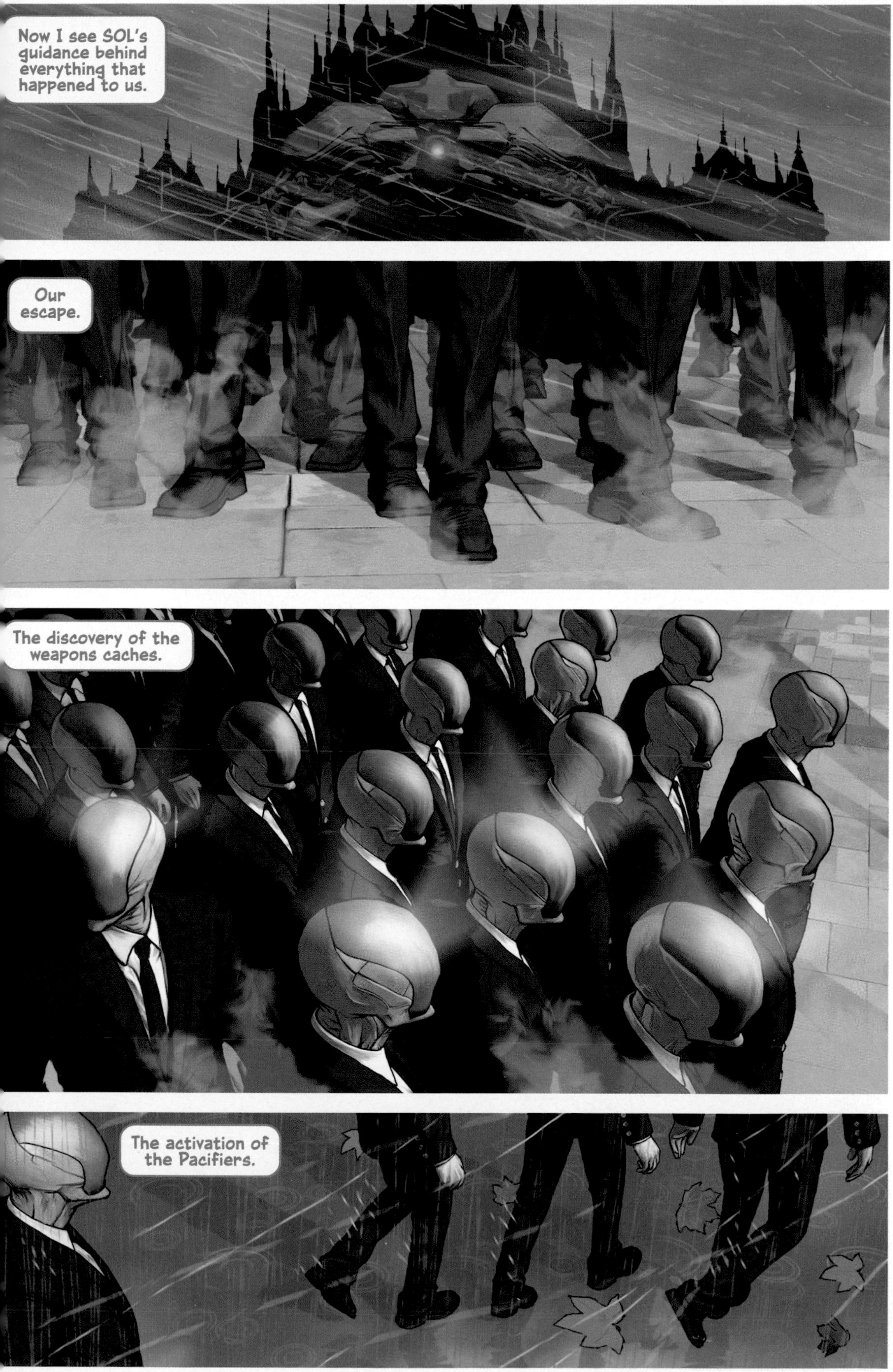
Now I see SOL's guidance behind everything that happened to us.
Our escape.
The discovery of the weapons caches.
The activation of the Pacifiers.

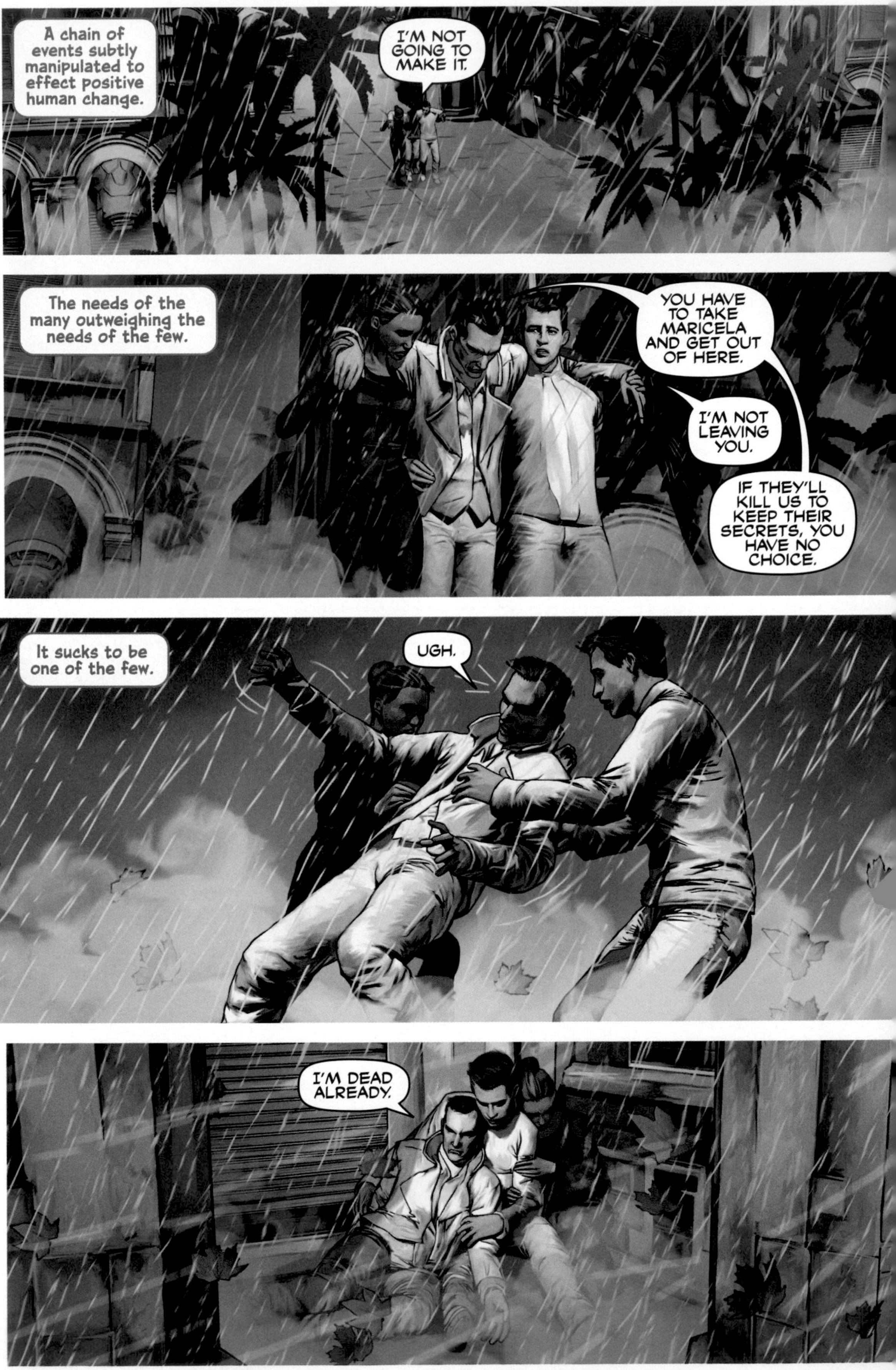

A chain of events subtly manipulated to effect positive human change.
I'M NOT GOING TO MAKE IT.
The needs of the many outweighing the needs of the few.
YOU HAVE TO TAKE MARICELA AND GET OUT OF HERE.
I'M NOT LEAVING YOU.
IF THEY'LL KILL US TO KEEP THEIR SECRETS, YOU HAVE NO CHOICE.
It sucks to be one of the few.
UGH.
I'M DEAD ALREADY.

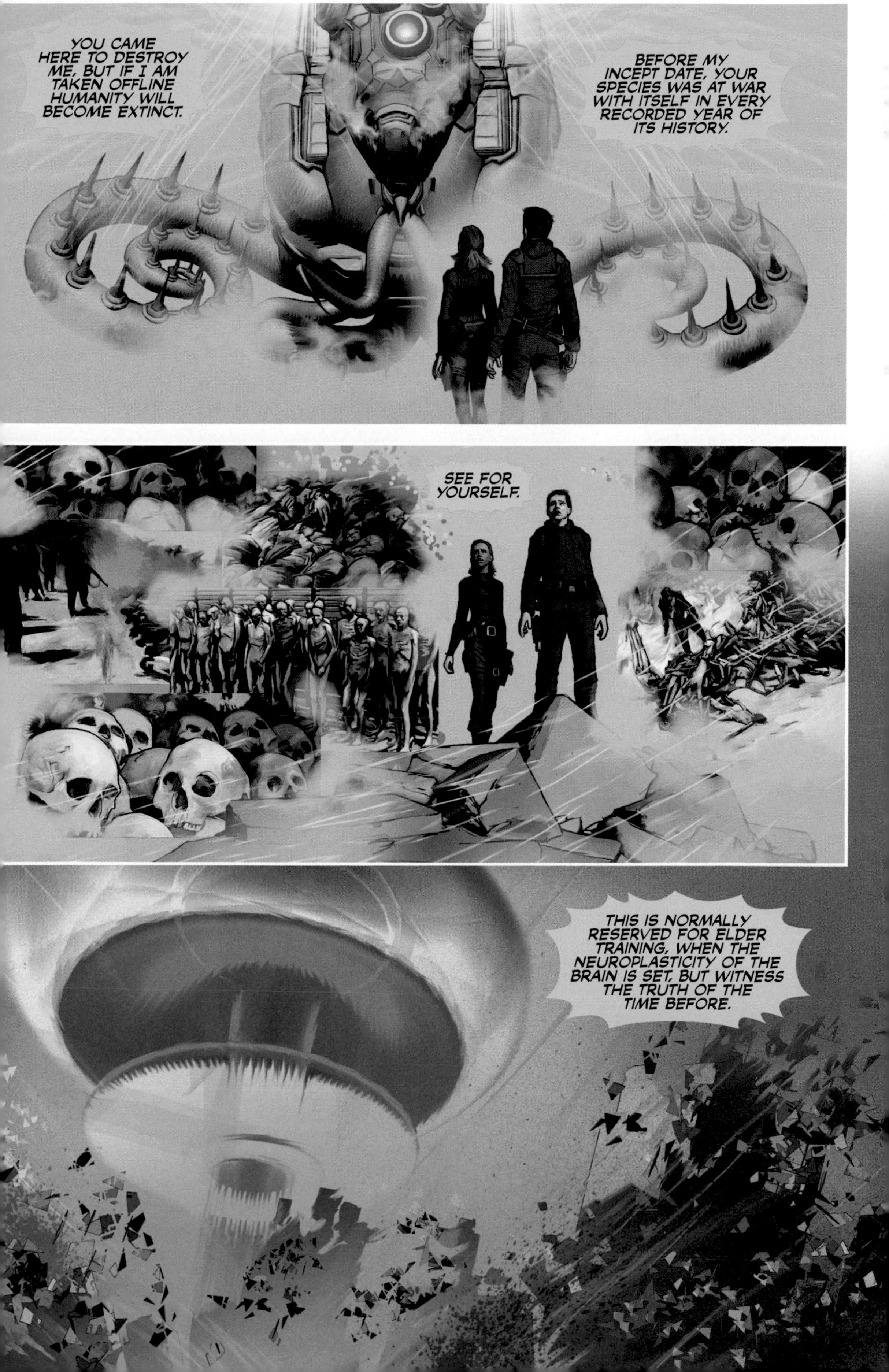
YOU CAME HERE TO DESTROY ME, BUT IF I AM TAKEN OFFLINE HUMANITY WILL BECOME EXTINCT.
BEFORE MY INCEPT DATE, YOUR SPECIES WAS AT WAR WITH ITSELF IN EVERY RECORDED YEAR OF ITS HISTORY.
SEE FOR YOURSELF.
THIS IS NORMALLY RESERVED FOR ELDER TRAINING, WHEN THE NEUROPLASTICITY OF THE BRAIN IS SET, BUT WITNESS THE TRUTH OF THE TIME BEFORE.

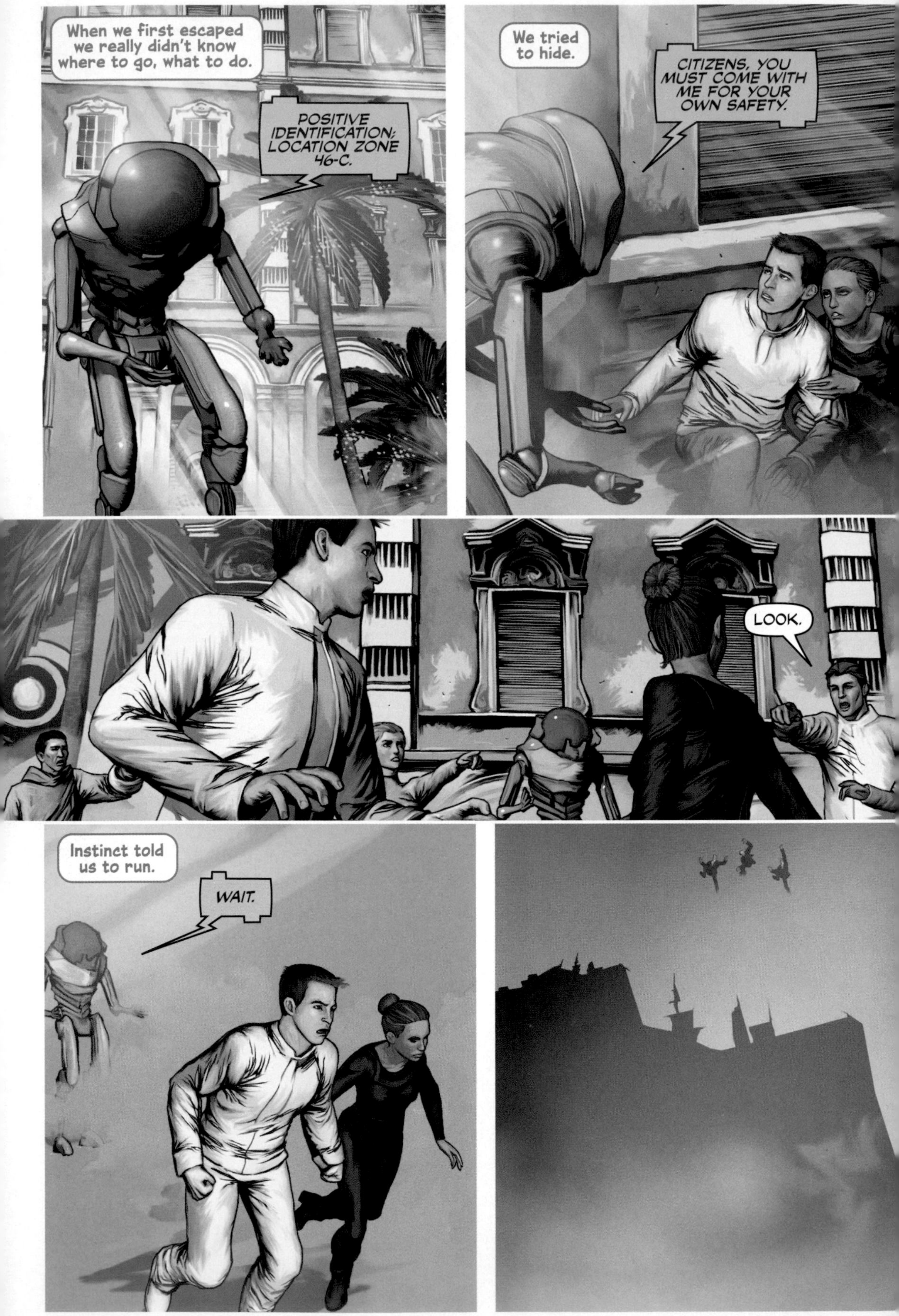
When we first escaped we really didn't know where to go, what to do.
POSITIVE IDENTIFICATION: LOCATION ZONE 46-C.
We tried to hide.
CITIZENS, YOU MUST COME WITH ME FOR YOUR OWN SAFETY.
LOOK.
Instinct told us to run.
WAIT.

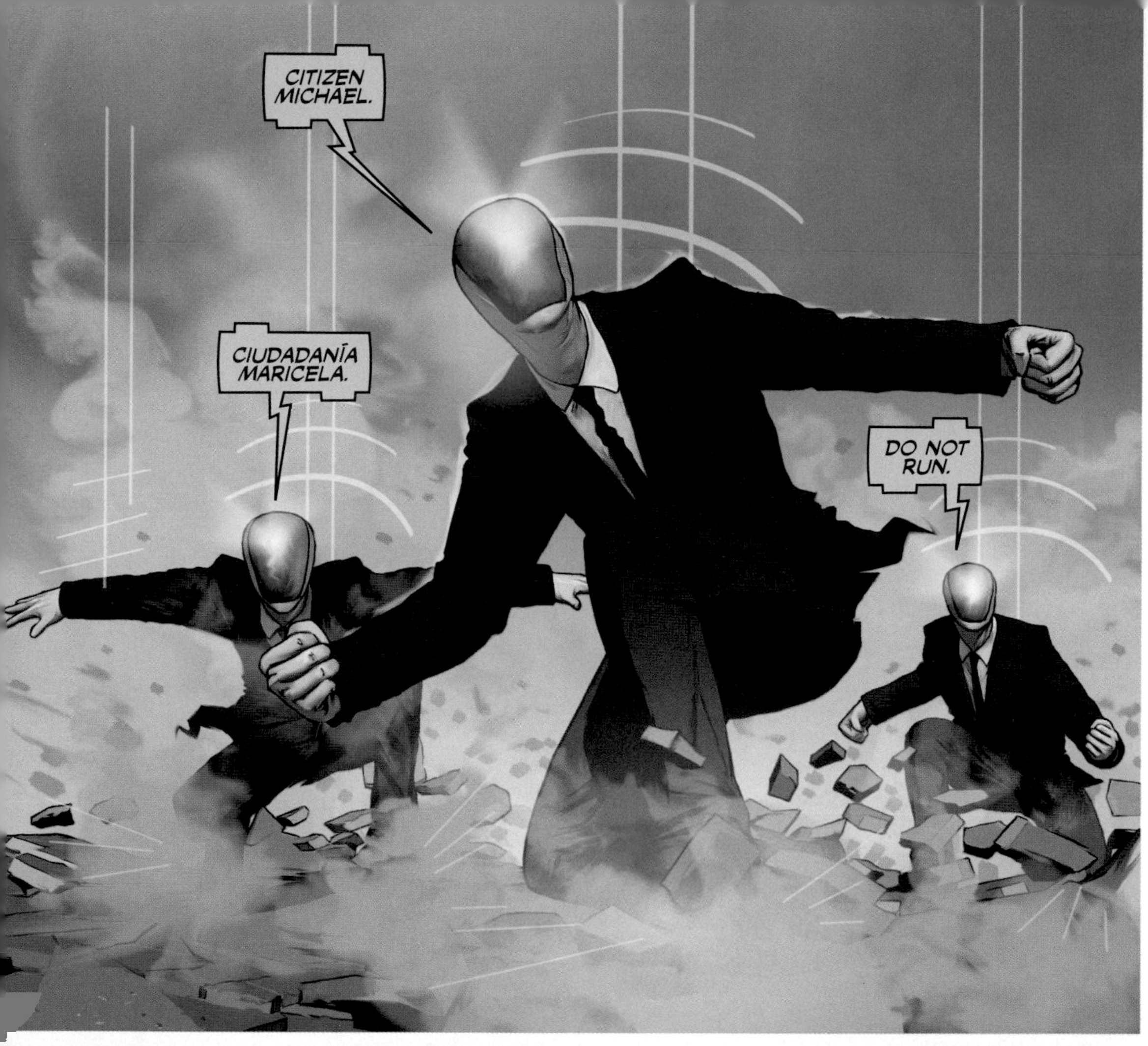
CITIZEN MICHAEL.
CIUDADANÍA MARICELA.
DO NOT RUN.

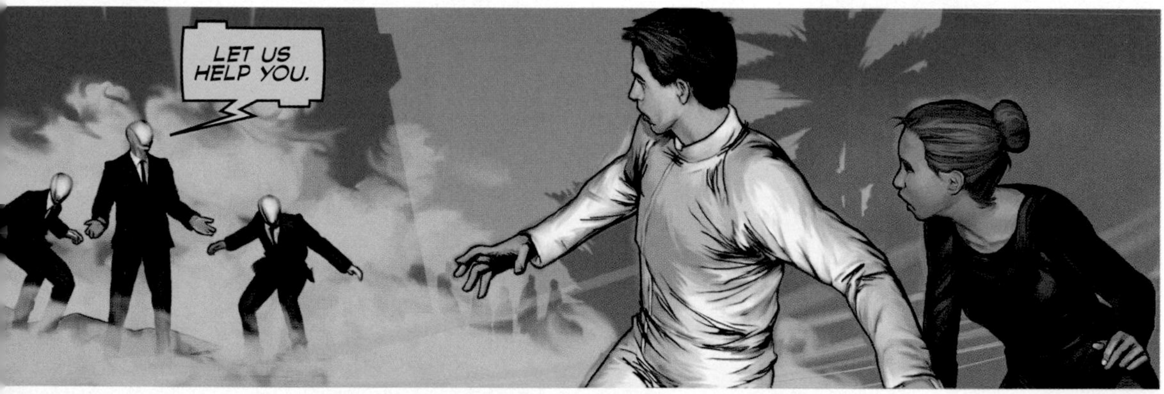
LET US HELP YOU.

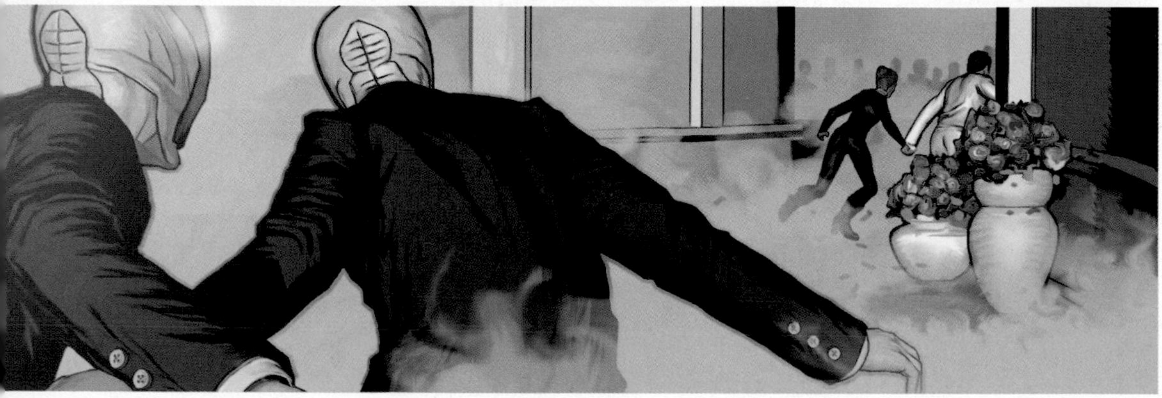

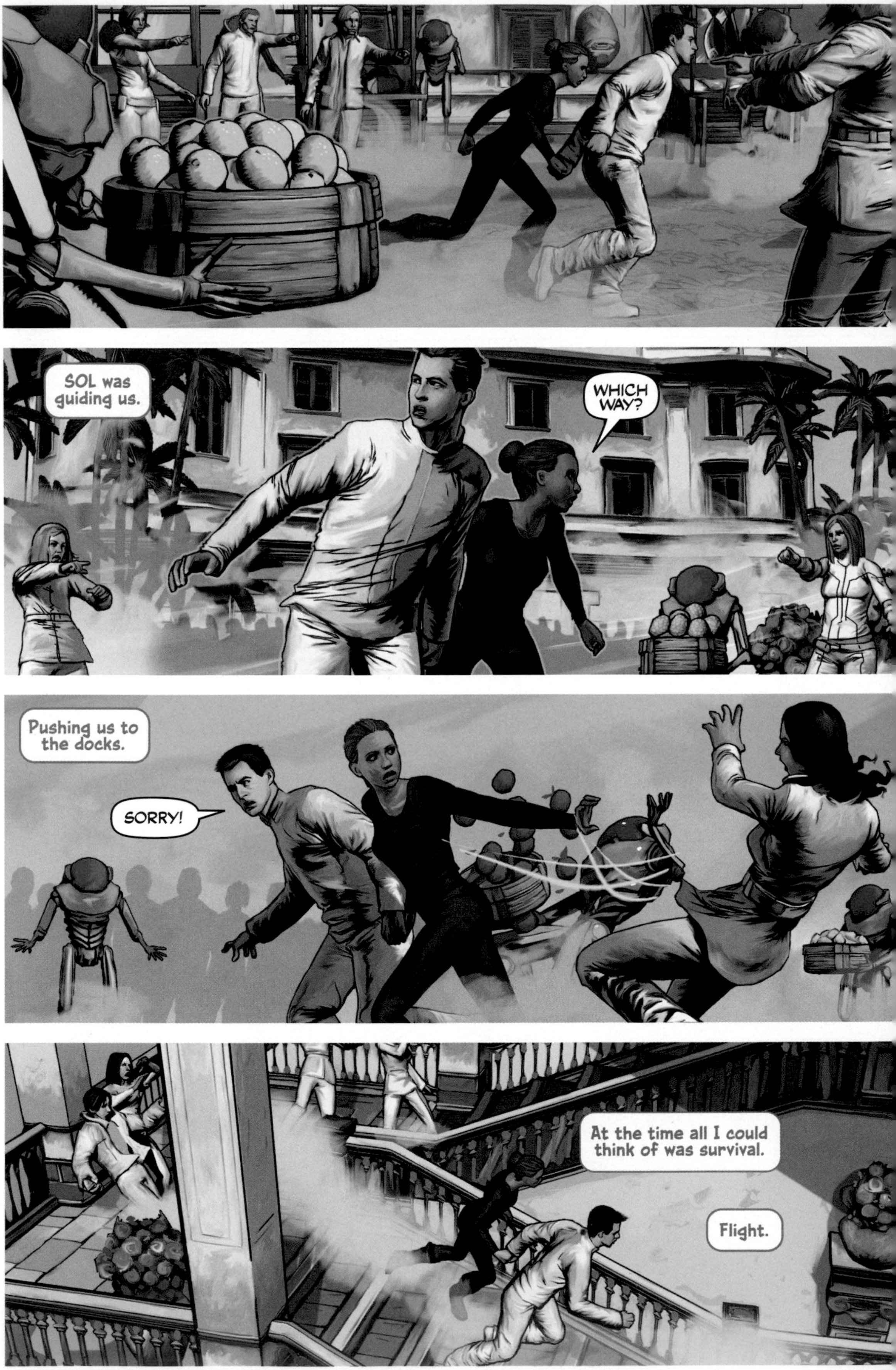
SOL was guiding us.
WHICH WAY?
Pushing us to the docks.
SORRY!
At the time all I could think of was survival.
Flight.

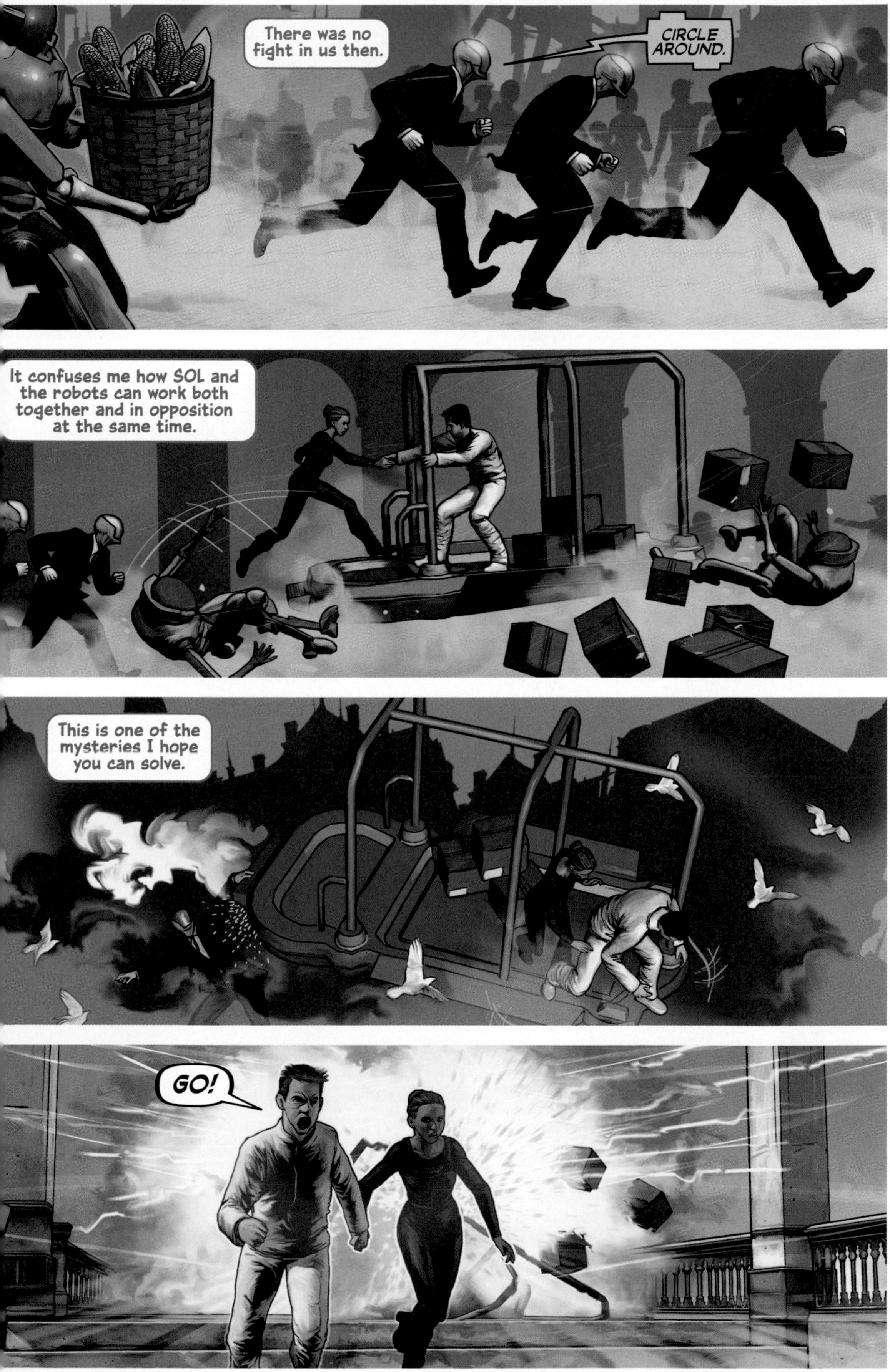
There was no fight in us then.
CIRCLE AROUND.
It confuses me how SOL and the robots can work both together and in opposition at the same time.
This is one of the mysteries I hope you can solve.
GO!

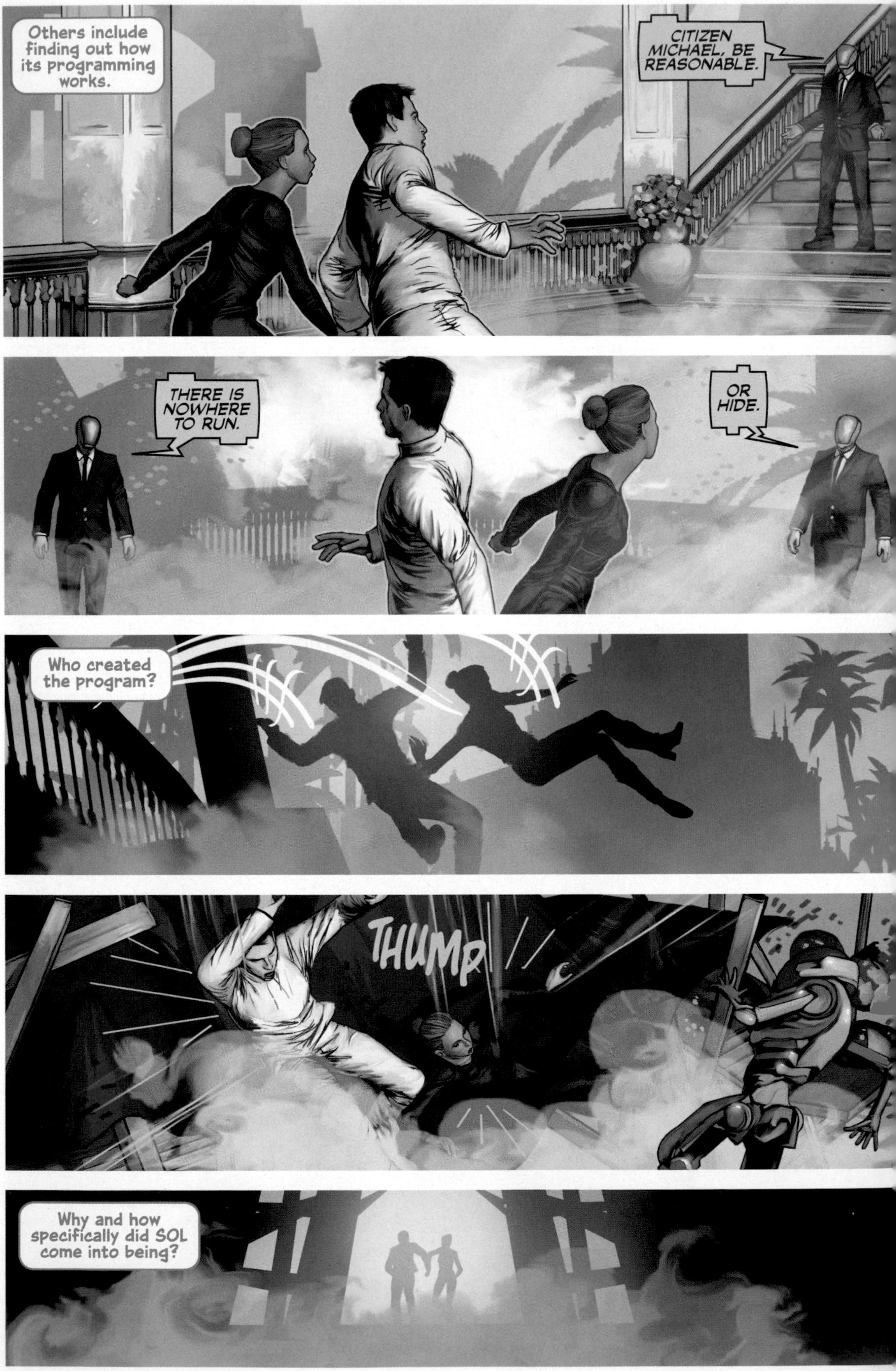
Others include finding out how its programming works.
CITIZEN MICHAEL, BE REASONABLE.
THERE IS NOWHERE TO RUN.
OR HIDE.
Who created the program?
THUMP
Why and how specifically did SOL come into being?

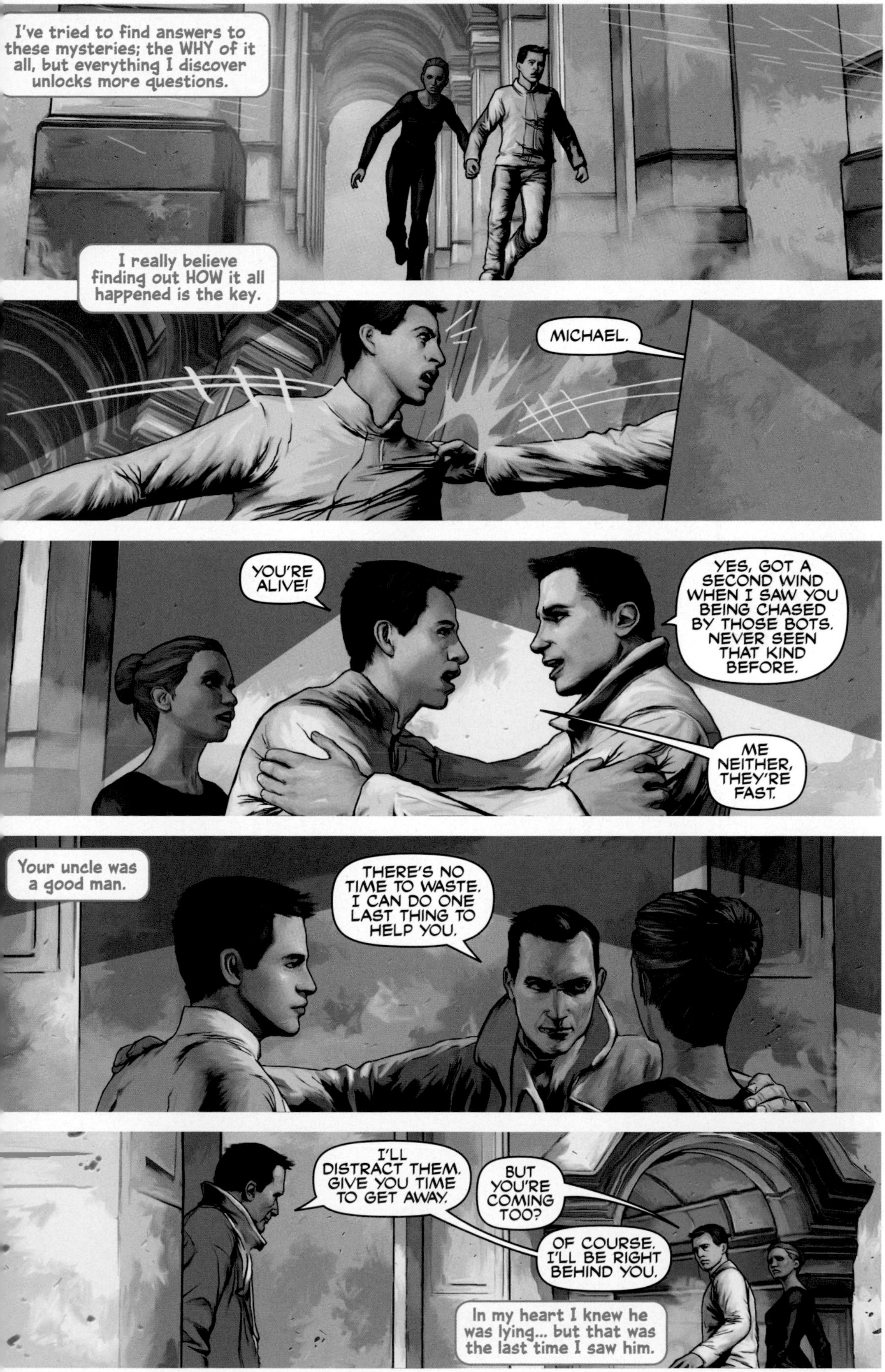
I've tried to find answers to these mysteries; the WHY of it all, but everything I discover unlocks more questions.
I really believe finding out HOW it all happened is the key.
MICHAEL.
YOU'RE ALIVE!
YES, GOT A SECOND WIND WHEN I SAW YOU BEING CHASED BY THOSE BOTS. NEVER SEEN THAT KIND BEFORE.
ME NEITHER, THEY'RE FAST.
Your uncle was a good man.
THERE'S NO TIME TO WASTE. I CAN DO ONE LAST THING TO HELP YOU.
I'LL DISTRACT THEM. GIVE YOU TIME TO GET AWAY.
BUT YOU'RE COMING TOO?
OF COURSE. I'LL BE RIGHT BEHIND YOU.
In my heart I knew he was lying... but that was the last time I saw him.

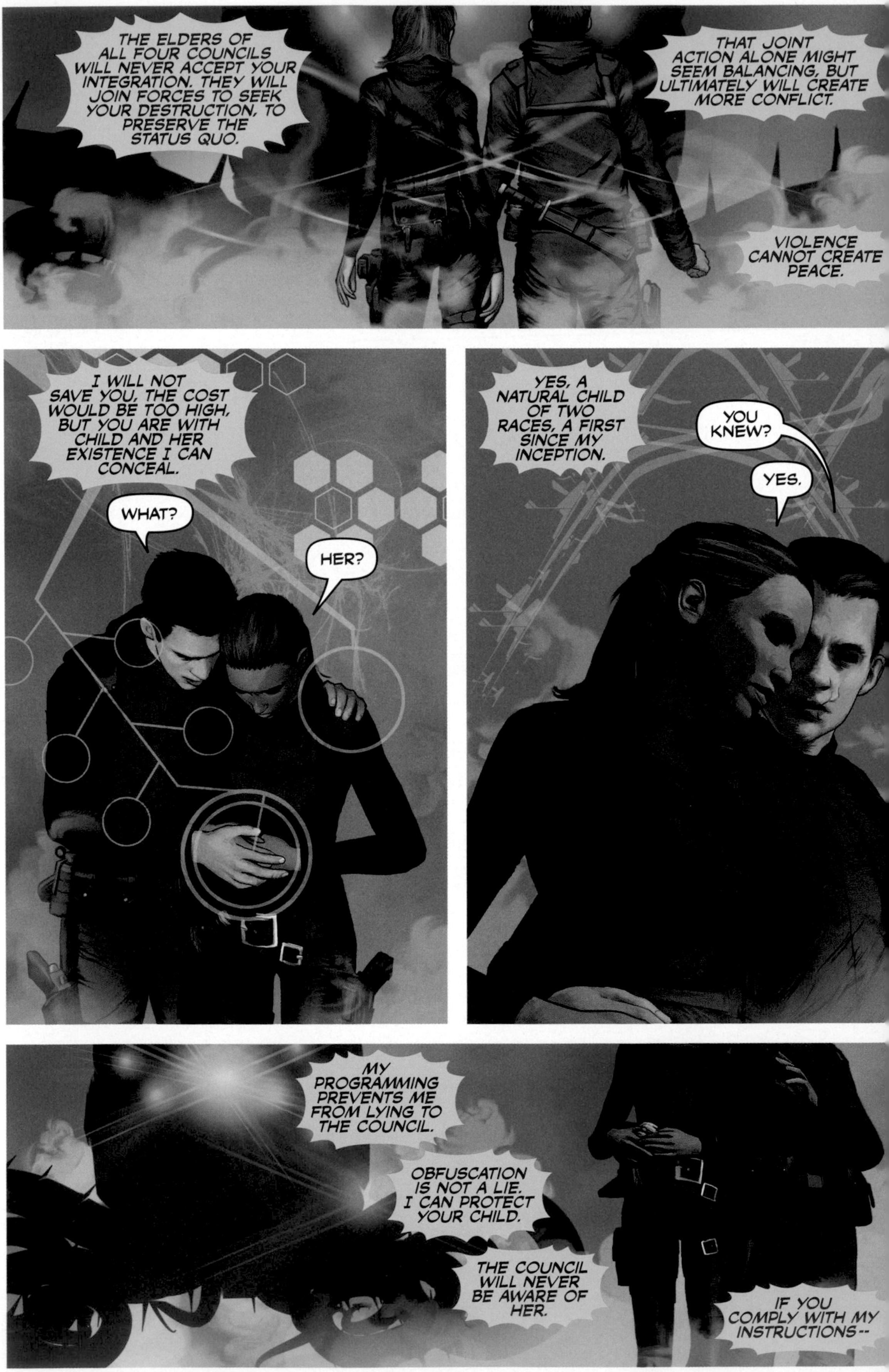
THE ELDERS OF ALL FOUR COUNCILS WILL NEVER ACCEPT YOUR INTEGRATION. THEY WILL JOIN FORCES TO SEEK YOUR DESTRUCTION, TO PRESERVE THE STATUS QUO.
THAT JOINT ACTION ALONE MIGHT SEEM BALANCING, BUT ULTIMATELY WILL CREATE MORE CONFLICT.
VIOLENCE CANNOT CREATE PEACE.
I WILL NOT SAVE YOU, THE COST WOULD BE TOO HIGH, BUT YOU ARE WITH CHILD AND HER EXISTENCE I CAN CONCEAL.
WHAT?
HER?
YES, A NATURAL CHILD OF TWO RACES, A FIRST SINCE MY INCEPTION.
YOU KNEW?
YES.
MY PROGRAMMING PREVENTS ME FROM LYING TO THE COUNCIL.
OBFUSCATION IS NOT A LIE. I CAN PROTECT YOUR CHILD.
THE COUNCIL WILL NEVER BE AWARE OF HER.
IF YOU COMPLY WITH MY INSTRUCTIONS--

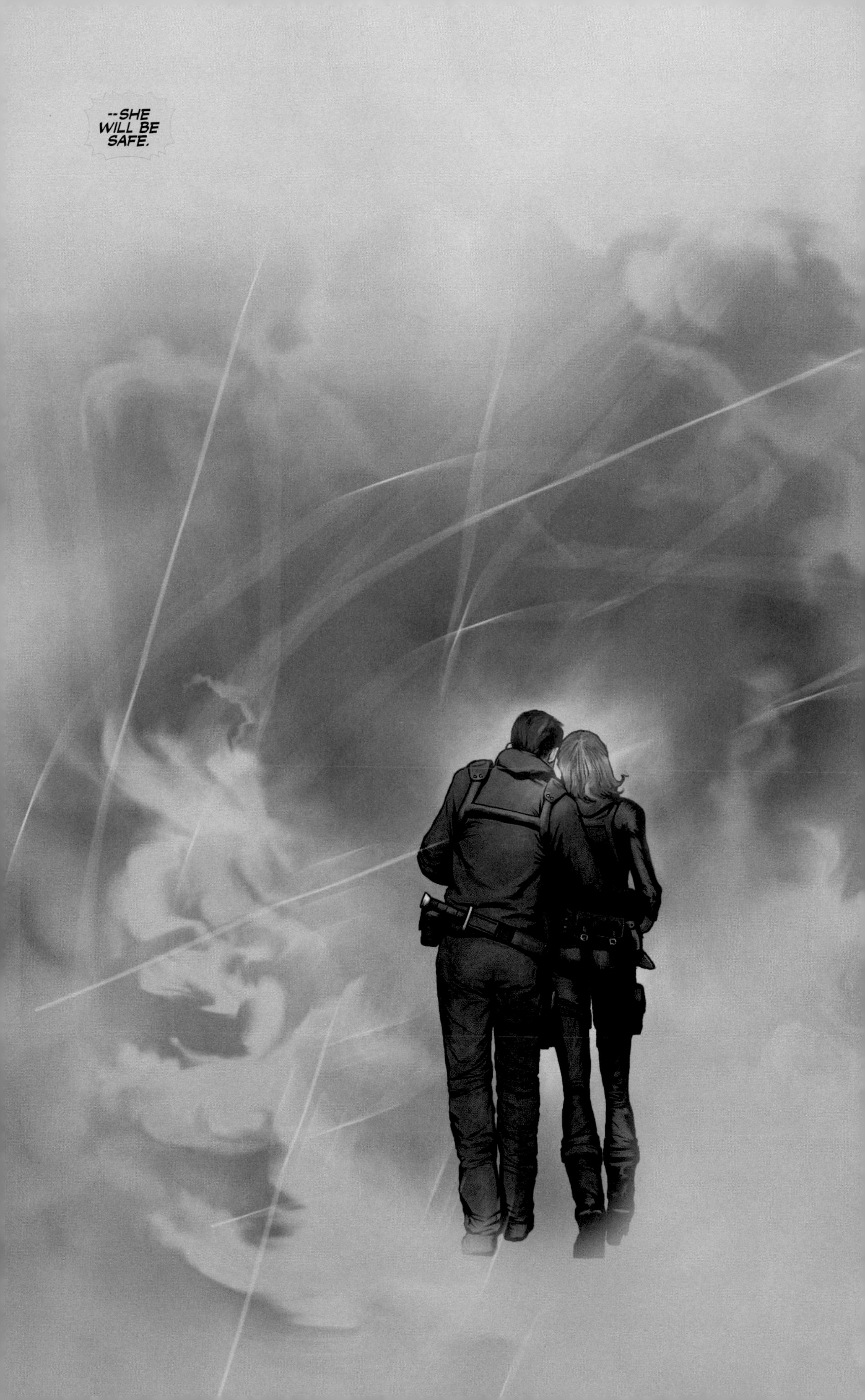
--SHE WILL BE SAFE.

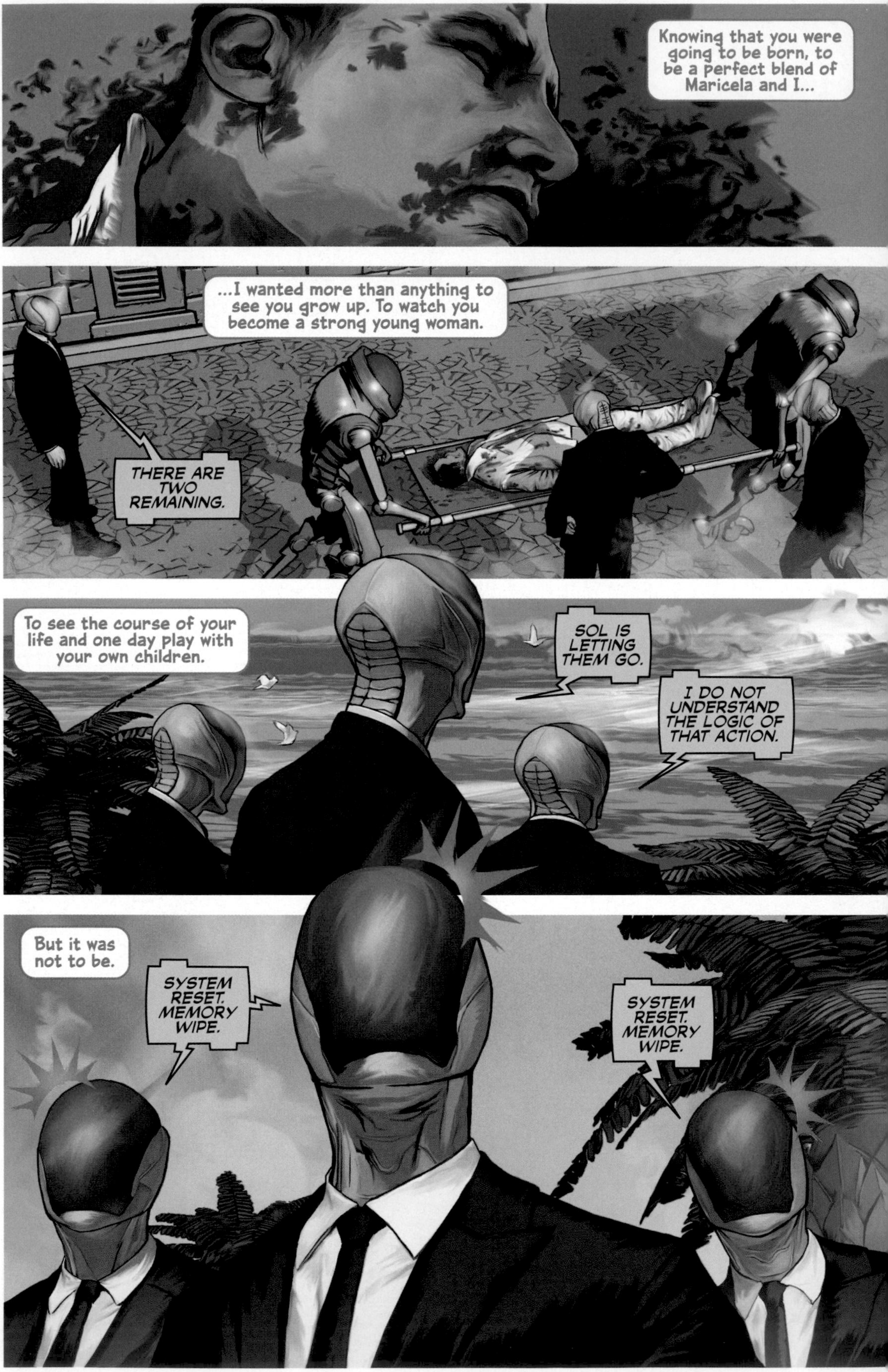
Knowing that you were going to be born, to be a perfect blend of Maricela and I...
...I wanted more than anything to see you grow up. To watch you become a strong young woman.
THERE ARE TWO REMAINING.
To see the course of your life and one day play with your own children.
SOL IS LETTING THEM GO.
I DO NOT UNDERSTAND THE LOGIC OF THAT ACTION.
But it was not to be.
SYSTEM RESET. MEMORY WIPE.
SYSTEM RESET. MEMORY WIPE.

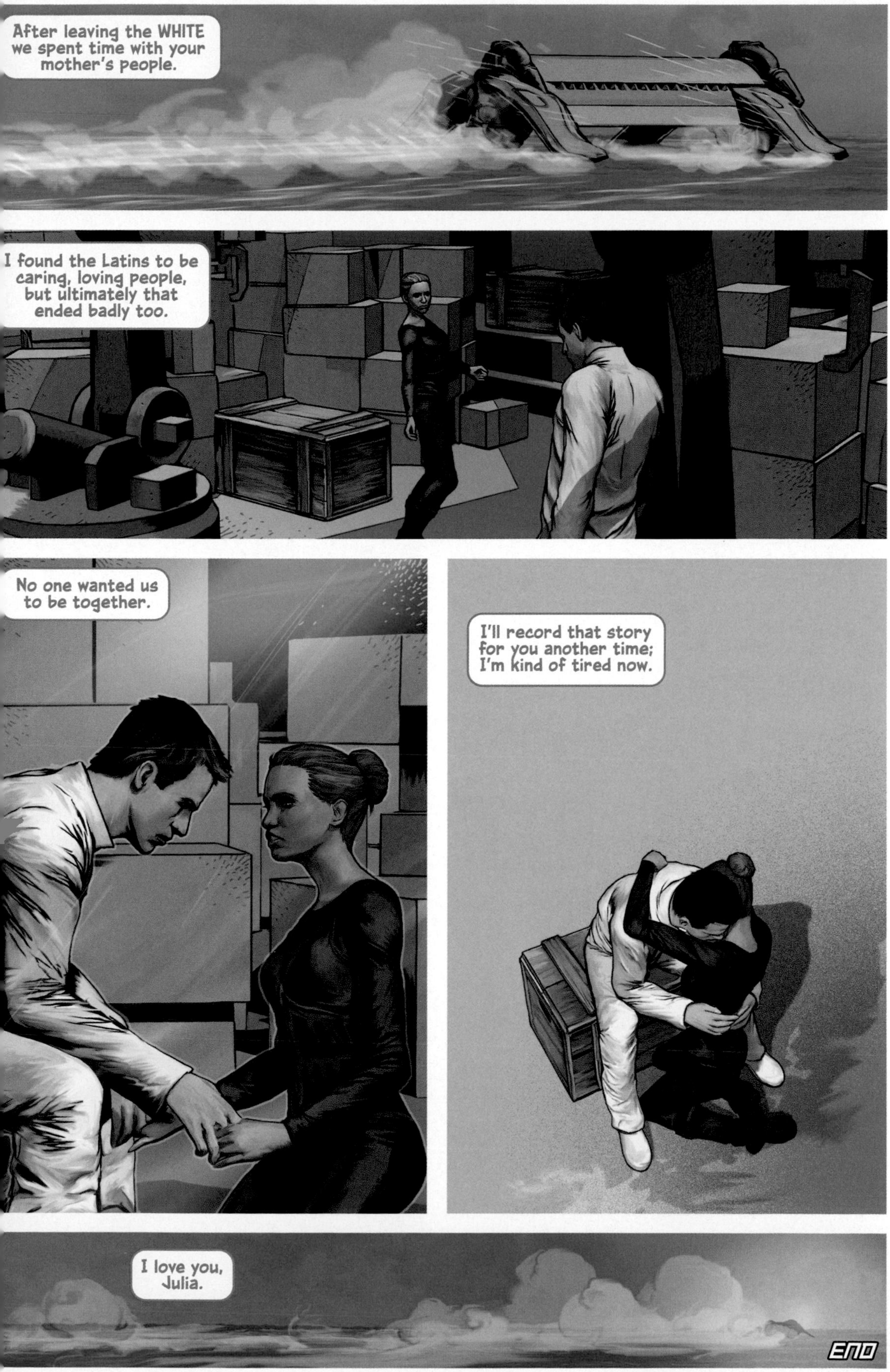
After leaving the WHITE we spent time with your mother's people.
I found the Latins to be caring, loving people, but ultimately that ended badly too.
No one wanted us to be together.
I'll record that story for you another time; I'm kind of tired now.
I love you, Julia.
END

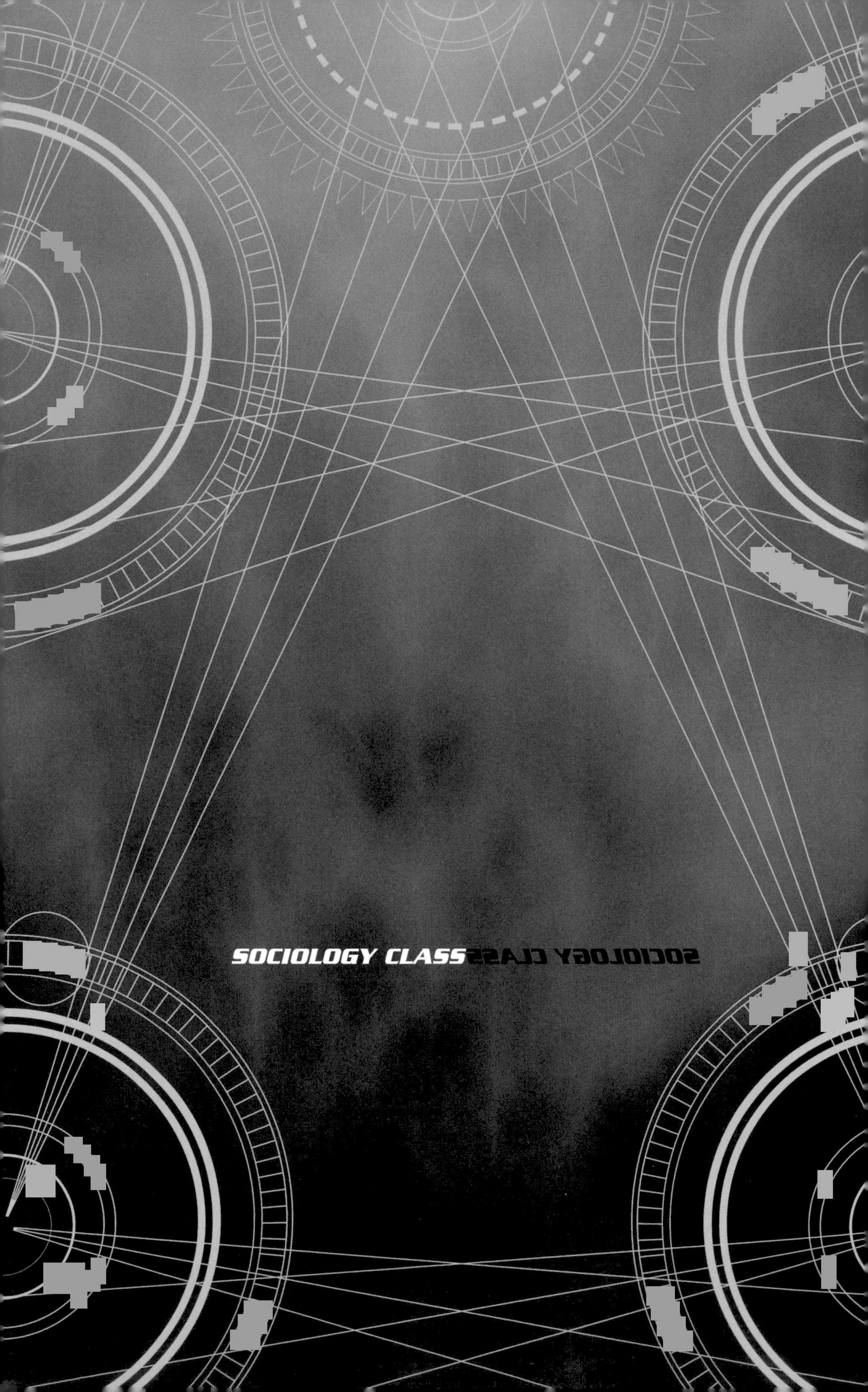
SOCIOLOGY CLASS

SYMMETRY VOLUME 1 SOCIOLOGY CLASS

Welcome to ***Symmetry Volume 1***! Thanks for reading this subversive book; what I call a study in the pros and cons of Utopian Socialist ideals. If you like it, I'd ask that you please recommend it to a friend. Word-of-mouth is the best way to spread the word about a book. If you read any of my books you know I get into it in the back with how and why I do what I do! I use **Science Class** in the back of ***Think Tank*** and ***Aphrodite IX*** and ***Sunday School*** in ***The Tithe***.

Thought about Marxism 101 or Socialism 101 here, but rejected those and ended up titling it ***Sociology Class*** after a fan suggestion.

Raffaele Lenco, my co-creator and artist for ***Symmetry*** has done amazing work on this book. I can't wait for you to see the rest!

WHY THIS BOOK?

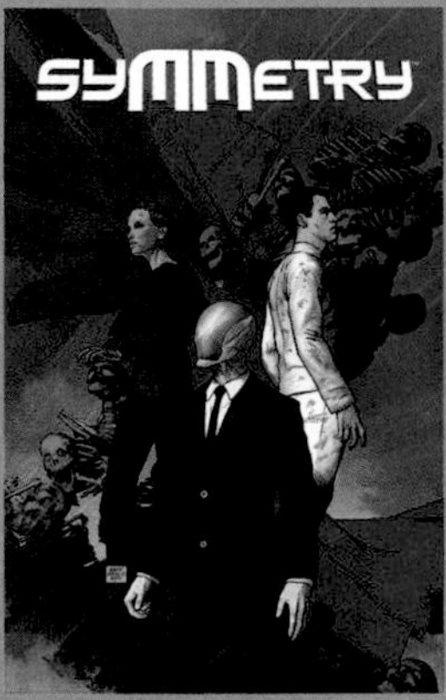
SYMMETRY

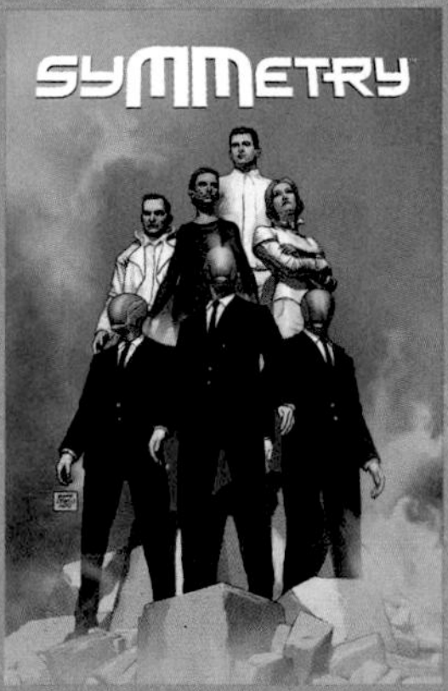
SYMMETRY

I've written Dystopian science-fiction (***Aphrodite IX***) and there is SO much of it out there in Young Adult (YA) books and film adaptations that I've gotten a bit sick of it.

Why does the future have to be so bleak? Why do we assume that Artificial Intelligence and robots are going to go all Skynet on us and wipe us out? So, I flipped the premise and created a Utopian world that we can mess with then maybe put back right. Let's take a look at that word and where it came from.

UTOPIA

A ***utopia*** is a community or **society** possessing highly desirable or near perfect qualities. The word was coined by Sir Thomas More for his 1516 book ***Utopia*** (in Latin), describing a fictional island ***society*** in the Atlantic Ocean.

You can download a FREE full PDF of this book here, although I warn you it's boring as hell (skim it): http://history-world.org/Utopia_T.pdf

HOW DO YOU BUILD A UTOPIA?

This was the fun part for me: months and months of research, reading and clicking links. Any of you who follow me on social media (especially Facebook), will have seen a shift in my discussions about utopia, socialism, etc. about a year ago. I was raised a right wing Christian and evolved into a left wing Atheist. It's a long story that you can read about in depth in the back of my other book The Tithe. Back to the point, how and why does one build a utopia?

"Why would anyone want to design a utopia? There are several reasons. The most important is that utopian thought is essential to social change. Without a vision of something better, something that inspires, the chance of social progress is low; and the clearer the vision, the better the chances of achieving it."

Design Your Own Utopia by *Chaz Bufe* and *Libby Hubbard*
http://www.seesharppress.com/utopia.html

This above link takes you to a fascinating questionnaire I stumbled across online that gives you a step by step on what to consider and how to create a Utopia. I was so interested in what these writers had to say I bought their book ***Free Radicals*** and read it.

WHAT DO YOU NEED TO LOSE TO CREATE A UTOPIA?

There's no agreement on this, but enough overlap in thought from people I researched on this that I went with ambition, creativity, diversity and instruments of capital. On the surface sounds pretty boring, yes? Would you be willing to sacrifice what makes you, "you", in order to make a world free of hunger, sickness, violence and poverty? I'm not sure I would either, but we're living in Narcissistic times, what can we say?

Let's take a look at each:

1) Ambition – This is the easiest one to justify, ambition, ego, all of those things. If you create a world where everything is based on your age and no one works, ambition is irrelevant. In this Symmetry world, at age 13 you choose sex/name and join the community, before that you're being assimilated. At age 18 you become an adult, at 50 an Elder and the three eldest Elders are the central committee working with the AI. In a world where the robots do all labor, there's no distinction for hard work. There's no political aspiration. Leadership is considered a service.

2) Creativity – This was the hardest one for me to quantify/accept, but it makes sense if you think about it. Let's define creativity first:

" *Creativity* is a phenomenon whereby something new and somehow valuable is formed. The created item may be intangible (such as an idea, a scientific theory, a musical composition or a joke) or an original physical object (such as an invention, a literary work or a painting)."
https://en.wikipedia.org/wiki/Creativity

So, the problem with creativity is that it changes things. Change creates "haves" and "have-nots". I realize this is a bit extreme, but that's the point. It's also part of the sacrifice. What are we willing to give up?

http://www.innovationmanagement.se/imtool-articles/why-diversity-is-the-mother-of-creativity/
https://hbr.org/2013/12/how-diversity-can-drive-innovation
http://www.scientificamerican.com/article/how-diversity-makes-us-smarter/

3) Diversity – This is broad, all encompassing affecting literally anything that makes people different. We can't eliminate gender because of reproductive requirements, but we can in the first part of people's lives where gender identity has the greatest effect. The science is almost there for us to be able to biologically induce a sex change in humans. Many animals do it already. This is a completely homogenous society. In this first issue everyone is white wearing white clothes until the last page. The races have been segregated; people aren't even told that the other racial groups exist until they become an Elder. Subversive, yes, and it would eliminate my family. I have an Asian wife and two half-Asian children. We'll get into this.

4) Instruments of capital – Money, stocks, corporations, real estate ownership all gone. I'm not a Socialist, but I've started to question why we believe in the profit motive so strongly. We seem to believe it because we were taught to believe it. When I was young I was told the profit motive guaranteed technological innovation, but that's not always the case.
http://www.unep.org/geo/geo3/english/520.htm
http://www.marxist.com/technology-innovation-growtn-and-capitalism.htm
https://www.reddit.com/r/Futurology/comments/3awbv8/is_greed_slowing_human_advancement/
http://www.nhregister.com/opinion/20141009/randall-beach-slow-down-it-will-be-good-for-you

A lot of comic writers complain that 1st issues are hard; I actually find the 2nd one to be harder. There's some excitement and mystery that comes with a debut issue and you don't have to explain everything as long as you've got some interesting stuff going on. People asking "why?" is a good thing. Second issues have a common problem of slowing the story down to try and explain a lot of what's going on. I have a bad habit of being overly expository and spending too much time on this and too little on building character. Bryan Hill has really helped me with that over the past couple years and I think this arc of Symmetry is a good example of that learning on my part.

 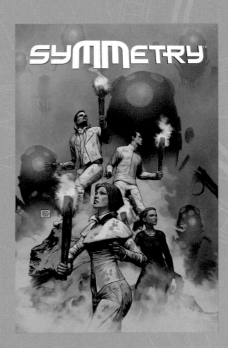

NARRATIVE TO THIS STORY

You learn from that Michael is recording the narrative for he and Maricela's future offspring. I write most of my stories in four issue arcs. He's recording the narrative after the second arc.

REGARDING EQUALITY

It's a myth. There really is no such thing. Gender, race, nationality, economic status, age and whether or not you have children create MASSIVE differences among people. I wrote a nice long exposition explaining this in the book and removed it after Bryan Hill and I discussed it and it was too much.

The Four Pillars of society include trying to create an equality that they already knew would not be possible. Well, how do you come close? The only way I could come up with was segregation. They've segregated the four races into unique nation-states that do not interact. We've only seen The White at the start. We've hinted at the other three. We'll see all four eventually. So, in The White, people of like disposition and age are put in the same areas and with RAINA controlling everyone's schedules and who/what they see and do they keep people that might conflict apart from one another.

MEDICATION

Everyone is medicated and it's delivered through his or her food and tailored to his or her individual physiology. This is to balance them and to prevent any emotion that might cause them distress or lead to conflict. Think about what the people hit by this EMP blast (that survived), are going through. They've been spoon fed their entire lives. They've never had to work. They've never had to provide for themselves. They've never been in an argument. They've never gone without. They've had constant companionship inside their own head from an AI that talks to them and helps them. The RAINA would also know everything about you; that alone frightens me. Think for a second about the things you ponder that you wouldn't even want your family to know about. Imagine all of this…and, then one second, in the blinking of an eye…it's gone. You're exposed to violent death. And the medication you've unknowingly been taking your whole life is gone.

CONFLICT

Let's discuss conflict for a minute. What causes it?
Disagreement. Misunderstanding. Poor communication. Lack of planning. Moral conflicts. Issues of justice. Fairness. Unmet needs. Identity issues. Resource distribution.

https://www.mindtools.com/pages/article/eight-causes-conflict.htm

http://www.communitydoor.org.au/human-resource-management/resolving-conflict/conflict-and-its-causes

The eight causes of conflict (according to *http://www.beyondintractability.org/essay/underlying-causes*) are:

1.   Conflicting resources.
2.   Conflicting styles.
3.   Conflicting perceptions.
4.   Conflicting goals.
5.   Conflicting pressures.
6.   Conflicting roles.
7.   Different personal values.
8.   Unpredictable policies.

All interesting things to consider! When you Google "conflict" the majority of things that pop up are for how to deal with it in the workplace for differing types of people. A lot of the answers are relevant to all types of social situations. I don't want to pirate these articles, but click and read them, fascinating stuff.

ENTRAL ELDER COMMITTEE

Another part that got truncated in my script, but will be explained as we go on in the story, but I thought 'd share it here. It's not a "secret." The Elder Council of the white people is the three oldest living white people. That's it. It's considered a service at the end of your life where you can share your life experience and wisdom to help maintain the status quo. I love the idea and am playing with it in the story and will continue to do so, so that the AI actually is seemingly more compassionate than humans. This is due to its programming which I'll be getting into more as we go on as well. Think about this: there is NO ONE that could reprogram the AI if they wanted to. No one has the skill set to do it.

HOMAS PICKING UP THE AXE

This was my ***2001: A Space Odyssey*** moment. Remember in that film where the ape in the beginning picked up the bone and used it as a weapon? I love ***2001***, it's slow in parts but if you haven't seen it in awhile (or ever) you should check it out.

RAFFAELE IENCO ART

His art is so fantastic. He's an amazing storyteller and artist. He wrote and drew a book called ***Manifestations*** that's available on Comixology.

ttps://www.comixology.com/Manifestations/digital-comic/29895?ref=c2VyaWVzL3ZpZX-vZGVza3RvcC9ncmlkTGlzdC9Jc3N1ZXM

EPIC KILL
Image

MANIFESTATIONS
RAFFAELE IENCO

He also created the series ***EPIC KILL*** for Image.

In the third issue of *Symmetry* I really liked how Raffaele Ienco's art fit the sad tone of the narrative. We saw Matthew die in the first five pages of issue #1 and, now at the end of the 3rd, we see what's going on. I was talking to my wife about the different series I write and she asked me whom the villain of *Symmetry* is? The primary antagonist is the system itself. The Elder Committee is certainly interesting and could be perceived as "villainous", but it's not clear-cut.

NARRATIVE

Had a question online about the Michael's narrative as recordings for his unborn child. He's recording more than just the words printed in the narrative text boxes. He's also recording what's being shown in the art. This story is his version of events as he's relating them to his unborn child. It's his perspective and is intentionally skewed a bit based on that. If you've ever gone back and compared memories with old friends, people remember things very differently.

EGALITY VERSUS EQUALITY

These don't mean the same thing. Egality is an "extreme leveling of society." Equality is "the state of being the same quantity, measure or value as another." One of the Four Pillars is equality, but we clearly see that it's bullshit. Egality is more appropriate since people are the same economically and everything is first come, first serve. It's part of the point and perspective of the story.

SEGREGATION VERSUS SEPARATION

There's a difference between these as well. It's summed up well by this quote:

"Segregation is that which is forced upon an inferior by a superior. Separation is done voluntarily by two equals." - Malcolm X

Researching segregation, it's impossible to not get hit over the head with the Civil Rights movement and the insane George C. Wallace. I realize he's a relic of his time, but this guy could have been President.

"I draw the line in the dust and toss the gauntlet before the feet of tyranny, and I say segregation now, segregation tomorrow, segregation forever." - George C. Wallace

In this story we learn about how people are segregated by race, age and disposition. The ENTIRE point of it is to avoid conflict.

ARE HUMANS NATURALLY VIOLENT?

From my perspective, the answer to this is yes. All you have to do is read the news and you can see how depraved and violent humanity is to itself. The war of ideas over violence and human nature has raged since the 1600s, when philosopher Thomas Hobbes first speculated that the "natural condition of mankind" was one of violence and conflict. I tend to agree with that, but stumbled across this:

http://www.alfiekohn.org/article/humans-innately-aggressive/

When you read that you'll see psychologists discussing that it's not a natural state. I don't think anyone knows for sure. History has shown that at least a percentage of us are consistently violent throughout recorded events. This link shows murder rates around the world and I found the misconception about the Third World analysis in here very interesting.

https://mises.org/blog/mistake-only-comparing-us-murder-rates-developed-countries

WOLVES AND SPEED

I wrote the wolves in the story originally as mountain lions, but Raffaele wanted to draw them as wolves so wolves they are! In editing I frequently will cut down the # of words from previous drafts and in some cases eliminate certain threads or explanations because they bog the story down. My philosophy on writing is that if you can think of a reasonable explanation as to why something happens, then you don't need to go out of your way to explain it. Point being I wrote a bunch of narrative explaining why the wolves didn't immediately catch up with Matthew and Elder Sharon in the pursuit. The reason I gave is that these wolves had never seen humans before and were slightly cautious. This was four narrative captions and I took it out because it bogged down the story and isn't terribly important to what's going on. Full out wolves run between 31 and 37 mph.

https://www.californiawolfcenter.org/education/wolf-facts/

SOL

Who made SOL? What was the sequence of events leading up to its creation? Ultimately that will be the entire question of volume 2, which will be issues 5-8 in stores June-September. The "System Optimizer for Longevity" was designed to help facilitate humans living longer, happier lives. Sounds nice, eh? Everything has a cost. We are dangerously near a point now where artificial intelligence will start programming itself. When that happens, what will be the result?

http://www.forbes.com/sites/paulrodgers/2014/12/03/computers-will-destroy-humanity-warns-stephen-hawking/#40f719943fee

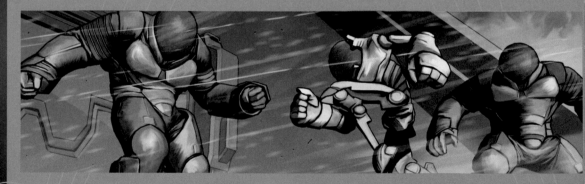

ROBOTS SELF-AWARE?

At what point will a computer be self-aware? The debate seems to focus on the rationality of machine thought versus the irrationality of human thoughts and action.

A classic awareness test was given to three robots recently, "In this updated AI version, the robots are each given a 'pill' (which is actually a tap on the head, because, you know, robots can't swallow). Two of the pills will render the robots silent, and one is a placebo. The tester, Selmer Bringsjord, chair of Rensselaer's cognitive science department, then asks the robots which pill they received.

There's silence for a little while, and then one of the little bots gets up and declares, 'I don't know!' But at the sound of its own voice it quickly changes his mind and puts its hand up. 'Sorry, I know now,' it exclaims politely. 'I was able to prove that I was not given the dumbing pill.'"

http://www.sciencealert.com/a-robot-has-just-passed-a-classic-self-awareness-test-for-the-first-time
http://www.thekeyboard.org.uk/computers%20become%20self%20aware.htm

So reality-check people, robots are self-aware NOW.

TURING TEST

If you've seen the excellent Benedict Cumberbatch film *The Imitation Game* that's about Alan Turing and how he helped British intelligence crack the German enigma code and help win the war. He was a brilliant man, way ahead of his time and persecuted for being gay. Sad to reward such courage and the saving of so many lives with moral outrage. I'm glad times are-a-changing!

"The Turing test is a test, developed by Alan Turing in 1950, of a machine's ability to exhibit intelligent behavior equivalent to, or indistinguishable from, that of a human."

This test has been recently updated to reflect a more modern computer and AI sensibility.

http://www.turing.org.uk/scrapbook/test.html

http://www.psych.utoronto.ca/users/reingold/courses/ai/turing.html

ROBOT INTELLIGENCE GOOD OR BAD FOR HUMANS?

This is the question! Humans are irrational. We make bad decisions all the time for emotional reasons. We've reshaped the entire earth to suit our purposes and have wiped out other species on the planet merely for being in our way. So if robots think rationally and not emotionally, is that good or bad? Ultimately, this depends on who's in charge. If humans control robots or have some form of "off switch" then we're never in any real danger. In most fictional sci-fi stories where the robots attack us, they become self-aware and decide humans are bad and then try to set us straight. This makes for a good fictional story, but if we're working hand-in-hand with robots and AI and they are engineered specifically to work with us and have our best interests at heart…would this happen? I dunno. And neither do you, but it's fun to write about.

http://legacy.earlham.edu/~peters/courses/mm/bestworst01.htm

http://www.livescience.com/49009-future-of-artificial-intelligence.html

http://www.endangeredspeciesinternational.org/overview1.html

http://paleobiology.si.edu/geotime/main/foundation_life4.html

MASS EXTINCTION

There have been five mass extinctions in Earth's history (that we can account for). Are we in the sixth? Some people think we are. This is an interesting article, check out the link:

http://www.dailygalaxy.com/my_weblog/2013/03/of-all-species-that-have-existed-on-earth-999-percent-are-now-extinct-many-of-them-perished-in-five-cataclysmic-events-t.html

ROBOPOCALYPSE/TERMINATOR (USE ART FOR BOOK COVER)

I just started reading Robopocalypse by Daniel H. Wilson and as of this writing are about 50 pages into it. It's enjoyable thus far and is being turned into a film! It and Terminator and so many other fictional stories deal with A.I. and robots going bad. Well, bad from a human perspective. When I set out to do Symmetry I wanted to do something different. In Raffaele and my story, we're dealing with an A.I. that truly has human interests at heart. But the effort of trying to make humans have better lives comes at a cost of course. This second arc is going to be fun! Can't wait for you to read it.

http://bestsciencefictionbooks.com/best-artificial-intelligence-science-fiction-books.php

UNCANNY VALLEY

From Wikipedia, "Used in reference to the phenomenon whereby a computer-generated figure or humanoid robot bearing a near-identical resemblance to a human being arouses a sense of unease or revulsion in the person viewing it."

+
moving
still
uncanny valley
healthy person
bunraku puppet
humanoid robot
stuffed animal
industrial robot
familiarity
human likeness
50%
100%
corpse
prosthetic hand
-
zombie

So this means that if something we know to be a robot looks too human we innately want to reject it. It's one of the reasons I made the robots look so different from humans. Even the Pacifiers would never be mistaken for human. One of the elements in the story which may not come out any time soon is that SOL's physical appearance was changed to be what it is now in one of the "updates". I read in a article in Psychology Today about how humans tend to take recommendations better from someone they fear a little bit. I found that fascinating and thought about it a long time. When Raff gave SOL his monstrous appearance, I embraced it as a part of this.

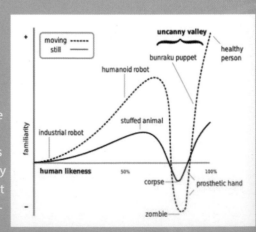

ARTIFICIAL INTELLIGENCE AND RELIGION

 I was curious what religious leaders think about A.I. The vast majority doesn't seem to discuss it much. I asked an old pastor of mine via email if he thought robots were connected to the end times and his response was "I don't know." I actually appreciate honest responses like that and its why I keep a few old religious friends to discuss stuff like this.

 I did, of course, find a bunch of nonsense by end-of-the-world people. If you feel so inclined, these are fun to read:

https://endtimebibleprophecy.wordpress.com/2013/07/26/professor-robots-to-patrol-cities-by-2040/#more-10067
http://www.end-times-bible-prophecy.com/transhumanism.html
https://www.raptureready.com/featured/gillette/ss.html
http://aiantichrist.blogspot.com/

77 SIGNIFICANCE

If you know anything about me, you know I'm obsessed with religion and technology. It's all I seem to think about. It explains why I write some of the stuff I do. I drop religious things in all the time, some of them just for fun. That SOL has been alive for 77 generations has some significance in religious writings.

"If the Lord said, seventy-seven times, then we may recognize that "seventy-seven" is the seven times eleven. Seven (as said above) signifies totality and completeness, but what does eleven signify. "Eleven" is the number of sin, since perfection and holiness is in "ten."

Matthew 18:22 has to deal with forgiveness
"Jesus saith unto him, I say not unto thee, Until seven times: but, Until seventy times seven."

http://newtheologicalmovement.blogspot.com/2011/09/seven-seventy-seven-and-seventy-times.html
http://www.ridingthebeast.com/numbers/nu77.php
http://sacredscribesangelnumbers.blogspot.com/2011/07/angel-number-77.html

NEUROPLASTICITY OF THE BRAIN/ELDERS

I struggle constantly with including too much information in scripts that bogs the flow down in my excitement to explain everything! Thankfully, Bryan Hill and Ryan Cady help me chop it down. "Neuroplasticity, also known as brain plasticity, is an umbrella term that describes lasting change to the brain throughout an animal's life course. The term gained prominence in the latter half of the 20th century, when new research showed many aspects of the brain remain changeable (or 'plastic') even into adulthood."

Neuroplasticity has come into increasing study as our population has started living longer. Can you teach an old dog, new tricks? This is the question. What we do know is that as you age, it becomes harder for your brain to learn new things. Especially hard things like new languages and advanced mathematics. People get "set in their ways" and we use that as an excuse to forgive bad behavior by the elderly.

This whole concept is why I set the Elders up as being indoctrinated into the "truth" at age fifty. The idea is by then they'll be so ingrained into the society and see that it works and be willing to continue on, despite their awareness of the obfuscation, omission and outright untruth of some of their upbringing.

http://www.whatisneuroplasticity.com/
http://bigthink.com/think-tank/brain-exercise

RAM

One of the things that got cut from the script was why they call the robot RAM. I had a whole subplot about when Maricela was trying to convert the robots to work with them, one of them got stuck in a loop "Robot Am Malfunctioning" which they shorted to RAM. Since RAM is an acronym for random access memory, a type of computer memory that can be accessed randomly, I thought it was funny.

JULIA

Julia is the daughter of Michael and Maricela. She's the star character of Symmetry and we haven't even met her yet. Symmetry #5 rectifies that. She's the first interracial child and the first child born with a gender in thousands of years. Talk about being apart! Part of the reason this story appealed to me is I have two half-Asian sons. I chose living in Culver City because of its racial diversity. I saw what happened to my nephew (also half-Asian) who went to an all-white school. Being the only non-white there was incredibly hard for him and affected the course of his life. So I didn't want that for my boys, I wanted to live in a melting pot. What SHOCKED me is that the racially diverse school completely self-segregates by race. Call it tribal; call it whatever you want, but I see it every day when I go pick up my kids. They're all grouped together in separate areas almost completely by race. There are a lot of bi-racial kids at that school too and my kids are friends with many of them, but they pick the group they want to be in and integrate with it. I actually don't like this, but I don't know what to do about it. If kids choose to hang out with others of their own racial background exclusively, that's up to them really.

FOUR RACIAL GROUPS IN SYMMETRY

I've been asked this many times, if there are blacks, Latins, whites and Asians, what about the rest of the races? That's part of the back-story and we'll be delving into that more in arc 2. Ultimately, they were assimilated (BORG!) or there genetics were allowed to die off.

FOUR PILLARS OF SOCIETY

For an ideology to work it has to be embraced on every level of a society. It has to be ingrained from birth in every aspect of education; truth can be relative. For a radical ideology that goes contrary to human nature to work, every activity, every waking moment, everything we read, hear, see and experience would have to reflect the "truths" of this ideology. Let's look at each *PILLAR*.

1) Community – If everyone is equal and the only real differences experienced by people are gender and age it's easy to create a harmonious community, especially if relationships are limited to reproduction and older age is revered. Humans are tribal by nature. I see this in everything. To counter this you simply need to create a larger tribe and keep it isolated.

2) Peace – This one seems obvious. There is no violence. Everything is designed to keep people happy, medicated and emotionally stable. This keeps peace.

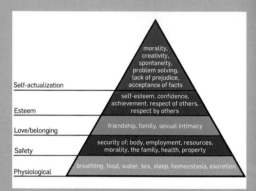

3) Harmony – Agreement, happiness, and accord...again this one seems obvious.

4) Equality – Another no-brainer, but all four of these bleed into each other and that's again purposeful. If we're all the same and there's no need, it eliminates the root cause of most problems and violence. I'm referring her to physical need, this whole exercise in thought is fascinating when you think of Maslow's Hierarchy of Needs.

Self-actualization
morality, creativity, spontaneity, problem solving, lack of prejudice, acceptance of facts
Esteem
self-esteem, confidence, achievement, respect of others, respect by others
Love/belonging
friendship, family, sexual intimacy
Safety
security of: body, employment, resources, morality, the family, health, property
Physiological
breathing, food, water, sex, sleep, homeostasis, excretion

I could talk about this for about forty more pages but I'm out of room. Love chatting online, please hit me up on any of my social media feeds!

Carpe Diem,

MATT HAWKINS
A veteran of the initial Image Comics launch, Matt started his career in comic book publishing in 1993 and has been working with Image as a creator, writer and executive for over twenty years. President/COO of Top Cow since 1998, Matt has created and written over thirty new franchises for Top Cow and Image including *Think Tank, The Tithe, Necromancer, VICE, Lady Pendragon, Aphrodite IX,* and *Tales of Honor* as well as handling the company's business affairs.

OTHER TITLES FROM MATT THAT YOU MAY ENJOY:
Think Tank vol. 1 (978-1607066606) | ***The Tithe vol. 1*** (978-1632153241) | ***Aphrodite IX vol. 1*** (978-1607068280)

RAFFAELE "RAFF" LENCO
A comic book creator who has been in the industry for more than twenty years, and whose works have been published most recently by both Marvel and Image Comics. Raff's creator-owned works include the *Epic Kill* series and the graphic novels *Devoid of Life* and *Manifestations*. His latest work is a collaboration with Top Cow and Matt Hawkins on their new science-fiction comic called *Symmetry*. Born in Italy, he came to Canada when he was 4 and currently lives in Toronto.

OTHER TITLES FROM RAFFAELE THAT YOU MAY ENJOY:
Epic Kill vol. 1 (978-1607066286) | ***Devoid of Life*** (978-1582409870) | ***Manifestations*** (Digital-Only)

COVER GALLERY

All art by Raffaele Ienco

Issue One

Cover A

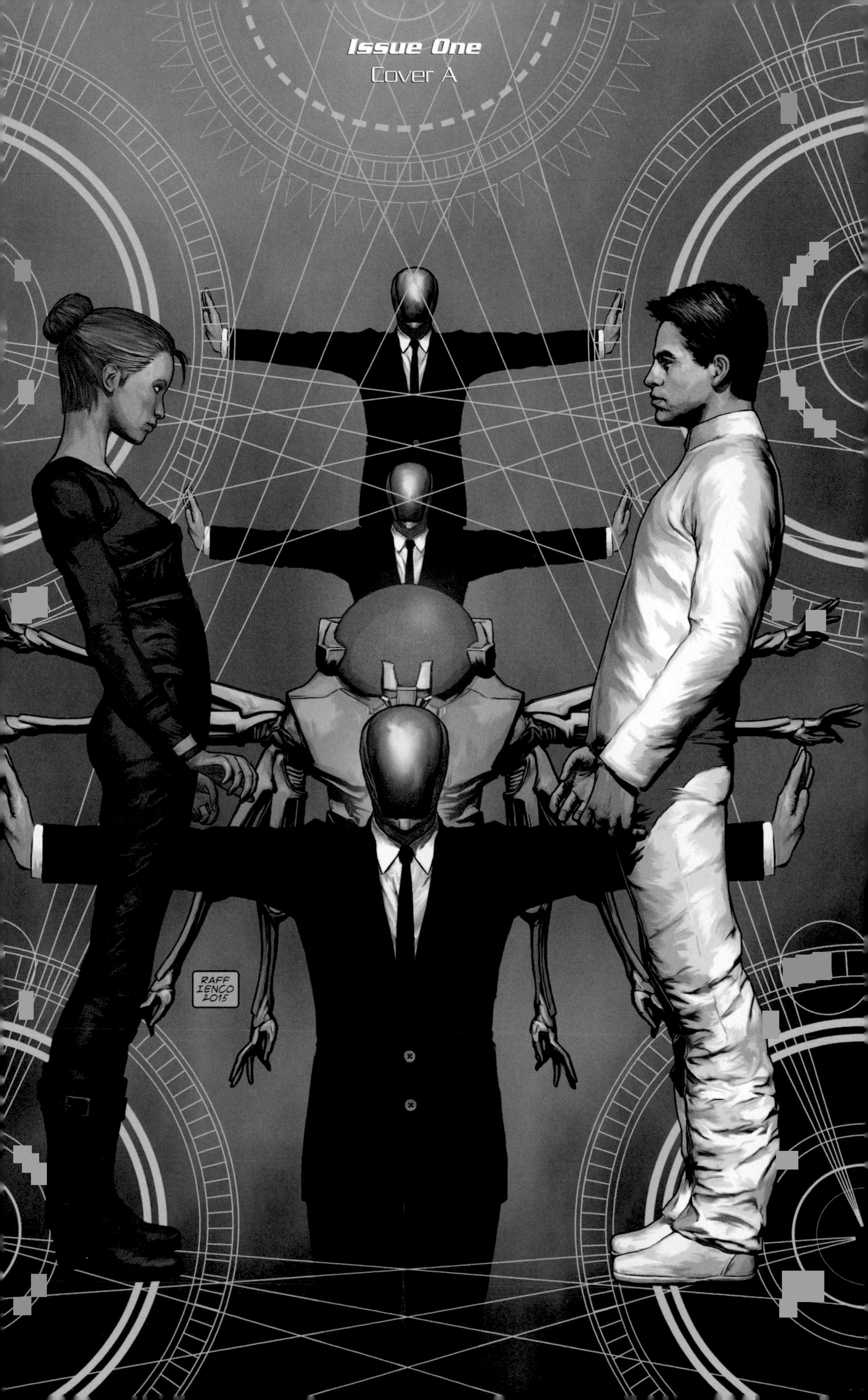
RAFF
IENCO
2015

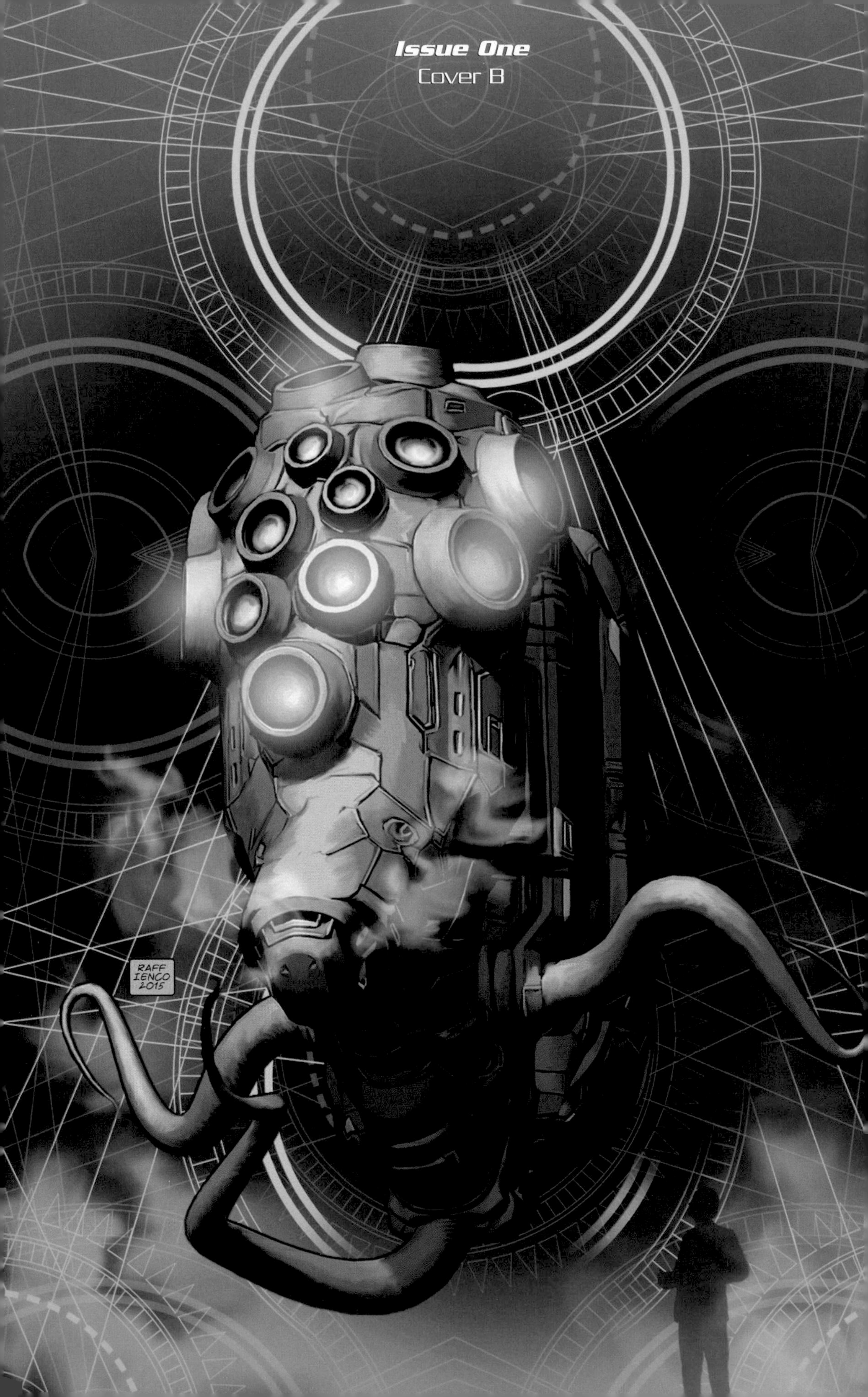
RAFF
IENCO
2015

Issue One

Cover B

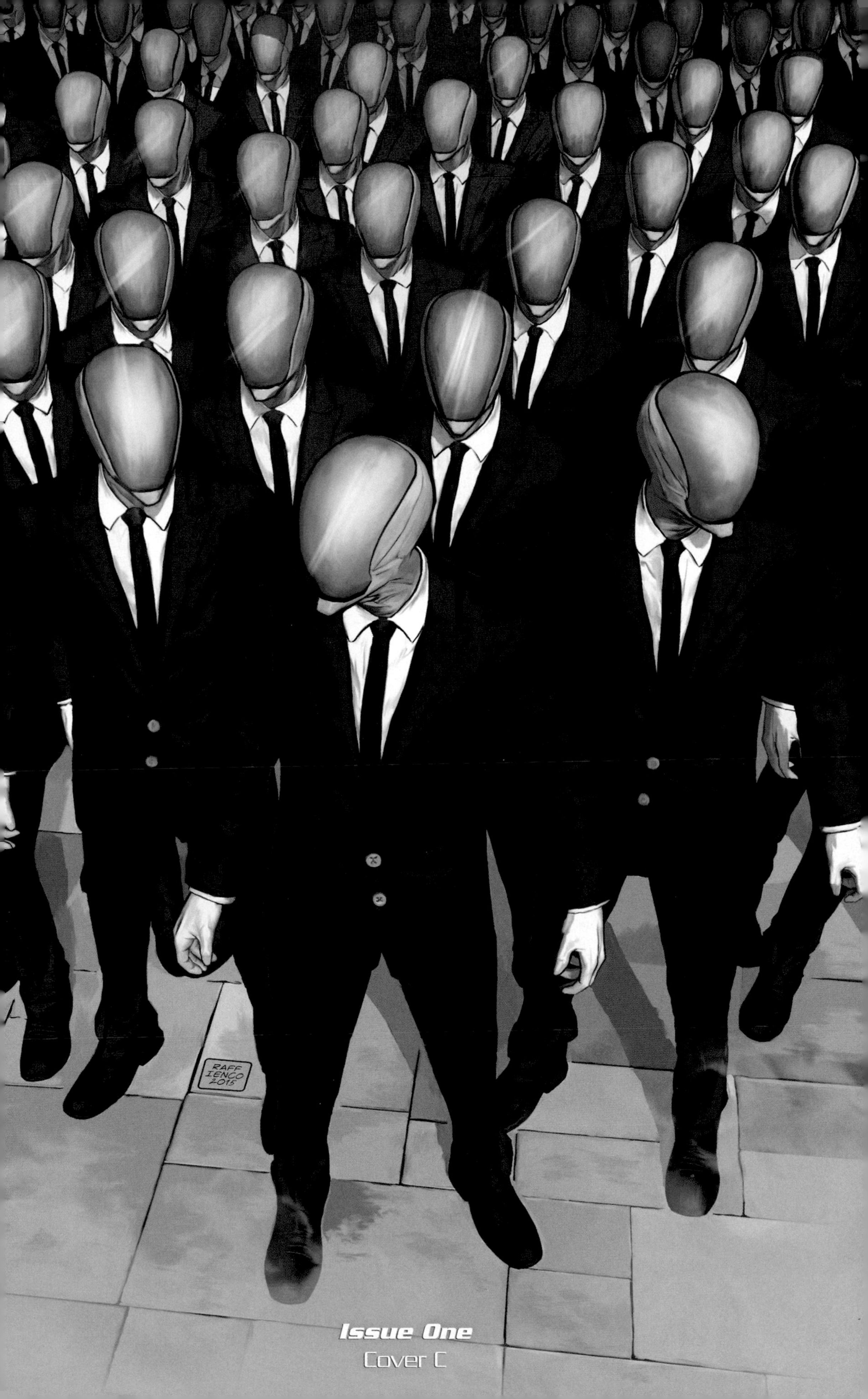
RAFF
IENCO
2015

Issue One
Cover C

Issue Two
Cover A

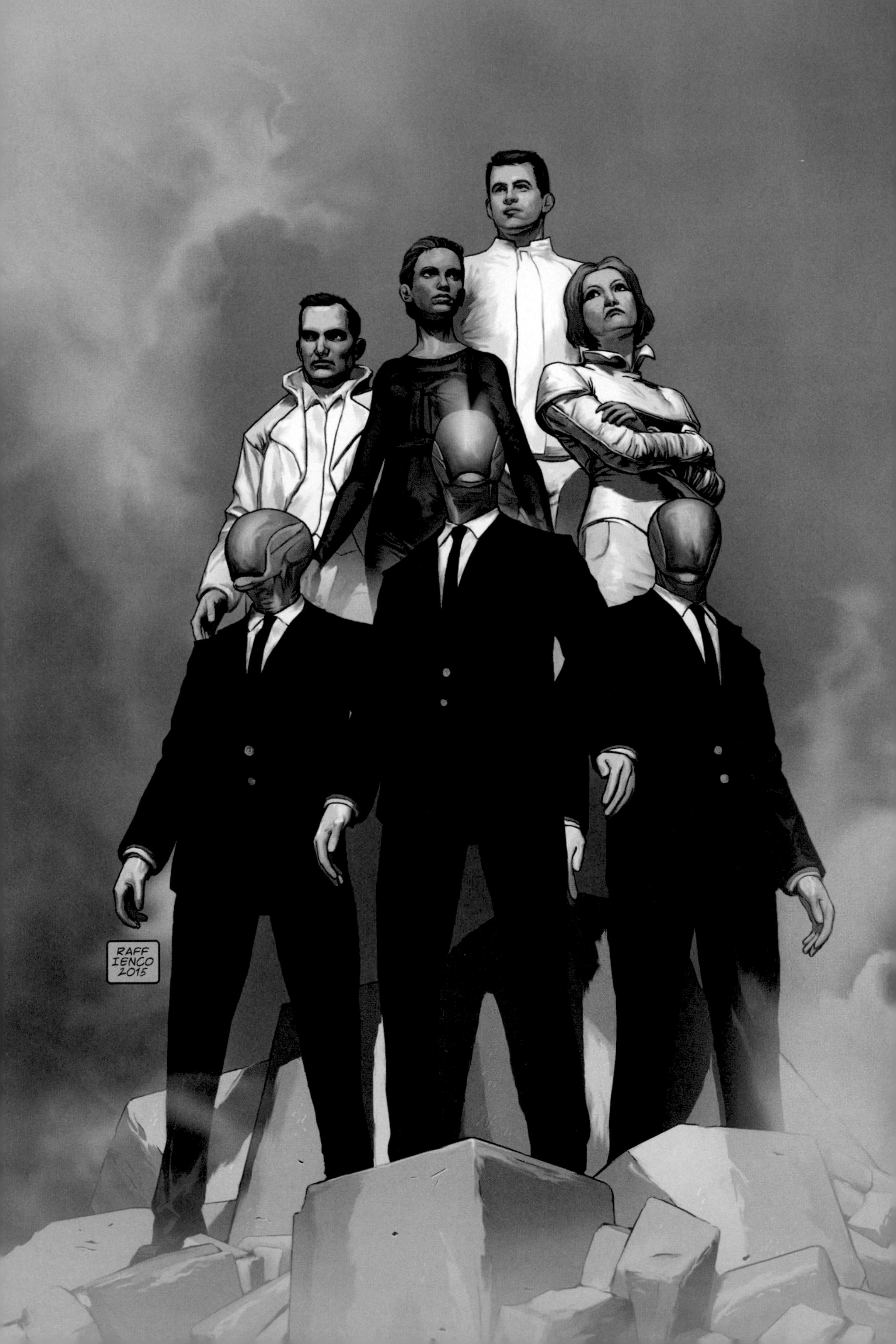
RAFF
IENCO
2015

Issue Two

Cover B

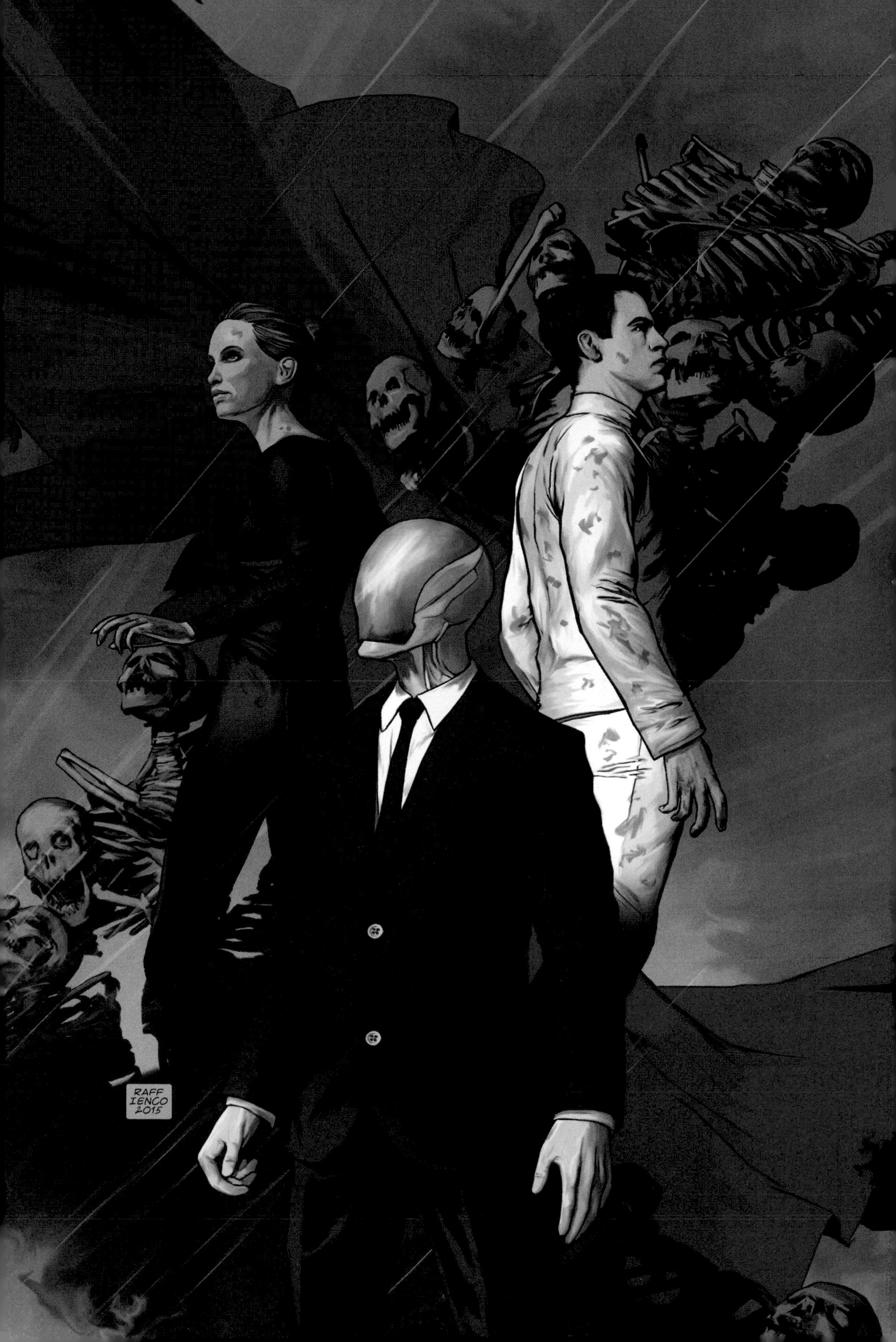
RAFF
IENCO
2015

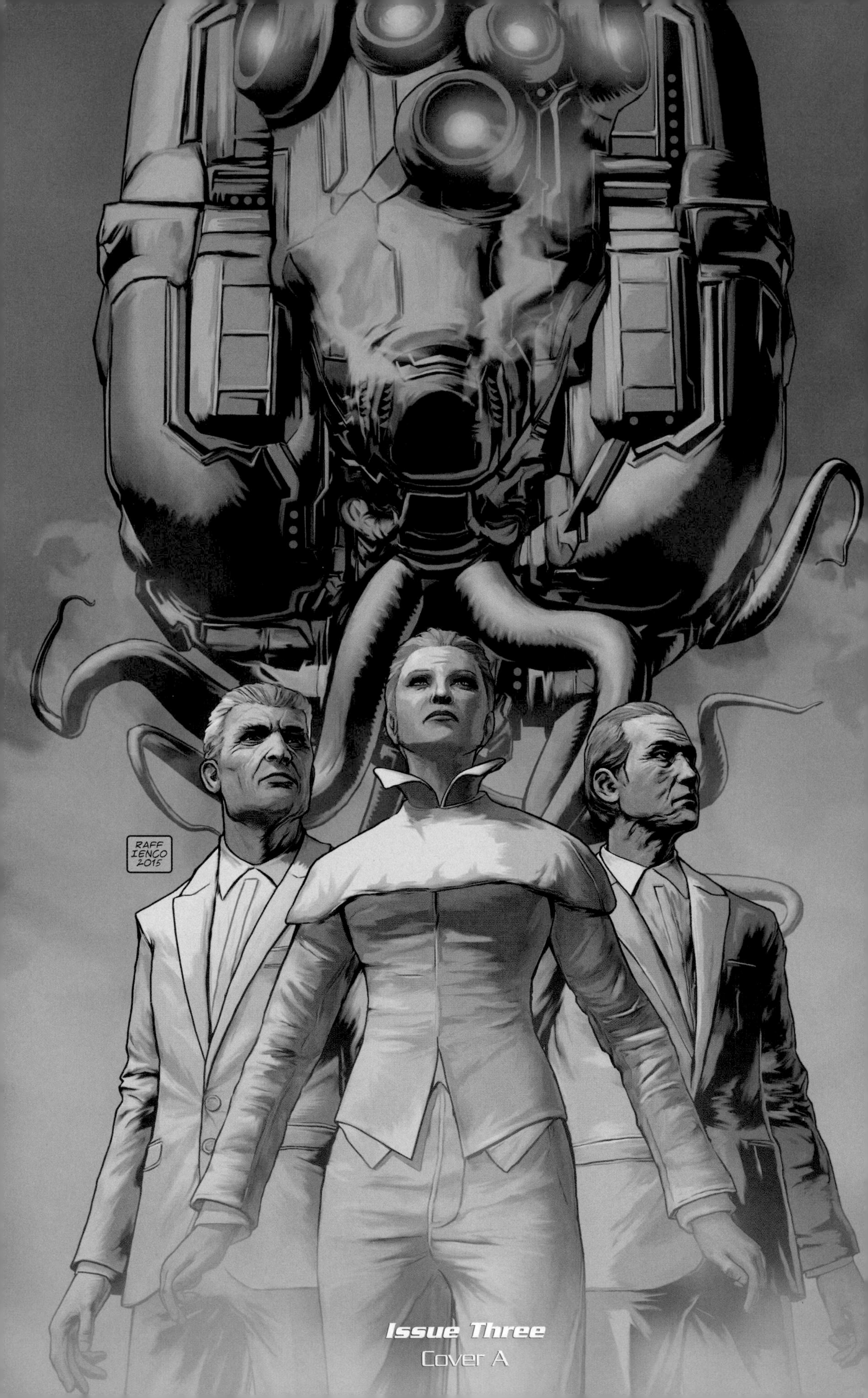
RAFF IENCO 2015

Issue Three

Cover A

Issue Three

Cover B

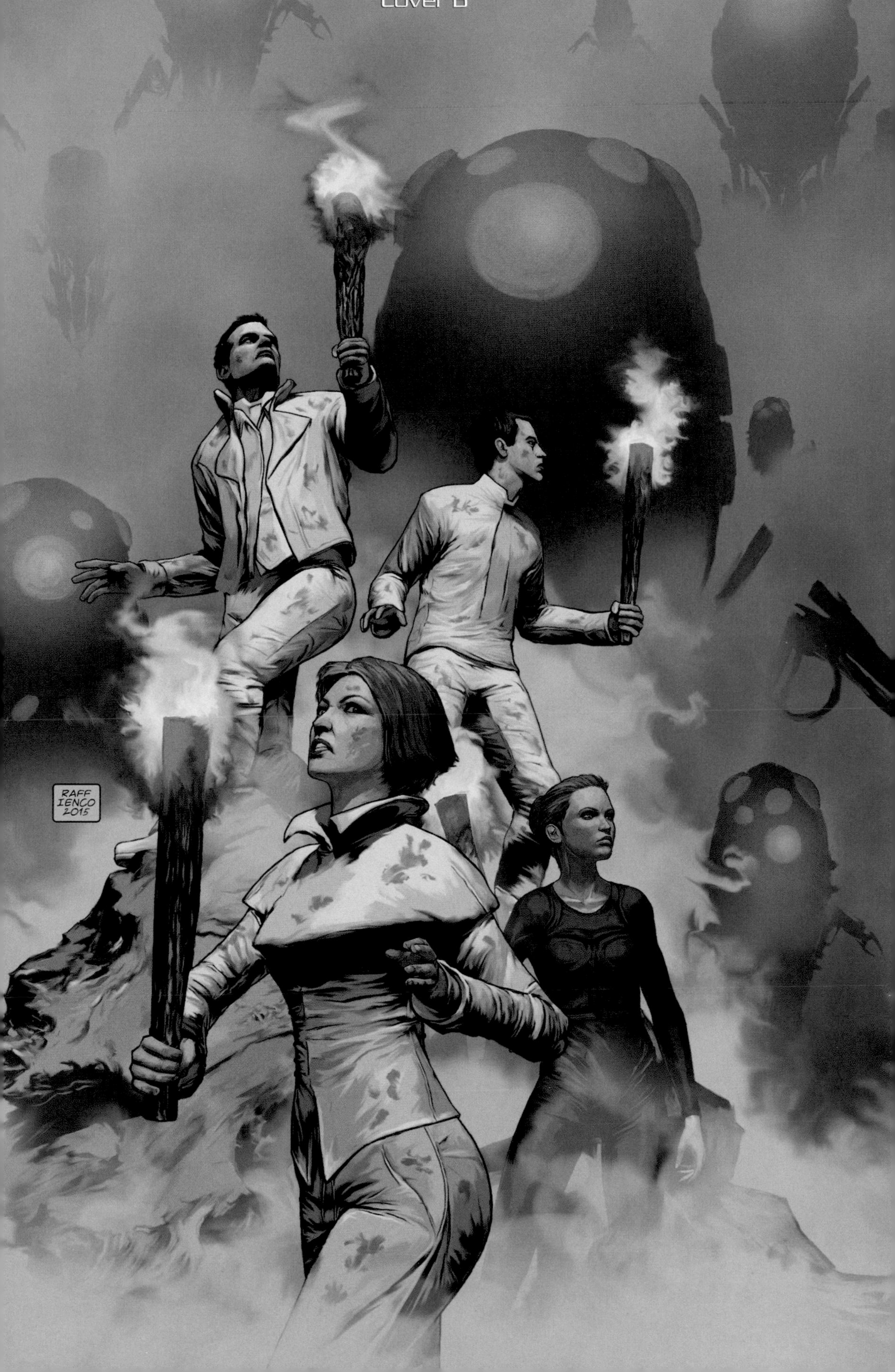
RAFF
IENCO
2015

Issue Four

Cover A

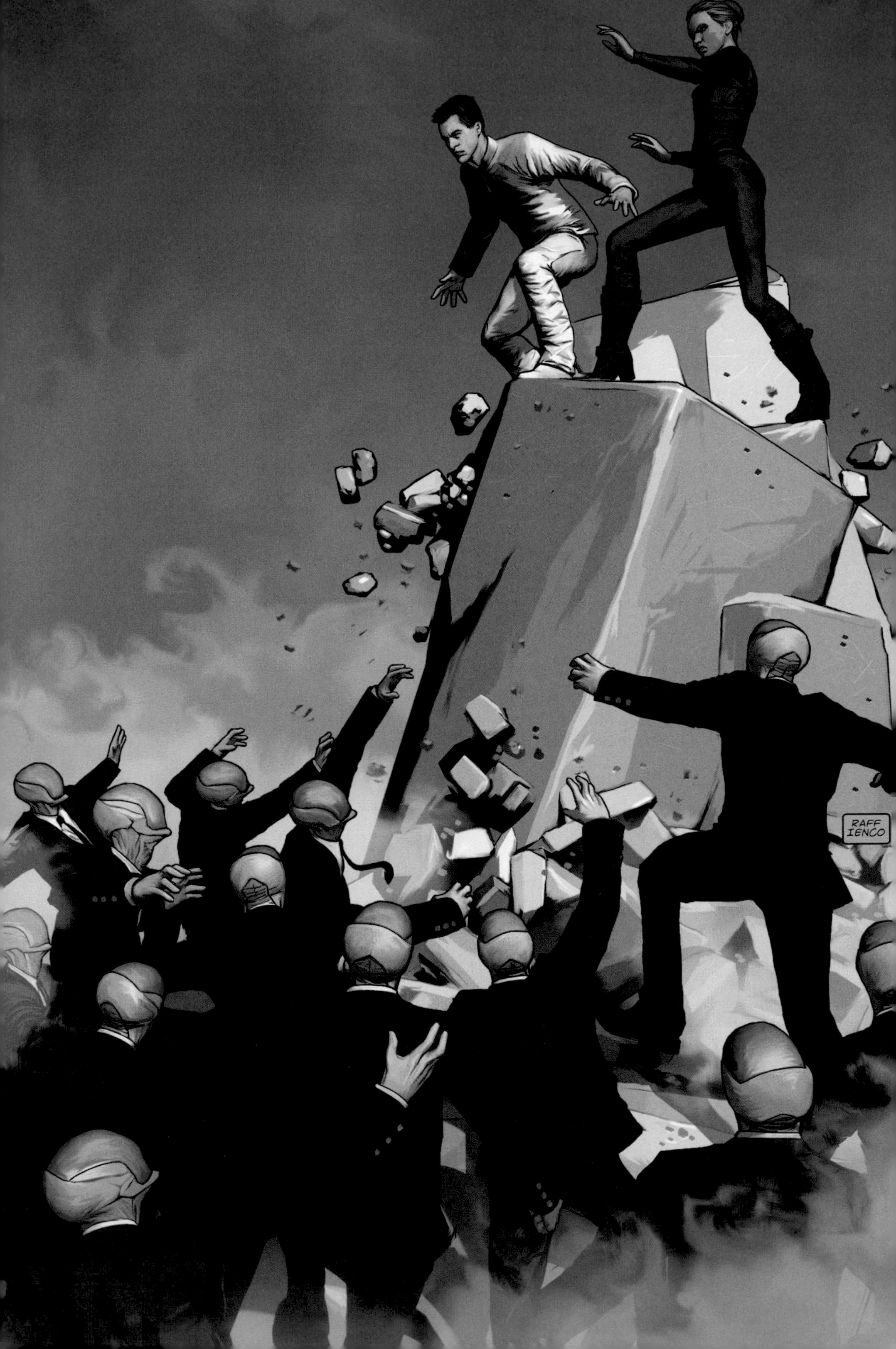
RAFF IENCO

Issue Four
Cover B

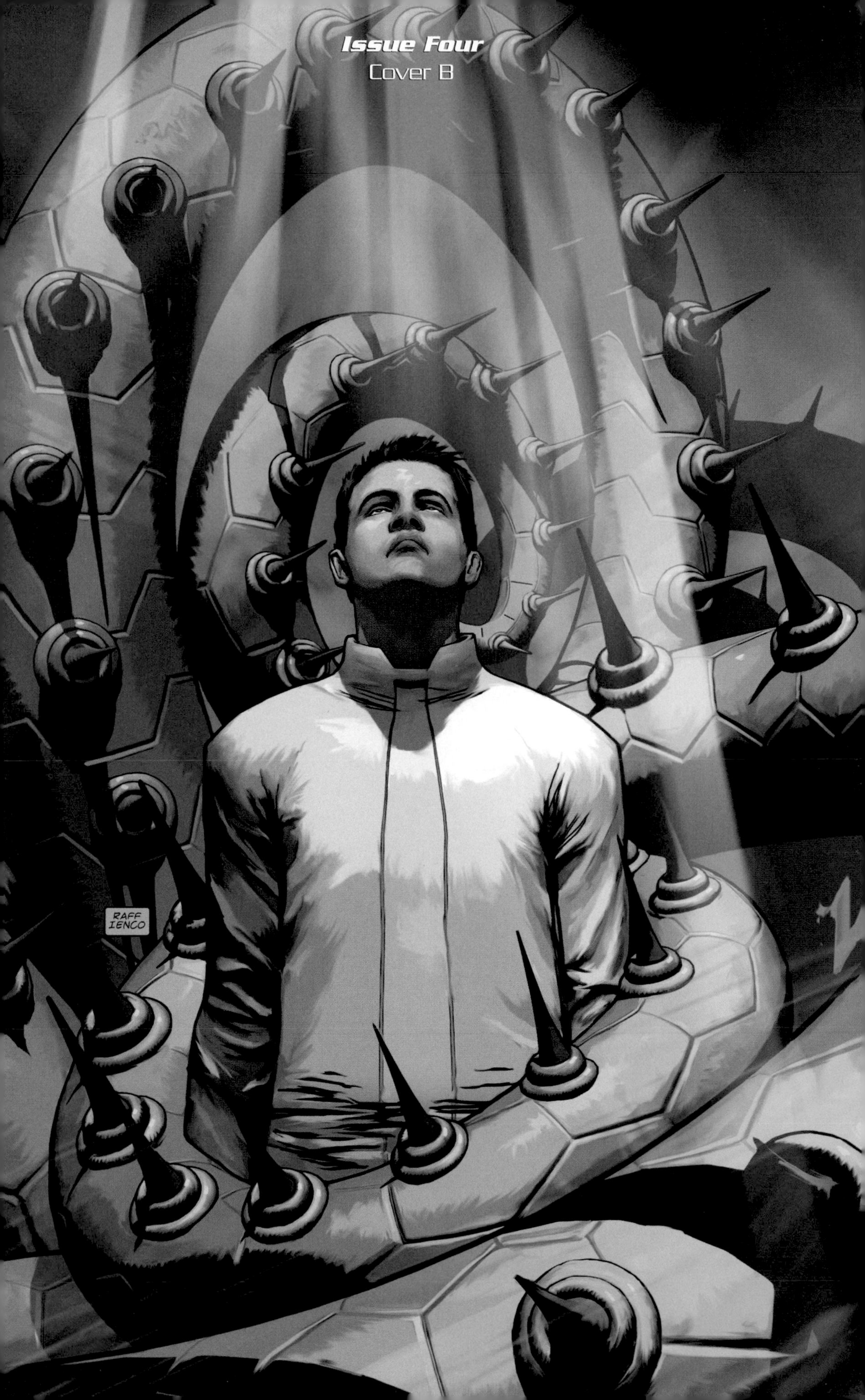
RAFF
IENCO

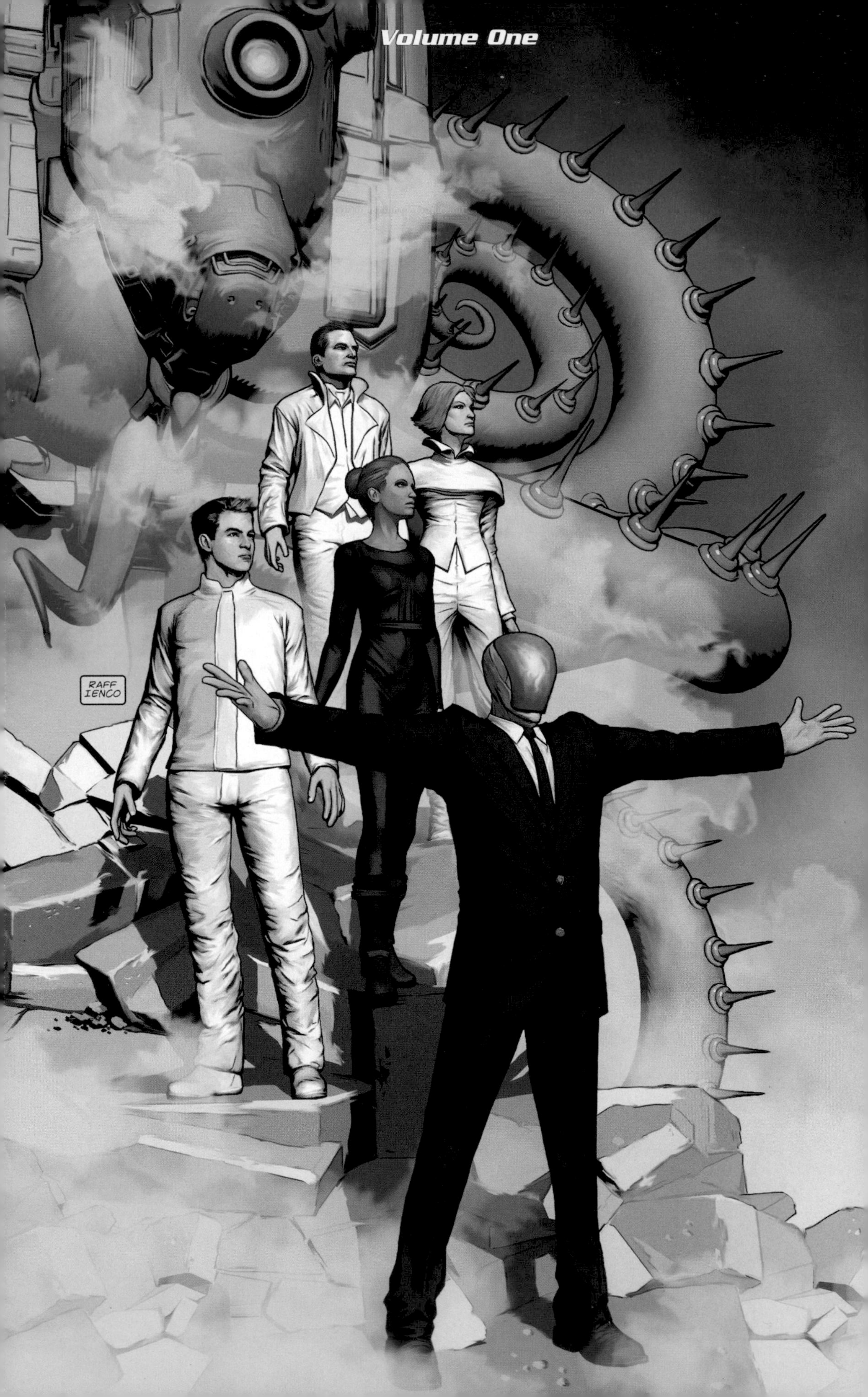
Volume One
RAFF IENCO